The Striped Tunic Trilogy

Jorge Armenteros

AIR
THE ROAR OF THE RIVER
THE SPIRAL OF WORDS

SPUYTEN DUYVIL

New York   Paris

© 2021-2023 Jorge Armenteros
ISBN 978-1-952419-49-2 hdc. 978-1-959556-24-4 pbk.

Cover: Tiraz Textile Fragment, late 9th–early 10th century,
Yemen (The Metropolitan Museum of Art)

Library of Congress Cataloging-in-Publication Data

Names: Armenteros, Jorge, author. | Armenteros, Jorge. Air. |
Armenteros,
   Jorge. Roar of the river. | Armenteros, Jorge. Spiral of words.
Title: The striped tunic trilogy / Jorge Armenteros.
Description: New York City : Spuyten Duyvil, [2021] |
Identifiers: LCCN 2021000992 | ISBN 9781952419492 (hdc.)
978-1-959556-24-4 (pbk.)
  Subjects: LCGFT: Novels.
Classification: LCC PS3601.R5723 S77 2021 | DDC 813/.6--dc23
LC record available at https://lccn.loc.gov/2021000992

To Possible Readers

This trilogy is something like an arena in which I invite you to join me in a game of the imagination. The books will not offer themselves to you like shelled pistachios. You will have to do the work of shelling through words, rhythms in prose, and the unconscious in order to savor them. It is the alliance between your efforts and my meditations that conjures this work of literature. A writer only begins a book, a reader finishes it.

J.A.

Air

1

She had no clear idea where to go, what hotel to look for, or where to eat. She decided to start walking south because that would take her away from north, and north was where Patricio would be looking for her this morning. Moving away was more important than finding a particular place. And with every step through this unfamiliar maze, Imena felt her pulse accelerating, and the oppressive weight of Patricio's questions lifting. She felt like flying, ethereally, over the medina.

Marrakech, Marrakech. The unrecognizable language, the tangled buildings, the mystifying maze of narrow paths, the medina ancient but brutally present. Women wore scarves on their heads while men stood on street corners waiting for the day to pass. An unanimous chant emanated from the top of oblique spires that grew from a legion of mosques. When Imena walked through the city gates, her dark hair, light complexion, and blue eyes wounded the day. Those who saw her walking knew she was in desperate need of answers.

A red door opened. Imena stepped inside a square courtyard containing a flowering orange tree in each of its four corners and a fountain in the center. The sign that led her there read *"Funduk."* If it had been written in French, she would have ignored it, as she was moving away from Paris now. At the reception desk, the innkeeper sat wrapped in a striped Moroccan tunic watching every move Imena made.

"Are you alone, *Mademoiselle?*" he asked in a grave voice.

Imena looked up and saw his storm-weathered eyes fixed on her. She did not know how to answer. She recognized the smell of the orange blossoms and the mint tea he was drinking, but she did not recognize this world.

"Are you alone, *Mademoiselle?*"

"I need a room for a week," she said. "Do you have one overlooking the courtyard?"

"May I offer you some tea, *Mademoiselle*?"

Imena moved closer to the innkeeper and the smell of the mint tea sweetened with rock sugar felt soothing. She noticed the striped tunic mended in several places and the sandals torn on top of the innkeeper's toes. The closer she came to this man, the more complex the smells became. She could now sense a variety of fragrances, some were floral, others spicy. But a strong animal smell, like musk or civet, overwhelmed all others.

"Yes, I would like to try some tea," she said.

At that point, Imena understood she was free to venture into this new world. She felt light again. And when the sweet, hot liquid filled her mouth, her mind opened to the sky.

*****

Patricio left his flat and hurried to *Au Père Louis* at the corner of *rue de Vaugirard*. Behind him trailed the disillusion, the anguish, and the internal metronome marking the rhythm of his anxiety. When he arrived at the bar, he ordered a coffee and an early glass of calvados while listening to the music in the old radio. He decided not to go to the university that morning. He was not going to receive his graduate students, he was not going to reorder his bookshelf, and he was not going to think about thoughts thought by others before him. Philosophy was dead for the day, and Patricio celebrated the occasion with a second early glass of calvados. He called René and instructed him to hold the morning seminar in his place. He also said he was at the brink of some revelation; that an idea had landed in the clearing of his mind, and it seemed possible it would explain the unexplainable. He did not believe this; nonetheless, he had serious thinking to do.

René did not question the request and in a distant voice said, "Yes, Professor." René, the taciturn assistant professor, was a gem; no one could be as René as René was.

*****

How is it possible, thought Patricio, that I'm here looking into this second empty glass not knowing what to do? All of these people around me in this filthy bar seem to know what to do. Look at them, they come, have a coffee, listen to the music, read the paper, and go on with their lives. Yet, I've no idea what to do.

How to deal with Imena? How to get closer to her? We've been close before, I thought we were… Yes, we were. How can I get close to a non-presence, to an absence? Is it possible to feel proximity, to relate, when the object is inanimate? Inanimate metaphorically, of course, because the anima was certainly there. But if it escapes and flies away when I try to hold her, how much closeness is there? A third calvados and a cigarette would surely explain the unexplainable. But I don't smoke and haven't surrendered my soul to alcohol. However, a third calvados is in order because that makes a triangle, and a triangle is a perfect figure. And at the count of three, one, two, three… It's gone, it's inside of me. Let it do what it has to do.

*****

At that point, the radio started playing an old tango and Patricio recognized the baritone phrasing of Carlos Gardel—*El Mudo*—as Argentines called him.

El día que me quieras
la rosa que engalana,

Patricio closed his eyes and the lyrics invaded his body. His breathing became deep and heavy, his fingers grasped the third empty glass and started compressing it.

"Carlos Gardel, Carlitos, what a son of the bitch you are," he said out loud. And with a deliberate swing of his arm, Patricio threw the empty glass away from him. It first hit the wooden panel at the bottom of the bar before crashing on the dirty floor, sending a constellation of tiny stars all over the feet of the patrons at *Au Père Louis*. The look on their faces mortified Patricio. He stood up slowly, and without saying a word, left the bar.

Forcing his way through the crowded sidewalks, Patricio reached the mouth of the Metro. He descended into its gut and looked at the signs for one phrase: *Porte de Clignancourt*. Any train going in that direction would bring him closer to Imena. He waited until the iron snake entered the tunnel with such destination on its forehead. A violent rush of people moved in and out of the train and Patricio had to force his way in before the doors closed. He stood and grabbed a steel bar to keep his balance. The motion of the train was syncopated, erratic: stop, go, stop, go, and stop. It screamed, it hissed, it jerked him around, swallowed people and spat them out, crawled on its belly and jumped abruptly, called out stations, and a stench of acrid sweat emanated unanimously. Patricio wished to scream in a high pitch to silence the voice calling out the stations, to make the train stop precisely at the moment it reached *Château d'Eau*. He wished for the power to silence the turmoil, but when he reached deep into the resources of his mind, he only found a soft memory transporting him to the time when Imena's fragrance possessed him like a lover.

He observed the changing tonalities on the walls of the tunnel and knew to release the steel bar when the train pierced its way to the *Château d'Eau*. He pushed his way out and ran towards the exit. The hope that Imena would be in her flat made him run faster. When Patricio rang the bell, he knew he was taking a chance. Her last words "I must go now," were still fresh in his mind, and like a basso continuo, they anchored the harmony of his every thought. He rang the bell again and again. Not a single sound came from inside the flat and the door did not open. He knelt on the floor, leaned against the door, and his head started banging the door with rhythmic tenacity, an implacable thump, thump… thump.

*****

Only yesterday Imena had reached *rue de Monttessuy* and entered the perfume laboratory at *Cinquième Sens* where she was studying to become a *Nez*. Her world was all there, hundreds of vials aligned like imperial soldiers on three levels of shelves. The bottom shelf contained amber, *santal d'orient*, *fruits secs*, and jasmine. The middle shelf had *lavande*, *muguet*, *herbe verte*, and *ylang-ylang*. And at the top shelf she had *fleurs fraîches*, *bergamote*, and *citron zeste*. On any given day her world assumed *fleurie*, *marine*, *poudrée*, or *boisée* qualities. Other times it turned *orientale*, *animale*, *épicée*, or *aromatique*. With a soft lead pencil, she would often write a number on the label of a small vial to identify her creation. This provided some order. Sometimes, when distracted, she repeated or confused the numbers. This provided some disorder. These scents spoke of mythical nights when the moon stood still and the flowers were transfixed, looking at the sky, trying to find the meaning of a thousand light points. For Imena this was music, the chorus of scents reverberating from the beginning to the end of time.

She spent most of her day listening to the souls of these particles while her master creation lingered in oblivion. She knew exactly the perfume she wanted to create but still needed to identify its components. She also knew its name: *La rose sauvage*. A sublime perfume, deconstructed, set to an atonal scale, capable of fascinating, mesmerizing, if it would only find its way into her consciousness.

Imena did not try to advance her master creation that day. She just wanted to compose a light and simple fragrance. Her nose worked hard, sampling multiple combinations of natural oils. But she failed. Everything she composed reminded her of drawers and closets. By the late afternoon, Imena had made up her mind. It was clear she needed time away from Paris. She wanted to fly, to run, to crawl fast. And that wish made her buy a plane ticket to Marrakech for the next day. She looked at the piece of paper with the itinerary and her fantasies exploded. When she remembered the telephone conversation she had had with Patricio that morning, especially the intensity of his questions, she squeezed the plane ticket so hard that the name of the city, Marrakech, entered through her skin and brought her mind two thousand kilometers south of Paris.

*****

The attendant showed her a room containing a bed, two chairs, and a washbasin. A lone window opened into the courtyard, allowing the scent from the flowering orange trees to fill and enlarge the small space. All lodgers shared the toilet across the courtyard. There was no shower. Imena entered the room with feathery steps. She imagined the mint tea as an ocean with soft undulating waves traveling through her body, touching her inner shores. The striped tunic stood at the door in silent observation.

"This is perfect," she said.

"You're welcome to more tea, *Mademoiselle*, whenever it suits you."

"Thanks, do you offer tea to everyone that comes in here?"

"No, *Mademoiselle*, only to those who need it."

"But how do you know I need it?"

"You came here alone and you asked for a room with a view to the courtyard."

Imena walked towards the door to inspect the maroon and golden hues of the striped tunic, but the acrid, civet stench made her stop in the middle of the room.

"What's so special about my request?" she asked.

"There's nothing special, *Mademoiselle*. Most people ask for a view to the courtyard."

"Then why do you suggest that I need mint tea?"

"You came alone and you asked for the view. Those who are searching need some relief because they never know for how long they'll be searching."

The striped tunic did not say anything else. After years of living the lives of others, he had become close-fisted with his words. And after a shallow bow he turned to the courtyard and walked away, leaving behind a trace of animal aroma floating in the air.

*****

I wonder what he means, thought Imena. I come here alone because that's what I want to do. I search, yes, but we all search. That's nothing special. For how long, for how long? Who cares for how long? For as long as long may be... then some more. Patricio must be looking for me today, or maybe he won't. He needs to understand that I cannot follow him, that the pressure is crushing me. I like dancing tango more than he does, but he insists in pressing forward. If I only knew where he was going I could follow. So stiff, looking who knows where. I can move backwards, I can do that. All over the ballroom, slowly, then across. Then on the side, the *salida*. The melancholic music gets to him. I just think it is soothing and beautiful. Maybe like mint tea. The flowering orange trees don't dance, they're great at standing still, but they can shake their hair to the wind and let themselves be felt… I can feel them inside me. How soft the wall is in this room, like an old bone, and the continuous elliptical curve joining the wall to the ceiling, forever around and around. This room could be an animal or the skeleton of an animal. I smelled the animal, civet, pure civet. I'll probably see him again. What if he offers me more mint tea? Maybe I need it as he said. I need the air and the space, a rhythm, a curve with texture and time, and a memory attached to it, and something else.

*****

After resting on the bed for hours, Imena covered her head with a melrose scarf and ventured outside the red door, following the immemorial stone paths of the medina. Her steps were driven by the light among the rooftops, the echoing sound from minarets, the children running, and the aroma of cumin, turmeric, and coriander. She felt free to run, to stop, to run again, to sample a fresh mandarin, to touch the walls of the primeval buildings, to laugh, to turn around, to feel the hand pressing her hand, to feel his chest pressing her chest, to rest her right hand on his shoulder, to keep her eyes gazing into the vacuous space, to cross her legs, the *salida*.

The pink buildings spoke to her in Arabic, in old Spanish like Quevedo, also in colonial French. She felt the weight of centuries, the weight of dead people that occupied the buildings, buried or burnt, debating, "whom do we belong to at this time?" But the voices of the living also bounce from wall to wall, in joy and anger, in ecstasy and despair, tracing a spider's web at the top of the medina, catching the dreams as they try to escape into the purple sky.

A man standing at a corner, lit a cigarette and blew smoky words out of his mouth, his right hand trembling while his left eye tracked her steps. "Are you alone, *Mademoiselle?*" Again those words, but coming from a different mouth. The question of belonging, the question of who we are and why we are here and for how long and for what reason and would you mind looking at me and what is your tongue, "Good morning," "*Buenos Días,*" "*Bonjour.*" These sounds twirled in the air and stopped in front of her eyes, now scratchy and teary, because the hours of sleep did not help her rest as much, because no one can rest while maintaining a latent awareness for that man in the striped tunic.

To the right, beyond a cat covered with layers of stupor, a yellow sign read "*Hammam.*" The idea of entering a gathering place and disrobing herself in front of others produced a sense of delight in Imena. She thought there would be water and marble, steam. She thought there would be hands, bare skin. Jealousy.

Imena followed three women entering the *hammam*. Once inside, she stepped into a cavernous room clad in white marble. She removed every layer of clothing revealing a transparency rarely seen by the other women around her. The steam embraced her body and her mind while she started to breathe rhythmically. With two empty black rubber buckets, one for cold and the other for steaming water, she stepped into the next room where women were crowding around the water source. They spoke while glancing at her from the corner of their eyes. She felt like a fish with no scales, her pearls and the seaweed between her thighs exposed. With no bench to sit on, she squatted on the marble floor and proceeded to pour steaming water all over her body to wash away the memories of Paris and Patricio, to drown the unfinished *rose sauvage*, to entice every pore to breathe, to expel a past that seemed far away, but in reality, lingered only two thousand kilometers north across the Mediterranean.

With the help of a rough mitt, Imena began soaping and scrubbing her body. Initially, the delicate motion of her hands felt soothing. She then poured some steaming water all over her body and continued to scrub. The weight of her gestures intensified. And as the room became hotter, she applied more soap and scrubbed herself even harder. When her right hand became tired, she changed the mitt to her left hand and continued flogging herself. She scrubbed more, and more. Her skin was flushing and red streaks appeared along her arms, legs, and torso. Her breathing broke into a different rhythm, a staccato, the humid air going in and out of her lungs with force. Like a desperate animal, Imena wanted to shed her infected skin.

The other women watched, and the whispers mixed with the sound of splashing water echoed through the *hammam*. When Imena saw the inquisitive faces of the other women, she turned her body towards the marble wall, covered the front of her pubis with one of the buckets and her buttocks with the other one. She did not say a word.

Imena left the *hammam* with a sense of spring. She meandered through the narrow streets emanating the faint scent of lightness. By the time she heard chanting coming from the top of the spires again, the shadows had cut a diagonal line across the buildings. Not knowing where she was, she continued to make random turns around the angular corners of the streets. A right turn followed a left turn, or a left turn followed a right turn, but always moving against time, opposing the clock, like in the *milonga*. The shadows advanced, eating the salmon pink of the buildings, until there was nothing left. She stumbled south until she identified the red door that had opened into the courtyard earlier that day. The striped tunic observed her in silence as she entered through the door. And as soon as she entered the courtyard, he poured mint tea into an opaque cup and with a gesture, ancient as the red clay under his feet, offered the cup to Imena.

"You need to drink this, you don't know how long you'll be searching," he said.

2

The smell of dead human cells was different from the smell of a dead rat. Not sweet… no, it was not sweet. And when his mother did not smell like Marilyn Monroe anymore, Patricio knew there was something seriously wrong with her. Not only did she have a different smell, but her eyes had an opaque curtain over them. She had started to look more like a corpse than like his mother. Her movements were slower, she took longer to answer his questions, and when she combed her hair, she looked at him with a vacant stare that scared him. Patricio would not speak loudly in the house because he feared his voice would destroy his mother. He walked around the house with a soft step, placing the toes first, softly, before rolling the rest of the foot, making his steps noiseless. He had stopped playing with his friends inside the house to avoid upsetting her. He thought she was so brittle that any abrupt movement would cause her bones to shatter. And there was the smell of death all over.

His mother insisted in listening to her favorite tangos. Patricio would play what his mother asked for, repeatedly. "*Piazzolla*," and he would find it and play it for her. "*La Cumparsita*," and he played that too. Every time he heard the beginning of a song, he feared his mother would not last to the end of the song. Three minutes felt like a very long time. And the lyrics went on telling stories of sorrow. But his mother continued to ask him to play the tango records. Melancholy was all over her face, but when the music was playing she seemed to come alive. She even sang with a frail charm.

Patricio did not listen to the music for he was frightened. He imagined his mother's limbs falling next to her body and her neck extending back while her mouth opened, gasping for life. The music would kill her, he thought. The music was the tango, was the melancholy, was the fear his mother would not hold him again. He wanted to be silent, to keep everything still so his mother would not be disturbed. But the *bandoneón*, that small square accordion, came bursting in with no consideration for his mother. The *bandoneón* had to tell its story; it had to announce that misery was pervasive.

Patricio worried silently that one day, while at school, his mother would die alone, that he would go back home to find her cold. Those thoughts kept him from paying attention to his primary school teacher. She believed he was the worst student because he would not answer questions when she knew, quite well, he had the capacity to answer. There was nothing he could do.

The morning when Patricio first had the dream was like any other morning. That is, he did not want to go to school. He heard a clear voice that told him, "Your mother will die on June 6th." Devastated, Patricio asked in his dream, "Why do you tell me?" And the voice simply responded, "Because you asked." Patricio never asked when his mother was supposed to die. He was afraid that thinking about her death would make him an accomplice. He thought he was killing her by worrying about her. But the more he tried to stop the thoughts, the faster they flooded his mind. And he could not tell his mother about his torturous thoughts because the shock would probably kill her.

When the morning of June 6 arrived, it was unlike any other morning. Patricio could not finish his breakfast. When his mother asked him if he was sick, he answered with a weak and frightened, "Yes." He did not go to school that day. His fears assaulted him like a tiger. Around noon, he looked at the clock and saw that half of the day remained. If he could only rush time, moving the clock past midnight, she may survive.

His mother then said, "Play any record you want." Patricio

looked at the many records and selected one by Gardel, her favorite. The record started oscillating at seventy-eight revolutions per minute, the familiar voice filling the room, the windows vibrating, the chandeliers quivering. Gardel told the stories his mother wanted to hear. Patricio, afraid the sadness and despair of the lyrics would deliver a mortal blow to his mother's heart, started perspiring profusely. He sat on the floor and covered his ears with his hands to block the music, to create stillness. But when he looked up trying to find his mother's eyes, he saw that her arms had fallen next to her body, her neck had extended back, and her mouth had opened.

3

"How are you?" Patricio asked.

He knew she would answer the phone because she did not have the strength to ignore him.

"How are you?" Imena responded. The words danced in the air as if they had no weight, no gravity.

"How am I?" Patricio said, but nothing else came out of his mouth. "How am I, why do you ask, does it really matter to you?"

Imena remained silent for a moment. Those moments were immense, mysterious, and contained all that was unknown to them.

"Of course it matters," Imena said. "That's why I asked you. If I didn't care, I wouldn't have asked. Why is everything so heavy with you?"

"What were you thinking?"

"Patricio, you just called me and I answered the phone. I don't know what I was thinking. It's too early to even think."

Without words, the silence grew and matured.

"Imena, are you still there?"

"I must go now," she said.

The telephone static ended abruptly.

*****

She may be thinking about last night, Patricio thought, but not as much as I do. It doesn't matter, she may think the tango experience was wonderful. Is she pondering my questions or is she traveling in her mind? I look around the room and study objects that relate to her: a wine glass, a flower bouquet, a picture of two people that seem happy, a copy of *Les Fleurs du Mal* that she didn't finish, air heavy with her presence. What can she be thinking?

In this morning hour the room is lit by a reading lamp and the moon, as it gives its life away. Nothing moves, there are no transfigurations—everything remains static. I still hear the static in the telephone line. It enters through my ears and quickly expands to fill my entire body. This is a different sound from the one last night at the ballroom. I know that tango music; I have run away from it before. I can see myself moving across the room last night, following that music from my youth, walking forward, pressing against Imena, my left arm suspending her right arm. That music had a different tempo, it began and it ended. This ache goes on.

*****

He does this every time, thought Imena, the cat and mouse game. How do I know what I'm thinking and why does it matter? I have been in this situation before and I know it doesn't lead anywhere. It creates a heaviness that doesn't feel right. It forces me to think about myself in a different way. I want to touch, feel, and smell, I want to see what is not there, I want to dance and let the music turn around me, covering me with a silk sheath, like the soft hands of a soft man.

The scents I study are soft, ethereal, and tender. And like a symphony, the top note dancing first, then the middle note piercing the heart, and lastly the base, the ground. A transformation over time as life emanates from the fragrances. I prefer that softness to the unbearable heaviness of his questions.

I have to admit, the music last night, the tango, was soft. It was there to intoxicate me, to deliver me to a lighter place, different from this one, a place where dreams are as real as the air that touches my face and musses my hair. He now asks me if I care for him. Why does he need to ask? I don't have all the answers. Sometimes, I don't understand his questions. He makes them too complex.

4

Imena surrendered to the peace of the small room. She closed the curtains of her awareness that night and slept over a sheet once white. The weight of her thoughts kept her head on the pillow and her consciousness yielded gradually to the indomitable architecture of her sleep. Towards the morning, she again dreamt of the swan. A white rush imposing over the paleness of her skin, his wings beating in the air, the feverish embrace, his bill pressed against her chest, the terrifying loosening of her thighs. The fear of procreation of a Helen more beautiful than anyone before or after. Every time she rose from that dream, her pulse was agitated and she felt surrounded by a smell of wet feathers. This time the smell was acrid, the animal smell of the striped tunic looking at her from the window. When she opened her eyes, the image of the swan dissipated giving birth to a musky creature studying her body.

"How long have you been staring at me?" she asked.

"Not for too long. I heard sounds coming from this room," he said.

"What kind of sounds?"

He would not answer. Imena stood up and extended her neck shifting her weight from foot to foot, as if she needed to see the flowering orange trees. His body filled the window blocking the light and the air from the courtyard. She felt the room shrinking and a need to fly again.

"I heard a cry and a song," he said. "It sounded like the song of a beast, I never heard a song like that, was it you who made that sound?"

"I don't like you staring at me as if I were something strange," she said.

"Seems like being alone makes you worry too much, *Mademoiselle*."

The room shrank even more and the air did not contain enough oxygen to fill her lungs. She went out the door, into the courtyard, and felt his eyes following her while the air sang an anthem of fear.

"The courtyard contains our lives," he said. "It's open to the sky and the winds are free to visit. The red clay anchors the courtyard, for what happened before holds our feet to the ground. I prefer to dream in the courtyard, it's the natural order of things. You, instead, were dreaming inside your room. The beast inside you sang."

"There wasn't any beast and I wasn't dreaming," Imena said.

"Then why do you want to fly away?"

Imena would not look at the striped tunic. She reached for an orange tree and ran her fingers over the blossoms. The rising angle of a thorn caught her middle finger. She moved it away quickly but the thorn had already pierced the skin and it dripped red.

"What makes you believe I want to go somewhere?" she said.

"You are here, but you are not from here, and you are alone, *Mademoiselle*. I know you are dreaming because your eyes seem to be elsewhere. And the sound of that beast..."

"But who are you to speak to me this way?"

"I'm your innkeeper. Like most men in this desert, I see people come and go, their dreams trailing behind if they come from the east or the south; but if they come from the north, like you do, or the west, their dreams are ahead of them. You're desperately searching for what's ahead or maybe inside of you."

Imena looked at his face trying to decipher him. She noticed the angular bone structure stretching the brown leathery skin from one side of the face to the other and the dark hollowness below his eyebrows.

"Even if I was looking for something I wouldn't know what that would be," she said.

"You came from far away, alone, and the first thing you did was to wander through the medina without any idea where you were going. Yes, you're searching."

Imena turned towards one of the flowering orange trees but its fragrance could not overcome the strong civet stench that permeated the courtyard.

"Why don't you tell me what I'm looking for?" she said.

"*Mademoiselle*, please, turn around, I am not the creator of your sorrow. Your face and your eyes spoke to me. They told a story, an old story, like those I've heard many times before. Then your hands were unsteady when you accepted a cup of tea. Those are the hands of people who reach but don't find. Then, I heard you crying this morning, and the song of that beast. I know desperate people do not sleep alone, they lie next to their demons, and those beasts can sing."

"Nobody slept next to me and I don't have any demons."

"We don't travel alone, *Mademoiselle*. Wherever we go, our mind follows. I must tell you about the last caravan that crossed the desert under the red moon." The striped tunic sat on the red clay and continued. "After arriving to the *Djemaa El-Fna*, a young man rested his head on a pile of oranges at the corner of the square. He fell asleep among the snake charmers, acrobat monkeys, storytellers, musicians, and dancers that filled the square every night. Nobody dared to interrupt his sleep, for he had arrived after a long journey and a thousand generations of dust covered his skin and dress, his face glowing with the color of amber. When the moon traveled far and the bottom of the sky boiled with light, the young man emitted an intense sound that filled the square and terrorized the balancing monkeys. It was guttural, animal—the song of a lonesome beast. When the sky heard his cry, a strong wind from the south invaded the square, lifting sparkle by sparkle the amber lights from the young man's face. The ebullient sky swallowed the amber glitter, creating a single star that now hangs low in the north of the night. The young man awoke in the minty morning. He was lost, and when asked, he could not pronounce his name nor say where he came from. But when the night fell again and he saw the glitter to the north, he knew his direction. He left his demons behind and walked in search of the star, unknown until then to those who crossed the sands under the red moon."

Imena listened quietly while keeping her distance from the striped tunic. When he finished talking, he remained in his sitting position without moving, like a statue made of salt.

"Do you have any mint tea this morning?" she then said. "I think I need it."

"What would it do for you?"

"I'm not sure."

"What do you hope it will do for you?"

"I can only hope to find relief."

"You won't feel liberated until you find your direction."

Imena felt the weight of expectations crushing her bones. She looked around the courtyard for a sign, a symbol, a star pointing north, east, south, or west. She only saw the salmon pink walls and the four flowering orange trees. She filled her lungs with acrid air and pressing her hands to her temples, released an inhuman cry, the ancient song of the lonesome beast. A whirlwind inundated the courtyard and dispersed the notes of the song one by one, until the sky had swallowed them all, no direction offered, no star favored.

5

The *18ème* was not a happy *arrondissement*, not for Patricio. And the confirmation that Imena was not at the tango lesson that night twisted his mood. The tango was certainly there, waiting to tell stories of disconcerted lovers, to seduce the senses into believing that passion was the sweet nectar of disillusion, that melancholy was ecstasy. Patricio sat at the corner of the ballroom next to the plastic flowers, and with his right hand covered the light from one of the spotlights. He could see the mass of aspiring lovers turn against time, step-by-step, chest touching chest, feet between feet, to the rhythm of the *bandoneón*.

*****

To be here and remember, to be here and not find her. Imena, where are you? There was nothing good when I left Buenos Aires and there is nothing good now either. Or is my mind just playing tricks? I try to embrace you and you turn into air. Yes, my mind is playing tricks on me. You're like the wind when you are with me. And with the *bandoneón* howling now, like a lone wolf—unbearable. But look at the lovers, flying, walking, looking ahead into the wallpaper or the plastic flowers at the corners of the ballroom. Here they are, next to me, flowers that exude the fragrance of petroleum and dust. And when I left Argentina, I did so without grace or fortune. To come to this room and find this music again when I thought I had left all of it behind, the absence of my mother, the absence of my tongue. Absence... the essence of you, even in your presence you are absent. But if I were to press with my left arm I might find your presence, and if my chest were to press against your chest I might find your breath. Fleeting, pulling away, walking backward away from me, disappearing.

The way I am today is so different from how I've been. Only one year ago an epiphany surprised me. I wasn't prepared. Something special drew me toward her, a chemical substance, a soft sensation that went directly into my brain, bypassing everything, a powerful and everlasting fragrance. Today, I couldn't remember its composition; I couldn't break apart the fragrance into top note, middle note, and base note, as she can.

I remember very clearly that day at *Pompierre* beach in *Terre-de-Haut,* walking on the sand surrounded by a universe of smells. There was the smell of ocean spray, sea grape, rust from the decaying beach shack, and there was jasmine. Burnt coal surprised me and the smell of laughter sprung from frolicking seagulls. The sound of her breath and the heat of her skin floated in the air. Walking down the beach was a prelude, a ritual, the preparation for something special and forbidden. We walked without saying much.

I wanted to climb on top of the roof of one of the brightly painted houses so nobody could see us. From that perspective we would see the entire beach. We would have the horizon in front with that evanescent line at the end. Once up on the roof, her fragrance became more intense, but I could not identify its nature. Primal, nubile, virginal, it enfolded me like a soft satin sheet. Imena murmured soft words, as if dreaming, and the moment she surrendered, I knew I was lost. I wanted to hold her close to me, I wanted to embrace her, but my arms could not grab her incorporeal body. And all I could feel was her delicate smell, that pure secretion of her vulnerable spirit, possessing me like a lover.

****

With the rhythm of his memories and the curse of lost hours, Patricio left the floor before the tango lesson was over. He could not bear the crowd, the melancholy, the sense that today was lost and tomorrow was uncertain. Once at his flat, the weight of his reality slowed his movements and made his breathing laborious. He sat next to the six-pane window and looked out to the field of Mansard roofs, punctured by fractured fingers reaching to the sky. He studied the colors and shadows of the buildings, the shifting figures behind curtains, the rhythmic steps of street dogs. He heard the sound of condensation forming as he breathed onto the window. Inside his flat, the wine glass, the flower bouquet, the picture of two people that seemed happy, and the copy of *"Les Fleurs du Mal"* were still resting where his eyes had left them, collecting particles of memory.

Patricio opened the bottom drawer of the worn-out bureau and searched for the glossy plastic disc bearing the name "Carlos Gardel." He recognized every song, *Cuesta abajo, Mi Buenos Aires Querido, Volver, Soledad, El día que me quieras*. His hand ached under the weight of the collected lyrics, the pain of his mother's death, the warmth of December and the chill of July, the exodus to his aunt's flat, the tow of forgetting. He paused to fill his lungs with the squalid air of his childhood before committing to listen to the tango. And then, note by note, with naked tenacity, the *bandoneón* pierced the silence inside the flat. The voice of Carlos of yesterday, the sensual baritone, brutally anchored in a hurtful time, unleashed an assault on the fragile security of Patricio's present.

He can sing the tango, he can tell how lonely we are, *El Mudo*, the bastard. And if I could only take her hand and lead her. Instead, the moment I press against her chest she takes a step backward. Coming here alone wasn't what a child should have done. What if I had screamed loud enough to get myself arrested. Everybody would have walked backward. Imena, do you understand that it hurts to see you fly away? Please, don't take to the air. *Cuesta abajo, cuesta abajo,* that's how my life goes. Can you hear the voice of *El Mudo,* Imena? He can tell you how it feels. And when he stops singing, the *bandoneón* takes over, telling it just like he does. *Soledad,* yes exactly, *soledad.* And when I look around my flat I see the book, unread, *Les Fleurs* that doesn't have the scent of delight but the stench *du mal.* Imena, your absence leaves me facing my past, alone. Carlitos, don't do that, please, don't tell me everything is hopeless, don't be a son of a bitch. While I try to talk, you sing an ode to misery. Imena, I know that up in the sky the air is lighter. And Carlitos insists on telling me that *Mi Buenos Aires Querido* is to be remembered, to be seen again. I would take to the sky with you, I would take a step into the void, holding you, while leaving behind the heavy load of *Mi Buenos Aires Querido.* The bitterness of the time I spent here in Paris, most of my life, with hope galloping behind me. Imena, what took you away from me? *Volver, con la frente marchita,* as if I had the chance to return to what seems far away. Could it be that a melody is all that is left? What if the entirety of our life was contained in a song? Past and present, joy and anger, apocryphal stories usurping the truth, all within three minutes of a tango. But if my life is all there, in the songs, then what remains is exactly what I want to forget. Can I ignore my past? If the songs were all I have, then you, Imena, would already be part of my past, a song, a melody. *El día que me quieras*, as if there would be such a day. Such a day can only flee from me. Can you hear Carlos sing for you and me? Can you hear the wind and the bells?

6

One, two, three…! Imena ran as fast as she could, touched the palm tree, and ran back to the porch. She lost, and to console herself, she drank a large glass of lemonade and looked at the sky. Another day, on her way home from school, a torrential shower cascaded over her, soaking her hat and feathers, her wet skirt grabbing her thighs, and her shoes squirting water at every step. Her mother, whom she called Beatrice instead of mother, scolded her for not taking refuge under a roof or a tree. This was the first time the smell of wet feathers assaulted her, an experience she would link forever to a sense of violation and shame. That was the time when smells started to explain life; a life her nose defined more vividly than words.

One afternoon, when the sun was visiting everybody, Imena sat on the porch, closing her eyes and covering her ears. She did not want to see, hear, or taste anything; she only wanted to smell. She let the air flow through her nose, carrying the fluttering atoms of the surrounding objects. She then identified a slow procession of scents. There was the wood of the porch covered with old paint, somewhat humid, different from the wood of the entry door covered with varnish, different from the wood of the rocking chair that was hard and bare. There was the smell of the white cockatoo, part feather, part saw dust, and part feces, the last one a combination of ammonia and decomposed seeds. There was the smell of seaweed that served as background to all other smells, a base note, a ground holding essence. And there was the salt suspended in the air, impregnating every element, flavoring tears and saliva, making the earth bow to the sea. Those were the basic fragrances, the ones that marked her youth, the ones she would identify many years later in different continents. And of all those olfactory experiences, salty air, suspended salt, volatile sodium chloride from the sea, left an indelible mark. Years later, she would imagine *La rose sauvage* in the context of its proximity to bodily fluids. The most sublime fragrance, the rose, construed as an earthy element, sweaty and salty, like the free air of the tropics, like tears and sweat emanating from a human body, a deconstructive reinterpretation. And she kept her eyes closed, because only through the sense of smell she understood the world.

When Imena played at *Pompierre* beach, she laughed hard and for a long time. She felt the sand, the salty water, and the sun on her skin, and that made her giddy. Her cousins invented all sort of tricks to make her laugh; they loved the spectacle. They would throw sand at her, sprinkle her with surf foam, and drag her body into the water, while Imena would laugh with abandon, savoring the childish torture. It was a naïve laugh, pure joy, a song from a child tickled by natural elements. One day her cousins dug a big hole at the edge of the surf line, right there where the water becomes vaporous and white while the sand tries to swallow its advance. And after a struggle, when Imena's laughter impregnated the sky with her youth and innocence, her cousins forced her into the hole burying her completely, her head, the only part of the body remaining above the sand. The cousins did pirouettes and ran around her while Imena continued to laugh, loud and long. In the middle of the mêlée, one of her cousins proposed to kick her head to score an imaginary goal, as if her head were a football, but luckily, the others did not let this happen. And with the same enthusiasm, everybody ran away to the other end of the beach leaving Imena buried in the sand.

The surf approached her timidly, only touching her for a second or two, before retreating into the full body of the ocean. And after a few moments, the white foam licked her neck and shoulders again. Imena could not move, the weight of the sand immobilized her while the air played with her hair and the sun kissed her lips. Her laugh died under the sound of the waves. And as the surf continued to lick her, the territory of her skin was gradually revealed. She lay impassively as the air and the water peeled layers of innocence away from her. Her body grew from the sand and floated over the low air of the shore. She felt a sense of fluidity, and the wind rushed to bring the aromas of the surf, the sun, the seaweed, and the sea grape. At that time, Imena knew her body wanted to feel the world, a time when her mind wanted to explore foreign shores, a time when Guadeloupe—the butterfly island of her youth—seemed desperately anchored.

7

When life comes to a standstill and today looks just like a used yesterday, that is the time to consider doing the opposite of what you would have done. Patricio, in such a time in his life, considered the DOM-TOM. Of all the places he could have chosen, Guadeloupe was the least philosophical. Patricio was certain not to find any colleague there, nobody to entice him to render a proof nor to consider an alternative angle. Guadeloupe convoked images of relaxation, abandonment, thoughtless nights. He arranged every detail ahead of time, even convincing René to water his plants in his absence. The summer was the perfect moment to escape and he seized the opportunity. His arrival was simple, one man, one bag, and one book: *Pride and Prejudice.* His philosophical considerations had no room on this island, what Patricio wanted was a taste of romanticism. An idea somewhat dangerous, since the concept of romanticism catapulted him to his youth. But he was eager to reinvent the concept in a new light. He thought he could let the breeze play around him without having to think, infer, cogitate. No deliberations, he only wanted sensations.

He did not expect to find the ethereal image of Imena, running for cover, when the torrential rain descended in the ripe afternoon. They both took cover under the imperfect straw roof of a fruit stand. The water leaked in a random pattern, and when Patricio took cover to avoid getting wet, he came in close proximity to Imena. She was looking at the gray curtain of rain that swallowed the view to the port. Patricio noticed how she grabbed a carambole and proceeded to savor its essence, inhaling the air close to its skin. She then grabbed a maracudja and a pineapple and smelled them too. Her lips opened and closed as if reciting a prayer to a mythical god, while her eyes remained closed. This image was sublime, magnificent, and Patricio could not keep his mind away from it.

*****

Her pale skin is luminous, in an island of the sun, contrasting with the skin of sun-drenched fruits, Patricio thought. A young woman who samples the air in such a way. I can feel the moisture of the rain, but I cannot sense whatever she seems to be sensing. No schemes for this, no system. And the rain falling, corralling us under the straw roof. And the softness of her eyes, blue when open. And the need to stay here observing, and the fear that senses can overtake the mind and ruin a lifetime of order. But who are you? And why does your hand cradle the fruit, as if it was precious? Who are you?

The rain lays a film of moisture over her skin, over her face, over her feet. The moisture that floods her triangle, I think, when she beholds a sensation deeper than the essence of fruits. The sense of me looking at her, the sense of me listening to her breath, the sense that my senses are painfully confused. And when the wind sprays sea salt and water over my face, I feel like she cuts my lips.

And when I ask who are you? You answer: I'm Imena. Imena, unknown to me. Imena never imagined or dreamt. Imena, as if the name itself could explain all I feel this instant. Imena, you're the skin of the fruit, the layer separating the carnal energy from the air that swirls around its corners. Imena, and the name sounds like it was always there, just waiting to reveal its essence.

38

✴✴✴✴✴

"All of my life," Imena said.

"And are you happy here?" Patricio asked.

"This is where I live, but I hope to learn about other places, perfumes, and music."

"I love music… some music."

"And I love perfumes."

"Interesting, but I cannot touch my music and you cannot touch your perfumes."

"But they're one and the same, a perfume has three sets of notes like a musical accord."

"Oh yes, I've heard this before."

"Well, the notes unfold over time, with the immediate impression of the top note leading to the deeper middle notes, and the base notes gradually appearing as the final stage."

"Can you hear the sound of smells?"

"Yes I can, I already know all the sounds that exist on this island."

"That's not possible, there must be thousands of different smells or sounds. Consider only the flowers, and the fruits."

Imena looked at the man standing in front of her. He was not an islander; that was clear. She always wanted to meet those who came from Paris. Those people were exposed to a different air and their breath smelled differently. As he stood dodging the rain, she admired Patricio's worldly aspect. And she noticed that when the rain fell, his eyes also fell over her, touching her moist skin. She found his demeanor elegant, but an essence of sadness exuded from him.

"Consider only the people, the human variations are even more complex than all the flowers and fruits together," Imena said.

"Do you actually smell people?"

"I don't mean to, but if they cross my path there's nothing I can do."

Patricio would not have ventured in this direction, but her comments invited him.

"So, what do I smell like?"

"You smell like sadness, an old sadness."

And with a quick gesture, Imena turned her face away from him, picked a curling stick of cinnamon, brought it close to her nose, and proceeded to inhale placidly, slowly.

"My name is Patricio."

"Patricio is how your name sounds like, but your name doesn't mean anything unless it suits your scent."

"How do you call the smell of sadness?" he asked.

"I don't want to know. There are thousands of other smells more interesting than the smell of sadness. Are you always sad?"

"No, only when I remember sad things."

Imena handed him a reddish-brown tamarind pod and asked him to savor its scent.

"Can you tell me what this smells like?"

"I'm not sure."

"I'm not sure either. Sometimes it's sweet, sometimes it's bitter and sour. Maybe your scent sounds bitter sometimes, maybe it sounds sweet sometimes."

*****

Imena's need for intimacy had grown as the world around her had contracted. And in Guadeloupe, she was suffocating. One day she found a way to continue studying perfumery in Paris and her imagination went amok. Nothing could compare to that dream. It was all for her to cherish, to caress, to throw up in the air and catch before it hit the ground. Imena saw herself in the company of other students who felt the same way. She imagined fragrances, forbidden flowers, discussions, long nights at cafés, and the change of weather with the seasons. She even wore a scarf, hat, and gloves for *La Saint-Sylvestre* when the temperature in Guadeloupe reached 32 degrees Celsius. Guadeloupe had its own aromas, but for Imena, they felt too sweet and sometimes even putrid. She wanted to smell the fragrance of northern flowers, of boulevards, the aroma emanating from *épiceries*, *boulangeries*, and the individual scents from a thousand different people. She dreamt of the butterfly island, raising from the sea and beating its wings high among the clouds carrying her to the city of lights. But in reality, the butterfly island would not fly away; it was anchored to the bottom of the sea by a thousand generations of volcanic rock.

She spent many afternoons sitting on the front porch of the old wooden house where she was born. She had not lived anywhere else, neither had her mother, nor her grandmother—they were a race of anchored women. And on this porch, she would rock back and forth in a rocking chair, dreaming of her future, while her white cockatoo gazed at her from the corner of its left eye.

"Beatrice, I'll be fine," answered Imena when her mother questioned her plans. She continued to rock on the rocking chair.

"What about that professor?" Beatrice said.

"That has nothing to do with my decision, you know that."

"I don't think you should live with him."

Imena was quiet for a while. She looked over the porch railing at the purple bougainvillea. The wind played with its leaves and flowers and she felt like joining in the play.

"Beatrice, that's ridiculous. I hardly know him, I'm not going to live with him."

"That's what you say now. Wait until you get there and the whole thing will be different."

"Don't you believe what I tell you?"

"I believe you…"

"Enough already."

"Well, he looks sad," Beatrice said.

Imena detested the snooping questions of her mother as much as she detested lying. She had decided to fly away a long time ago. She had wished for an escape from the heat of the tropics that putrefied everything alive. Patricio was different from anyone she had met before. She found his eyes evoking, his slender body inviting. He was capable of listening and he did not question her fascination with scents. He would also walk on the sand while singing songs from his childhood. He said he had to sing them to defeat them.

Imena spoke to him about her dreams, the idea of learning about the world of scents in the city of lights. Patricio devoured her innocence, this intensity a fresh experience, unedited. The notion that a mysterious bond existed between them flooded Patricio's mind, and he took her hand trying to decipher his own destiny, an imposition that Imena ignored then but would later resent. But those were the days of oneness, when the sounds merged composing a delicate sonata, balanced by her sensorial intensity and his inquisitive force, a melody he found as sweet as a tender word, while for her it was beautiful as the green morning dew. And without effort, they glided over the sand, they breathed the sultry air, they constructed a magical world with Paris at its center, a world containing their unconscious projections.

At *Les Saintes,* she knew the morning colors looked different the day she walked on the sand with him—the *tourment d'amour* were sweeter. She walked next to him, and with every step, the wind lifted her higher and higher. She could see herself flying away, and from the sky, the *filets blues* looked like small dream catchers dotted with orange tears. And when he insisted on climbing up to the roof of the brightly painted house, she thought he was trying to get away from the earth and travel high into the sky. But he was not. He seemed absorbed by the smell of her hair and neck. And his face seemed bewitched when his hands touched her skin. Paris then seemed so close to her. And as he touched her, she touched Paris. She noticed the angle of his jaw, like a boomerang coming back to his neck, while he looked at the horizon with interest, as if trying to find the answer to some deep metaphysical question. And Paris so close to her, so close.

8

Paris, Paris. The recognizable language, the oblique sunlight; people wore a pale skin, just like her, and the air heavy with a million dreams floated above all. Imena settled in a modest flat in the *11éme arrondissement* far away from abundance but in the center of herself. The flat had enough room for her dreams with two windows opening to the vastness of the city. The smell of the streets was a novelty for her. In the mornings, the warm aroma of early baked baguettes provided a gloriously fleeting top note. The middle note was composed of moist air rising from freshly rinsed sidewalks, mixed with dust and cigarettes butts. At the bottom of these, she perceived the scent of her own body, a heavy and lasting presence, an animal emanation—the sign that she was no longer a simple island girl but a desirable woman. This world, vast and anonymous, penetrating her senses, removing veil after veil, allowed her carnal self to soar. And all this exuberance needed an anchor. And without her full awareness, Patricio, by way of his paucity of thought and grave demeanor, held Imena firmly to the ground, while her arms reached to the sky and the thin air above.

At *La Sorbonne*, the walls were dark and the air heavy with too many thoughts. Imena avoided entering that world, Patricio's world. There were thousands of books but only a handful of flowers, an unsettling discrepancy. She preferred to wait until the end of the day, after layering bergamot over jasmine or rose over fougère, to visit Patricio in his flat. There she could look out the window, over the Mansard roofs, to contemplate the territory of her dreams. Patricio spoke in a soft voice, illustrating the beauty of life, past and present, delivering a sense of peace and calmness, a sense she did not know existed. Their dissimilar worlds became interconnected.

The profundity opening to the freshness of the flowers, the light breeze molded by a thought, the gloomy past relieved by an exuberant present, the beautiful nothingness coming into being.

They spoke of their silences, their senses, *la raison d'être*, all with softness, under the slanted light of her lamps, both firmly attached to the present, or tomorrow's present, a subterfuge to silence memories from the past, a beautiful escape. Imena read numerous books, all procured by Patricio, his attempt to remedy her lack of literary exposure. She could recognize the most furtive essence, but the most common words sometimes eluded her. He brought her books by Dumas, Flaubert, Yourcenar, translations of Hemingway, Faulkner and García Márquez, short stories by Chekhov and Poe. He would not share with her Borges, Cortázar, or Sábato, the homeland heroes, the dangerous ones. The latest book, "*Les Fleurs du Mal*," proved to be a challenge to her interest. She felt this was an imposition, a desire on his part to make her conform to his interests, the first sign that her freedom would be threatened, an impression that would grow, gradually, every afternoon. And when he would ask her about a certain verse in the book, she would answer with a languid sigh looking out of the window, trying to smell the rain drops that beaded on the outside of the glass.

Their days were long, their afternoons longer, their nights started to become interminable. Imena remembered how she left the butterfly island hoping to find a grander world, with more scents, with a larger sky, large enough to accommodate her spirit. And Patricio showed her a grander world, and the *Cinquième Sens* provided a universe of scents, and the Paris sky seemed limitless. But the delicate shell of her self-esteem experienced an attack every time he made a suggestion, her interpretation of an imposition, an assault on her independence.

9

The red door kept reality from entering into the striped tunic's hotel. The dry air had free access into the courtyard by sliding from tile to tile until it filled the open space, and then, after carelessly swirling around, rapidly ascended, escaping into the medina. Loose dreams and confused thoughts trailed behind the air. The red door also kept beggars out on the street. But Jacques walked through it, effortlessly, wearing a red beret covering half of his left eyebrow. He crossed the courtyard diagonally, from corner to corner, and disappeared into a guestroom directly behind one of the flowering orange trees. His step was firm yet light, his shoulder carried a bag full with tools to carve marble, limestone, or maybe granite. Imena followed his movements from her window. He walks on water, she thought, while sensing a faint aroma that reminded her of salt and seaweed. She stepped out of her room and into the courtyard to fill her lungs with the smell she perceived. But when she tried to capture the smell, it escaped like a bandit up into the sky. Imena could only grab the loose dreams and confused thoughts left behind.

She resolved to take to the streets and follow the trace of this familiar aroma. Amid the turmoil of thoughts, her feet moved quickly over the cobblestones, and the pink walls applauded her tempo. She passed people, doors, monkeys, a scream, while still feeling the warmth and dryness of the air. People looked at her as she rushed by them. They reacted with surprise. The sight of a lone pale woman crossing the medina, hovering in the air, was strange. She saw shadows again, cutting in angles, swallowing entire buildings. She felt her pulse accelerating and her skin becoming moist with sweat. But after hounding the medina, the aroma did not materialize.

His step was light, thought Imena, as she returned to the courtyard, he didn't press on the red clay, and he floated, even with the bag on his shoulder. I can always remember the salty air. It covered everything and everyone on my butterfly island. And the seaweed stretching itself at the edge of water and sand, resting under the sun or swallowed by the surf. All of the same sensations but now in this courtyard. The salty air was oppressive, and then I flew away to Paris. The intensity of Patricio's questions became oppressive, and then I came south. And the striped tunic, no…, not him. He may know something, he seems to know me, growing out of nothing at my window, that civet. He said I was looking for something unknown to me. I don't know whether I'm searching or not, but I know how the salty air feels. But why do I follow the air now? If it felt oppressive then, it will feel the same way now. And look at me now, persecuting the saltpeter from which I escaped. It's time for me to let go, it will be better if I go into my room and rest my head on the pillow. I should let the wind blow away the salt of my youth.

Imena returned to her room and found relief from the openness of the courtyard. She closed the window to shut out the air. She was now free to sleep without the burden of her salt. When she finally rested her head on the pillow, hundreds of thoughts had come together to dance in her mind. It was a feast, a bacchanalia. The color purple floated, the white cockatoo gazing at her, *La rose sauvage*, Patricio's hands, *ylang-ylang*, oceanic, ozonic, that red beret walking across the courtyard, Paris so far away, and the civet, and the fear of not finding anything, the white wind and the golden sand, the butterfly, her butterfly, seaweed at the base, the heart of narcissus, a head full of mimosa, and the lightness of her spirit, and the heaviness of her dreams, all the colors of dusk.

The stillness, the darkness, and the soundless space, conjured a weightless silence for her head to rest. Once again released, the whirlwind of dreams went amok in her mind while the closed window kept the air from the medina outside of her room.

In the morning, when her body was perfectly paralyzed and her eyes were moving rapidly under her closed eyelids, Imena dreamt again of the swan. And when she finally opened her eyes and the morning light became thin enough to fit through the crack between the window and the wall, Imena felt as if she were surrounded by the smell of wet feathers. She decided to clear the air in her room by opening the door and her window, letting the air circulate freely. The same aroma of salt and seaweed that had assaulted her the previous day surprised her; it was freshly present, greeting her that morning. And then, her eyes saw the silhouette of a man sitting at the other end of the courtyard, in front of one of the flowering orange trees, smoking something that could have been hashish. She crossed the courtyard and stood in front of him.

"What happened to your red beret?" she asked, after noticing his uncovered head showing a receding hairline and eyes the color of wheat.

"You must be the one who watched me, I thought there was someone there," he said while pointing to the window of her room.

"Not many people come here, you're the first in the last couple of days," she said.

"Are you expecting someone?"

His words propelled her to consider her situation. She was alone in this forsaken part of the world accompanied by her need to search. But her curiosity forced her to ask him again,

"What happened to your red beret?"

"I only wear it when I'm away from home."

"Does that mean you live here?"

"No, but I feel comfortable here, I can do my work."

"What do you do?"

"Why do you ask?"

Imena felt the familiar heaviness of questions. The continuous inquiry, the need to explain in a rational way. She could look around the courtyard and absorb the light and colors reflected from the walls. She could identify the components of the acrid salty air and the pungent seaweed. But she could not answer his question. She felt like leaping into the air from the very place where she stood. She felt the need to fly away.

"You don't need to answer. My name is Jacques."

She landed. And with her two feet on the ground, she extended her hand to him and said that her name was Imena and that she was here on a short holiday and that the medina had a mysterious maze quality; that the air came from above and that the innkeeper was somewhat strange and stunk of civet and that something happened yesterday that made her remember the butterfly island of her childhood.

"This place doesn't remind me of anything," Jacques said. "I just find it peaceful."

"But what is it that you do?"

"If you ask questions, I'll ask questions in return."

Imena felt the threat. Without responding, she turned around and walked to the center of the courtyard where the fountain was celebrating life. Her hands brought water to her face, washing away the memory of past interrogations by Beatrice, by Patricio, by her own self.

"I make sculptures, primarily out of stone," Jacques said. "I shape them like the human body, womens torsos, many of those, you may like them."

"I suppose you make them look real, do you?"

"Sometimes the wet marble shines like your wet skin."

"Do your sculptures smell like real people?"

Jacques never considered the smell of his sculptures. There were dust and stone particles in the studio, but no discernable smell. He then traced the angles of her torso with his eyes and found it slender and gracious.

"Live torsos have a lovely fragrance, but you are correct, my sculptures don't."

"That's tragic, gravity and shape, but no animal fragrance."

*****

I could chisel a hard stone, Jacques thought, and make it look like her body. Her expression… that's more difficult. But if I watch her closely, I may see beyond her skin, beyond her shape. I come here looking for peace and she enters the courtyard with questions. So many times in this courtyard, but never a torso like hers. When I asked, she turned her face away from me. Marble would be best since her skin is pale. Marble, smooth and maybe white. And if I follow my hand, it will create her shape in the air. And if I swing my hammer, it will eliminate the excess stone and reveal her shape. I can almost touch her shape, her skin, the marble, the coldness, her warmth. There, there, looking at me, from the center of the courtyard, her hands wet, her face wet. The torture of wanting to hold her but not wanting to destroy the image. The same situation again, the same agony of holding and destroying. The hammer, swinging high, creating shapes. I never thought about the fragrance of a stone. She's right, how tragic, what a loss. But if the stone could emanate a fragrance, it would be the fragrance of pale skin, like her skin. If I could only carve what I see, it would be lightness, but if I were to carve what I smell, I would be lost.

10

I knew she would accept the mint tea, the striped tunic thought, because she's desperately searching. If I would bring out dates, she would accept them as well. But she does not know the beast is inside her. I heard it the other night; it was horrifying. I had to go and see what it was. Through the window, it was only she. The beast is inside. And like so many others that come here, she's deeply lost. But her freshness is different, she's light as the mist, she flows like dry air. I sit here and I see them come and go. I sit here…, and I sit here, for there is nowhere for me to go. And when the sun shines, and when the sun dies, the air and the shadows are like my brothers and sisters. My guests believe the answer is in a realm outside of their own selves. That's why they come here—to look. They all go to bathe themselves, to shed the layers of memories. As if the water would do the magic. As if the water would deliver them as new people. And they don't understand that our lives stick to us, like a layer of sweat drying on our skin in the hot desert air. I know them, but they don't know that I know them. Otherwise, why? Otherwise, why do they react to me as if I were a hideous creature? She was definitely scared of me. She avoided my proximity but accepted my tea. But foreigners are always that way. They come here looking for something. And when they find other realities they deny them, they destroy them.

My guests despise my attire. Yes, it's old, my tunic, with all the stripes, wrapping my body and my soul. It contains the essence of who I am. They don't know what came before them. They don't know the wind already occupied their spaces. That's why I offer them tea. Because the ones before them needed it just as much as they do. They just don't know it. Only the search brightens their horizons. But the search is futile by itself. Only when the air comes into the courtyard do they find a direction. And even then, when the star shows the way, they don't see it. I wish for the air to fill the courtyard so she may find her direction that way. But what does that mean for me? If the air comes into the courtyard or if it returns to the sky. What does it matter to me? Perhaps it matters because my soul is now sedentary, no caravans, no horizons burning. Perhaps because the blood in my veins feels cold, coagulating my dreams. The life I live is the mirage of the life I have lived. Today so silent, living the lives of others.

Jacques doesn't know about her as I do. And when she finds him fascinating, she's only living as so many others have lived, mistakenly absorbed by their primeval impressions. Magically convinced, not knowing that what seems so perfect is only the projection of their unfulfilled fantasies. And with ease and distraction, the world will turn, and the result of erroneous projections will solidify a life, and make it almost real, livable. How sad.

"Imena," she wrote down on the passport document, a beautiful African name that means "dream." That's her essential temperament, for a dreamy substance constitutes her nature. I can see with my gray eyes the path that brings her to this courtyard. I can sense the need and the disquieting elements of her soul. I can feel her need to search, the same way I can feel my need to contain my impulses. She makes me feel entire, she tempers my instinct to revert to the desert. I can watch her asleep as she struggles with the beast. I can almost see through her eyes. But she doesn't know any of this. She doesn't know about the beast. And when I offer her mint tea, she thinks I'm invading her life, not knowing that my gesture is meant to alleviate the anxiety, the apprehension, the deep feeling of loss, of an incomplete self. Imena, I'm your innkeeper, I can be the tamer of the beast.

11

WHEN the sun flooded the courtyard and three of the flowering orange trees were bathed in the light, the striped tunic appeared from one corner and offered them mint tea. Imena became stiff as she recalled her previous conversations with the stinking civet. Jacques, more familiar with the creature and apparently not affected by his scent, accepted the offer graciously. Imena watched while Jacques swallowed the first sip of tea and recognized that he was lost, just as she was, and that he was also searching. She then took a sip from her cup and waited for the air to circulate freely, to revive the aroma of salty air and seaweed, to slide from tile to tile into the courtyard, filling her lungs. And when her senses were satisfied, she decided not to fly away.

"Is the hammer separate from the hand?" Imena asked. "Can the hand shape the stone without the hammer? Can the hammer shape the stone without the hand?"

Delighted by the fresh presence, Jacques looked at her.

"There's a conversation between the stone and the hammer", he said. "When they understand each other and there's synchronicity, my hand is no longer necessary. The blows follow a rhythm, like music, without effort on my part. But when the conversation turns sour between the stone and the hammer, my hand needs to take control, a futile endeavor, since no human effort can transform stone into art against its will. That's when the work of the sculptor becomes violent, when instead of creating shapes we destroy nature."

The winds had stolen the words between the stone and Jacques' hammer, creating chaos and misunderstanding, reducing him to a violent sculptor, his artistic illusions long vanished, his life in the middle of quicksand, sinking.

"Why do you come to this place?" she asked.

"I've been coming here for years, It's a familiar place. I feel I can swing my hammer freely, destroying nothing, maybe creating nothing, maybe looking for you."

Falling in the dry terrain of her sensitivity, Imena heard the sound of his words, a non-inquisitive style, igniting her need for softness, sequestering her imagination, akin to the very essence of her search.

"And if I were not here?"

"I would still be swinging my hammer."

An honest answer hiding a dishonest truth, for Jacques knew his hand did not command the hammer any longer, and his artistic effort accomplished no more than the mere destruction of nature.

"I wasn't supposed to be here, but here I am", Imena said. "Unlike you, this is an unfamiliar place for me. I'm taken by the colors and the scents that permeate the morning and the night. Can you feel the air when it fills the courtyard?"

Jacques felt the pressure to answer imaginatively, to polish the artistic veneer of his barren core, to produce a phrase that would entice her interest.

"The air speaks to me of a maiden voyage, of the desire to find new sands to imprint," Jacques said, a deliberate attempt to define himself as a romantic, a sanctuary for the wind.

"Can you tell me about the stones and the shapes you want to create?"

"I can show you the sculptures I'm working on at this time. Most of them are incomplete, works in progress."

Jacques went on to speak about the stones and the shapes he knew he could not create. He spoke extensively and colorfully, invoking ancient myths and deities, dreams and desires, all in an effort to fulfill Imena's expectations for an answer, the lucidity of his discourse only matched by the hollowness of his reality.

*****

This night is not like the others, and I will not close the window to the courtyard because I want to feel all that comes from outside, I want the air to bathe my skin, I want the sound of beating wings to echo in my room, I want the scent of marble, granite, and onyx to invade my space. I want to feel. And if the swan returns in the morning, I will caress its feathers. And when the morning comes I will be open, for I can feel the lightness, the fragrance in the air, his soft and gentle word. This night is crisp and clear, not like the heavy and condemned nights of Paris. Perhaps this is the reason for coming south, to find this other night, to feel the lightness. If I travel through this night, weightlessly floating out into the courtyard, up into the purple night, following the sparkle, I may be liberated. As I sleep serenely in the small room, the desire for liberation grows within me, impatient to fly over the roofs of the medina, feeling like his hammer may lead the way out of my hole. And on the other side of this night, after the moon traces its dark orbit, escaping the rapacious chase by the wolf, a creature from ancient times that still howls within my body, I will see the lightness, and my body will rest there, open.

*****

The fusion between the aroma of mint tea and chants from ancient spires invaded the small room arising Imena to a day of rapture. She removed several layers of veils, some made of dreams, some of time, others of memories, and looking out into the courtyard she felt radiant, a state of mind that occupied her entire self, all her senses, all her cognitive resources, propelling her into a new uncirculated space, eager to greet Jacques and enter his inviting world unknown to her but full of liberating promises. Imena approached his corner of the courtyard, and extending her hand to Jacques she said, "*Bonjour*, are you creating shapes today?" Jacques held her pale fingers between his hands and recognizing her vulnerability, calculating the distance between the courtyard and his working studio, imagining the possible seduction of such a wonderful creature, responded in a soft and comforting tone.

"*Bonjour, Mademoiselle.* Yes, I'll create shapes today, and if you are curious, you may be witness to the process."

Through the red door they left under the observing eye of the striped tunic. They ventured deep into the medina and once at his studio, Imena felt a sense of lightness. She walked over the white and gray dust particles that covered every surface of the studio, entering a world where shapes were transformed and liberated from rough stones. She attempted to find the scent of round figures, some standing, some reclining, scattered all over the studio, but the stones had no smell of their own.

Jacques stood behind Imena, remaining silent, while she studied the series of sculptures that had been in the same spot for several seasons, gathering dust and shame. He had not completed any sculpture in the last two years, perhaps because his muse had died, perhaps because his sensibility was an artifice, a pretense for a life molded by a bohemian ideal, perhaps because his inner landscape was barren. But when Imena asked about his latest creation, he pointed to a reclining nude, claiming it had taken the best of his efforts over the past few months, the weight of the marble as heavy as the malice of his deception.

She traveled through the room, she touched the smooth surfaces, exploring the space surrounding the sculptures. They spoke of divine creation, the game of playing God, about the transfiguration of matter into shape, flowers into fragrances, about suffering and ecstasy, all under the dim light of the afternoon sun, a light that filtered through the wooden shutters, a light so weak that it failed to expose Jacques for what he really was, a dilettante.

But the afternoon continued to grow, and the words that carried hope, desire, and salvation floated in the air, like symbols of an aspired life playing in the theater of their dreams. And when his hand reached the back of her neck, under her hair, Imena felt the blow of the hammer, a seductive force shining like the star she wanted to find, south from north, in the dismal air of this simulacrum.

✶✶✶✶✶

The softness of his hand, his voice, the softness of not asking or expecting, the softness of sharing the games of God. It all feels precious to me. And when his hand makes a circle in the air, a shape is born out of the hardness of the stone, like pressing a thin petal and filling the air with the world of irises. And when my body sings songs of tomorrow, the light so intense, lifting me, liberating me, I feel I'm being born today. Imena, my name sounds as new as the morning, for today I see the afternoon as a glowing morning. And the morning is the time for the arousal of my senses, not a swan, but a shimmering me, Imena, open to a field of lights, absent of mist.

The peace of not having to fly over the medina, for the red clay holds my feet warmly, kindly. And if I smell the air, the scent of salt and seaweed feels like home, no need to run, no need to escape. I can be here, calmly, embraced by the extensions of the hammer, not wanting to talk of the past. Paris, Paris, so distant from me.

12

Imena, the shell may be hard; the shell may not allow you to immerse into me. The thoughts are my shell. I find them here, at the university, among my books and students. Imena, there's a tender interior, believe me. And when you look through the window at the field of Mansard roofs, it is my spirit that watches you, not my thoughts, for they are incapable of feeling your creation, the world that you formed and lives in my interior, hidden from your senses. There, there, in the inside. Imena, can you hear the wind and the bells?

13

My mother always spoke of Paris, "a fabled city," she said. There, in my fairy tale city, I was certain to find all kinds of candy, and even better, the best croissants. So by the time she turned deadly ill, she had already imprinted an extensive collection of Paris images in my mind. There were the parks, the boulevards, and the iron tower—places I had not yet seen. That was her way to deliver me to the brutal unknown, to the place where I was to grow in constant assault from the past. But the promise I remember most was not that of the boulevards, but of the angels in the sky, up there, above the clouds, where they dance and laugh, floating, calling me to join them in their play.

As a lone child leaving my country, I released the hands that escorted me, and waited for the silver bird to fly high above the clouds, to the place where the angels play. But when the clouds came together to form a velvety carpet outside my window, a soft and white horizon, the sun shining above all, I did not see anyone playing, there were no angels, the light intense, the emptiness—immeasurable. So when the stewardess brought me a soda, I asked her about the angels. She smiled and padded my head. "They're there," she said, and my dreams remained suspended. I slept, waiting to arrive in a Paris winter having left the summer of Buenos Aires.

My aunt waved at me from among the crowd of people standing on the other side of the rope. She took my hand and squeezed it hard before planting a kiss on each of my burning cheeks. I can still feel the burning sensation, a mixture of fear and excitement about the unknown. There I was in Paris, taking my aunt's hand, having left the falling hands of my dead mother, all in the absence of playing angels. Imena, you should have seen how vulnerable I was. And the first thing that I asked my aunt was to take me to eat croissants. She laughed and said those things were not good for me.

It wasn't until I was paid a few francs for watching the neighbor's dog that I managed to buy my own croissants. I remember carefully handing the coins to the old woman in the *boulangerie* in exchange for two little golden half-moons. Imena, they were perfectly shaped, with a crispy buttery texture—delicate. But I only ate one of them, because the image of my mother's hands falling came rushing into my mind. I think I wept. I hid the other croissant under my pillow, stuffed between the bed and the wall in the little room my aunt had improvised for me. Every night, before falling asleep, I touched the drying golden half-moon, hoping to see my mother, hoping to dream of angels playing above the clouds. But a week later, when my aunt changed the bed sheets, the dry croissant disappeared. Imena, I haven't eaten another croissant since.

14

The howling was revolting last night. I saw her again through the window, thrashing the air in the heart of her nightmares. But this morning she looks radiant, as if the nocturnal odyssey didn't affect her. I know what I heard. I will bring her mint tea without comment, I will be a shadow—an invisible man.

She turns her face away from me in repudiation of my fetid tunic. And when the dry breeze and the stillness break the morning spell, her eyes brighten and her face becomes splendid. How sad to see this fleeting image, beautiful in its levity, soaring high to the sun, only to redden the sky when it burns in its presence. Jacques will probably join her in the courtyard. I know his soul. His search ended a long time ago. I'm not clear what he found, but it must have been horrifying; maybe he found himself. He doesn't repudiate my presence for he's aware that I know about him. Sometimes he seems scared of me. And when he's uncertain, he looks at me with an anxious face, just like he's doing now, fearing I would expose him.

But today I'm an invisible man. Nobody can behold me, nobody can address me with words, I'm not material, past or present. For today I exist only in my mind, I'm only a conscience today. And when I watch Jacques take her hand and lick the dripping tea from her fingers, I hold myself back, knowing what I know, I still hold myself back. For today, the nature of me is incorporeal.

As an observer, I accumulate life within my skin, inside my external perimeter. I drink the life of my guests, not their blood, but their dreams, their nightmares, their selves. And growing old in this desert, where the air comes and goes like a universal tide of people's dreams, makes me a man, a hard and humble man. But as a shadow, today, I don't have a presence.

Imena, there's a beast within you, howling at night, the sign of a vigorous search, making you a splendid creature. Imena, Jacques won't tame the beast. For he's only a force of falsehood, tired and pretentious. His hands, Imena, those hands that force themselves upon you, aren't mythical, not the hands of Thor or Vulcan. This I see with my ancient gray eyes. But as a conscience, I'm not available to you, Imena. I can only see and feel your bewilderment from my corner of the courtyard. And when your tears fall on the red clay, my conscience will materialize. For only after your search claudicates will my words be relevant to you. Imena, I'm an old conscience, and the desert taught me how to vanish.

15

Of all the squares in medieval Paris, the symmetry and elegance of *Place des Vosges* offered Patricio the most calming balsam. He walked under the arcades when his spirit needed cover; but when he felt supreme, he stormed the courtyard and ordered the white stone and red brick to stand in parallel attention. Inside this envelope, he would surrender to his memories, sometimes, other times he would attack and conquer them valiantly. And in this empty afternoon, Patricio went to *Place des Vosges* seeking cover under the arcades. Because she left no sign of her destination, no indication of purpose, no emotional register, he could do nothing but walk under the arcades, a walk as laborious and preposterous as his escape from his lost past.

He walked counterclockwise, like an Olympian, to undo time. And the more he walked, the louder her voice became, defying the natural order of things. "I must go now," sounded softly, "I MUST GO NOW," sounded loudly. Patricio feared the odds of holding her again were vanishing, like daylight at dusk.

✶✶✶✶✶

Once in his flat, Patricio read verse after verse from *Les Fleurs du Mal*. A certain remote strangeness held him captive until the ringing of the telephone startled him. The unexpected sound of her voice barged into his solitude.

"Patricio", she said.

He wanted to answer at once, but the words crowded his throat choking him.

"Patricio", she said again.

The telephone static was dense, the night was dense, his thought process—coagulated.

"Imena, where are you?" he finally said.

"In Marrakech."

"What are you doing there?"

"It doesn't matter. I'm calling to tell you…"

"But where are you exactly?" Patricio interrupted.

"In a small hotel with a red door near the *Djemaa El-Fna*. But that's not important."

"What happened to you?"

"Patricio, many things happened to me."

She paused for a second while the scratchy static expanded, like the pulse of a malevolent creature, filling the silence, sustaining the conversation.

"I'll be back in a few days but I'll need space and time to be alone," she said.

"Imena, I need to see you."

"Do you understand what I'm saying to you?"

Patricio understood that something indeed happened. He recognized her distant tone, but her words surprised him. He perceived gravity in her words, a heavier quality, different from her ethereal self.

"Imena, I miss you."

"Yes, I know, but I must go now."

The static ended abruptly and Patricio hung up the telephone. He then started to hear the familiar thump, thump, thump, filling every corner of his hollow self.

✶✶✶✶✶

A bizarre call, thought Patricio, a warning, maybe a prophecy of disgrace. Many things have happened to her, she said. I don't really know what that means but the words sounded ominous. Then… Marrakech. Why not Rome or Amsterdam? But Marrakech. And like in that ungodly morning, she says "I must go now." But where's she going? Yes, her presence can be an absence, but there was more than an absence in her voice, there was boldness. Is this flight like the others, Imena? Are you walking backwards while still holding my hand? I wonder what dreams haunt you now? But every time I ask, you fade away, and your eyes look at the sky where the air is lighter. Imena, I don't know what dreams or fears took you to Marrakech. I don't know if the air is lighter in the desert. But I can see there's a door, red, an entry to your world, and a purple sky that wraps your spirit.

*****

With clear and intense determination Patricio opened the window and his gaze traveled south, above the roofs, until it reached the empty sky. He stayed at the window for what he thought an eternity, enthralled, attentive to the street sounds. He then moved slowly through his flat and collected several items, placing them on top of the bureau. There was a wristwatch, a pair of sunglasses, three shirts, two pairs of pants, underwear and socks, his passport, and the unfinished copy of *Les Fleurs du Mal* with a picture of Imena in-between its pages marking the place where a verse read:

> *Comme vous êtes loin, paradis parfumé,*
> *Où sous un clair azur tout n'est qu'amour et joie,*
> *Où tout ce que l'on aime est digne d'être aimé,*
> *Où dans la volupté pure le cœur se noie!*
> *Comme vous êtes loin, paradis parfumé!*

He needed to venture into the unknown, he needed to place his known world on hold. And his first step was to call René.

"René, I need you to substitute for me in the morning

seminar tomorrow, maybe the next morning too," Patricio said. "Or better yet, keep doing it until I come back."

"Yes Professor, but, for how long will you be absent?" René asked.

"I won't be absent; I'll be here in spirit."

"I see, is there anything else you need done while you're away?"

"No, just don't say a word to the rest of the faculty."

"Professor..." René paused for a second and hesitated before continuing. "Professor, the last time we made this arrangement you seemed very distraught afterwards."

"Don't worry, René."

"No I won't... But, may I ask you where you are going?"

"I'm going south to Marrakech to open a door, a red door."

16

He remembered how his mother turned her face the day the uniformed guards escorted his father away, his hands still red with jealous blood. They grabbed him by the neck and dragged him through the streets in front of the towns people who stood on the sidewalk watching the spectacle. He learned that the misery of one was the entertainment of another. And when he looked up to his mother, hoping to find comfort and warmth, he saw her stony face and her afternoon eyes. That was when he lost his father for the first time and when he hated his mother for the first time.

And when he sought the comfort of his mother, he only found indifference. During those days, the air and the light felt closer to him. And the days became longer, and the nights became shorter, and he learned that people can harbor a beast inside their bodies, a horrid creature. Those were the days before the caravans, before he took to the sand and the wind, before he ran with the forsaken, the days that still contained a place with a name, holy or unholy, but a known place.

Many years later, the striped tunic would not recognize his father when he finally stepped out of jail, a blind walking specter. His old man looked older, broken, his vacuous eyes hovering in the dead center of round shadows. And when he went to kiss him, the old man did not move, he looked through him, as if he was made of air. And for the rest of that first night, the striped tunic looked at the sky and told his father about the shapes formed by the stars. His father remembered the shapes, and told stories about gods and beasts, and the men in-between them. The striped tunic did not wear a tunic then, he wore trousers and a shirt opened at the neck, like other youths. He was free and fast, like the wind, before the burden of caring for the broken blind became imprinted on his soul. He needed to see for his father and for himself. He learned to touch the colors, he started to hear the space, and he began to smell fear, anger, joy, and sadness. And while sitting under the purple sky, the stories his father told became real, and darkness spoke in a clear and diaphanous language.

One day, when he walked to his father to offer him mint tea, he noticed his father's eyes to be heavier, as if the weight of the shadows had become unbearable. He then called his name but his father did not answer. He tried to raise his father and bring him up to his feet, but the body had no lift, no upward movement, it simply sank. And when the rigor stiffened his father's body and the air stopped moving through his lungs, he understood the finality of his imperfect father.

The striped tunic became a striped tunic during the funeral. His family prepared the body at home, with the help of a neighbor experienced in caring for the dead. Men chanted Muslim professions of faith as they carried his father's body to the burial site. They buried him on his right side with the head facing south toward Mecca, ready for resurrection. No one knew whether his father's soul would enter heaven or hell, most likely hell, he thought. In the midst of the turmoil, he found a tunic striped in traditional fashion and donned it with the spirit of a person who fears the past and hopes for the future, wondering how the people in the village would regard him. After all, the son of a murderer, the striped tunic was.

He harbored the sordid loss of his father. And the arbitrary loss of his mother did not settle his spirit. Her inability to comfort him, her ambiguous smile, her hard hand, and the silence about the murderer, still his father, but a murderer in her eyes, all of these created an enormous distance between them. And when the excitement grew and the destitute spoke of the desert, he felt the beast revolt inside of him. Securing the tunic around his body, he joined the disjointed and followed the caravan leaving the town. The air and the sand seemed eternal, the inner beast, inconsolable.

17

Marrakech, Marrakech, completely unknown to Patricio, conjured wild images, sand, heat—even death. Those were only images, he was aware reality would certainly be different, revealing, and perhaps epiphanic. He grabbed his valise and left his flat, descending quickly onto the crowded street. With precise steps, one hundred twenty nine to be exact, he turned the corner and entered the bookstore. This time he did not buy *Le Monde*, he went directly to the travel section where maps of foreign countries were kept. He found what he needed, a city map of Marrakech. He purchased the map, traversed *Le Luco* at a fast pace, and hurried once more to his little oasis, *Au Père Louis*. He sat at a table under the watchful eye of the bartender and opened the map with Marrakech at its center. A labyrinth of streets and little squares that followed an ancient and mysterious logic, or no logic at all, a spider web capable of containing Imena's dreams, a walled city with an open sky. He studied the map carefully until his eyes stumbled upon the unreal square—the *Djemaa El-Fna*. With precision, after consulting the scale in the map, he drew a circle with the fabled square at its center. If the small hotel with the red door was near the *Djemaa El-Fna*, it should not be any further than five hundred of Imena's steps.

Patricio ordered a first glass of calvados, and afraid of having a second, or a third, proceeded to breathe in and out, slowly. He concentrated on his breath, not listening to the music. For what he needed most were lucidity and an even temper, knowing that later that day he would be two thousand kilometers south of Paris, in search of Imena.

I go because I need to go. I knew this would happen the moment I saw her moist skin bathed by the sun, a moment that still shines in my mind, saving me from poisonous memories, working the miracle of redemption, a moment that prophesied her vanishing light. Imena, don't let my longing for you take you away from me. The very essence of you and me, like two winds flowing apart, like a parted ocean, must come together, one impelling the other, in unison. The separate parts, stained with memories, scattered, must find each other and merge.

Volver, volver, yes, but how can I return if I don't know my way? I search after her, moving in an undulating line into the unknown. And when your silhouette settles in the distance, parting the horizon, I cut the ropes and sail to you, just to find you parting the horizon further away, interminably. You went south away from me, but I follow, knowing that your retreat could be, perhaps, only a gesture, an elegantly measured step required by the dictum of the dance, that diabolical melody, the role assigned to you, Imena, as a woman. And as I take to the sky, propelled by fuel and engine, unlike the natural you who floats in the evanescent sunrise, as I move through the dry air, hoping to reach you, I begin to feel how liberating this exodus can be.

What amazed him most was how the salmon-colored walls collided with the red ground under the unattainable blue sky. He thought the ancient city looked like the Saturn of Goya, a hungry beast devouring its offspring. There was tension in the air, as though something horrible was about to happen soon, maybe this moment. And with tentative steps, Patricio moved through the gates and into the old medina of Marrakech, carrying his valise in the right hand, the left hand clutching his hope to find Imena. He fought the crowds and walked over orange peels until reaching the center of the maniacal *Djemaa El-Fna.* He then sat on his valise, unfolded the map of the ancient city, and started studying the area inside the traced perimeter.

He triangulated the spot where he was sitting and made it the axis of his exploratory walks. The strategy was complicated since the small streets did not radiate from the square in an orderly fashion, their erratic arrangement looking more like a frenetic maze. Nevertheless, he started walking methodically, dragging his valise and his hope. He went by many dilapidated doors, the color of decay, mainly. Some open doors offered a limited vision of the cavities they guarded, cavities dark and shallow, with the occasional surprise of a bright courtyard. The white doors were the most beautiful—but those were not red. Patricio continued walking, like a spider over its web, covering the territory marked in the map. Every time he returned to the epicenter at the *Djemaa El-Fna,* he felt as if he came to the end, as though he had touched death itself. After several hours, the failure to find that red door started to feel like a heavy burden. His steps became leaden and the internal metronome started its attack once again.

The only red door he found was closed, and after knocking for a while, an old woman answered, her opaque eyes protruding out of her face like white eggs. Her blindness was enough to convince Patricio that no young woman had procured room or board in her place. By the time the sun vanished and the sky turned purple, Patricio had covered about half of the area on the map. And with desolation as his companion, he entered a plain-looking hotel and obtained a place to rest for the night. He ordered a glass of cognac but there was none to be found. He then decided to abandon this day and went to sleep, thinking of the day to come.

When the angular morning arrived full of light and heat, Patricio felt he would find Imena that day. He only needed to cover a small area; besides, he was now familiar with the intricacies of the medina. He knew that if a street turned left or right, it did so capriciously, not following any logic or plan. All he needed to do was mark on his map the streets he had already explored, turn a new corner without fear, and then move into the unknown. Once he felt prepared for his quest, he entered the decrepit bar of the hotel and ordered a *café au lait*. The server looked at him with disdain and brought him Nescafe. "This is what we have," she said.

He could stumble upon the red door at any time of the day. If he found it in the morning, for example, his disposition would probably be the best—he would be rested and full of confidence. But if the day went by without luck, his hope dying slowly like a forgotten flower in a vase, his reaction upon finding the red door could unveil what he really was, a desperate and perhaps, illogical man. And after setting his emotional bearings, Patricio walked for a second day in search of the red door and his ethereal muse. People did not look at him too much, he was not noticeable, he was rather, invisible.

*****

I think I know what to say first. No…, nothing first. Whatever I think will be first may end up being last. I may just touch her face. I may just look at her. I may look at her and touch her face, and say something later. But if I just imagine the encounter, with all its details and fantasies, most certainly it will not be that way, for things never happen in the way we imagine them. It doesn't matter what I think now or what I say later. Today I must walk the streets of this ancient town, leaving a burning path behind, a path covered in memories, a path turning to the unknown, constantly, until I reach the luminous object of my desire behind the red door.

*****

That day was no different from the day before. The heat was there, the dust floated in the air making translucent curtains when penetrated by the sunrays, the people where there, a boiling mass, in the alleys the children ran past him. His triangulations worked well since he never walked the same street twice. However, every time he approached the epicenter at the *Djemaa El-Fna*, the screaming monkeys looked at him with derision. This made him uncomfortable. His steps were regular, covering the same distance and maintaining a precise rhythm. For a moment, he thought of the tango. The walking forward, *la salida*, inundated his mind, threatening to build a wall of memories in front of him. In spite of this, Patricio looked ahead and continued his systematic search, unyielding. And as the day advanced the intensity of his luminous desire started to grow exponentially. And after many more steps, after turning to the right and to the left, after facing the unknown angles of the streets, after looking into unfamiliar eyes peering from the depth of dusty tunics, and after hearing the monkeys scream once again, not yet finding that red door, Patricio felt overtaken by a sinking feeling.

Finally, the word *"Funduk"* caught his eye, he looked to the left and a red door emerged. An immense calmness descended on him. Patricio caressed the red door with the back of his right hand, as if it was a precious object. He pushed it open, stepped inside the courtyard, and saw the flowering orange trees in each of the four corners and the fountain in the center. He walked around and looked into several of the open windows. Nobody seemed to be in the rooms at that time. The dry air spiraled around him, and for the first time since he arrived in Marrakech, he distinguished the smell of the medina—a spicy and floral explosion that brought the image of Imena abruptly into his consciousness. He sat by the fountain and closed his eyes. He remained motionless for a century. And the images of Imena danced in front of his mind's eye, conjuring unedited sensations, the past revolting as a new present. And the images were ambrosia in the desert, nectar in the dark of his fears. He thought he had found her, her air, her trace; he thought he had entered her world away from him.

But without pronouncement, unexpectedly, Patricio felt a light tapping of fingers on his left shoulder and the acrid smell of an animal unknown to him until then. When he opened his eyes and turned to look at the striped tunic next to him, he felt the urge to vomit. The stench emanating from the apparition was violent, a putrid experience that infused him with fear and repugnance.

"Are you looking for a room, *Monsieur?*" the striped tunic asked.

"No, not really, I'm looking for a person," Patricio said.

Patricio stood up and took a few discrete steps toward one of the flowering orange trees to gain distance from the fetid apparition.

"May I offer you some tea, *Monsieur?*"

"That's very kind of you, are you in charge of this place?"

"How can I be in charge of this place? Here the wind comes to fill the courtyard when it pleases. The sun comes to kiss the walls when it has to. The dust settles on the surfaces continuously. And people from all places, like yourself, walk through that red door unannounced. As you can see, I'm not in charge."

Patricio observed the striped tunic and felt a strange sense of bewilderment. Here was, in front of him, a person who thought about the absurdity of life, vulnerable and exposed to chance circumstances, a person who, because of a physical quality—the repugnant smell—was certainly rejected by others. But in spite of this realization, Patricio kept his distance from the striped tunic and moved toward an upwind position.

"As I said, I'm looking for a person, a young woman in her late twenties with blue eyes, dark hair, and very pale skin. You would easily recognize her as a foreigner. Her name is Imena, Imena LaSalle."

The striped tunic stared at Patricio. He did not blink, he did not move, and for a while it seemed that he did not breathe. Not a word came out of his lips, and the only impression that Patricio perceived was the animal stench that swamped the courtyard, nauseating him.

"Has anyone like that stayed in your hotel?" Patricio asked.

"*Monsieur*, you're looking for a ghost," the striped tunic said.

"No, she's real, entirely real, and I need to find her."

"Many people pass through this hotel, *Monsieur*. I may have seen someone like that, perhaps."

"You couldn't have missed her."

"Yes, I could have."

The striped tunic disappeared abruptly, leaving a vacuum behind him rapidly filled by the cascading air of the medina. Patricio remained in the courtyard, his sense of hope trembling, as if tip-toeing on a rope, this rope a tense filament tying Paris and his life from before to this dry patch of clay behind a red door, fearing the rushing air could make him tumble, sending him into the precipice of his memories.

✳✳✳✳✳

After an attack, while bleeding from its wound, the sublime creature flees, and the hunter follows its trace. The hunter has no option; he needs to look for her, he hopes to find her. And he enters into my courtyard searching for her trace, I suppose, following her aroma. Instead, my odor, the unexpected odor of a scoured man from the desert assaults him. But how to tell him? How to tell him that he won't find her here? I can feel the pain and the anxiety in his heart. His pain is his own, and I may not be able to soften it. I'll offer him mint tea because he is searching, and he doesn't know that his search may never end. I'm sure he doesn't know that the beast resides within her. I'll walk into the courtyard with a tray, balancing rock sugar and mint tea. I'll speak to him softly. I'll tell him. I'll feel his pain. I'll share the dry air and the endless sunlight. I'll let him know that in the desert there's only barrenness.

*****

"Can you look in your records for Imena LaSalle?"

"I don't keep records, *Monsieur*," the striped tunic said. "Please accept some tea, it may suit you well."

"She has blue eyes, dark hair, and very pale skin."

"I heard you say that before. What makes you believe I notice the appearance of my guests?"

Patricio grabbed a cup from the tray and drowned a few pieces of rock sugar into the hot liquid. He could not understand this offering creature. The striped tunic gave him something he did not ask for, while with facility, dodged his questions. Patricio did not trust his leathery face, he could not see into the gray eyes, and he could not stand the stench.

"She mentioned a red door close to the *Djemaa El-Fna*. I walked every path and street for the past two days. This is the only hotel with a red door."

"How about the blind woman?" the striped tunic asked.

"Yes, I knocked on another red door yesterday and a woman with bulging eyes answered. She, Imena, couldn't have been there."

"You probably didn't ask."

"The woman couldn't see anything."

"Just because she's blind it doesn't mean that she's…, blind."

The striped tunic stared at Patricio; for a long time he stared at him. There was no expression on his face; there was no movement of his arms. He just stared at Patricio, softly, as though he wanted to merge with him. And he uttered no word, and his breath was shallow, and he showed no expectations. The passage of time did not seem to matter to him; the time simply did not seem to pass. The orange trees grew and the fragrant blossoms fell to the ground. The water in the fountain danced in a perpetual rise and fall.

"I'd like to stay in this hotel for a few days. Is there an available room with a view into the courtyard?" Patricio asked.

"All the rooms open into the courtyard. That's where the air comes from. Do you like the tea, *Monsieur*?"

"Yes, the tea is fine, but, is there a room available for tonight?"

"There's no need to stay here if you are searching for an illusion, those you will find outside of the city walls, in the desert."

"As I said before, I'm searching for a person."

"I know you're searching, and you may cross that tenuous line between an illusion and a person, or perhaps not."

The striped tunic stood up and asked Patricio to follow him across the courtyard. They entered into a small room with the basic arrangement of a bed, chairs, and washbasin. A lone window opened into the courtyard barely allowing the stench of the striped tunic to escape.

It's inevitable, they follow their animal instincts. Once the desire is in their hearts, once the need is established, they set out to search. I'm tired of being witness to this undying cycle. And why should I be the beholder of reality? I renounced all attachments to such pursuits; I renounced the ephemeral. For a time as long as time, I have ruled over this courtyard. But in a lost place, like this place where there's nothing but dryness, dust, and air, the lost ones come for shelter. And those that came before were the caravans, human and animal agglomerations, and their quest was for life and richness. There are no caravans today. Now they come as loners, consumed by their yearning. My presence, the spectrum of my presence, revolts their senses. Unbeknownst to them, I'm the tamer of the beasts and the unreal. Between these walls, with my mind open to the sky, and my feet anchored, I hear everything and I see through their fears. But why should I be the beholder? If a day came and found me hiding in a corner, my face turned to the wall, the air stagnant, without tea to offer, that day I would find relief, perhaps. Or if I stepped out of that red door, for the first time since I stepped in, my putrid shell would fall off my body and I would run through the streets, naked.

He says he's searching for a person; that's what he says. But he doesn't know. He followed her trace, coming south from north. Now, installed in one of my rooms, he'll have to face his incomplete self. For he has the intensity of those who fear the day is over, those who fear the red moon will ascend and remain suspended forever a night. He seems to want her, or maybe he wants her essence. And when the night comes, I'll listen. I'll walk through the courtyard and I'll listen. He doesn't know about the air coming from the medina into the courtyard, swirling, moving sand mountains, and robbing memories under my command. Unlike her, he doesn't know the fragrance of the flowering orange trees. For he has the intensity of those who use the present to shield the past. And for that reason, I may not hear the beast inside of him, its song strangled, asphyxiated by the ever present unreality. The night will come again, tonight, and I'll lay myself down on the red clay to listen, to behold, the red door closed behind me, my scent floating to the purple sky.

18

Guadeloupe, south from Paris and so distant from the natural order of his days. René felt the embrace of the oppressive humidity as he walked from the plane into the airport security. He presented his French passport, the last official document of his life as a man. Nobody expected him to arrive in Guadeloupe, just as nobody expected him to leave Paris and his post at the university. He was an absolute stranger in a strange land. Patricio had travelled to Guadeloupe, obligating him to teach the morning seminars during his absence and to water his plants. That was all he knew about the island. He wore khakis, a light blue button-down shirt, and black shoes. And when the passport control officer looked at his picture, René smiled, aware that his known image will soon disappear, forever.

Once he arrived at the little rental apartment in the old Pointe-à-Pitre quarter, he noticed the peeling paint of the surrounding buildings, the piles of uncollected garbage in narrow alleys, and the irritating noise of the motor scooters. This place would serve him well while he arranged for the arrival of his female side. He would not rush this. René knew he had to follow his instincts, the direction that promised an answer, the direction that would deliver him as a different person. He also knew that embodying his female self could send his life into a terrifying spiral.

René spent many days traveling through the island, collecting sights, and looking at dark-skinned women—mostly the muscular ones. He was, for the most part, unnoticed, due to his plain features and shy manners, typical of many Europeans that descend on the island. One sultry afternoon, he sat at a café to savor some Caribbean rum. From his position at the café, he observed people with a keen eye for their facial contours under the tropical sun. He noticed every angle of the cheekbones, the rate of ascent of a nose, the shape of the chin, the thickness of the lower lip, and above all, he noticed people's eyes and tried to decipher their expression. René was interested in the truth of people, not their convenient truth, but the very truth, the one beneath. He studied the way women dressed, how they let the air play in that space between their clothes and their skin. While observing those women, René imagined them dressed in men's clothes. The image nauseated him. That afternoon he imagined love. René loved infrequently, but when he loved, his love was brave and unruly.

*****

If I remain here, René thought, the world would forget me, if I remain… But the essence of me is not in remaining. I walk through a door and I'm greeted with *bonjour Monsieur*. I walk through that door leaving myself behind and I'm greeted with *bonjour Madame*. As I dream of my complete self, its totality, I see the opposing elements merging as one. One day, a woman will show me how to be with another woman, I can only hope. I'm so far from everything. I'm so far from myself. How many faces can I have, how many lives can I live?

And if my body sinks in clear water, would it reemerge from the ocean on a shell, luminous? Botticelli, so far away, I wish your brush could touch me. All my life looking at myself in the mirror, all my life staring at the shell, the sexual appetite repressed. I remember when a young woman placed her soft hand over my hand. I wanted my hand to shrink, to disappear in shame. I wanted her from another perspective barely known to me. The dark-skinned women on this island, how real. I marvel at the length of their necks, the delicacy of their arms, the softness of their profile. Unknown as I am to them, I float like a spirit, through their hair, around their breasts, between their thighs, with envy.

*****

This island reminds me of my father, René thought. Up and down, up and down, the head heavier than the handle, nailing his dreams into place, my father swung that hammer. Its nose was round and the ears set back like those of my cat when she went around chasing lizards. Bang, bang, bang, it sang against wood, ting, ting, ting against zinc. My mother hated that place of desolation so the hammer was not her friend. She feared staying alone in the house; she feared that horrible things could happen when left alone. My father did not care. "Nonsense," he said, and continued to paint his dreams with the strokes of the hammer. At the right angle, the sun would reflect on the hammer's head. That was years ago. "This is where the window goes," my father said. "You'll see far out to the line where the mountain's edge and the sky come together." Poetic, but my mother didn't care. "There's nobody here to talk to," she would say.

The hammer's handle was made of black rubber, nothing special, slightly curved. But it allowed itself to be held funneling my father's force directly into its head. Bang, bang, bang, ting, ting, and ting. "If she wouldn't be so hard headed, as this hammer, she could see that I'm painting my last dreams," my father said. The dreams he never touched. But I picked up that hammer and made it mine. I can swing it to build what he didn't build. And when I look out to the ocean surrounding this volcanic island, I can imagine where to place the windows and the walls—my hands can build.

And my broad shoulders will remain with me after I'm transformed. And my wide hands will remain as well. I may need my shoulders and my hands to build, to carry the weight of a thousand eyes on me, to deflect the humiliating words. The mind, the study of the mind, the study of the study of the mind, I'll leave behind eating dust at the university. Like a child learning how to walk, how to talk, how to love, like a child with an entire life ahead, I landed on this island. And as I enter this new world, I laugh at the voices from before, even when I fear the voices from tomorrow. I now sit motionless trapped in this alien body, with my flat chest, manly attire, and angular face, hoping for the chrysalis to open and reveal me.

19

Jacques and his lies led Imena to Nice, to a flat in the *Musiciens* quarter where a view of the Mediterranean sea graced an elegant parlor. The idea of learning about his sculptures intrigued her, but the scent of the southern flowers, the herbs, and the sea were a more powerful allure. Imena heard him talk about his family, how they left Russia, how they struggled, how they settled in Nice almost one hundred years ago. She saw images of times past when walking by the seaside boulevard across the street from the flat. That woman with a parasol, that man with a hat, the bathers frolicking on the pebbles. She wanted to touch them.

Jacques introduced her to several of his friends. Most were in their twenties and thirties and seemed to have an inordinate amount of free time. At their first gathering in Jacques' flat, the champagne flowed and the conversation revolved around jewelry. Imena sat on the tired divan and saw her image reflected on the spotted mirror under the dim yellow light of an ancient candelabra. The revelers saw her as a pale young woman with a long bare neck. She heard the broken words travel from wall to wall, from mouth to ear, and a laugh, then another. And from the mouth of a young woman, a cloud of smoke emerged—*bocanada de humo*. She observed the movements of men and the gazes of women. She then closed her eyes and sampled the air. She identified *bergamote* and *citron zeste, orientale* and *épicée*, in delicious combinations.

Partially covered by an oriental screen depicting graceful cranes among blooming plum trees and bamboo grasses, a young woman with a naked torso rubbed her body against a man. Imena knew they were looking at her but she averted their gaze. Then a scream of ecstasy came from behind the screen. It was the sound of pleasure, abandoned, guttural, and orgasmic. And the revelers responded with a clamor and an enthusiastic clapping of the hands.

When Imena was admiring the reflections from the chandelier in the middle of the parlor, she felt a soft hand caressing her bare neck. Surprised, Imena grabbed the hand and pulled it away from her neck. It was a hand with elongated fingers adorned with perfectly manicured nails. The delicate wrist wore a pearl bracelet twisted around two or three times. The unknown woman attached to the hand smiled slyly and turned her head back to swallow a glass of champagne. The woman sat on the divan next to Imena and said her name was Charli and that she was a friend of Jacques—like everyone in the room—and that she admired her pale skin and her long neck. Charli did not wait for Imena to say a word, she just kissed her on the lips while caressing her neck once more. She then stood up and walked away to join the others. Imena closed her eyes, she trembled. In the background, the voices of Billie Holiday and Serge Gainsbourg struggled to reach over the noise of the crowded room.

The night went deep. The convoluted interactions between men and women, between women and women, between men and men, between women and men and women, were exquisite. Imena did not participate in the carnival, she remained on the divan, observing and trying to catalogue the numerous scents that permeated the fragile air. The bodily odors assaulted her with intensity, all confused in a single room. There was sweat from black and white people, there was the aroma of dried champagne over bare skin, there was the smell of semen, and there was the smell of Charli's saliva on her lips.

I feel open, Imena thought, permeable like the edge between the sand and the sea. I have no limits, and around me, there are no walls. To fly, I just need to extend my arms and the wind will lift me. My feet barely touch the floor. And if *La rose sauvage* came to me already composed, pure, I would weep. I can imagine that moment. In a grand space, with air all around me, the light like liquid crystal, the sound of wings fluttering, myself standing naked, my senses open. Yes, I can dream of that moment. But no one around me dreams that way. Everyone is tied to something grave, so it seems.

Charli kissed me, and for a moment, I felt light—only for a moment. Jacques was watching, I know he was. Perhaps that's why I felt uncomfortable. He waited for Charli to find my mouth. He must have liked when her lips touched mine that very moment. Then came the heaviness and the need to fly. But why? I don't really need to fly now, there's no pressure, and I'm here because I want to be here. The rose, my *rose sauvage*…, escaping among her lips, with no trace or fragrance left behind. That's my hope, to follow a trace but leave none behind. If I could just find that mystical scent, with a top note of marvel, a middle note deep, and a base note strong to hold me. If I could consume every drop of that scent without wanting to take to the sky.

There's a certain looseness here in Nice. I can move around people, through the streets, alone or with Jacques, and something always touches my skin—the sea breeze, the sun, Jacques' hands, even Charli's kiss. It's like a constant imprint on my skin. And when Jacques walked through the courtyard in Marrakech, he entered my body like the smell of salt and seaweed. And Charli—she's beautiful—with her elegant hands and her soft lips, and the gentle touch of her mouth over my mouth, and the faint and distant sweetness of her saliva lingering on my lips, she also enters my body. Am I missing the nectar of the gods by only tasting and smelling semen from the wolves that hunt me? Am I sensing the world in its entirety? I wonder.

✶✶✶✶✶

Imena explained to her faculty supervisor at the *Cinquième Sens* that she was in Nice exploring the natural essence of the roses in the *grassoise* hills. This was partially true, but at the same time, partially false. She was in Nice—and Grasse was nearby—but she was exploring herself more than any rose or hill in Provence.

One morning, after an evening filled with social encounters, discussions about the color of ecstasy, and the correct number of pearls in a 19th century Prussian collar, Imena asked Jacques to take her to his studio as he had promised. Jacques explained that his studio was in a seedy part of the city, and that they were meeting Charli for lunch at the *Café de Turin*, where the shellfish was so fresh that it swam away from you. Imena insisted, she wanted to touch the curves, the hard body shapes made of granite and marble. Jacques agreed to visit the studio after lunch. He looked at Imena in an unfamiliar way, and he mumbled something about Charli that Imena could not understand.

Once at the restaurant, a variety of critters from the bottom of the sea covered the small table while Charli spoke about a new champagne lounge that was the rage of town. Her hand, that ornamented hand Imena had admired before, balanced a cigarette with lazy abandon. When the waiter asked if she wanted more wine, Charli said, "but of course." The words, the smoke, the aroma of oysters and lemon, the image of her ruby lips, all of those sensations penetrated Imena. She felt

88

her mind detaching from her body and floating lightly, free to observe herself between Jacques and Charli. She thought her body looked fragile, like the body of a nubile girl in the butterfly island. And when the waiter asked if she wanted more wine, Imena said, "How about champagne?"

People came, ate shellfish, and went on their way down the streets of Old Nice. Imena watched every person and tried to link their image to their scent. Sometimes the match was perfect, like when a round young woman emanated the essence of pears or apples, and when an old squalid man infused the air with the stench of desiccated cod. At other times, the image and the scent did not match, like when the handsome Italian opera singer left a trace of death floating around him. And with every mollusk that entered her body, Imena felt in communion with the sea. She felt magnificent as she allowed the sea life to penetrate her, to reside within her womb. And when the cold champagne clouded her awareness, Imena knew she could now kiss Charli's lips.

The door at *Rue Pertinax* guarding Jacques' studio had no particular sign, and once opened, Imena, Jacques, and Charli entered a room illuminated by an angular light that filtered through the wooden blinds. The expected magic of shaped granite and marble appeared in a ghastly glory. A thousand generations of dust particles covered every surface. Every tool rested on its side, lifeless, or simply bored from the wait. There was a chisel reclining on the edge of a wooden table, considering jumping off into the abyss to end its life and enter the white oblivion of ignored tools. And the stone sculptures, those that had eyes, watched the intruders with an empty expression, the expression of fallen angels with no hope to return to their God's grace. The process of creation in Jacques' studio had been dismantled, deconstructed, rendered useless by time. Like unborn babies abandoned in the middle of labor, Jacques' sculptures hardly came to the world complete. The bastards, a conglomerate of bastards.

Jacques did not explain much. He moved around the studio, pretending to be engaged in some creative process. He never looked at the sculptures fearing they could see through him. But as an expert dilettante, he was triumphant in his crumbling stage.

He then grabbed Imena and brought her to the center of the studio where he held her tight. Charli followed them, and with a fluid motion, grabbed Imena by her waist. Imena yielded to the two of them. They stood motionless looking at the stone shapes, no comments uttered, no further movements made.

20

In the morning, the hotel room looked unreal, maybe because his eyes were dry or because he had forgotten where he was. He felt an urge, Patricio, forcing him to leave the room looking for the toilet. Diagonally across the courtyard he ran, rounding the fountain and dashing by one of the orange trees, its flowers dancing in the dry morning air. He emerged pallid and when he reached the center of the courtyard, the voice of the striped tunic reached him at the same time as his putrid stench.

"*Bonjour Monsieur*, may I offer you some tea?"

"I'll have your tea, but we must finish our conversation from yesterday."

"Are you referring to the words we exchanged, the thoughts we had about each other, or the dreams that assaulted each of us last night?"

"I'm referring to my questions about the young woman."

"Yes…, I see. You want to talk about your dreams."

An uneasy feeling came over Patricio. And like a child, he could not control his sphincter, and a shameful watery excrement ran down his legs. His intestines were contracting, screaming, revolting against himself, and exuding fluids from inside. He sat on the ground curled over, his head between his knees, while a violent cramp strangled his insides. His skin, covered by a shiny layer of sweat, became clammy and cold. That was when the chills started. And like a fine tremolo, every muscle of his body started to vibrate. And even when the hot and dry air of the medina inundated the courtyard, he felt like ice.

Patricio stood up from the red clay and walked back to his room. He lay on the bed and covered himself with a blanket

made of coarse camel hair. The striped tunic followed him
and stood at the side of the bed, observing Patricio in desert
silence.

"I'm cold," Patricio said.

"You feel cold outside, but inside you are burning."

"I'm cold."

"Your insides are revolting."

Patricio felt as if his body was sinking in a clear blue ocean,
drowning slowly. The sounds were distant but his thoughts
were unquiet.

"You must have some of this other tea, *Monsieur.*"

The voice of the striped tunic pulled him from the bottom
of the ocean. He helped himself to a dark and bitter liquid that
did not taste like the sweet mint tea he drank the day before.

"Have you seen her, Imena, with her pale skin and her blue
eyes?" Patricio asked.

"You're very insistent, *Monsieur.*"

"Just tell me, have you seen her?"

"I've seen every man and woman. Eyes or skin color have
little meaning to me. I did meet a young woman who seemed
lost and ethereal. She came to the courtyard, drank the dry
air, and then left to search for a star."

"Did she come from Paris?"

"She came from the north, Paris perhaps, and she was
alone."

"Is she still here? Where is she?"

"*Monsieur,* the young woman was searching, just like you
are. I heard when she approached my red door the first day.
Her steps were light, an imperceptible touch of the ground.
After resting her spirit, she wandered through the streets and
alleys, searching, and naturally, finding nothing. The man
with the red beret, the sculptor, distracted her. It appears she
sensed something about him. That young woman is no longer
here, she left with the sculptor."

Patricio could not hear these words for his senses were confused. The dark and bitter tea had muddled his awareness.

✶✶✶✶✶

No, not here..., she doesn't want to die here. Turn down the music, turn it down I say. You don't listen. TURN THE MUSIC DOWN. She'll die again. I can still hear it. Motherfucking Carlos! *Mudo hijo de puta!* You're going to kill my mother, I'm telling you. You are Carlitos, right? But you smell so bad. What happened to you? I'm fine, sleepy, but fine. Are you the one who smells so bad? Or is it me, I think I have shit all over me. No, no, no, don't take me deeper, this is dark as it is. But please, turn the music down. Carlos, I thought you were dead, and she's dead too. Why do you come here to kill her again? Not deeper please, no. I cannot move, I cannot move. Stop singing or you will kill her. Fuck *Mi Buenos Aires Querido.* You're killing her. I'm not touching the records, I'm not playing them. Can't you see? I cannot move. Oh no, where's this going? She's looking at me but I cannot move. I must lower the volume. Carlos, that's it! No more *Volver* or *Cumparsita.* I cannot move. You killed my mother. No, I didn't kill her. Or maybe I did. It smells like death and shit all around me. And the other one, Imena, she went flying. Is she dead too, you dark creature, tell me, is she dead too? Don't look at me that way, I just need to know. She said she had to go. Did she go that far? Is she dead? Yes, she floats away. Up, up, up. Cannot touch her. No more, no more, I may never see her again. Mother went down, Imena up, and I'm down here, so dark. No, no, no, not deeper. I'm sinking, I'm sinking motherfucker, where am I going? Pull me up from here. I cannot move. It's dark, inside is dark. I didn't kill them. Don't look at me. I told you motherfucker, don't you listen? Inside, I'm inside, so dark.

21

The first doctor asked him to leave his office and to pray to the Lord for help. He had grown up nearby Lourdes, and would not deem René's request acceptable—the Virgin would be mortified. That was the first one. He then consulted an American surgeon who listened carefully, and after René described his plan, he said he did not dare, and that he better look for help elsewhere. Yet another doctor asked him to consult with a psychiatrist. René refused. Disappointed, he continued to travel across Guadeloupe, looking at the women, seizing their hips, their legs, especially their breasts, and weaving images of him as a rounder more voluptuous other. One night, in his dreams, René approached a beautiful woman who was reclining by the shore, precisely where the surf dies over the sand. Her breasts were bare, and her nipples pointed to the sun, asking for rays. He came close to her and his hands caressed the pyramidal shapes. He whispered to the woman, "I want you, and I want to be you." The woman looked at him and laughed. René woke up.

The shell, the envelope, the skin, betrayed him. Inside of him was clear and luminous, a world like no other, even serene. But the outside was ever-present, visible to all, and people regarded him according to his looks: a young man with a pleasant face and timid demeanor—nothing more. But René was no Orlando, and the desire to desire a woman as a woman seemed unattainable. His doppelgänger continued to live outside of him, turning away from him, while he led the life of a taciturn ex-assistant professor.

The mirror showed his face, freshly shaven and smooth, he then took a step back and saw his naked body. The familiar image disgusted him, so he closed his eyes and inhaled the soothing cigarette smoke for a long time. Hair grew everywhere, under his arms, over his chest, between his legs, even over his shoulders and back. He had to remove or conceal it all. And as he had done so many times, he started the ritual of the false metamorphosis by sheathing his legs with black stockings. To prevent any tears, he placed his hands inside a pair of white sport socks and pulled the stockings firmly until he felt the pressure against his toes. He gazed at the mirror and admired the sleek image of thin, yet muscular, legs. He then attempted to conceal his penis and testicles by wearing tight athletic suspenders. He was not ready to eliminate his sexual organs, he just needed to suppress them. The mirror showed a triangular flattened crotch but no womanly characteristics, no ravine. He smoked some more and the night began to open—the birth of Venus. He then confronted the flat and barren chest. To build a shapely torso, René stuffed the cups of a brassiere with torn newspapers and wore it, as a deceiving woman would. He smiled when sine and cosine interrupted the vertical line. He then slipped on an elastic black dress that embraced his modified silhouette. Another puff and another look at the mirror—enchanting.

The shoes were uncomfortable, so much weight concentrated on the fine stiletto heels, but the elongation of the legs and the presentation of the buttocks were all worth it. Another puff. The eyes grew black lines around them and a smooth blue-gray tone drenched the periphery of the orbits. While looking straight at the mirror, without blinking, he covered his head with a curly wig the color of *vin de Bourgogne*. Finally, he spread a field of red fatty emulsion over his lips. René looked deeply into the mirror and drew the soul out of the cigarette. From behind the mirror, a woman returned the stare. After taking the final puff, he squelched the cigarette against the bottom of the ashtray and left it in oblivion, a rim of red color imprinted on its dead body.

Under the moon and through the shadows he walked, the salty air following him everywhere until he entered an establishment that served alcohol and played Broadway pseudo-operatic tunes. Sitting and standing everywhere, women and men drank while mimicking gestures and poses of their favorite idols. Cher stood tall and Tina showed her thunder thighs. René struck a pose, inviting. And soon, a young man dressed like a sailor approached him, and said his name was Alain, and that he loved her athletic build and the color of her lips, and that he would like to share a cigarette with her, and that he was in Guadeloupe for a week, and if she wanted she could join him for a drink by the beach where there were fewer people. But René was not looking at Alain, he did not care for his boyish face or his green eyes, he was not yearning for the hand of a man. René continued smoking, puckering his red lips to inhale and then letting the white air out, placidly. His arms and legs stayed close to his torso as he walked, maintaining a womanly rhythm, softer than his manly walk of earlier hours. He reached the bar and rested his left elbow on the counter, the forearm extending vertically to the sky, the left palm opening up like a flower while holding a cigarette between his index and middle fingers, the little finger curling into the palm. He shifted all the weight of his body to his left leg and assumed an accentuated contrapposto, the relaxed right leg wrapped around the left, the toes pointing to the floor. The right arm rested on his waist and the elbow pointed backwards, opening his enhanced chest while his head turned away from the cigarette to scan the room. Twisted, he continued smoking and yearning.

Across the bar a blonde girl with a sweet smile and a silly demeanor stood next to a brunette with a determined expression while their conversation jumped with gestures and gazes. René approached them and learned that both were tourists and had not known each other until that evening. He joined them and started to gesture and gaze, just like them. They spoke about Guadeloupe and the soft breezes, the sun, the local girls with their dark nipples, the strong marijuana, certainly laced, and what if the three of them played together. The words flew back and forth through smoke and shadows among the three. The brunette went to the bathroom with a little metal box tightly held in her fist. She returned more determined than before, her eyes intense. She gave the little metal box to the blonde girl who went to the bathroom as well. She returned with a bigger smile. They passed the box to René and urged him to try it. He stood up and walked across the bar toward the women's bathroom. He went into a stall, closed the door behind him, and sat on the toilet without lifting his dress or lowering his stockings. When he opened the box, the mirror in the inside of the cover reflected his image. He was pleased to see his red lips. He put them together and blew a kiss at himself. He snorted two lines and looked at himself again. He released his female dreams and they looked more real than ever.

René returned to the bar, his heart punctuating every step, the pulse quickening. He sat between the two young women and continued an emboldened conversation. He talked in a woman's voice but with a manly quality. And the cigarettes burned one after the other, and the smoke carried his words like the air carried his dreams. He was sweating, and a martini did not satiate his thirst. He smoked some more and another martini flooded his throat. The tourists continued to gesture, jabbing words at each other. And the three took turns going back to the bathroom with the little metal box clenched in their fists. Each time one arrived from the solitary stimulation, their intensity seemed to raise, their pupils dilated, while the hurricane roared inside of them.

When the last call of the bar had expired, the music stopped, the ceiling lights drenched their bodies in a sickly whiteness, and empty glasses pounded the wooden counter. Confused bodies straggled out of the bar into the warm ocean breeze, looking for the next adventure, perhaps looking for a small amount of death. The two women and René walked toward the beach, their arms over each other's shoulders, the blonde girl in the center, René and the brunette on opposite sides. When they reached the sand, the tourists sat with casual abandon. René kept his knees together and sat sideways, hiding the opening between his legs.

The three bodies were burning, the hearts pumped faster, the blood pressure climbed, the pupils opened wide to fit the thousand light points. And then all hands broke loose, dancing over thighs, faces, and breasts, and the lips found other lips, and the sand and the shells scratched the sweaty skin of the blonde and tore René's stockings. That was when the brunette stood up from the sand abruptly.

"I don't want to touch this filthy queen," she said.

The blonde girl started giggling, "but he's a sweet queen," she said.

And with force, the brunette pulled the blonde away from René.

"Fuck you, you pathetic queen."

The brunette dragged the blonde girl down the beach with possessive force. René heard the stupid giggle fainting in the air as they drifted further and further, and when there was nothing but silence, he took reign of his incongruous kingdom.

22

I'm a woman. And if Charli desires me, I'm still a woman. And if Jacques desires me it is because I'm a woman. They grab me and kiss me without asking. Why is her arm around my waist? The taste of her saliva hunts me. But why does her arm hold me in the center of this room? And when I look around this studio I see more death than life. The dust everywhere, as if the shelves had gone to sleep centuries ago. And he said he worked here, maybe he dreamt here, maybe he dreamt he worked here. Yes, these are the shapes of incomplete dreams. The stones don't have a fragrance and their souls reveal emptiness. Jacques, where are you? Jacques, simple, empty, you bring me to the center of this studio where there's nothing to hold.

I know I can fly away and over the stones. The air will hold me. But the memory of the salty air mixed with seaweed chains me down. Her arm does not retain me, it proposes. I yearn to fly away, but also to remain and embrace her. My skin is permeable, sensations enter as they wish, and my mind holds nothing and allows everything. This day I'm everything and nothing, and their frenzy penetrates me.

$$*****$$

She left alone, Imena, and followed *Rue Pertinax* for one block before she started to feel light again. She continued walking aimlessly, without looking at people's faces, just keeping a rhythm, like dancing tango. The walls ignored her, they remained yellow, and the shadows whispered her name in purple. She knew the open sea was south of *Boulevard des Anglais*, so she followed the sky until a precipice was born in front of her. There was a band of human flesh, a band of pebbles, and a band of blue that extended far into the horizon. She sat at a bench and forgot about time, for Imena was not anchored to the moment. She could see herself as a child savoring a maracudja and dreaming on the front porch of her house, Beatrice and the cockatoo talking incessantly. And like a child, she let the breeze play with her hair and her skirt, her eyes closed and the world singing. Time passed, and Imena remained at the bench. A myriad of sensations paraded in front of her, sometimes inundating her, sometimes just flowing past her. That was when she thought about Patricio. She also remembered the melancholic melody of a tango, and at the same time, she recalled the position of her right hand and her legs moving backwards. She also remembered "*Les Fleurs du Mal*," forgotten and unfinished.

> *Elle se répand dans ma vie*
> *Comme un air imprégné de sel,*
> *Et dans mon âme inassouvie*
> *Verse le gout de l'éternel.*

After one or two hours, Imena left the shore and went back to the *Musiciens*. When she arrived at Jacques' flat, she did not expect to find him standing by the window with a cigarette in his hand; but there he was.

"Why did you leave so abruptly, we thought you were ill, or mad," Jacques said.

"I left because the air felt stagnant."

"Were you scared?"

"No, I wasn't scared, I just had to leave."

"Charli wanted you to stay, you know, she was upset when you left."

"You deal with her, she seems to do whatever you want."

"Well, we had fun."

Imena looked over the flat while Jacques' voice continued to resonate vacuous and far. She observed the dining room table, probably from the 19th century, the wild oriental screen, the antique samovar, the collection of plates, all of the above beautifully arranged to create a sense of elegance and comfort. And when Jacques finished talking, Imena looked at him with saturnine eyes.

"Tomorrow I'll leave this place," she said.

"You cannot leave, you don't know where you're going."

"I know where I'm going, I know very well," she said.

23

Why do they come to my courtyard? One after the other, walking through my red door. Look at him, it all came out of him, from the inside, his deeper side. And the tea I gave him only facilitates what has to happen, it opens the door. One only expels inner fears when they are unknown. I have seen the desert sand accumulate forming mountains, and then blown away by the wind overnight, many times, a thousand times. Still, the desert remains the same, with or without mountains, with or without the wind—there's no revolution. And his excrements are cathartic, like the desert wind, blowing his sand mountains away. But there will be no revolution for him. Not today, for his search is young and his internal landscape virginal, untouched. Patricio, he calls himself, like a patriarch of sorts, not even of his own reign. He's nothing but a man-wolf who follows his prey, far into territories unknown, sinking his rabid teeth into himself. That's when the wounded wolf growls, and shits everywhere. I've seen the white shadow of the rabid wolf, the one that feeds from the horror inside, when the man is unaware of who he is. But when the man knows his inner horrors, he must decapitate them or excrement will ooze from his body like a river.

He's delirious now, and delirium is the royal road to the horror inside, like dreams in a soft night. And when a man loses touch with reality, his derailed thoughts reveal his fears. And I heard him, I heard the tragedy of his words exposing his inner conflicts, for he thinks he was a murderer. Or maybe he thinks he's a murderer now. He speaks of killing and wants to prevent more killing. And there's a deep abyss inside of him, a dark horror, where the murderous fears seem to lurk.

The fear of the abyss, so intense, he fights it in the mists of his delirium. So intense.

He cried about a previous death, one surrounded by music. Must have happened during his youth, because the sadness seemed long, extended over time, tired. He seems afraid of the sounds and that music. And how and when the music bore a hole in his happiness, I don't know. But it was a long time ago, and in the confusion it all comes to the surface.

Because my feet are buried in the red clay, because my soul is ancient, because I must stay within these walls. The courtyard holds the dry air and the sky opens to the purple night, and my observing self is in the middle. For the red door is closed to me, and my kingdom is within the courtyard. And the flowering orange trees grow in the corners of the courtyard, offering their fragrance and thorns, growing despite the dry air, reaching up, maybe to nowhere. All as it always was, I'll behold him and all others like him, from within these walls, unveiling their demons.

✶✶✶✶✶

When he started having thoughts that made sense, Patricio knew he had not died. Around him were his emanations, but his body was intact, and he began to breathe with life again. Everything was quiet, and a faint morning light entered the room from under the door. He saw the filthy crust covering his clothes and decided to remove them, piece by piece, as if peeling away a bad omen. The shameful smell of dry feces forced him to open the door and exit his room. Outside in the courtyard, it was luminous and open, and for a moment, he could not see. When his eyes adjusted to the light, he saw the striped tunic looking at him from across the courtyard, as if he was guarding this claustrophobic universe. Then the striped tunic began to approach him, and to his surprise, he did not detect the stench that had stemmed from this creature the day before.

"May I offer you some tea, *Monsieur*?"

"You, you tried to poison me last night."

"You're mistaken, I was only trying to help you. Your body needed to rid itself of its inner fears. I only provided needed assistance."

"What fears are you talking about? I was sick, and you knew that, and you gave me something that made me worse."

"That bitter tea came from the finest poppies, cathartic, yes, but the best. And I may say, *Monsieur*, that the problem is not that you were ill, the problem is that you don't know why you were ill. And your derailed mind spoke of death, and your fears left your body in the form of excrement."

"I don't understand what you say."

The striped tunic stared at Patricio without blinking, his face reflecting no emotion, as if frozen a thousand years ago, or dead perhaps.

"Where's Imena?" Patricio asked.

The striped tunic did not give an answer, he just waited in silence, as if time did not matter, as if the world could wait forever. He finally spoke.

"Why do you need to know? You seem obsessed with the young woman."

"I came from Paris looking for her and I need to find her."

"And what makes you believe that you will find her?"

"She said she was in a hotel close to the *Djemaa El-Fna*, behind a red door."

"As I already told you, the young woman is no longer here, she flew over the roofs of the medina."

"You don't believe that, people don't fly."

"But you believe it. For you know her spirit is lighter than yours. And while you wail in the thickness of your excrement, she searches for her answers elsewhere."

"This is nonsense."

"You may say so, *Monsieur*, but the reality is the same. It's like a sand dune, monstrous and heavy."

"You're not answering my questions."

"I listen to your plight, but I have no answers to give you," the striped tunic said, still looking at Patricio with the same glacial expression.

"I know where to find my answers, I don't need you."

"If you knew where to find your answers you wouldn't have come to Marrakech."

"I don't need to talk to you anymore."

"As you wish, your denial is formidable, *Monsieur*."

Patricio realized he could not argue with the striped tunic. He looked around the courtyard and grasped the strangeness of his situation.

"Look, I feel horrible, I have shit all over my body, and there's no bath in this place."

"Are you disgusted with yourself?"

I'm disgusted with you, Patricio thought, but did not say the words.

"Can you at least tell me where can I take a bath or a shower?" he did say.

"There's a *hammam* not far from here, go through the red door and turn right, the sun will shine on you. After a few dispassionate thoughts take another right and walk straight until you feel the light air flowing through the alley. Make a left and make an effort to remember what it feels like to be naked and free, like a child, at that point, no sooner, accelerate your pace until you feel like flying, but don't take to the sky, instead, look to your right and the sign for the *hammam* will be visible. Of course, if your denial is obstinate, as you just demonstrated, you may not find the *hammam*. But if you find it, you may identify a familiar fragrance, perhaps. Good luck *Monsieur*, I'll see you at dusk."

He walked through the red door and Patricio felt the sun shining on him, but his thoughts were not dispassionate, to the contrary, his yearning for Imena grew larger and deeper, making him miss the right turn and the alley inundated with light air, and instead of remembering what it felt to be naked and free like a child, he remembered the music that buried him in the ground of three continents. And at that point, Patricio knew he would never find anything.

24

René was the tenth, the last one. All he knew was that his seven sisters wore dresses and that his two brothers, the only ones that wore pants, had died when they were young. René walked up and down the stone paths of Saorge, played in the small squares, and during *La Saint-Sylvestre,* danced to medieval songs with his mother, all his sisters, and a few other children, *marginaux* all of them, who shared the joy of being there, that was all. He liked dancing more than working.

The work was brutal for a child, especially carrying olives from the steep hill nearby the *St. Croix.* But the time working as a mule, away from his sisters, allowed him to fancy himself a wonderful Russian princess from the nineteenth century, spending luxurious summers on the lazy hills east of Menton. One day he saw a book with pictures of the Russian Ballet, the dancers were beautiful, and the dresses divine, a spectacle for his imagination that only knew of grey shoes and rustic shirts. He believed the dancers were magical fairies and secretly aspired to be one of them.

He stayed young for a long time, maybe longer than his sisters who wore lipstick by age ten and rejected their mother by age twelve. He held on to childhood until puberty ruined his dreams of becoming a princess. His breasts did not swell and his penis and testicles grew larger—a terrible disappointment. So he continued to play as a boy/girl until another boy kicked a soccer ball so hard at him that he cried in pain, like a girl, and all the kids started calling him *Mademoiselle* Renée—if they only knew.

And at age thirteen, René met Antonia, a young girl from the Roma people, with a soft body, dark skin, and those eyes. And he wanted to be with her, but Antonia would turn away from him. And he would look at her but she never looked at him. Antonia, there's nothing I want more than you, he thought. He walked around Saorge dreaming of her. But Antonia was not there for him, she looked away, she walked away.

Antonia loved René's sisters, particularly the older one. Many times, Antonia and the older sister planned expeditions into the back hills of the town. They would prepare a picnic basket with beer in the bottom, hidden by *tourte saorgienne* on top. They did not allow the younger sisters to join in those excursions; they did not know how to play the games they played. Other times, they descended into the deep gorge and swam naked in the rushing waters of the Roya river. One day, René followed them at a distance. He saw them eat and drink, he saw them frolicking and rolling over each other on the dry autumn grass. At that point, he knew that his body was not the body he wanted, that it had to be something else, something Antonia would notice, like the body of his sister. He wanted to be close to Antonia, he wanted to touch her like her sister did. But he was too young to know the language of the butterflies.

And when the time came to smoke and dance at the *Fête de la Musique*, René retreated to his bedroom and dreamt of another place, a place away from his sisters who blossomed as delectable women in a small town. Alone, in front of a mirror, he would wear scarves and dresses, replacing his masculine figure with the dream of Renée, a girl Antonia would notice. He would pull his penis backwards between his thighs, hoping that it would disappear, someday.

25

Once he lost the dominant position in front of the caravan to a younger merchant, he knew the desert had died for him. The vastness of the land had defeated him. To make a living, he would need to stay inside the city walls, a reality that upset him deeply. After years of traveling through the desert, he did not anticipate this ending.

With no one to call his kin, he wandered through Marrakech unable to rest his head. The passage of time did not affect him, the sun could not crack his leather any deeper, and the wind twisted around his striped tunic without touching his skin. After walking all the streets of Marrakech, he decided to look for a courtyard open to the sky—a receptacle for his mind. He believed the conversation between the sky and the ground was sacred, that living creatures had no choice but to look to the sky for their true selves. Eventually, he found a decrepit building with multiple rooms around a barren courtyard where a fountain grew green algae. Perfect for a hotel, he thought, and paid for it with the money he made trading spices and opium poppies.

The place was right; it was the right place. He bent down and grabbed a fistful of red clay, kissed it, and threw it up to the sky, the wind lifting the particles higher and higher until they disappeared over the roofs of the medina. Wanting to link the ground to the sky, he planted an orange tree in each corner of the courtyard. And every seven days he would use water from the fountain to satiate the elemental thirst of the orange trees, their leaves turning dark green and their thorns becoming sharp and strong.

He restored the building, opening windows into the courtyard, painting the walls ochre, and furnishing all spaces in a simple manner. He painted the front door red. And when he was satisfied, he opened the hotel for business.

Before the trees flowered, before their fragrance filled the courtyard, he attempted to trim a few branches, those that grew in a radical angle, the rebels. He was searching for a natural order, the natural order of things. And accidentally, a thorn gored his skin and came to rest deep, almost touching the bone. Blood dripped, staining his extravagant idea that living creatures could be tamed. And at that time he understood his role as an impassive observer, a silent beholder. Living the life of a learned man became his next goal. And he read, and he learned, and he talked to people and observed their behaviors, until he finally understood the highs and lows of the human condition. He had learned the sand was many sands.

He used to go into the Medina to procure for his needs and to converse with a few men at the *Djemaa El-Fna*. He was always alone; he kept no company. And after arranging for the delivery of tea and other bare necessities, he gradually started spending more and more days inside the hotel, observing the guests and cataloging their behaviors. One morning, while drinking mint tea in the courtyard, he realized he had not left the hotel in the past six months. He looked at the red door and did not feel the urge to step through, or to traverse the streets on the other side. Wrapped in his striped tunic, he had another sip of mint tea and looked up to the sky above the four flowering orange trees.

*****

The striped tunic accepted the bread and roots from her giving hands. He looked at her face, the beloved mole clinging from the corner of her right eye.

She came to the hotel once every week to bring the meager sustenance. It had been two years now. She did not come for money, there was very little to make, she came because she wanted. His presence exerted a strange force on her. What it was she did not know, but she could feel it was strong, like a tempest. He always took what she brought without asking. And at the very moment when she handed the bread, the roots, or whatever she had to give that day, she felt as if her hands where drawn towards his hands, as if pulled by a magnetic force. But they never touched each other—except once.

She had known many men at the café. From all parts of the world they came, played backgammon, and went to the little backroom to see her, to take from her. This she did in a mechanical way, never feeling a pull or force from any of the foreigners. She was caring but careful. And if her blood did not come, she knew what to do.

But after the striped tunic touched her, she did not do anything, even after three months had passed without blood. She continued to bring him the weekly rations without mentioning her little secret. They did not speak much to each other, they barely exchanged greetings. And in spite of their weekly encounters, he could not have detected her inner turmoil. So when her body changed, a growing bulge shifting her center of gravity, she hid under colorful *djellabas*.

One day she came to the hotel carrying the newborn baby wrapped in wool. She had thoroughly wrapped him so that only the top of his head could be seen. The striped tunic laid a wooden look on her, took his food, and did not speak a word. She then started to bring the baby along every time she came to the hotel. Even when the baby was resting his head between her breasts, a few centimeters below the mole, the striped tunic ignored him completely.And the force pulling her towards him became even stronger.

"Is this food enough for the rest of the week?" she asked.

"This is the same as last week, and the same as the week before, why would it be different today?" the striped tunic said.

"People change sometimes."

"Have you changed?"

She wanted to say yes, she wanted him to hold the baby, and above all, she wanted to touch him again. But her wishes were blown away by the dry desert air as it flooded the courtyard. She then stood in front of him, close enough to hear the slow rhythm of his breath, and staring at him asked:

"Do you want to hold the baby?"

"I cannot touch that creature, and I should have never touched you."

"But you did."

The striped tunic turned his back on her and walked away to a corner of the courtyard. She felt an unbearable weight pressing down on her. And with her natural and open voice she sang a lullaby so tender that the orange trees dropped countless flowers on the red clay.

26

The mist and the green leaves are in the same corner I left them, protected from direct sunlight. That's how they survive. Perhaps I survive because the sunlight evades me, or perhaps, because I evade the sunlight, I survive. But I didn't evade anything, I went south and exposed my face to the sunlight and the dry desert air. I think I flew… I know I flew. But here I am now, north from south, in the glorious but opaque Paris of mine. For this Paris of mine contains a putrid essence, and for that reason, belongs to me.

I long for lightness, and I long for truth. And the striped tunic possessed a piercing truth, and Jacques and Charli embraced an artificial truth, a lie that is. And Patricio… I don't know about Patricio. What could his truth be? And as for lightness, he is lead. But tomorrow, after I rest my mind and sleep long and deep, I may look for Patricio, perhaps.

The wolves follow me, and Patricio is one of them. I have seen the white moon eaten by wolves. And sometimes I feel as if my white skin, like the moon, glows in the dark of the night. That's what the wolves look for, that's what they want to eat. And when I run away beyond the horizon, the wolves follow me, hoping to eat my white flesh. I want to be light, but this lightness invites the wolves, and I'm bitten, ferociously bitten.

My body wants to exist as a fruit, a frothy substance without a skin, not covered by a thickness, emanating freshness and a pungent fragrance. My body wants to feel the air, get wet with the morning dew, smile exhausted under the sun. My body wants to be in contact with my dreams and the world around me. And that's why I went south, and that's why I tasted Charli's saliva. For my body is fluid, the boundary between the external world and myself is porous, and I feel the movements of the air, the playing of the sunrays, and the warmth of the wolves' semen.

Leaving this Paris of mine was easy, I just went south. Returning is different. But Patricio, where is he? What can he be thinking? I told him I was in Marrakech, behind the red door. But in reality I was behind a layer of fear. Patricio, can you see my fears? Can you tell that I'm afraid of losing myself?

✻✻✻✻✻

Dusk came and the shadows turned the ochre walls of early morning into a maroon, or reddish purple. He walked through the red door, Patricio, and the disillusion and anguish trailed behind him, as they had done in the streets of Paris. He never found the *hammam*, and he never found a fragrance familiar to him. Inside the courtyard he waited. Then he waited some more. And without noise or clamor, the striped tunic emerged from across the courtyard and approached Patricio slowly.

"You seem anxious, *Monsieur*," the striped tunic said.

"I didn't find her."

"What makes you believe that you would find anything?"

"You said that I would find some familiar fragrance. I thought you meant I would see her somewhere."

"That's what you thought, perhaps that's what you wanted to think. In reality, I never mentioned any specifics."

"She's not here, she's not anywhere around here, and you know that."

The striped tunic turned around and left the courtyard. Patricio did not move, he remained in a state of anticipation while his anxiety weighed him to the ground, the ground of pure red clay binding his feet. When the striped tunic returned to the courtyard, he was carrying a tray with two glasses, a jar with mint tea, and some rock sugar. Patricio felt a sudden stab through his chest, a visceral scream, and his palms started to sweat, an uneasy sweat.

"No, you won't poison me again," Patricio said.

"*Monsieur*, I never tried to poison you."

The striped tunic remained emotionless. He proceeded to pour tea in both glasses, and with the softness of an angel, he offered one glass to Patricio.

"You seem angry, *Monsieur*. Perhaps you're tired from searching in the wrong places."

"I know she was here and I'm certain you know where she is now. So, let's stop this idiotic game and tell me where she is."

"What makes you think this is a game?"

"Because you sent me out there to the streets knowing that I wasn't going to find her."

"*Monsieur*, your thoughts torture you, preventing you from feeling naked and free, like a child. Why are you afraid of flying?"

Patricio did not answer. With his right hand, clammy from the cold sweat, he grabbed the glass of mint tea and brought it to his lips. He sipped a small amount and found it bitter. He put two pieces of rock sugar into the glass and stirred it with his index finger. He sipped a little more, and finding the tea agreeable, he continued to sip slowly until the glass was empty. He stopped thinking about Imena, he stopped thinking about the vomit of the night before, and he stopped thinking about the striped tunic. He arrived at a stage of passive alertness, where the dry air of the Medina circled around him, and the beast inside kneeled, putting its head against the ground.

"I'm not afraid of flying," he said.

27

René saw himself as Christine Jorgensen, April, and Aleshia, all exceptional transgender women. If he could, he would be, as he wanted. The university in Guadeloupe accepted his academic credentials from Paris and gave him permission to use their library. And after numerous blind leads and a few historical articles, he learned about Dr. Burou and his *"Clinique du Parc"* at 13 *Rue La Pebie* in Casablanca. But that was in the 50's and he needed current information. He read more, made several inquiries and telephone calls, and discovered that Dr. Leduc, a former intern of Dr. Burou, was still making miracles in Casablanca.

And from that moment René started to plan his life as Renée. He did not have friends, and with the exception of his night outings in drag, he remained a virtual recluse. That would facilitate the disappearance of a man and the birth of a new woman. During the daytime, he went to the beach where he could not stop watching the dark-skinned women. He wanted them; he ate them with his eyes. At other times, he worked in construction, building wooden porches, fixing roofs, and working the land, all in an effort to earn a few francs. Away from Paris and the intellectual torture of the university, his mind was free to imagine and to dream, his masculine body still keeping him in wraps.

And the days piled, one of top of the other, and the desire grew, but the money was not sufficient. His thoughts became strange. That was the time when his mind conceived the monstrous plan. He had thought about it many times, but the aberrant behavior seemed beyond his capacity. But he crossed the line of reason that night after he was left alone at the beach, when he heard that stupid giggle fainting away in the air. René returned to his apartment late that night, or early that morning, when the light had not yet turned humble. He stood in front of the mirror and observed the reflection of his impersonation, an unreal image. He remembered his youth, his sisters, his inadequate boyish figure. He thought about Antonia who would not look at him, and he wanting her. And he felt the pain of abandonment when dreams die suffocated.

He thought he was able, and his hand was certainly able. And he did not think about the pain; that was irrelevant. Even under the squalid lights, the view of the mirror was clear, and his frontal reflection rushed over him like a tempest. He peeled off the elastic black dress and undid the brassier construction. What appeared in front of himself, what he despised most, were his hanging testicles and his flaccid penis, a grotesque sight, an indelible stain. He looked at himself, at his anatomy, and the echo of the stupid giggle suffused the room.

René went to the kitchen, opened one of the top drawers, and grabbed the knife he used to peel potatoes and apples. The blade was thin and almost sharp. He returned to his position in front of the mirror and continued to observe his reflection. The red lips were not as bright as they were earlier that evening, the lines around his eyes were still dark, and his dilated pupils let the light straight into his retina. He saw everything sharper and fiercely intense. He lit a cigarette and took two big puffs, he exhaled and the floating smoke blurred his reflection, only for a moment.

*****

This isn't me. This isn't what I want to be. It looks like me, distorted, but it's not me. This body isn't my body and what I see isn't my true self. They laughed at me at the beach because they could see I'm a fake. And I want to be real, not a fake. And this image is abhorring, an abomination of hanging

117

organs. All of my life dragging this anatomy…, all of my life. The triangle between my legs, clean, without eruptions, with a crevice instead, the chest opulent, the silhouette desirable. That would be my true self. And I can be the instrument of my own change, I can deliver me to where I want to be. My own hand, the instrument of transformation, will perform the change. Let the fear die, fear is not within me. I know how to build, but now, I need to learn how to destroy to create something new.

Antonia, you would like me better. You didn't look at me when I was looking at you. I know you looked at my sister, and I saw you loving her. You didn't want me, not a sissy boy—you wanted a woman. Antonia, my gypsy, the edge of the knife divides my two disparate selves. I can see how the blade, this blade, can cut away my shame. And if I transform my anatomy, this repugnant reminder of what I'm not, you may like me better.

*****

In front of the mirror, under the poor light, René held his flaccid penis and testicles with his left hand, pulling sideways to allow ample room for the operation. He remained in that position for a few minutes, evaluating the best strategy. The knife had to enter below the scrotum on the right side, continue diagonally upwards towards the left, ending about ten centimeters below the umbilicus, severing testicles and penis along the way. It had to be a firm and continuous action, without hesitation, without fear. His mind had rehearsed the act numerous times, but that night, after the ridicule and rejection at the beach, he felt empowered. And after two more puffs from the cigarette, René held the knife on his right hand, thinking about Antonia, thinking about those who endured this pain before him, and looking straight at the mirror, the knife proceeded to carve into his own flesh, opening a chasm in his groin, the blood dancing, his right testicle falling away from his body, while his consciousness abandoned him.

28

And if I'm mistaken? After so long inside the courtyard wrapped in my tunic, without venturing into the streets, I could be mistaken. If I were mistaken, my observations would be meaningless. What an absurd idea. But after facing the sun, the sun that bleaches doubts and fears, I cannot be wrong. Even if my mind finds a hole in my precepts, I cannot be vacuous. I understand, or at least I understand better... so I think. But what if I'm a petulant monkey? What would happen if my beliefs are flawed? Just like that, flawed. But if the time inside these walls had warped my senses, if the loneliness and ascetic practices had weakened my reasoning, if the absence of another reasoning mind made me an obstinate fool..., how would I know? I think my mind is sharp, I believe my perceptions are accurate.

And when I sense the beast inside my guests, I'm not imagining an illusory monster, I'm describing their inner drives, the dark ones. Those drives are not an illusion; those drives are real. Even if I see their longing for each other, their mistaken passions, their imperfect selves, their unbridled beasts, does that make me knowledgeable, or does that make me an accomplice of their primitive nature?

A woman flees; a man follows. There's nothing special about that. A woman dreams; a man yearns. Basic..., elemental. And I behold them, I speak to them and I behold them. My words, they listen to my words as if there was some hidden meaning in them. And I have to pronounce my words because that's what I do. And I declare my words because they are the only personal expression that travels beyond the red door. My body is bound, my eyes fixed on the visiting creatures, but my words travel in their minds.

But what if my understanding was a mere farce, an erratic exercise, an artifice of my twisted mind? What if my observations were a reflection of my fears and weaknesses? What if I had created a courtyard like a spider web, a natural capturer of the weak and confused? What if..., what if? And if what I think about them is nothing more than what I think about myself? I don't leave this courtyard, I don't venture outside the red door. But I propose for them to traverse the streets, to fly over the medina, to search for the North Star. That's what I propose. And when they see me approaching them, my tunic floating, my bodily odor encroaching, they hold their breaths and turn away. But they still listen to my unnerving thoughts. They know that I know something, or at least, that I have thought about them in a different way. The time under the sun and between these walls has given me another way of looking at life. And I'll behold them and cut through their lives with my words. For the only meaning in my life is to allow the creatures to dream, to search, and to conquer their beasts, even if I have to remain in this courtyard for years, occult from the world outside.

29

When Imena walked down the *avenue de La Bourdonnais* and turned the corner at *rue de Monttessuy,* the comforting iron tower grew behind her and her senses felt at home. The orchestra of fragrances was still playing. She vibrated. The other students at the *Cinquième Sens* greeted her as if nothing had happened, because they did not know that anything had happened. And when she spoke with her faculty mentor, she declared that the natural essence of the *grassoise* roses resembled the saliva of a young woman. Her mentor was perplexed. She looked at the scent vials on the shelves and her mind opened like the flower of an accelerated spring. There were colors and shapes, fragmented images, undulating sounds, perhaps the wind, all traversing through her mind, caressing her skin in unison. A world she could play with; a world that would not hurt her.

That morning, Imena intended to find something savage. She sampled hundreds of vials, one by one, sometimes in duos, or quartets, looking for wildness. She wanted to fuse the naked nature of a *grassoise* rose with the violence of Charli's saliva. Her goal was the juxtaposition of opposite poles, a bipolar madness contained in one fragrance, a conflicted fragrance. But the essence of Charli's saliva was of an animal nature, and if left unbridled, would subjugate the soft rose. She remembered the opening words, a kiss..., a caress. She struggled to sequence the smell of Charli's mouth and the air that moved through the room at the *Musiciens.* And drops of a vial mixed with drops of another vial, and her mind registered a song, a song that was pure blue, and her skin felt the color of roses, and a wetness formed between her legs, and the light became untouchable, and she heard the sound of the beast, a sound brutal and deep, and her pulse accelerated, and she closed her eyes, and her fingers found the wetness, and the color purple cried, and the taste of Charli's saliva assaulted her, brutally, and the moment exploded, while her torso undulated in a state of arousal, her breathing wild, her sensorial world expanded, *la rose sauvage* experienced, in her sex and mind.

She could not feel anything else, and for a moment, a clear light suspended her. And when the world materialized again, Imena knew she had touched the line between the flower and the animal. Her senses exhausted, she walked out of the *Cinquième Sens* and sat at a little table in *Bistrot Firmin* where she had a coffee.

A tide of thoughts and unanswered questions overtook Imena, propelling her to leave the perfumes behind and search for Patricio that afternoon. She went south because of him, and now she came back north…, because of him. And with a resolute step, Imena took to the streets of Paris, following the scents to the building where Patricio had contemplated the Mansard roofs. All familiar to her, the path of the wolf that hunted her.

Once at his door she knocked, and after a moment, came the silence, the stillness, the absence. She called his name aloud, as strongly as she could, knowing there would be no answer. And there was no answer. She then knelt down and placed her nose at ground level in front of the narrow gap between the door and the floor. She wanted to sample the air that escaped his apartment. And the air brought him, faintly, the air spoke like him, softly. And all at once, she remembered the books, the flowers, the lazy afternoons. She knocked again, once, twice, and with force, thrice, only to feel the pain in her knuckles, for Imena knew that Patricio was not there, that he was looking for her elsewhere.

At the end of the day, her mind still unquiet, Imena dared

to enter the department of philosophy at *La Sorbonne*. And just as she remembered, the walls on the second floor were dark and the air heavy with too many thoughts. She stood in front of Patricio's office and read the name on the door. It was his name, she was at the right place, but there was nobody there. She walked down the hall, the wind of thoughts behind her, until she reached the desk of Huong, or the Vietnamese secretary that Patricio called Huong. And before Imena uttered a single word, Huong said,

"He's not here, *Mademoiselle*."

"What a son of the bitch."

"Excuse me, *Mademoiselle*?"

"Nothing, nothing."

And hastily, without looking back, Imena walked away looking for René's office. She did not know him very well, but if anyone would know the whereabouts of Patricio, it would be René. But he was not there either. Again, she walked down the hall to where Huong was looking up, expectantly.

"*Oui, Mademoiselle?*"

"Do you know where I may find *Monsieur* Liprandi?"

"Yes, I think I know," Huong said.

"Where would that be?"

"Not here."

"Then, where would that be?"

"He left for Guadeloupe, the DOM-TOM, you know."

After a second or two, she understood there were no more doors to try and no other scents to follow. And with a gentle gesture, born from the softness of the air, she waved Huong goodbye, and left the hallway of the second floor, wondering where would people go when their yearnings are on fire.

*****

Yes, he can. Yes, he can be in Marrakech, roaming the streets and looking behind one, or many red doors. I can almost hear his questions, I can almost feel the heavy breathing. And when I went to the *hammam*, and exposed my body to the scalding water, I thought I had washed all the past away. I thought I had tossed it away, in my nakedness. And Jacques made me believe that I was fresh, born that morning in the comfort of salt and seaweed. And Charli gave me her mouth, her bodily fluids. But why? Why do I come back and bury my head in the ground? After flying away, why? And here, among these grave walls, the absence of Patricio penetrates my skin. His absence disrupts the structure of my fragrance. I feel groundless, all *bergamote* and *citron zeste*. But when he's present, I feel the oppressive weight of amber, *santal d'orient,* and jasmine. That's why I left. I left because the base note was devouring me—that wolf.

Starting at the top, and progressively reaching the base, one layer swimming into the next, one life expiring as another is born. And the story developing gradually, sustaining the ecstasy, allowing for my senses to savor the nuances of a thousand molecules, as they vibrate in the air. My way, I live my life that way. And the more I run away from him, the more I want to find his middle note, his top note. I am certain those notes are there, maybe in the form of the tango, that melancholic music of his past. Maybe the tango is that space above his base, the space he doesn't share, his volatile and playful essence. But he doesn't want to inhabit that space, he doesn't want to explore it. The fear and the horror holds him down, at the level of amber, preventing him from being playful like the *fleurs fraîches*.

The air that floats above him remains a secret to himself, his balance, the rest of his composition. I'll decipher it. I'll break down his notes: the base binding me to the ground, the middle conjuring survival, and the top, eluding him but finding me flying above the roofs of our lives.

30

Not too far from the acrobatic monkeys, Patricio found another door, white, and behind it, an old store selling books in several languages and old records. The titles spanned a universe, from *Don Quijote* to *Light in August*, from *Birth of the Cool* to *Le Sacre du Printemps*. The cumulative thoughts and the vastness of the artistic expressions excited him. Inside the store, the languid horn of Chet Baker exuded from an old phonograph, painting the air blue. Patricio approached the owner, Mr. Sanford, a retired British colonel who wore a glass sphere in lieu of his original right eye, and without forethought asked him for employment at once. Mr. Sanford half-looked at him, and after placing his Siamese cat on the floor, determined that a man requesting employment from him must be either very serious or seriously mad.

"Did you say you want to work for me, is that what you said?" Mr. Sanford asked.

"Yes, that's what I just said."

The proposition perplexed Mr. Sanford. He had managed his store for a long time, always alone, and never considered he needed help.

"But I don't know you."

"I don't know you either."

"What would you do in this old store?"

"I just want to be here."

"But that's not a real job, or is it?"

"I can think for you."

"But I can think for myself, you don't have to think for me."

"I can think in a different way."

Mr. Sanford was use to all sorts of characters entering his

store. But Patricio was different, he did not ask for any specific book or record, he proposed to think on his behalf.

"What are you, a prophet, or a magician, or what?" Mr. Sanford asked.

"No, I'm a philosopher."

"So you're a magician after all."

"I want to fly," Patricio said as if he was telling a secret, something he was not supposed to admit.

"Wait, wait…, now you want to fly. You just told me you were a philosopher. "

"Yes, but I need to take to the air."

"So you're a philosopher who wants to fly who wants to think for me." With a big laugh, Mr. Sanford turned away from Patricio and ran after his cat. He managed to get a hold of the Siamese, cradled her in his arms and approached Patricio with a wide grin.

"There's no order in this place," Patricio said. "The books are disorganized, the records are everywhere."

Mr. Sanford looked around his chaotic store, petted the annoyed cat, and turned to Patricio.

"And what's wrong with that? It's been like this forever," he said.

"You could sell more if this place were organized."

"But I don't care about selling books or records, I just want to show them off."

"There's no one here to show your books to."

"What makes you believe that? You walked through the door, or maybe I should say you flew through the door because of my books. How do you explain that, Mr. winged philosopher?"

"What attracted me was the chaos, the disorder."

"You're lying. The books attracted you, the pile of disordered records attracted you."

Patricio continued to walk through the store, moving

carefully among the innumerable piles of books and records, dusting a few covers, reading the titles until he reached an old desk under a window open to the southeastern sky.

"I would like this to be my desk," he said.

"Are you planning to fly away from the sill of the window?"

"I speak in a figurative way. As you know, I cannot fly away *per se*."

"Then, what do you mean?"

"I only want to be among books. If I'm lucky, I may float a little. And if I'm by the window, I may be able to experience a little lift, that's all," Patricio said.

"That's a wonderful idea. You may just reach the moon, Mr. Lunatic."

"Mr. Sanford…"

"Call me Sanfy, that's how everybody calls me around here, even the monkeys call me Sanfy."

"Mr. Sanfy…"

"No…, you don't need to use mister. I'm no mister."

"Sanfy, can I work for you?"

"No you cannot."

Patricio had never been rejected that way. He was not sure if the problem was with him, or simply with Mr. Sanford, or Sanfy, whatever his name was.

"Why won't you hire me?"

"Because you seem to be crazy and I don't know how to deal with crazy people," Sanfy said.

"Mr. Sanford…"

"Sanfy, Sanfy, please."

"Listen, Sanfy, I'm not a crazy person. I'm a professor of philosophy at *l'Université Paris-Sorbonne*. I plan to remain here in Marrakech for a while and will need some money, you don't have to fear me."

"Most interesting, and where are you staying?"

"I don't know the name of the hotel, but it has a red door."

"Really, and who's the proprietor, the blind woman?"

"No, a man with a striped tunic, but I don't know his name."

Sanfy proceeded to look at Patricio with his good eye, as though he was scanning the surface of the moon.

"Very, very interesting. Are you a writer?" Sanfy asked.

"No, I told you I'm a professor."

"Yes but what is the purpose of your stay in Marrakech?"

"A friend of mine may be here somewhere, I came looking for her."

"A fool then, a fool looking for another fool, that's what you are."

Patricio's face disbanded. He was not used to this type of confrontation. And reigning in his emotions he said:

"She doesn't know that I'm looking for her."

"A secretive fool then. Is there any explanation for that in your philosophy books?"

"I cannot explain much, the last couple of days have been very confusing. At one point I thought I was going to die."

"Were you trying to fly, did you jump from the top of a roof or something like that?"

"No…, not really. I drank a bitter tea that made me sick."

"I see, I see…the striped tunic provided you with that tea, didn't he?"

"Yes he did. Do you know him?"

"I know him like I know my cat."

"But do you really know him?"

"What do I know? I don't know anything or anyone." Sanfy became quiet again for a few seconds while his inquisitive eye continued to observe Patricio.

"I haven't seen him in a long time; he has been hiding inside that hotel for a long, long time. He's studying you, I'm sure he is."

The Siamese cat came close to Patricio and pressed her

head hard against his ankles. She then turned around and charged against Patricio again while pointing her tail straight to the ceiling, her back arched, her eyes halfway closed. When Patricio tried to pet the cat, eager to show Sanfy that he cared for his pet, the cat squirmed away and went to sit on the floor three feet away from Patricio, her back and tail pointing at him but safely away from his reach.

"Just like your friend, isn't she?" Sanfy said pointing at the cat.

"When can I start?" Patricio asked.

"You've started already, professor."

31

The crooked scar made him look like a rag doll with limbs clumsily stitched to the body. He had gone as far as he could by himself. And when the psychiatrist asked him if he wanted to kill himself, René denied such a crazy idea. He had attempted to start his life, not to end it. The doctors repeated this question at every eight-hour shift during the three days he spent in the hospital. They were more amused by his intellectual discussions about the ambiguities of the self than by any suicidal intentions he may have had. And after the third day, René resuscitated and was allowed to leave the hospital on his own—limping.

The wound turned into a mocking reminder of what he was not. If the knife had completed its oblique course, all the organs would have been detached, and René would have been closer to his ambition. But only the right testicle fell off, the left one continued to produce testosterone, chaining him to a hormonal maleness. With patience, René awaited for the wound to heal. He did not return to the beach, the bars, or any other place he frequented as a woman impostor. And after several nights and many more visits to the front of the mirror, René concluded he needed to return to Paris, settle his accounts with the university, and complete his transformation under the skillful knife of Dr. Leduc, in Casablanca.

René called Huong and learned that Patricio was missing and that a young woman had been searching for the two of them. And with the softness of a wounded lamb, René reassured Huong that everything was fine and that he was on his way to Paris after much needed respite.

René foresaw the difficult situation awaiting him in Paris. He needed to arrange for a longer permit, a sabbatical of sorts, or some other stratagem that would permit him to proceed with his plan. He suspected the young woman who went looking for him and Patricio was Imena. He did not really know her, but knew that Patricio was infatuated with her. He thought of her as a very attractive female, but her skin was pale, unsavory, maybe tasty for Patricio, but not for him. However, the fact that Imena was looking for him was interesting, for nobody ever cared much about him. She could help his cause, she would know the whereabouts of Patricio, the only person for whom he felt an attachment.

Once in Paris, after the brutal reencounter with his life of before, René felt mortified. He walked through the streets with a limp, frequenting a few restaurants in the *5ème arrondissement*, and answering questions with vague answers. Where he had been, nobody knew, why he limped, nobody guessed, and where he was going remained a mystery. And when his colleagues asked him if he was ready to resume teaching, René laughed and ran away, muttering words that had no meaning—the language of the butterflies.

✳✳✳✳✳

I must leave. I must leave this cell. The force of the wind behind me, pushing me to the edge of this instar, my Paris instar. And with violence I catapult myself into the red precipice, crashing my chrysalis. For this is the path I must follow. Antonia, with your soft body, your dark skin, and your eyes. You didn't see me, you looked through me. But what if I had scales and the light shining on my body reflected another self, with colors. What if I were like my sister, but brighter? Would you then look at me, Antonia? I must leave, not leave exactly..., I must evolve, into a different shape, the same body, the same core, but another shape, with scales. And if the horizon opened a sliver of light, dark on top, dark in the bottom, I would fly to the light, for my scales would reflect my essence. Antonia, can you see the four eyes? No, don't be afraid, they should not scare you. You can even touch them, I won't die from your touch.

And the time will come, and the knife will be lifted, not by me this time, no. And I'll repose, my torso pressed against the ground giving birth to the contour of my breasts, my left leg bent at the knee, the light breathing into my flower, my face placid, glowing, my flesh and the stone as one, a living version of the Borghese dream. Myself..., the imago of myself. And as I evolve I'll savor nectar and dung, I'll dance over rotting fruit, I'll flutter over decaying flesh. But the colors will be wonderful, radiant, and the lightness, exuberant.

Antonia, you never saw me, and then you closed your eyes forever. But I never stopped looking at you. When the water filled your world, when the air left your life, I continued looking at you. I imagine the coldness, the thickness of the water, the darkness. And my sisters running around under the sun. Myself, the undesirable self of that time, hiding under a pine tree. I could not hear you because I didn't exist. Then the grey flesh, the body bending, the arms touching the sand, the sun ashamed. Antonia, you left without knowing you were leaving me. And when a cry was heard, I secretly bit into my skin because I needed to feel, because the pain of others ignored my pain. Antonia, my gypsy Antonia, if your eyes could see me, you would notice me. Antonia, look at me, I'm turning.

With courage I'll go, to the edge of the knife I'll go. The knife will travel, as far as it needs to travel, eliminating the ambiguity of my persona, delivering me as I dream of myself. And the sun of the south will darken my skin, and the chest will develop a contour, and the triangulated ignominy of my old self will give birth to a new horizon, with valleys and ravines. I'll emerge from the sea, the shell under my feet and gold leaf in my hair, a radiant nymph.

32

Marrakech, under the sun, beaten by the wind. Imena returned to this ambit with an open mind, her senses fully aware. But this time she was chasing the wolf. Her nose captured every nuance in the air, her eyes detected the salmon color of the walls, and her ears welcomed the eternal chant. And without much delay, she set to the streets to find the red door. She walked fast, looking in all directions, but the labyrinthian madness of the medina confused her. She continued her frenetic walk until she heard a fountain singing and felt a strange familiarity in the play between light and shadows. She then recognized the hotel. Imena walked straight to the red door and tried to open it. But the door was locked. She thought of calling the striped tunic to come and open the door but she did not remember his name, actually, she never knew his name, she only knew his stench.

Imena tried to walk around the building looking for another entrance, but the confused streets led her astray. There was no backdoor, the only access to the hotel was through that red door. But she knew the real entrance, the one used by the air, was not from the street but from the sky, through the open courtyard. She studied the cramped facades of the adjacent houses, looking for a way to climb to the roof. There were balconies, closed windows, half-dried clothes hanging from black wires, other doors of various colors, and a lamppost. If she could climb to the top of the houses, she would be able to walk over the jagged roofs, like a cat, until reaching the edge of the courtyard.

She remembered the day at *Pompierre* beach when Patricio helped her climb to the roof of a brightly painted house. The horizon was pure and the air pulsated with the smell of salt and seaweed. She remembered. She could almost feel his hands touching her skin. Those hands were different from the sea spray that had caressed her all her life. She was not pale then; her skin was the color of cinnamon and tasted bitter. She remembered how the birds celebrated in the air. And she remembered when she dreamt of the butterfly island rising from the sea, beating its wings high among the clouds, carrying her to the city of lights. But today was different, she was not anchored to the bottom of the sea, today she could fly. And with the dry lightness of desert air, Imena walked over the roofs of the Medina until the courtyard opened in front of her. She sat at the edge of the roof and contemplated the courtyard below. There was the fountain in the center, singing, and the four flowering orange trees seemed to vibrate with life.

*****

I can see the sound of the air as it moves among the orange blossoms, thought Imena. I can hear the humming heart of the red clay. I can smell the fragrance of my dreams. This time I fly to encounter, not to escape. Because I'm not anchored, because I'm not bound by memories. I feel transparent, my skin is a thin veil, and all the atoms in the world can travel through me. And if the wind were to blow furiously, my body would not shift. And if the arrow tried to penetrate my body, it would pass through, like a song. I capture nothing. I retain nothing.

He wants to hold me, Patricio. He needs to touch my skin to feel me. He needs to bite into my flesh. But there's no flesh to embrace like there are no thoughts to hold. I want to live inside his mind. I want to smell the scent of his ideas, but they are vast, and they disseminate in the air leaving no trace.

From my butterfly island to the city of lights, to the desert. From Patricio to the south, to the north, to the south, to Patricio. How violent the flow. But it doesn't hurt me, it is fluid and runs through me. And if I were to stop the flow, I would fall out of the sky. That's why I let the winds take me, and I let the lights shine through me. For my existence is insubstantial, I'm made of distant particles, all traveling and vibrating to the tune of my inner chaos.

And at the right time, only then, I'll distill my fragrance. The rose as an animal. Patricio, the wolf, can he be a rose? Can he be more than a thinking animal? Could a thought, an idea, have a scent? And if a thought were to travel through the gentle *grassoise* hills, would it return as a fragrance? I cannot be a rose, but I can be the scent of a rose. Here, on the edge, as I look down on the courtyard, I feel neroli running through my veins. And I'll descend to meet the ground, to sing with the fountain, to flower with the orange trees.

✶✶✶✶✶

He liked books, but not every book. He read essays in philosophy during the daytime; at nighttime, he only read fiction. He needed the miracle of imagination after sundown. When Imena came to his flat, in the late hours, Patricio felt as if a flower opened inside him. Those were the fiction hours, when the rational monster was asleep. He read with Imena, he read to Imena, he loved when Imena read to him. And when the words percolated through his inside, his face became radiant. So when Sanfy asked him to report to the bookstore in the morning hours, Patricio knew his life was about to change. Daytime would no longer be thinking time; it would become softer, erratic, even musical. He felt light, and scared.

After a day full of words at Sanfy's store, Patricio walked back to the hotel, twisting and turning through his rehearsed path. And when he finally arrived at the red door, he also found it closed. He pushed, he leaned with his shoulder, he kicked, but he could not open the door. He wanted to call the striped tunic, but like Imena, he did not know his name. The striped tunic never said his name, and never gave him a key to the door either. For a moment, Patricio doubted that he was at the right place. But when he surveyed the street and the adjacent buildings, there was no doubt he was at the right place. That he had no key, and did not know the name of the stinking creature, was an unsettling truth. He decided to walk around the medina for thirty minutes, more or less, maybe less, and return later to see if the door would be open. The thought seemed rational, but he knew it would be futile. Not completely convinced, he started to walk, always turning left, tracing a big circle that would eventually bring him to the place where he started, he thought.

But all the streets looked the same and the corners did not want to turn in right angles. And Patricio worried he was not going to find his way back. He started to walk faster. He turned left, always left, until a point where the only way to turn was right. He turned right against his will, because there was nowhere else to go. And when he looked ahead, the street laughed at him. He started running, without speed, a dead run following a right curve, the opposite angle to a left curve, decidedly away from the red door. And when he came to the next corner, it was not possible to turn left either, again the street only offered a right turn. Patricio stopped and looked down the street as far as he could. There was nothing special; the street continued twisting away from his desired direction as if the world did not care about the red door. And he heard the street laugh again.

Patricio stood at the side of the street to catch his breath. The aroma of uncertainty invaded him, entering through his nostrils and reaching the base of his skull. He did not move. He just stood there.

"Have you found your woman?" the blind woman asked.

Patricio turned towards the voice. He recognized the face and the bulging eyes.

"No, no… I don't know…"

"At least you found a place to stay, I hope."

"Well, yes, but I'm having a hard time finding it again," Patricio said.

"Who's your innkeeper?"

"I don't know his name. He wears a striped tunic."

"Everybody here wears a striped tunic. Does he have a musty smell?"

"What do you mean by that?"

"I mean, does he smell like a trapped animal?"

"Well, the innkeeper smells horribly, like something rotten."

"Yes, yes, he needs to come out of that place sometime soon. Just go back the same way you came and you will find that dirty place. Turn left two times and then right as many times as needed. You'll get there."

"You seem to know this man."

"No, I only know he hides inside that hotel, we haven't seen him in years."

"But, could you actually see him? I mean, can you see anything?"

"You think I'm a pitiful blind woman, don't you?"

"Well, not really, but can you see me?"

"No, but I can feel everything. I can feel you."

"Can you feel her, the woman I'm looking for? Can you hear the wind and the bells?"

"I don't know anything about that woman. But I can feel your fear… Enough! Go back now, to that courtyard, and maybe you'll learn to live without fear. Go now, go."

Patricio looked back to the street where he came from and started walking in that direction. He turned left two times and then right. Behind him, the mutterings of the bulging eyes crashed against the pink walls. I must go now. Go now, go. I must go now. Go now, go… go.

33

Casablanca, at the edge of the sea, at the edge of the knife. The look he received, René, was one of compassion when the nurse gave him a paper robe to cover himself. Instead of putting his arms through the openings leaving an open slit exposing his back, he reversed the procedure and left his front exposed. That was when the nurse saw his maimed genitalia. "You'll be fine," she said. René wanted her to stay next to her, but she left the room to inform Dr. Leduc that René was ready. While waiting for the doctor, he looked down at his botched groin and pulled the paper robe trying to cover it completely. But there was not enough robe to conceal the act. He sat straight, clasping his hands together and gracefully placing them on top of his groin, assuming a statuesque posture, arms extended, chin lifted, his eyes looking at the door in expectation of Dr. Leduc.

He waited. And a short film played again inside the dark room of his mind. A familiar film. The rag doll, with a long and narrow scar stitched with barbwire, limped and ran, trying to escape a hideous creature. The creature had the head of lion and the body of a snake covered with feathers. It persecuted the doll while dragging its own large and putrid phallus. And the faster the doll limped and ran, the deeper the barbwire cut, the blood dripping and soaking the rags red. And when the creature finally reached the rag doll, it devoured it utterly. But the creature would not stop there, it devoured its own putrid phallus while roaring, hissing, and howling.

"I see, I can see. When did this happen?" Dr. Leduc asked.

"Not too long ago, but it seems years ago," René said.

"What kept you from cutting everything off?"

"I think I fainted."

"Did it hurt you, or did you feel a soothing relief?"

René had not thought about that concept before. He remembered how it happened but not exactly how he felt. He remembered seeing the right testicle falling off, and the blood, but he did not remember seeing anything else. As for relief, nothing of the sort, to the contrary, images and creatures hunted him, eating him alive.

"Doctor, I've not rested since."

"I understand."

The doctor put his hands inside latex gloves and proceeded to touch and handle the desecrated area. René closed his eyes, and allowed the doctor to examine him, hoping the creature, the feathered snake, would not catch up with him this time. He felt every touch of the doctor's fingers. For a moment, he felt as if the right testicle still hung from his crotch. A phantom, a nervous memory of his image in the mirror, when the grotesque sight propelled him to carve. But even when this turmoil jammed his mind, René managed to remain supine, his legs opened, his vulnerable soul exposed.

"Tell me about yourself," the doctor said.

"I'm René Liprandi, born in *Saorge, Alpes-Maritimes*. I'm a professor of philosophy at *l'Université Paris-Sorbonne*. I don't want to be a male anymore."

Dr. Leduc laid a phlegmatic look on René. He continued to examine his anatomy, like a general planning a battle. He looked up at René and asked, "Are you sexually active?"

René looked at the doctor and saw his unemotional face, his half-closed eyes not blinking, and his steady hands. He felt cold and tried to cover himself with the paper robe. He fidgeted and changed his position on the examining table.

"I'm a virgin," he said.

"That's fine, but do you get aroused by men, women, or both?"

"Women, primarily women. Ever since I was a child I looked at women. But I've never been with one."

"Why not?"

"Because I'm a man. I want to be with women as a woman," René said, turning his face away from the doctor.

Dr. Leduc continued his examination in silence. He asked the nurse for some instruments which he used to poke and explore. He then wrote some notes on a piece of paper. When he was finished, he asked René to get dressed.

"*Monsieur* Liprandi, you'll become what you want to become."

"I didn't ruin my chances?"

"You were lucky. You could've severed the femoral artery, and then there would be nothing to repair."

"I had no option, I needed to cut away that monster."

"But tell me *Monsieur* Liprandi, what do you want to see when you look at yourself in the mirror?"

"I want to see myself."

"Isn't that what you see now?"

"No. I look at myself, but what I see is not myself."

"Are you referring to your anatomy, or are you referring to yourself as a person?"

"Doctor, I don't know anymore. When I dress as a woman, pretending I have breasts, pushing down whatever is left of that monster, it makes me feel empty. I feel I'm lying."

"Who do you want to be?" the doctor asked.

"I just want to be who I always was," René said.

34

Imena stepped into the empty courtyard and felt the red clay grabbing her feet. She stood by the fountain and savored the refracted light dancing around her. She imagined the striped tunic would be around, watching her from some oblique angle, but decided to stay calm. The only noise she heard came from the orange trees, as the leaves caressed each other while the white flowers watched in complicity. She remained quiet, in expectation. Then, an abrupt reverberation of air particles ushered in an animal aroma. She closed her eyes and concentrated, trying to identify its origin. But by the time she recognized the stench of the striped tunic, his voice was upon her.

"*Mademoiselle*, I've been thinking about you."

"I tried to open the door but it was closed."

"Yes, I know."

"Why did you close the door?"

"Why did you try to open it?"

"I needed to come back into the courtyard."

"I needed protection against my impulses."

"Oh, what impulses?"

The striped tunic looked at Imena serenely, his breathing was slow, and his lips formed a placid smile. He appeared whole, as if a universal peace had entered the courtyard.

"I don't have those impulses any longer. I'll open the door today," the striped tunic said.

Imena walked toward one of the flowering orange trees, inhaled the fragrance, and with a quivering voice said, "I need a room."

"Are you looking for a room and a cup of tea?"

"Both, I need both," she said.

The striped tunic walked across the courtyard, and with a strong push of his shoulder, he lifted the heavy wooden crossbar, unlocking the red door. He did not open the door; instead, he crossed the courtyard again and sat next to Imena.

"What brought you back to my hotel?"

"I thought I may find a friend of mine here, in this hotel."

"Why would your friend come here?"

"I told him I was somewhere in Marrakech, behind a red door."

"Interesting, but why would he be looking for you?"

"Why do you want to know?"

"For the same reasons that you want to know. You continue to search, this time outside of yourself."

"Has anyone come here asking for me?"

"A wolf, a desperate man, came here a few weeks ago."

"Was he looking for me?"

"I don't know, *Mademoiselle*. To say exactly what anyone is looking for is impossible."

"Did he mention my name?"

"*Mademoiselle*, who are you?"

"You must know, I wrote it in your hotel papers last time I was here."

"I know your name is Imena, but that does not tell me who you are. I can say your name but I cannot pronounce you. And if anyone came here asking for you by name, I would say I don't know who that person is."

"Imena, Imena," she whispered to herself, almost imperceptibly.

She needed to hear her name to rescue it, to make it her own. She felt her body disintegrating, her limbs falling off, and her organs melting to the ground. Under the stern look of the striped tunic, Imena composed herself and ran out into the street, leaving her essence floating behind like an atonal melody.

****

My impulses are brutal. They wrap my mind as the tunic wraps my body. My anger about the outside world, that diabolical force threatening me every day keeps me inside these walls. And when she left following Jacques, I felt like rushing through the red door behind her. I haven't crossed that door in years, and I won't cross it now. But the animal nature of my instinct, an instinct driving me to revert to the desert, is wicked and powerful. In despair, I howl, and saliva comes out of my mouth like a song.

This courtyard contains everything I am. And solitude tinges the clay and the walls. For I live like a hermit, in isolation, with tea and time and a few pieces of bread and roots. And then there's the nauseating fear at the center of my solitude. For when I want to escape and rejoin the desert, fear is the instigator. She didn't bring fear to me, but she accentuated my solitude when she left. And from the center of my solitude I felt the fearful urge to flee.

I must counter this force. These impulses can only destroy the harmony, the delicate balance of the courtyard, of my mind. As I sit here, beholding everything and everyone, away from the outer world, my interior is serene. And I indulge in the air from the medina because it enters the courtyard like the sound of a flute, in peace. This body, ascetic, yearns for tranquility. And I'm not joining the air when it escapes back into the medina. I'm not crossing that red door. I resolved to block the entrance, not to keep the outside from invading, but to arrest my impulses from breaking through.

She came here searching and then left to search elsewhere. But the same search brings her back to the courtyard, to the wolf sniffing around for her. She seems as lost as before, and for that reason, the more delicate. I see her nervousness, the dubitative shyness of a child. But her eyes don't search my eyes, she's not coming back for me.

And as she descends again into my courtyard, not because of love, or carnal passion, but because of her diaphanous presence, I feel entire. My fears and solitude dissipate. I can continue as before, wrapped in my tunic, beholding the world contained within my courtyard. Now I dare to unlock the door because my impulses lie dormant again.

*****

He took a long time, Patricio, but at the end of numerous turns, after facing dead-ends, tortuous alleys, and uncertainty, he finally arrived at the hotel. This time he found the door open. When he stepped into the courtyard looking for his room, a disquieting aroma overwhelmed him. His mind rocketed to Paris, *Pompierre* beach, *Château d'Eau,* his flat with pictures and books, the tango lesson, her last words. A sense of vertigo assaulted him and Patricio fell on his knees. He recognized the fragrance. And with the beautiful force of despair, he called her name: "Imena, Imena." The air, leaving him alone in the center of the courtyard, carried his words. No one answered. The sun attacked the south wall of the courtyard and the flowering orange trees chanted a joyous song.

Patricio staggered into his room. He decided to rest, breathe, and recuperate his poise. He savored the agonizing possibility that Imena could be somewhere near. But he could not help thinking about the striped tunic, and a blast of doubt shattered him. What if he offered Imena the same bitter tea that almost killed him? Patricio thought. He was not certain about the stripe tunic's intentions, as he was not certain whether Imena was in the hotel. He only knew her fragrance floated in the air.

145

With caution, Patricio opened the window into the courtyard and stood at its edge in silence. From the protective shadow of his room, he surveyed the entire courtyard. He waited. And anticipation charged at him, like a bull goring through his mind. But nothing happened. He stood in silence for some time, and then, for some more time. The striped tunic was nowhere and Imena did not answer his call. The world he observed did not coincide with his anxiety. In fact, the air felt placid, layering itself over roof tiles, fountain, and clay, while the sunlight bounced from wall to wall, uninterrupted. Nothing around him shared his intensity; nothing validated his suspicions.

Patricio felt obligated to return to the courtyard and search for the striped tunic. He walked slowly but deliberately, and the images of before danced in front of his eyes. "Imena, where are you?" And when he believed the courtyard was completely empty, a shadow materialized from behind an orange tree and confronted him with unexpected words.

"You seem to be looking for something," the striped tunic said.

"Where did you come from?" Patricio asked.

"I come from everywhere, and toward everywhere I go."

Patricio stood in front of the striped tunic wanting to decipher his mystery. But he could not sustain that position. And taking a few steps back, he said, "Do you remember the woman I spoke to you about?"

"I could not forget her."

"You haven't touched her, have you?"

"*Monsieur*, I haven't touched a human being in a long while. But why do you ask that question?"

"I think she's here in the hotel. I sense something. Maybe you know where she is. Maybe you won't tell me."

"What makes you believe that?"

Patricio thought he entered a minefield. Perhaps he

revealed too much. If the striped tunic had not seen Imena, his questioning could easily entice his curiosity. He resolved to prevent any commingling between Imena and the striped tunic, and decided to avoid mentioning her completely.

"*Monsieur*, you seem mortified. May I offer you some mint tea?"

Patricio felt obligated to accept the venomous substance. To refuse, he thought, would only alert the striped tunic of his apprehension. He needed to sit with him, drink the mint tea, and talk about the desert, Sanfy's bookstore, and Paris, but nothing else. There could be no further mention of Imena, or his search for Imena. And when the striped tunic brought the worn tray with tea and rock sugar, Patricio realized he was performing a survival ritual as ancient as the desert sand.

35

René could not sleep the night before—his thoughts were on fire. He looked at himself in the mirror, the last time as a man. That image would soon die. His mind entertained other visions, other images. And after entering the hospital, removing all his clothes, grabbing the nurses hand, lying on a cold surface, and letting go of his consciousness, the one image he admired, "The Birth of Venus," reigned supreme.

Dr. Leduc removed the penis and the remaining left testicle. An expert dissection through the muscles of the perineal area created a vaginal cavity. He then turned the penile skin inside out and divided it, using part to form the floor of the vulva, and part to form the anterior wall of the vagina. With a flap of the left scrotal tissue, he formed the posterior wall and apex of the vagina. He constructed the labia from scrotal tissue as well. At last, René was surgically demasculinized.

When René regained consciousness, he had several tubes connecting his body to plastic bags. He did not know where he was or what had happened to him. Everything around seemed unfamiliar, even menacing. But the dull pain coming from his groin, and the sight of the nurse's white hands quickly reoriented him. It happened, he thought. And with a faintly anesthetized voice he spoke to the nurse.

"Are you there?"

"Yes René, next to you, here on the other side of the bed," the nurse said.

"Did he change me?"

"You had your operation. Everything went well."

"Did he take that thing away?"

"Well, you had a reconstruction."

"Can I see?"

"The area is swollen and tender, you shouldn't touch anything there. You cannot get up from bed yet."

"I want to see, I want to see."

The nurse understood the immediacy of his request. She went to the nurses' station and pulled out a small makeup mirror from her purse. With clinical skills, she removed the dressings, unveiling Dr. Leduc's fine work. She then positioned the mirror at a correct angle, offering René a view of his neovagina.

"Venus," he said.

36

Imust run away from him, the civet. He seems to know everything about me. I feel he can see into my mind. He's looking in. And he takes advantage, he knows I'm vulnerable.

I must run faster. Run away, but toward me. I need to find myself. When I try to capture the sound of my thoughts, there's only an echo. When I try to touch my body, there's no substance. That's how I fly. For nothingness is ethereal. Even the perfumes, what I control most in my life, are vaporous elements without a body.

And where's Patricio? He can be here in Marrakesh, he could have found the red door. And the striped tunic mentioned a wolf. That must be him, Patricio. How could he know Patricio hunts me like a wolf? That civet is aware of everything.

But if he knows about Patricio perhaps… No, I cannot speak to him. He may just use me, enter my mind, and use me. I know he can smell my anguish. He can smell my sex, I'm certain. He tells me he doesn't know me, that he doesn't know my name. I really fear him. He doesn't touch me, but he may try to posses me. I don't fear Patricio, his pressure is of a different nature—he needs me. That's why I am looking for him. I need to return to the courtyard. Everything is there now. Even the air of the medina wants to visit. I'm not different from the air, where else could I go?

✶✶✶✶✶

I can feel the warmth of the mint tea making its way down my throat. I'm accepting his poison. I should resist. No, I shouldn't. He knows where Imena is. I need his help to find her. She must have been here at some point. I know this because her presence is in the air. What presence? Always hard to define. When she's next to me I cannot touch her, but when she's away, her reality is overwhelming.

He serves tea as if he was serving life. And I accept it as I accept death. Could I be wrong about this repulsive creature? But why do I fear him? Maybe because he knows what I want to know. I don't know his name, or the address to this place, or if it is a real place. What's the reality of this man and this place? Maybe desert sand is all there is, and this city, the walls, the red door, and the orange trees are illusions. But I know I'm here, and I'm certain the fragrance in the air is that of Imena. As if she were real.

I used to be a professor, I'm a professor. Was I ever a professor? Now I sell books. I have not sold a single book, I just read them. Does it matter? Here I have no possessions. In Paris I have objects, worse even, I have rotten memories. This creature seems to live without attachments. He's wrapped in that tunic that seems to contain him. He must have horrible memories buried somewhere. I wonder how he sees me. Can he see my wrinkles, my irritated eyes? Can he tell what I'm thinking? For if he saw me, I must be real to him, then he must be real as well. I should fear a real man, or creature.

He talks but he doesn't say anything. He mainly asks questions. That's how he knows about Imena. Could he know who she is, who I am? But if I'm not certain about myself, how could he understand who I am by simply asking questions? Maybe his existence is relative to mine, and my existence is relative to Imena's, and hers to mine, and mine to hers.

37

Huong did not know how to answer when people called the philosophy department inquiring about Patricio or René. This was a most unusual situation: two professors missing—at the same time—leaving only vague information on their whereabouts. All she knew was that René had returned from Guadeloupe but had disappeared again, and that Patricio had gone somewhere south. Their mail accumulated, their lessons were cancelled, and wild stories about their absence began to circulate. Finally, the chair of the department instructed Huong to say they were both on sabbatical. This did not solve anything—it only prolonged the intrigue.

One morning, when she was distracted rearranging schedules and organizing files, Huong received a call that complicated the mystery even further. She immediately recognized René's voice on the telephone when he said, *"Bonjour Mademoiselle."*

"Professor Liprandi, where are you?"

"That's not important. Have you heard from Patricio?"

"No, everyone is asking about you, and about him."

"Do you know where he is?"

"No, nobody knows anything. Professor, all your mail is here and people keep calling you. Are you well?"

"I'm very well, but I need to speak to Patricio. When did you last hear from him?"

"We have not heard from him since he left almost four months ago. He went south somewhere."

"I see. *Merci, au revoir.*"

And that was all Huong and the department of philosophy would ever hear from René. He never called again, he never wrote, so eventually his chattel was donated to charity, except for his books that were distributed among his ex-colleagues who accepted them happily, not asking too many questions.

René had obtained the information he needed. When he learned that Patricio had not returned to the university, he knew he was in Marrakech, probably looking for Imena. René did not speak about his personal life with anyone, not even with his family in Saorge. His limited acquaintances never saw him wearing lipstick, high heels, or the simulacrum of breasts. He kept his inner world a secret. At this point, he felt he could confide in Patricio and wanted to find him. But a more powerful reason drew him toward Patricio, an unknown instinct, he thought.

Burdened by the continuous need to dilate his neovagina, René waited in Casablanca until the swelling subsided and the hematomas cleared. He then arranged for a supply of hormones to last him several months, and prepared to travel to Marrakech in search of Patricio. But what he could not have considered, was that a creature smelling like a civet would allow him to build what he had never built.

38

She walked, Imena did, over the neural tissue of the streets, each step sending a jolt down her spine. Every mouth uttered a word, silent or bewildering, all lodging in her raw consciousness. Steadily, Imena approached the core of the medina, the ancient *Djemaa El-Fna*. Many hands gestured at her, many eyes perused her body, and many men desired her. She moved among acrobat monkeys and spellbound serpents until she found a tranquil place. And from a comfortable stillness, Imena opened her mind to the ebb and flow of sensations. She heard ochre, the color of rust and time. She heard turmeric, the smell of dry land. And the sense of salt invaded her mind and her peace. And when the snake erected its body, charmed by the sound of the flute, she thought of Jacques. And when the memory of seaweed threatened to leave, she inserted her fingers into her vagina and tasted them. The sweet aroma of tango, with its cadence and violence, entered through her pores, making her think of Patricio. She savored amaranth and auburn, bright pink and bronze, and cried at the sound of dark sienna. The soft touch of ancient echoes seemed to call her name as she observed orange peels laying flat on the ground making a map of her butterfly island. And when the songs of the multitude at the *Djemaa El-Fna* silenced her inner whispers, Imena felt small.

She did not want to move, she did not want to alter this oceanic experience. And when a vendor stood in front of her, hawking rugs and wire bracelets, Imena looked through him. She ignored the clamor of his hands. Unlike before, she did not take to the sky, she remained grounded. Everything she needed to feel was present in the air. Slowly, as if entering a cold lake, Imena lost her sense of reality and fell asleep under a veil of sounds and aromas. That was when the beast sang again. Her inner turmoil howled with brutal force, terrorizing people and animals alike. And a strong wind from the south invaded the square.

*****

I can hear the beast, thought the striped tunic. That atrocious song travels in the air and reaches my courtyard. I know it comes from her. Nothing else could sound as tormented. She must be asleep somewhere in the medina, alone. I could go looking for her and bring her back to the courtyard. Then I could tame that beast. I know I can. But if I venture outside… No, I cannot. But there it is again…, that haunted song. I cannot tolerate that cry. This is torture. But if I left the courtyard to find her, I would perish. If I were to cross that door, I would cease to exist. I must stay within my boundaries, beholding everything, resisting the impulses.

I know she sleeps unaware of the epic battle inside her. If she became conscious, her dreams would turn to stone. The beast hides deep inside her, away from her awareness. And it needs to be tamed and destroyed. If she were to hear the howling with her own ears, if she were to gain insight, the consciousness would kill her. She doesn't know. How could she know? She moves as if gravity didn't exist, from one petal to another, ignoring the dead weight inside.

She sleeps now. And I cannot watch over her for she's beyond the red door. I can only walk in circles around the courtyard waiting for her return. Impotence is death, my familiar death. But death also awaits for me outside this courtyard. At least the death inside is alive; the death out in the medina is dead. I died once before when I renounced the world, and I'm afraid of dying twice. But I know she'll wake up, and not remembering her name, she will search for herself

155

among these flowering orange trees. And once she returns, I'll confront the beast inside of her.

*****

Sanfy saw Patricio approaching the bookstore with his hands in his pockets and a distracted look. He could tell Patricio was conflicted. He then rushed to the door and held it open for him. "How's the moon?" he asked, as Patricio entered the store. Patricio did not respond, he went straight to his desk under the window and plopped himself on the chair. In silence, he listened to Mozart's Clarinet Concerto as it played on the phonograph. Sanfy did not approach him—he sent his cat instead. The Siamese cat traced a sinusoidal path until she arrived at Patricio's feet. She rubbed her whiskers against his shoes and ankles, and not getting any attention, she darted away from him. When Sanfy saw that Patricio did not care for the cat, he knew Patricio was in a sour mood and decided not to interfere.

Patricio looked out the window at a sky, unlike his mind, impossibly clear. He felt the familiar weight of the songs of his youth, the death of his mother, and the etherealness of Imena. He opened a book and read a passage at random just to calm his mind. And the harder he tried to keep his eyes on the paper, the more alluring the openness of the window became. But when he looked out the window for a sense of tranquility, all he saw was a dirty puddle, muddled by worries and fears.

He then stood up and rushed around the store like a tornado, turning and turning. Under hundreds of books and in every pile of records he looked. His fingers moved quickly through sonatas, concertos, boleros, jazz, more jazz, old rock, mambo, even Gregorian chant—but no tango. There had to be a tango record somewhere. Sanfy observed the frantic search—or lunacy, as he would say—of his employee with

156

curiosity. Patricio continued to look in every corner of Sanfy's jumbled universe for most of the morning. Eventually, stuck between a decrepit empire divan and the dilapidated wall, Patricio found a stack of Latin American records. He looked at the faded covers and recognized *Orquesta Aragón*, *El Trío Los Panchos*, *Pérez Prado*, and finally, the Golden Age of tango: *Carlos Gardel*.

Patricio extracted the old record from the cover. He contemplated it as if contemplating his life, a flat surface inscribed with a spiral groove. To know its content, to hear the music, a needle had to scratch it slowly at 78 revolutions per minute. He felt flat as the disc, his grooves scratched by Imena and by his memories, producing unamplified sounds. He was afraid of following the spiral groove in the record of his life. At the end of the spiral, in the center of his flat cosmos, was that little boy in Buenos Aires, the one who felt guilty for the death of his mother.

His chest tightened, but Patricio managed to put the record on the antique phonograph. Slowly the spinning started, and with trembling fingers, he placed the needle in the groove. Then the sound grew, filling the space, pushing the air out of the store, leaving Patricio gasping. And the songs that killed his mother whispered softly in his ears.

39

The suitcase contained a few old skirts and old shoes, but the rest of the wardrobe was relatively new. She had folded and arranged everything perfectly. She was particularly fond of her lingerie—the garments she enjoyed buying the most because now she could. She also carried a small *nécessaire de voyage* tightly packed with tools for her hair, emollients for her skin, eyeshadow, liners in various colors, beautiful blushes, and lipstick the color of plums. That was all she needed to bring. She left everything that belonged to that man behind. She would never return to his world, she would never reclaim the past.

The train stood motionless, hissing, waiting for passengers to settle with their bags, their cigarettes, their known and unknown destinations. She boarded a second-class cabin, accommodated her luggage on the aluminum shelf above the seats, and took her assigned place next to the window. A man wearing a fez hat sat across from her smoking short unfiltered *Gauloises*. Their crossed legs did not touch. She watched the river of passengers on the platform and thought of the world left behind, of Paris and Saorge, her former colleagues at the university, the anguish. And it wasn't until the train started moving that she reconciled her mood and felt capable of reading Sartre.

She noticed how the man sitting across stared at her between one *Gauloise* and the next. Sometimes he took advantage of the smoke screen to look at her for several seconds. He did not appear threatening, just pathetically curious. She uncrossed her legs, placed the book down, and looked straight at the man trying to catch his eyes. But the man averted her gaze and continued smoking. Outside the window, the trees and the villages became a blurry substance, like her past, dashing fast into oblivion.

By that afternoon, the atmosphere in the cabin had changed. An old woman sat next to her, and a young man dressed in military uniform took the seat diagonally across from her. The military man started to smoke, contributing to the stuffy air in the cabin. And when the conversation ignited among the three other passengers she decided to stay quiet. Nobody addressed her for a while, until the man with the fez hat finally offered her a cigarette. He looked at her with the inquisitive eyes of a child. She accepted the cigarette, he lit it, and she began to smoke while looking out the window. The man scrutinized her movements. Her hands, the veins in her hands, their quiescent strength, and the manicured nails, absorbed him.

The train ignored several stations and stopped at a few others, but the composition of the passengers in the cabin did not change. It seemed all passengers were following a similar destiny across the desert. In the background, a whistle pierced the air every time the train reinitiated its march. The old woman kept a lively conversation with the military man ignoring everyone else. This created a sense of dichotomy in the cabin. Meanwhile, behind the smoke screen, she contemplated the contrived expression of the man with the fez hat, while he contemplated her hands.

When the train stopped at the next station, the old woman collected her belongings and stepped out of the cabin. Her seat remained empty until a younger woman, dressed in earthy colors, occupied the seat. Her smile was as ample as her skin was olive. The military man shrank in his place and avoided eye contact; the man with the fez hat continued smoking and pretended not to care. But she could not resist, she stared at the newcomer, drinking her exuberance, desiring her deliciously. She then asked the man with the fez hat for another cigarette—

which he lit—and turning to the young woman next to her asked if she wanted to smoke and offered her the cigarette. The young woman took the cigarette between her fingers and began to smoke, completely disinterested in the passengers around her. She smoked as if she was all alone in the world.

At that time, the conductor opened the door to the cabin and requested the travel documents from all passengers. The military man produced a letter with official orders, the man with the fez hat and the young woman, a Moroccan passport, and she gave him her falsified French passport. The conductor reviewed the documents and returned all except hers. He looked at it closely and asked:

"*Mademoiselle* Renée Liprandi, what's your final destination?"

"I'm going to Marrakech."

"And for how long do you plan to stay?"

"Not for long, a day or two, three the most," she said, knowing it was a lie.

The conductor looked at her. He did not look into her eyes; instead, he focused on the angle of her jaw. He then returned the passport, closed the door, and continued walking down the hall. Inside the cabin, smoke impregnated the air.

40

When Imena woke up in the tumultuous *Djemaa El-Fna*, the familiar smell of wet feathers surrounded her. She looked for a sign or a direction, but neither appeared. People walked by her without showing any particular interest. She knew she was alone then, unattached for the moment, and she felt clear. Seizing her freedom, she resolved to finally attempt her elusive composition: *La rose sauvage.* She then asked directions to the *Souk Haddadine* and followed the meandering path north from the *Djemaa El-Fna*. The clanking of metal and the light bouncing from thousands of pots, pans, and plates announced the location. Amid a deafening clatter, men bent over metal shaping all sorts of forms. Imena needed two flat trays, sturdy, with a low edge. The metal had to be polished but not chemically treated. She evaluated several samples until she found the perfect pair: two round brass trays without decorative inscriptions, about fifty centimeters in diameter, reflecting her inspired image. The merchant asked an exorbitant sum and she offered half of that. He cried. She ignored him. He spoke about his children and she spoke about her perfumes. They had a cup of tea. She walked away with the trays, and he was happy.

Imena then found her way to the butcher and asked for fat, pork fat. "Nobody wants that much fat," the butcher said when she asked for all the fat he had in the shop. But Imena needed all that animal fat. She did not care for the meat, and asked the butcher to "clean out the meat." So the butcher provided her with two kilos of translucent pork fat, no meat attached. Then she arrived at the spice market where she obtained unadulterated musk pods, a large quantity of sun-cured Turkish tobacco, vanilla beans, myrrh, clove, and Roman chamomile.

Finally, Imena entered the flower market, her domain and her universe. She visited stand after stand and spoke with numerous merchants. She inquired about the wild Moroccan roses that grew in the desert, in the High Atlas Mountains, at the coast of Essaouira. She wanted to know their color, their aromas, and their growth patterns. And when she sampled the raw petals of the Atlas mountain roses, grown among villages without electricity, exposed to violent heat and cold winds, she discovered their savage souls. And after selecting dozens of the finest roses, Imena joined the tumultuous streets of the medina and made her way back to the hotel.

The striped tunic observed as she entered the courtyard carrying the absurd combination of items. Imena became aware of his presence, a presence that overwhelmed even the strong scent of the Atlas mountain roses. She ignored him— her mind was not concerned with the old civet cat. And, as if repeating ancient gestures, Imena approached each of the four orange trees in the courtyard, caressed the blossoms, and collected hundreds of tiny white petals saturated with neroli oil. After placing the pork fat, the flowers, the brass trays, and the spices in the middle of her room, and after making sure the window to the courtyard was closed and secure from the inside, Imena went searching for the striped tunic.

"Can I use your kettle, the one you use to make tea?" she asked.

"What do you need it for?"

"To boil water."

"*Mademoiselle*, what's the water for?"

"Do you need to know everything?"

"No... Only your thoughts."

"My thoughts are elsewhere; my senses are the ones inside my head."

"You seem confused, *Mademoiselle*."

"I'm not confused," Imena said, turning around and

walking away from the striped tunic who watched her without saying another word.

"Bring me boiling water," she added before disappearing into her room.

The striped tunic obeyed her order with the willingness of a possessed monk. He would bring the kettle to her door and she would take it inside her room without letting him see what she was doing. After some time, she would place the kettle outside the door containing undecipherable residues and cold water. In silence, they repeated this operation until nighttime.

When the red moon rose later that night, Imena stepped out of her room and walked to the fountain at the center of the courtyard. She was completely naked and her pale skin glowed under the opalescent light. Standing motionless, in peaceful observation of the stars, she let the dry air touch her intimately. Equally motionless, but from the shadows of the courtyard, the striped tunic watched, until the moon turned dark, until Imena vanished. The song of the beast was diabolical that night.

*****

Sanfy could not stand the sight of Patricio weeping. He shuffled through the store, pushing books and boxes, opening drawers and cabinets, until he found what he needed—a bottle of gin. He poured two glasses and sat across from Patricio. The Siamese cat jumped on Sanfy's lap and together with her master remained expectant. Patricio took a sip of gin and nodded.

"There must be another way to forget Sanfy."

"Perhaps, but this is what you have now."

With the tango still playing in the background, both men had three or four glasses of gin. Patricio's eyes had dried but his expression remained distant. The memories of his conflicted childhood fluttered in the air, playing games with the musical notes. But gradually, he began to settle. And he reached for the cat and started petting her under the chin.

"She liked you from the first day," Sanfy said.

"Do you think she likes the music?" Patricio asked.

"I don't know, you have to ask her."

The cat started kicking with her back legs, freed herself from Patricio, and jumped on the floor. She disappeared under a table following a fast moving insect.

The evening filled the store as the gin escaped the bottle. Both men told stories, some miserable, others laughable, but honest. Sanfy made haste to close the store and went out on the streets with Patricio. "We're going to see my friends," he said. And he dragged Patricio through unknown parts of the medina.

In the darkness, the buildings loomed over them, but Sanfy knew his way and walked with a firm step. They went into a café where two men were smoking and playing backgammon, otherwise the place was empty. One of the men recognized Sanfy immediately and offered them a seat at their table. They spoke in Arabic all the while looking at Patricio as if he understood everything. Then Sanfy grabbed Patricio by the arm and asked him to follow him. They went to the back of the café where a silk curtain covered the entrance to a small dark room.

Before his eyes grew accustomed to the darkness, the room spoke to him in the language of sounds and smells. Under the penetrating smell of incense, sandalwood, and saffron, he heard a nervous giggle. He then felt a small hand grabbing his hand leading him to seat on a low pillow. When he could see through the darkness, Sanfy had already left the room and he found himself alone in front of a young woman, attractive in her simplicity, with a round face adorned by a sensuous mole at the corner of her right eye. She smiled and whispered to him in Arabic. The soft cadence of her words, mixed with the floating incense produced an inebriating sensation. The mystifying environment seduced Patricio. He allowed her to remove his shirt and accepted her caresses. His mind escaped the room and traveled to Paris, to a time when Imena seduced him with her perfume creations. He thought about Imena when the lips of the young woman covered his shoulders. "Imena, Imena, where are you?" he said. She did not understand his words and responded with her own unintelligible whispers.

The young woman helped Patricio lie on his back with his head resting on the pillow. With two delicate kisses on his eyelids, she closed his eyes, while Patricio continued to dream of Imena. In the darkness, she started humming a simple melody, like a lullaby, while moving around the room with the softness of mist. She then knelt next to Patricio and started to rock her body and arms, slowly, while cooing and humming. Patricio then felt the weight of a mound of warm flesh on his chest. He opened his eyes and saw a naked baby curled in a fetal position lying just below his chin. The young woman, also naked, leaned against Patricio and covered his hands with kisses.

Patricio felt an eruption coming from inside his stomach. He pushed the baby away while turning his body to the side. He expelled a large amount of bile, gin, and sorrow. He stayed on his side, and started to weep. The young woman held him tight and pulled him away from the vomited carpet. She spoke softly to him but he was inconsolable. She then put the baby to sleep in a corner of the room, donned a colorful *djellaba*, and went out of the room looking for Sanfy.

The café was still empty except for the same two men still playing backgammon. They told her that Sanfy had left and asked if there was a problem with the foreigner. She told them everything was fine, that the foreigner needed to cry, that was all. She returned to the room and helped Patricio sit up and put back his shirt. With a towel, she cleaned around his mouth. Patricio complied when she grabbed his hand and escorted him out of the room, through a narrow hallway, and through a side door into the street. She saw him walk away under the red moon. Back in the room, the young woman sat at the corner where the baby was sound asleep. Sobbing interrupted the soft melody of her lullaby. She found the towel dirty with vomit and folded it lengthwise. She then stretched the towel across the small face of the baby and pressed down with her two hands. The tiny arms and legs shook spasmodically; the towel covered the purple lips and the innocent cry.

The night, the shadows, the weight of the vulnerable baby on his chest, and the twisted streets confused Patricio. The sound of his disoriented steps filled legions of empty streets that night. He walked for several hours, never arriving anywhere. But when the aurora bathed the pink walls and silver cobblestones, Patricio finally found his way through the red door and into the courtyard. He staggered towards the fountain and simply sat on the ground next to it. He remained transfixed, looking at the flowering orange trees under the morning light and listening to the water dance.

"*Bonjour*," the striped tunic said, who had been watching from the moment he came into the courtyard. "You don't look well," he added.

"I don't know what happened to me."

"What do you mean?"

"I don't mean anything."

"We always mean something, *Monsieur*. What happened to you?"

"I'm not sure... I need to find...," Patricio stopped before saying: "I need to find Imena." He wanted to scream those words but he held back.

"May I offer you some tea? It may suit you well," the striped tunic said.

"Yes, yes…it may suit me."

When the striped tunic went to prepare the mint infusion, Patricio felt relieved. He noticed how the air turned unusually light and entered his lungs with ease. He also noticed the fresh scent of roses and bergamot. Once again, like in the previous day, Patricio felt the nearby presence of Imena. She must be somewhere near, he thought.

The striped tunic returned and sat on the ground across from Patricio. He served tea for both and began to drink it while staring at him. Patricio felt impaled by his stare—an unrelenting gaze that burned his skin. And with every minute of silence, he felt increasingly violated, exposed, and helpless. A sense of inevitable doom flushed through his veins.

"Please don't hurt me," Patricio said.

The striped tunic did not react, the stretched leather of his face did not reveal a twitch, and with a grave yet soft voice, he asked:

"Do you think I'm about to hurt you, *Monsieur*?"

"Please don't hurt Imena, don't hurt her.

"*Monsieur*, your fears are devouring you. What makes you believe that I would hurt anyone?"

"I think you can, I think you will."

"Yes I can, and so can you. We are one and the same."

"You're not part of me, stay away, stay away from me."

"You came to this courtyard on your own account, searching for her, searching for yourself. I didn't invite you."

"I came because I know she's here. I need to find her, before you do anything to her."

The striped tunic took a final sip from his cup of tea. He stood up in front of Patricio sustaining the impaling stare for a few more seconds and said, "*Monsieur*, you seem disturbed." He then turned around and walked away leaving behind an odiferous imprint.

Once alone, an uneasy feeling weighed Patricio down. He

felt like a small child afraid of the dark. And with the need for a sense of safety, he left the courtyard and headed back to Sanfy's store. He traversed the known geography of the medina following a rehearsed zigzag pattern. When he arrived at the store, he was exhausted. At that early morning hour, neither Sanfy nor the Siamese cat were there. He grabbed the phonograph and the tango record he found the previous day. And with urgency, Patricio returned to the hotel courtyard looking to reconcile his mind, not knowing that two days will pass before he would find more than he was looking for.

*****

I can see through them, the striped tunic thought. I can see their fears, their hopes, and their desperate search for something they cannot see. I can see the vacuity that comes from not being whole. They behave as if their lives were intact, not knowing that they walk in one direction only, without looking to the right or to the left to find more of themselves. And when the doubt that there is more to their lives invades them, they break apart.

I saw him shaking this morning, afraid that I would hurt him—a fear so displaced for I'm not the assassin my father was. Looking for Imena, a self-inflicted pain that hurts him more than anything I could do to him. And she, Imena, locked in her room brewing potions. They look for each other because they feel a need, an emptiness. But even if they were to mesh into each other, an inevitable void would remain.

How many parts can there be to a person? I don't know, hundreds, a handful. If a full man is broken in two—and every part is complete—then each part is a perfect half. And put together he will be one again. But if the same man were broken into incomplete halves, he will never come together as one. They look for each other as perfect halves would.

But I can see they're not complete, there's more about them elsewhere, outside of their selves.

He needs to expose himself, peel the skin off his body, and share his thoughts with the sky. He needs to return to the cradle of his fears and strangulate their young. She, Imena, needs to descend before the sun blazes her wings. She needs to open her eyes in the middle of the night and scream. This they need to do—without me—for I'm only the beholder of their incomplete selves.

The courtyard contains us. All missing parts need to convene within these walls: the wisdom of the desert, the memories of childhood, the taste of blood, and the scent of mint. We're all fragmented, and parts of us live and die elsewhere, as imperfect doppelgängers. But within these walls, inside this courtyard, we may all come together as one consciousness—a sight to behold.

41

Renée did not expect luck to help her find Patricio—she counted more on fate. Luck was capricious, but fate was determined. And she entered Marrakech through *Bab Agnaou* with fierce determination. And she did not settle until arriving at a quiet riad inside the medina. There she registered as *Mademoiselle* Renée Liprandi and requested complete privacy. Her concern was not time, she had all the time she needed to find Patricio. Not knowing the real reason for her search was her real concern, and that made her feel uneasy. The moment Dr. Leduc's knife delivered her, the moment she raised from the waves, between the wind and the flowers, not surprised by her beauty, accepting her position as her due, that moment she began her search for Patricio. Yes, Patricio would understand her, but so would a prostitute, or a psychic. There was more to her search than an anticipated acceptance of her new gender—she just could not imagine what it was. But she had followed her instincts in the past and this time would be no different.

Renée shed all her clothes and immersed her body in the warm tub of the riad. She cleaned herself carefully, caressing her skin, appreciating every angle, feeling the roundness. She touched her body as if it was the body of another woman. Her hands traveled through her landscape while her mind rejoiced in images of her youth. The image of Antonia materialized. And when she touched her skin, she was touching the dark skin of Antonia, and when her hands caressed her nipples, it was Antonia's nipples she was caressing. She wanted to bring Antonia back to life, she wanted to swim with her in the warm water, and she wanted to share the miracle of her new body. Renée imagined herself as Antonia and a sense of peace inundated her. You're within me, she thought.

Renée opened her *nécessaire de voyage* in front of the mirror and pulled out all the tools necessary to adorn her face. She had a steady hand and a dignified sense of beauty. And with precise strokes, she created a visage, sublime and alluring, like no other. She donned an elegant white robe, attached a whimsical belt made of colorful stones around her waist, and put leather sandals on her feet. Before leaving the riad she asked the attendant for directions to any café frequented by foreigners. She believed that at some point, Patricio would cross her path. In the meanwhile, she desired to see women, and be desired as a woman.

Renée walked through the crowded streets of the medina with an elegant cadence. When going through tight passages, she delighted in the occasional friction with a stranger, two bodies pressing each other at random. She welcomed every stare, every comment, but answered none of them. She was living the life of a daring woman. And carried away by a feeling of self possession, she soon lost her way. She was walking aimlessly but gracefully—that meant more to her. The tumultuous streets, such an tantalizing stage, belonged to her that moment. And she felt as if strangers clapped at her every step. And when chanting came from the minarets, she bowed to the ovation.

A young man with a goatee arose from a side street and started walking by her side. He seemed cheerful and greeted Renée with an enthusiastic "*Bounjour, Mademoiselle.*" Renée ignored him and the young man greeted her again, "*Buon Giorno.*" Without looking at him, Renée continued walking. She turned a few corners and crossed a small square while his steps trailed behind her. He matched her pace and from behind said, *Wie geht es Ihnen?*" Renée did not turn around, did not acknowledge his presence—the chase excited her.

She went into a jewelry store and pretended to be looking for a gift. She admired the adornments, the hammered silver teaspoons with striped ebony and enamel handles, the turquoise earrings, and Tuareg-inspired cocktail rings that looked like hypnotist's props with concentric circles in dark wood and bright orange enamel. The young man stayed outside the store and waited with the calm determination of a jackal.

When Renée reemerged from the store and tried to avoid the young man, he cut in front and confronted her. She saw his goatee moving up and down forming the following words: "I know you're alone, and I won't let you be alone." His tone was harsh, abrasive. She turned around, and moving away from him, started walking at a much faster pace. He followed her. She went by people, shadows, windows, and cobblestones. He followed her closely. She felt as if the streets became narrower with every step, as if the walls were leaning against her. He continued to follow her. And when she feared being trapped, she stopped abruptly and turned around to face the young man.

"What do you want?" Renée asked.

"I know you're alone," he said.

"Money… is that what you want, money?"

"You're alone, and I won't let you be alone."

Renée went past the young man and turned into a wider street. She was trying to lose herself among the crowds. The incessant steps of the young man trailed behind. She then saw the entrance to a café and headed inside rapidly. The young man did not follow her inside the café. He stayed outside guarding the door from across the street.

With a cigarette in her lips, Renée sat at a table, ordered some tea, and waited for her fear to subside. Small drops of sweat had accumulated over the well-shaven skin of her face. She wanted to feel the excitement, the thrill of persecution— she wanted to be desired as a woman. An intense fear stabbed her like a knife, both exciting her and making her shiver. She needed to believe that if a man wanted her, so would another woman. She smoked one cigarette after another, sipping her tea and watching as people entered and left the café. After about one hour, Renée dared to look out wanting to know if the young man was still there. She saw him sitting across the street, his goatee resting on his crossed hands, looking toward the café, like a sentinel. Renée trembled.

As if stepping into an abyss, Renée stepped into the street abandoning the temporary security of the café. She moved hastily without looking over her shoulder. She navigated the river of people around corners, through passages, deep into the medina. And the heavy echo of trailing steps revealed the continuous presence of the young man. She was certain he was following her from a short distance. But she did not look back. And while keeping her fast pace, she felt a flood of ecstasy and fear.

One turn followed another, one street lead to another, and at last, she came to a blind alley. There was nowhere else to go. The young man came close to her. His fast breathing and dilated pupils made him look menacing.

"You're not going to be alone," he said while pulling a jackknife out of his pocket.

Her excitement died under the heavy weight of fear. And when Renée tried to run through the narrow space between the young man and the wall, the jackknife blocked her escape.

"You look pretty," he said.

He then grabbed her wrist and bending her arm forced her to kneel on the floor. The knife found its way to her throat where he kept enough pressure to make her feel the edge without cutting her skin.

"You keep quiet now," he said.

Renée leaned back away from the knife and fell on her side. The young man sat on top of her and grabbed her tightly by the hair immobilizing her head.

"Still, still," he said, while keeping pressure on the knife.

The young man kissed her. And emboldened by fear, Renée caught the young man's lower lip between her teeth and bit out a piece of flesh. The young man moaned and wiped the mixture of blood and saliva from his goatee.

"You bitch," he said.

He then lifted her white robe and proceeded to thrust his body into hers, with force, violating her neovagina. Renée could not endure the pain, she dissociated. Her mind flew to her childhood in Saorge, the beauty of the mountains and the river carving the gorge, her sisters, the magic of his father's hands, the green light of the olive trees in spring, the water running through the old fountains, the sweet honey flavored by wild flowers; and above all she thought about Antonia, so vulnerable in her death. And as her body was assaulted she felt no pain because her mind had escaped, leaving her body alone to endure the abuse. When the young man was satisfied, he disappeared down the alley, spitting blood, cutting the air with his goatee, while pulling up his pants.

42

Like an alchemist, Imena went into hiding inside the hermetically closed room and started working with her collected ingredients to bring nature to perfection. The musk pods and tobacco provided a base but not as strong and fixative as she wanted. The *rose sauvage* had to be *sauvage*, not only *rose*. And searching for that savage edge, she added her own urine and feces to the distillate arriving at a base note *animale*, closer to her expectations. To the vanilla beans, myrrh, clove, and Roman chamomile, she added strands of her own hair arriving at a middle note, the heart of the fragrance. She then thought of Charli and the taste of her saliva—a semi-sweet juice that ignited her heart in Nice. As she remembered the viscous fluid in her mouth, she dribbled some of her own saliva into the composition. She was going into herself in this creative process, deep into her every cell, exploring her living and excreted nature.

Imena had not stepped out of her room since the night before and was not prepared to leave until *La rose sauvage* was born. The hours paraded slowly, silently, while Imena created sublime fragrant notes. The sun rose and collapsed; the wind flooded the courtyard and left in a fugue. That night, the dream of the swan assaulted her sleep again—the white rush imposing over the paleness of her skin, the terrifying loosening of her thighs yielding to the pressing bill. She felt her humanity usurped by the bestial impetus of the bird-god.

The striped tunic had spent the night in vigil hoping to see Imena approach the fountain, as she had done the previous night, naked. With the patience of an unfathomable mind, he waited. But Imena did not appear that night. And having missed her, he knocked on her door that morning. But Imena did not answer. She was not going to answer any call until she had finished her composition. And as it turned out, she was not going to eat either. The striped tunic called Imena knowing she could listen across the door. "Let the beast out *Mademoiselle*," he shouted. And indeed, she was exuding the beast through every one of her pores.

Imena thought hard about the next step—the top note. It needed to be strong yet delicate, ethereal yet present, a balance of light molecules evaporating quickly, an infatuating experience. She applied a thick layer of pork fat to the inner surface of the brass trays. She had no use for the remaining fat so she simply threw it on the floor of her room. And then she applied, one-by-one, a harmonious combination of rose and orange flower petals to the surface of the fat. She calculated the ratio of the two different kinds of petals to permit the sumptuous rose essence to shine over the deep neroli oil. She then stacked the trays against each other to prevent the petals from drying out. During the next two days of this *enfleurage*, the fat would gradually absorb the perfume of the petals. As the petals got exhausted, she replaced them with a fresh supply, over and over.

*****

Inside his room, Patricio did not feel as safe as he wanted. Yes, the striped tunic was outside, but he could burst through the door at anytime, he thought. His wasted body needed rest, and the turmoil inside his mind needed a calm morning. And with hesitation, he played the music of his youth.

I really don't want to look back, thought Patricio. It hurts to confront the images imprinted in my mind. I didn't create the images of my childhood in Buenos Aires—they were handed down. One day, I thought about my past and the images were already there, lurching in the shadows, anxious to launch an assault on me. And that music… it was always there when my world was imploding. I can still hear the *bandoneón* filling the air, echoing the words of my mother. But today that music seduces me with an unsettling power, it enters my mind, and with every chord I die a little.

*****

Attracted by the foreign sound, the striped tunic approached Patricio's window and saw him lying on the bed. He remembered the earlier conversation they had and was careful not to let his presence be known to avoid frightening Patricio. He was not familiar with the tango, but understood that the melodious instrument, the *bandoneón*, was crying. He remained immobile while watching Patricio through the window. And when the music ended, the only thing he heard was the scratching of the needle around the paper label glued to the center of the disc.

When Patricio noticed the shadow projecting inside the room, he arose and silenced the phonograph. "What do you want?" he shouted, hoping not to get an answer. He would not open the door, nor did he look in the direction of the window.

"What do you want?" Patricio repeated.

"*Monsieur*, I'm just listening to the music," the striped tunic said from outside the window.

"What do you *really* want from me?" Patricio asked.

"I want the same thing you want from me. I need you the same way you need me."

Patricio turned to the window and saw the impavid face of the striped tunic staring at him.

"Well, what is it then? Tell me, what is it?"

"I need Imena, I need her to stay here with me," the striped tunic said.

Those words sent Patricio into a raging panic. His body quivered.

"She's here, isn't she? Where is she?"

"*Monsieur*, compose yourself. You see, I also need you to stay, I need you both."

"This is nonsense, tell me where she is."

"She's in the hotel in voluntary seclusion."

"You must show me where she is."

"I won't show you where she is, and I won't let you search for her," the striped tunic said in a paused and grave tone that paralyzed Patricio. "You may see her when the red moon rises, if she comes to the fountain," he added and then disappeared leaving Patricio alone.

Patricio could have followed the striped tunic and forced him to tell where Imena was. After all, he was younger and very likely stronger than him. But a strange sensation held him back. He felt a certain connection, an affinity, to the striped tunic. This hideous man wants the same woman I want, but he also wants me, Patricio thought. Then, an unforeseen touch of humanity overtook him. He felt powerless, disarmed. And without a clear understanding of this experience, Patricio found himself facing his loneliness and impotence, as he observed the striped tunic walk away. Alone in his room, he resorted to playing the old tango record again. The scratchy melody infiltrated his mind, but unlike his mother, he could not sing along.

Later that afternoon, an embattled Patricio emerged from his room carrying the phonograph and the record. He placed the phonograph in the center of the courtyard and started to play the tango. He then sat by the fountain and listened to the music grow among the ochre walls of the courtyard. The striped tunic watched him with interest and kept his distance for a short while. Slowly, he approached Patricio and sat next to him in silence. Patricio continued listening to the music while he felt a deep pull from his past.

"There's sadness in the melody," the striped tunic eventually said.

"The sadness belongs to my past," Patricio said.

"What about your past?"

"I wish I never had one, it doesn't leave me alone."

"The past is our company when there's no other company."

"I don't want that company."

"Then, why do you play your old music?"

"I play the music to cauterize, to forget my past."

"*Monsieur*, we never forget."

"But I need to forget… I need to forget."

"And if you did, for whom would you play the music?"

Patricio grabbed a fistful of red clay and threw it up in the air. The desert wind invaded the courtyard making eddies, spreading the fine clay particles in all directions. The music, the sadness within the music, reminded the striped tunic of his days in the desert, the endless passages of caravans, watching the burning horizons. And when the striped tunic heard the voice of Carlos Gardel singing,

> *Mi Buenos Aires querido,*
> *cuando yo te vuelva a ver,*
> *no habrá más pena ni olvido.*

he felt a longing that went beyond any language, known or unknown, a human longing.

Sitting next to each other, Patricio and the striped tunic continued listening to the record until it ended. None of them spoke another word. They shared unspoken sadness, disillusion, and a yearning for human touch. No two other men could have differed more from each other, but the communion of music allowed them to share, albeit briefly, a common plane. Within the courtyard, the music expanded, entering that part of the brain that made them both human.

And when stillness reigned in the courtyard, the two men kept their awkward sitting positions. The striped tunic felt an uneasy vulnerability that prevented him from looking at Patricio, while a low grade fear made Patricio feel tense. They avoided each other's gaze. And for a while, both men remained self-absorbed. But an understanding of their shared loneliness had descended over them.

*****

I can hear the tango, thought Imena, the music reaching where the air doesn't dare. I can feel Patricio's presence. But this time it's not a menacing presence. Not the wolf… no. He must be out in the courtyard, sharing the air with the flowering orange trees. Sharing the air with the civet, that unctuous cat. But he's playing his music. He feels little when he plays that music, sometimes he weeps. He needs to hear that music and weep, not for me, but for himself.

Inside this room, with my petals and my animal secretions, I feel the aura of creation. And the top note makes me feel light, my *rose*, and the base note makes me confront my animality, my *sauvage* self. For this is how I can talk to him, through the sense of smell. I can only fly if unanchored. He knows that. The very reason for his following me here, to this reddish part of the world, is to ground me. Better yet, to stand over my vaporous self and try to reach the sky himself. I know he needs to fly, and I know I need to land. What a treacherous discrepancy. When he touches me, the distance between solid ground and my flying self shrinks to a mere breath. And he can make that space, that sliver of breath, magical and insufferable at the same time. But when he plays the tango, that music he loves to forget, that music that describes him in ways he would never accept, he loses touch with everything. Those are the moments when the memories of his childhood revolt him. I threaten him, the same way he threatens my volatility. But I'm creating for him and for me. I'm composing the perfume that could lighten him, the perfume that could throw him up in the air. The same perfume could help me touch the ground, find a base of security within the realm of gravity. Only then, under the spell of *La rose sauvage*, could we exist together, as one.

I can hear the music. And he probably knows that I'm here in the hotel. He knows that I'll never finish reading *Le Fleurs du Mal*, he knows that I need to detach myself from the volcanic rock of my youth. He knows all of this, and for that reason, he plays his music loudly, to talk to me, to make me walk backward. He wants to lift my left arm and press against my chest, all the while looking past me, ahead, toward another place away from his past. I can see the steps, on the side, backward, a cross, the *salida*.

I'll remain inside this room until the petals are consumed and exhausted. All the elements joining in a primal orgy, blending our needs, fears, and hopes. I won't let the air enter my room. The music can enter, for there's no way to stop it. I'll produce a perfume like no other. I know my creation, *La rose sauvage*, will be rendered in its absolute form. Only then will I face him.

*****

The night entered the courtyard silently, like a thief, and found the striped tunic, Patricio, and Imena in retreat, away from the water fountain, all expecting a private miracle. The striped tunic had seen the marvelous scene two nights before, when a completely naked Imena stood in peaceful observation of the stars, letting the red moonlight and the dry air caress her. Patricio, however, never imagined Imena would actually emerge from hiding to bathe in the moonlight. The night continued to fill every corner of the courtyard, eating away the pink reflections from the walls. And when the moon showed its full red face, the dark cloth of darkness behind, it seemed to be calling for the children of the destitute.

Patricio and the striped tunic had not spoken to each other since the afternoon, but a tacit expectation floated between them: Imena would come out to the courtyard that night. For Patricio, seeing Imena meant he would come close to completing his search, a search whose ultimate result lingered, for finding Imena was not his quest, merging with her was. For the striped tunic, the sight of Imena was his comfort, the balsam that could soothe his brutal instincts. And both men, independently, awaited the radiant moment.

The red moon crawled to the top of the courtyard obscuring all other light forms pinned to the sky. Unabashedly supreme, it lured the destitute to step out into open spaces and admire her. The moon did not regard anyone as an individual, but everyone regarded the moon as his or her own personal prophet. And when Imena stepped out of her room and walked to the fountain in complete disregard of Patricio and the striped tunic, the indifferent moon bathed her in red light. And when the dry air joined the red light of the moon, Imena felt the intimate touch of a lover, and her skin glowed in the darkness, in full sight of Patricio and the striped tunic.

43

Renée's intimate dreams did not include men or violence, but she encountered both in the narrow alley. Renée had come to a strange land, a land of heat and desert, a land where she found the edge of the knife that transformed her. And just as Renée had lost her boyish innocence when Antonia died, she now lost her newly minted female innocence to a brute.

She did not give part of the incident to the police, fearing senseless interrogation, humiliation, and guaranteed extradition. She simply returned to the riad to care for herself. She was not physically hurt, but the rape would certainly leave a scar, a scar that would remind her of the precarious nature of her identity.

Renée decided to stay in the riad for a day or two before facing the outside world again. She needed to soothe the pain and regain her confidence. She spent hours in front of the mirror looking at the purple skin around her groin. The image disgusted her. She would try to distract herself by reading or smoking, but she would inevitably return to the front of the mirror. And there she was again, a victimized woman.

*****

Why did I become a woman? To be abused? This is ridiculous. And the coward pulls a knife. To be the man he's not he needs a knife. What a pathetic creature. I'm sure he feels like a big man, a big fucker. What an aggressive, idiotic bastard. But I'll be fine, I know I'll be just fine.

And why did I leave Paris? No, no, no… I won't question that. I left because I had to leave, and that's all. This is where I need to be now. A strange power compels me to be here. I don't know the nature of this power but I can feel it. I feel a yearning that goes beyond finding Patricio, a primeval longing calling me. I cannot run away from here, abused or not, I must stay and face that call. That longing must be calling Patricio as well, and the young woman he desires, and everyone else who forms part of me. They're all here, somewhere, under the same spell—I know.

I thought the real search was for my other, for that woman, but that's an incomplete search, a mirage, real to the extent it satisfies a part of me, but not the entire self. The mirror, honest and truthful, returns a vision of my other, and I love that vision. And this longing makes me feel that I'm more than one person, that all of my doppelgängers are near. This longing brought me here, now I must find my others.

But I must rest now, soothe my pain, and care for my pride. I'll look in the mirror for myself, the lonely self. Then I'll dream of the others. And if I were to dream them with intensity, they may come into being. And perhaps this powerful longing is a call for imagination and dreaming. Or perhaps, all of us are only a mirage of ourselves. I'm not sure, I really don't know. But I'll remain here dreaming and looking for others in the mirror, afraid for what would happen if I stopped dreaming about them.

44

The morning light penetrated every possible corner of the courtyard, but respected the room where Imena was practicing alchemy. Her window and her door remained closed, as they had for the past three days. No sounds came out of the room, only silence. In the courtyard, the four flowering orange trees looked exuberant, gracious, and seemingly unaware of the theater of human life. And in that morning hour, the air had a crisp minty quality, falsely foreboding tranquility.

Knowing Imena was inside one of the rooms in the hotel, Patricio called her name out loud, "Imena, Imena," but there was no answer. He wanted to believe the striped tunic was keeping her inside a room against her will. But her apparition the night before was fluid and certainly voluntary. Patricio thought she was retreating, walking backward like in the tango, seductively stepping away from him.

The day ahead seemed long to Patricio. He was anxious for the hours to roll by quickly, setting the stage for the night and, perhaps, another Imena sighting. But he could not stand waiting in the open courtyard while the suspicious striped tunic watched his every move—intolerable. He knew Sanfy's store would offer him solace and decided to go there and spend most of the day among books and records, as he had done every day for the past three months. Besides, he had not seen Sanfy or his cat since the night they drank gin in excess.

When Patricio arrived at the store, he found the front door completely open. He looked inside but did not find Sanfy anywhere. There were no clients either. A strange situation, he thought, because Sanfy would not leave the store open. He looked around once more and found everything in perfect disorder, the natural order of things at the store. Wherever

Sanfy went, he thought, it would not take him long. Patricio had more important concerns than looking for Sanfy, he needed to put his mind to rest. He knew the hours would pass easily if he dove into poetry, or perhaps a novel. At this moment, he needed to suspend his worries and expectations, he just needed to stay afloat until nighttime.

But as soon as he sat at his desk by the window, he heard the front door close behind him and a man starting to yell in Arabic. The language was undecipherable, but the high volume, the staccato rhythm, and the intensity of the man's voice, helped Patricio understand he was being insulted, and possibly threatened. For a second or two he did not move, a sharp fear paralyzed him. But the instant he turned around, he recognized the man advancing toward him. He had seen him playing backgammon at the café where he met the prostitute and her baby. He only got a glimpse of his features that night, they were ordinary, but this moment they appeared distorted, filled with rage. The man charged towards Patricio and the closer he came, the larger his fury became. Patricio did not have time to move out of the way, he could not even utter a word. In an instant, Patricio felt a freight train crushing him against the desk. A sharp pain below his umbilicus made him bend his knees and fall to the ground. There was blood on the floor.

He lay on the floor for one day, one hour, one minute, or one second. He did not know exactly, but he knew his life had just changed. With effort, he grabbed the chair and pulled up the weight of his body until he stood by the desk. He was alone now, the man, the horror of the man, had left. His lower abdomen felt heavy and wet, and dullness ran down his legs.

In pain, Patricio started walking out of the store. A veil descended over him, blurring the pink color of the walls and dampening the street noises. He tried to scream, but his voice broke. He walked, and with every step, a sharp pain lanced his lower abdomen. He left behind an interrupted trail of blood: several drops in some places, but none in others. And the people in the narrow and crowded streets walked past him, madly engaged in their daily hustle, unaware of his open stab wound. And like every day in the afternoon, chanting came from the top of oblique spires that grew up from a legion of mosques.

The faster he tried to walk, the more laborious his breathing became, he was panting. He walked a few steps, grabbed a lamppost, walked a few more steps, took in air, as much air as possible, tried to run, panted, pushed a woman out of his way, heard her protest, turned a corner, turned another corner, spat saliva mixed with blood, and at one point, emptied his bladder completely. Patricio then felt a wetness covering his skin and he started feeling cold.

Through the red door he staggered at last. The courtyard looked small to him, as if the walls approached each other, trapping him in the middle and squeezing the air out of his lungs. He lay on the ground, shivering. And for a moment he thought he was in Buenos Aires next to his ailing mother. But when he looked around, it seemed as if he was in Paris, looking over the Mansard roofs. He did not move anymore for he was dizzy, wet, and cold.

When the striped tunic saw Patricio lying on the red clay like a dying gaul, he approached him and sat next to him. The nauseating stench emanating from the striped tunic brought Patricio's mind back to the courtyard.

"I'm hurt, I'm bleeding," Patricio said.

The striped tunic observed Patricio with the coldness of a winter lake. He noticed the paleness of his skin and the drenching sweat covering his body. The wolf is hurt, he thought, and felt as if a fragile part of him was melting in front of his eyes. The dejected face of Patricio reminded him of the slaves from the south—their horrid expressions—

when abandoned to die alone in the desert. He recognized the terror and the anguish. That bitter memory produced an uneasy sense of shame in the striped tunic.

"I know where the young lady is, *Monsieur*, I can bring you to her room."

Those words resounded inside Patricio's head like auditory hallucinations. He was not sure who was doing the talking. For a moment he thought it was his mother or his own voice as a child, perhaps. But the stench once again pierced its way directly into his brain, forcing him to recognize the grave tone of the striped tunic's voice.

"What did you say about Imena?" Patricio asked.

"Yes, Imena; I know where she is."

"Did you hurt her?"

"You're the one hurt, *Monsieur*, you must stand up and follow me."

"I can't feel my legs."

The striped tunic grabbed Patricio's arm, placed it around his shoulders, and lifted him to his feet. Patricio's limp body fluttered. The striped tunic helped him walk from the courtyard to the room where Imena was secluded. He knocked on the door several times but Imena did not respond. He knocked again, this time with more force, but still there was no answer.

"*Mademoiselle*, your search is over, open the door," the striped tunic said in a voice that sounded ancient, as if coming from the bottom of existence.

Imena opened the door and stood facing the man she feared and the man she came to find. As in the previous night, she appeared radiant in her nudity. A dense vapor saturated the room: a mélange of fetid smells, flowery scents, and earthy aromas. The striped tunic held Patricio on his feet while Imena placed her right arm under his shoulder and grabbed his left hand, holding him tight against her bare breasts.

"This is the wolf that chases you. He needs you now, *Mademoiselle*," the striped tunic said before leaving the room. He then went to take possession of his courtyard, his fate.

*****

The sight of an injured Patricio seemed unreal, everything seemed unreal, for the strong miasma inside her room had confused her senses. She saw Patricio as a wilting flower, and in desperation she tried to hold him up, but his petals fell off to the ground.

"Press against my hand, make me walk backward, Imena said.

"I'm pressing," Patricio said.

"Press hard, press hard."

"I'm pressing."

Imena felt the weight of Patricio's body as he leaned against her. Her hands and chest were drenched with his blood and sweat.

"Patricio, Patricio," she whispered.

"I'm not afraid of flying. I'll take to the sky with you," Patricio said.

Imena could not hold up Patricio's body as his legs gave from beneath him. He fell on the floor like a broken dream.

"Patricio," she said.

Imena tried to lift his head but it felt heavy and limp. She took his cold hands and pressed them against her chest, but they dripped away like water through her fingers. Patricio's body lay on the floor, pale, wet, lifeless. She then removed all of Patricio's clothes, liberating him from earthly attachments. She wanted to lighten his body, to make him float in the air. The same wolf that had pursued her ardently, appeared placid now, yielding, absolutely serene. She understood his desires and thought that Patricio had understood hers. Imena caressed his soft and clammy skin and felt as if she was caressing herself. When the back of her fingers glided around the angle of his jaw, Imena felt a gentle touch on her face. And when she pressed her hands against his chest, soft caresses rounded her breasts. A deep sense of oneness overtook her.

*****

Imena's hands abandoned Patricio and turned to the completion of her perfume. As in a trance, she mixed the volatile materials, completing the last few steps of her creation. Gradually, she worked into the fat the intense distillate she had carefully produced. The resulting pomade, emerging from her extravagant efforts, excited her. She could not describe the fragrance as *fleurie*, or *animale*, or *épicée*, for its composition challenged known classifications. It was a violent perfume, violent it was. And when she spread a thin layer of the pomade on the inner side of her left wrist, testing the interaction between the fragrance and her skin, she knew *La rose sauvage* was born.

With tenderness, Imena applied the fragrant pomade over Patricio's entire body. *La rose sauvage* contained all of her— the ethereal self and the animal self—and she wanted to share it with him. She then covered her entire naked body with the pomade and lay on the floor next to Patricio. She felt close to him, and she wanted to be one with him.

Like a slow caravan in the desert, the ingredients of the pomade started their journey. They steadily abandoned their emulsified state and penetrated her bare skin. The ravishing Atlas mountain roses marched first, accompanied by the glorious orange flowers and semi-sweet saliva. An intricate mélange of vanilla, hair, myrrh, clove and chamomile followed. And at the base, grounding everything, were the slow movements of musk, feces, and sun-cured Turkish tobacco.

The air in the closed room was pregnant with the intensity of the new fragrance. The skin, rejoiced in the calmness of the chamomile, inadvertently allowed the passage of a deadly concentration of nicotine exuded by the sun-cured Turkish tobacco.

Then came the afternoon hours and the stupor. Imena lost touch with her consciousness and fell asleep. There were no sounds, the light was clear, and her body felt weightless. In her mind, she saw her body leaving the courtyard and flying over the medina. She felt pure and timeless. But minute by minute, the lethal nicotine molecules broke through her skin reaching her blood rivers and spreading throughout her body.

After a few stuporous hours, a sudden burning sensation in her mouth and throat jolted Imena. A copious amount of saliva threatened to choke her, leaving a horrible taste in her mouth that she could not spit out enough. Her stomach cramped violently. She stood up, but the nausea and vomiting brought her down to her knees. Imena felt all her strength slipping out of her body. She rolled on her side and leaned against Patricio's cold body. And like a sand storm, her heart roared. Imena's senses were overwhelmed, she became confused, and could not comprehend that her own creation, *La rose sauvage*, was poisoning her. Her muscles suddenly tensed, pulling her arms rigidly towards her body. At that point, she uttered a loud moan—the song of the beast—an animal grunt that perturbed the peaceful expectation of the striped tunic. Then a violent shaking of her arms and legs made her roll and stretch. At the end, the room became dark and she could not see anymore.

45

Renée found the mint tea too sweet for her taste. She preferred a good strong coffee, but none could be availed. At the *Café Arabe*, foreigners mingled with locals in a cordial and voyeuristic atmosphere. She did not reject gazes or absorbing looks, although feeling vulnerable, she was determined to regain her confidence. But what Renée really hoped for was to encounter Patricio at some point, sooner or later, but expectantly sooner than later.

While disagreeably sipping her cup of tea, Renée got a glimpse of *Le Matin,* where an article on the second page referred to a suicide pact by two French nationals. A bold picture showed the naked torsos of a man and a woman in close embrace. Renée clearly recognized the man as Patricio, the face of the woman resembled that of Imena. According to the article, a certain professor from *l'Université Paris-Sorbonne* and an unknown young woman were found dead inside a room of a fourth-class hotel. The hotel location was very close to where Renée was sipping her tea at that very moment. When found by the hotel attendant, whose name was not mentioned, the man and the woman were naked and covered with a greasy, but exquisitely aromatic substance. The police deduced that the man had stabbed himself in the lower abdomen, while the woman had poisoned herself. According to the article, the motives of the suicide pact were unknown.

She feared the dead man was Patricio and the young woman Imena. And after corroborating the address of the hotel, Renée resolved to find the place and verify whether her suspicions were true. She wandered through the maze of the medina that afternoon until the number on a red door matched the address in the paper. And when she entered the courtyard, she felt a sense of wholeness she never knew existed. She admired the simplicity of the courtyard with the fountain in the center and four flowering orange trees in each corner. Renée had never been in that place, but every angle of the courtyard spoke to her in a familiar tongue. She felt a sublime scent conjuring Imena, she felt Patricio's earthy warmth, and she felt the presence of a mind, everyone's mind, perhaps. A peculiar proximity burned her skin while an acrid stench impregnated the air. When Renée turned around, the striped tunic was watching her, dispassionately, as if he had foreseen her arrival.

"*Mademoiselle*, there's a familiarity about you, have we met before?" the striped tunic asked.

"No, I don't think so," Renée said.

"Perhaps not, but may I offer you some mint tea?"

"Please, tea would be perfect," Renée said as she observed the striped tunic's slow gestures and impenetrable face. She saw him walk away and wanted to follow him to say she really detested mint tea, but a strange force retained her in the center of the courtyard. When the striped tunic arrived carrying the tray with mint tea and rock sugar, he exhibited a composed face and a sense of enlightenment.

"You're searching for something," the striped tunic said.

"Yes…, or something is searching for me."

"May I ask what are you looking for, *Mademoiselle*?"

"I think I knew the man and the woman that died in this hotel."

"They are not dead, they are part of us. But I'm certain that's not the reason for your visit. I feel you needed to come here because you belong here, as they did."

"I don't know where I belong, but I sense part of me lives here."

"Everything is contained within this courtyard, we are all inside these walls."

"Could I stay in a room with a view to the courtyard?" Renée asked.

"You may choose any room you want, the entire hotel is at your disposal."

Renée walked around the courtyard admiring the state of abandonment of the plaster, every window and door, the lonely toilet, the broken tiles. Like her father, she could build with her hands; she could orchestrate a renaissance in this hotel. And with a sense of belonging, Renée occupied a room in the hotel. She sat on the floor and allowed the air to play with her memories of Antonia.

When night fell, and Renée slept in a bed of dreams, the striped tunic walked under the red moon to the center of the courtyard. With a piece of yarn he tightened the tunic close to his body. With his bare hands he grabbed a fistful of red clay and swallowed most of it. And with resolute determination, he broke free through the red door, out into the streets of the medina, his unshackled self chanting. Behind remained the four flowering orange trees, reaching for the moon in pure whiteness.

The Roar
Of The River

"No man ever steps in the same river twice,
for it's not the same river and he's not the same man."

Heraclitus Of Ephesus

EXPOSITION

THE STRIPED TUNIC

The roar of water flowing over dark pebbles mutes the sound of my steps. I run on the river's shallow edge, one foot sinking while the other barely surfaces just to sink again in a circular race with no beginning or end. Now I know the fear and the fear knows me.

The serpent river turns, hissing, all while the deep green water runs under me, and I glide. Inside, my blood rivers run, pulsating, fear gushing through my arteries, veins, capillary deltas and brain barriers, flooding me,

the fear…

A hollow past runs behind me, what happened vanishes, and the only thing that remains is restlessness, or the uncertain color of dusk coming down to touch the river's edge. How hard to move forward when my past keeps on dying.

One step crushes against the pebbles, water splashes, another step seeks grounding, but the slime dressing the rocks causes me to wobble. I look for a branch to hold on to, but the brush is far, far in the shadows, away from the edge of the river. Ahead of me lies the water path, supine, taking my steps like a virgin.

I am running through you,

I am running away from you.

The air feels thick, miasmatic, a dripping curtain of particles bathing my face, my chest, embalming my urge to flee, and with every step I sink, and with every step I rise through the thickness.

A dirt path descends from the surrounding hills, through the brush, kneeling by the river's edge. The lunar light accentuates a boulder as the shallow water licks the pebbles at the edge.

I step into the dirt path leaving behind an uncertain trace.

Let the river carry my scent, let it swallow it.

Dry land now.

Dodging tree branches and shadows, I follow the dirt path, undulating, ascending, covering my before without offering a clear after. I climb a hill and see the streetlights of a perched village announcing life.

Whose life?

The path delivers me to an open plaza flanked by two sycamore trees and a dozen solitary café chairs. I turn my face away from the faces that turn my way, not in shame, but in fear that my wet appearance may ignite their fantasies,

phantasmagoric fantasies,

or thoughts and opinions about where I come from, why I stand erect and wet, what my next step will be, or whether I will approach and touch them, kiss them, violate their purple spaces, consume their air.

I stand breathing a shallow air and setting my eyesight low, like a mule, or like another creature ruminating life. I know what happened, I think I know, but my body projects a dejected image, not luminous or enlightened, but the image of dilapidated life,

I stand,

and the faces turn away from me.

Maybe my face, maybe the acrid smell emanating from my body, or the striped tunic that wraps me, perhaps the absence that stains me.

They turn their faces.

I close my eyes and try to ignore everything around me, but the roar of the river carving deep into the gorge betrays me. The river gargles on the trace I left behind, spitting my scent as white foam over the rocks.

An old woman, bent, carrying a load of groceries in plastic bags, passes close to me. She struggles under the weight of her bounty, limping on her right leg. A few steps later, she stops and turns to look at me.

—Are you..?

That question. No answer for that question. Not at this moment.

I ignore her. I need not take notice of anyone.

And the river roars.

Three different paths radiate away from the spot where I stand erect as before, three different destinies,

probably.

One of them ascends to the top of the village, another turns quickly to the left and falls away behind a stone wall, and the third disappears into blue shadows,

enter them, the shadows,

there, there.

Seeking cover from illumination, I penetrate the blue path. Several wooden doors and a few small wooden windows interrupt the stone walls that surround the path. Locked, all of them. I follow the path deeper into the shadows.

—Come inside.

—Who's talking?

—Come inside.

A sliver of light cuts vertically as a door opens to my right. The opening frames the face of a severely bearded man, a long grave face.

—Come inside.

I trespass the threshold and find myself inside a room as dark as the path outside. The unknown man stares at me with the expression of,

expression.

Dirt on the floor, empty bottles, one gas lamp nervous in a corner, the rest, I do not know. The air is damp and I smell moist earth. I sit on the floor and feel my wet tunic wrapped against my skin. Words filter through the thickness of his beard,

indiscernible words,
they stumble down and vanish in the lost corners of the room.

—What're you saying?

—Come inside.

—I'm inside.

—Good.

The man shuffles through the room and disappears behind a curtain made of strings. I hear him thrashing around and mumbling incessantly. He then comes back into the room, his hands holding what appears to be raw meat. He breaks a piece of it and hands it to me.

—Have some.

—What is it?

—Have some.

I bite into a cold and glandular substance,
bitter,
 fatty.

—What's this?

—My friends.

He laughs a jagged laugh, mumbles some more, and laughs again. The words sound like the chirp of a wounded bird, perhaps a language of his own. He moves around the room kicking dark objects I cannot recognize. He then brings a tin flask and holds it right in front of my face.

—Here.

—No, no.

—Here, here, here.

His eyes stare at me, nailing me, brutally. That is all I can see of his face, the rest is covered under the thickness of his beard. He may be an old man, or a young man, but a man of a clear decrepitude. I consider stepping out of the room and returning to the path outside,
 shadows there,

people looking for me.

I accept the flask and swallow some of its content. A rancid wine burns my throat.

—Blood of Christ!

He grabs the flask away from me and takes a mouthful. His eyes soften and he starts again his chirping mumble and laughter. Ignoring me, he sits on the dirty ground and starts to rock back and forth while taking sips from the flask. I sit in silence. I look at him and look at the door wondering what keeps me from bolting out,

out of here, there is a river.

All at once he stops mumbling and rocking. For a moment he appears to have died. Not a chirp. His presence deflates and his bearded face turns vacuous. His body becomes tense while he pulls his arms towards his chest. A loud scream, a death scream breaks the silence. His limbs then start twitching violently, shaking and vibrating. He falls to the ground, scattering the detritus of that glandular substance and the flask of acrid wine all over the room. He rolls and stretches his back, I fear he will break his spine. And in a second or two, he becomes as peaceful as an angel, blood coming out of the corner of his mouth, urine pooling around his recumbent body.

The chirping man

it hurts, my back hurts, is it night? the floor again, looking at me the floor, I think I fell again, my face is fine, my eyebrow, how long ago? it may be night, Blood of Christ, where's the Blood of Christ? this is urine, I'm wet, who's breathing? I hear someone breathing, you there, you, you came inside, did you push me? you motherfucker you, don't take anything from me, where's the meat? maybe he took it, I don't know, Christ, Christ, so salty in my mouth

—where's the Blood of Christ?

what's he doing there looking at me, and breathing? did I ask him in? maybe I did

—what are you doing here?

—I was out on the path and…

—I asked you in, motherfucker, I asked you in

is it blood? so salty in my mouth, he did come in from that dirty path, does he bring money? I need money, he's looking at me

—money, I said, money, money

I'm getting up from the floor and then I'll get money, or something, it hurts, my back, I think I seized, fuck me

—can I help you?

—get me money motherfucker

he does not listen, he's breathing my air but he doesn't listen, I'll stand and crack his skull open

—what did you say?

he, I asked him to come inside, where's the meat? where's the wine motherfucker? Blood of Christ, don't steal from me

—what did you say?

what do I say? what do I say? I say nothing, I just need to get up and hit him hard, crack him open and find some money, my back hurts

—can you hear the river?

—what motherfucker?

—the roar

I hear nothing, him breathing, no roar, no buzz from the blood, he talks to me as if I care, my tongue feels heavy, sticky on the right side, this salty piece of meat

—what do you want from me?

—nothing, you asked me to come inside

—don't motherfucker, don't

The striped tunic

As if from a bad dream he stares at me. Still lying on the floor, he poses like a broken man, a collapsed soldier. I lean closer to him and offer my hand. I want to help him. But he twists and turns his body while retreating into a corner of the room,

a hunted animal,

leaving a trail of blood and urine.

Outside, the path remains quiet, no steps, no voices, only the distant roar of the river. I must leave, this man will talk about me, he will tell them. I turn my back on him and start walking towards the door.

—Don't go.

He grabs an empty bottle from the floor and throws it my way, missing me, breaking into pieces when it crashes on the floor.

—Don't go, you. Stay inside.

—What do you want?

—You're wet.

—What do you want?

—You came from the river.

The man pulls himself up and staggers out of the dark corner into the center of the room. He looks around for the tin flask, finds it lying on the floor, and drinks the remaining wine.

—Blood of Christ! Best cure for the fits.

A sense of gravity descends on me as I observe this man, pure animalism, subverting my wish to flee. The path is now quiet, I must go. He can fall again, die if he wants to, but I must go,

somewhere,

away from the paths ordinary people follow. Everything

horrible happened already. Can he smell my past? No, how could he tell I smell of sulfur when he lives in decay? I am safe,
    I think I am,
    this moment.
    —From the river, I say, your shoes are covered in mud.
    —I come from everywhere.
    —Easy, drink some.
    —You seem dead to me.
    —Don't let my fits fool you. I, I, I, I…
The man starts chirping again, revolting, a sound cerebral for an animal, but unintelligible to me. His presence uncovers an uneasy feeling, a sense that life is wasted on substandard creatures. Who am I to judge, who am I to flee? And finding solace in a dark room, who am I to lay anger against a man who chirps? He asked me to come inside this room, and I did. The simple gesture is generous even if all he wants is money,
    the creature,
    noticing my wet tunic, my coming from the river.
No coincidence can explain his interest in me. He was the first one to speak. He asked me to come inside. I did not request to enter, I did not force my way inside this room. I was expecting nothing. No, more precisely, I was not expecting anything at all. I am not running away from the river. The river is a path, a road for water to descend from the heights of the mountain, or a passage,
    life, the river is,
    I am running towards life, not away from it.
    Not too long ago I thought life was resplendent. What an abrupt change,
    brutal,
    and then this journey by way of the river. To come face-to-face with this man who recognizes I need something. And now he asks me to stay inside this cave to witness his convulsions, his decadence.

The chirping man

Yes he comes from the river, that striped tunic wet, wet, the money must be wet too, why is he looking at me like that?

—do you want more wine? I have more

—no, you need it more than I do

—I need money, do you have some?

—no

lying, he's lying, coming from far away with no money, don't believe that, wonder what brought him here, and why did he go in the river wearing that tunic, I wear no tunic, nobody here does, no we don't wear that, he, he, he, he wraps himself in a piece of cloth, my own clothes are torn, why? where's my tunic? don't have one, no, no, I've nothing, money, does he have any of it?

—do you have any money?

—no, I told you

my meat, my people even, maybe my friends, is a rat a friend? they live so close to me, how could I not call them friends, my friends, my meat, the meat I share with him, he's not my friend, but he may have some money, he said no, I hear no all the time, the rats, no, they don't speak, they chirp, I chirp too, I'm not a rat, a rat, no, no, sometimes we eat the same thing, no, no, I'm not a rat, he may be a river rat, wet, keeping his head above water, he wants to go, to the river, the rat

—don't go back there

—where?

—to the river, you came from the river

—I come from everywhere. I told you.

—motherfucker, you

—what?

—the river, don't lie

he, he, he jumped from the dark path outside my door into my place, dark this is, he came in and drank my wine, the rats, well, he didn't have to eat them

—the river was a passage

—where from, motherfucker, where from?

—do you have more meat?

—yes, my friends are here, do you like them?

—I'll have more wine

—Blood of Christ?

—I'll have any blood

—yes, motherfucker

The striped tunic

The wine warms me. I need the warmth. And a place to replace the one I lost. This cannot be my place, this place belongs to him, or he belongs to this place, or the place exists without caring for any of us, not for me, I am certain of that, and how could anyone care for him?

he has friends,

do I have anyone?

I have myself and a past to carry with me, and at this moment what I need most is another path, not a river, a solid road to hold my steps, moving from, moving, from to, from a heavier from,

to a lighter to,

moving,

away from this room that rots.

Turning my back on the chirping bearded man, I reach for the door. I fear he will try to stop me again, but he does not move, he just watches me with an incomprehensible expression on his face, insulted, abandoned. When I open the door, no light filters through, the path outside remains dark, promising nothing.

—I'll remember you

—money motherfucker

I will remember him like I remember people from before, ghosts, vapid substances, makers of my destiny,

are they?

functionaries of what happened. I will carry his image, and his chirping voice will resonate tomorrow like it resonates now. Above all, he shared his food and wine with me, a stranger, a stranger even to myself, something he cannot see but somehow feels, for he called me into his decrepit cave hoping for something.

Out on the path, I hear the river roaring like before, an echo bouncing from wall to wall, traversing the village, the plazas, combing the hair of trees, reaching my ears and reminding me that my steps are liquid, that I recently arose from its banks, dragging water and moss because nothing else would suffice,

I drag nothing,

from before,

I think.

An array of erratic paths opens up in front of me. To my right a turn leads to a lower plaza where children practice the barbaric rituals of life. To my left the path keeps on ascending to the highest point in the village. I turn left, ascending with the path, higher, my tunic still dripping blood, or river water, and with every step over the stones that form the path, I leave something behind. Am I invisible? Can people see my profile and tell I am a stranger? Can anyone tell me where to go?

Many stones from many walls stand in procession as I hike the path through the village, making my way higher, higher, in the wake of laughter, screams, and the dissonance of the children's voices. What is the name of this village? Where are the faces of this village? I suspect that people are hiding from me behind closed doors and shut windows. I pull the hood of my tunic over my head,

my face hidden,

my reflection on the river lost.

Did I reflect any of my likeness when I ran through the shallow river? Did the turbulent water fail to reflect me? Did my image become a thousand fractions of a discontinuous,

me,

leaving no trace, or multiple traces, or a flow of confusion?

As I ascend, I ascend. And the path leads into the woods away from the last houses that remain standing one kilometer away. A black thorn protruding from the long bluish agave tongue tears my tunic. What grows in the wild is wild and unrepentant,

we should not grow that way.

After a fig tree, the path turns on itself and gradually descends onto a ledge, where the ruins of a farmhouse sleep. The partial roof on the house has a soft curve and rests gently on the robust stone walls, half-fallen now. The window openings remain but the wooden shutters are long gone, so are the doors and the frames. The house is the color of the mountain, beaten by sun and rain, and the oblivion of people. Inside, dirt makes up the floor, and numerous weeds grow from the crevices where stone and dirt come together. This house can host me, a forgotten kingdom for an errant,

vagabond,

the roar of the river inaudible,

only the sound of the wind as it slides down the face of the mountain, whistling when it goes around bushes or tree trunks.

I can occupy this amphitheater, wrap my tunic tight around my body, and lay my head on the ground. I can rest here and ignore the incessant stride of a dying past. I come to this. I must come to this.

The one-armed man

What could he be doing in there? He looks like a goat, at least he smells like one—putrid. He seems to be alone, nobody else with him. He could be a criminal, or he could be lost, or he could be a lost criminal. Maybe he is not a criminal at all, just a lost hiker, or maybe he is not a criminal nor a lost hiker, but a fetid apparition. Fetid he is, no doubt. I got a whiff of him before I saw him. And that striped tunic…

Why does he stay inside that ruin? I wonder if he is sleeping. He could be eating. No, he is not eating, he carried nothing with him when he went in. What if he is spying on me the way I am spying on him? He may be as scared of me as I am scared of him. He could be waiting for me to continue walking down the mountain. What if he has a knife under his tunic? I also have a knife. But why would I attack him if he has not attacked me? He could be waiting for me to start walking down and then come from behind and attack me with his knife. He could have a gun, a rifle. But I did not see him carrying anything.

No sound. He makes not a single sound. He must be keeping quiet, just listening to me. But I am not making any sounds either. If he does not move I will not move, and if I do not move, he will remain static. He could be planning his escape, how to leave that ruin and make his way down the mountain, into the village. But from where I am hiding, I would see any move he makes. I would know the moment he gets out of the ruin, no doubt. But if he waits until the night falls, I may not be able to see him in the darkness. But then he would not see me either, he would not know that I would still be spying on him. He would not know if he needs to hide, if hiding is what he is doing.

I can sit here, all day, waiting for him to make the first

move. And how do I know that something horrible is about to happen? There is no clear way to know, but the fact that this rancid person went into a ruin on this mountain, surrounded by nothing but scattered trees, creates a perfect scenario for trouble.

He remains as quiet as a dead body, so much so, that I decide to walk towards the house to capture any signs of life. He could be asleep, he could be meditating, he could be watching me in silence—he could really be dead. No, not dead, he prepared for his arrival to this place in a meticulous way, you could tell because every move he made seemed rehearsed. Do people plan their gestures and moves for the day? Why, why? Nevertheless, those gestures would look pathetic, especially in a cold-blooded murderer like this one. But how do I know that he is a murderer? I do not know, but I imagine he is one.

I make my way closer to the house in the most inconspicuous way, walking in a zigzag, as if the final destination had no particular meaning to me. I even stop and bend down to pick a little red wildflower, pretending I have no concern for anything or anyone occupying the ruin. I smell the flower. This one being fresh and placid, nothing like the smell that emanates from the ruin. When I come upon a flat rock at the edge of the path, I decide to sit down and look at the trees, the mountains, and the ravine that harbors the river. He could not imagine that I imagine him observing every move I make. But at the same time, he may think I am ambushing him, making my way closer and closer with the only purpose to surprise him, to reveal him—to kill him. Is that what I want to do? I have this knife that I have never used on a person, or animal. I have sliced bread with this knife, nothing more. But if he gets a glimpse of the knife, he may think that I am intent on pulling it on him. He has not seen my knife, like I have not seen any knife on him. But he could have one, and very likely, he thinks I have one, why would he not?

As I move closer to the ruin, a sense of asphyxiation comes over me. The air becomes thin, as if the oxygen had been extracted from it. I struggle to keep my head heavy when it wants to be light. Standing on my feet feels risky, so I look for another rock to sit on, this time I pick no flowers or pretend anything. I fear what he may do when I get closer to the ruin. He may shoot me with that gun I have not seen, or he may burst out of the ruin and stab me multiple times with that knife I have yet to see. He may also not dare to move one inch, fearing that I may charge at him with my knife or blast him with a gun I do not have. There is no way to know.

Each fresh step takes twice as long as the previous one. And I approach at a slow, slower rate, finally reaching the stone wall that stands holding nothing, for the roof of this decaying house collapsed decades ago. I know he waits inside, resting, spying, and deliberating what to do next. I deliberate with him. Should I try to surprise him with a sudden attack, delivering a blow to his malicious plan? But what plan does he have? Could he be plotting to surprise me with a sudden attack as well? What if he is standing just behind this wall, opposite to me, listening to my breathing? And if I were to rush inside this ruin hoping to find him on the floor, weak, smoking or sleeping, but instead find him with the blade of his knife ready to carve through my ribs? There is no real way to know.

I lean my back against the wall. I hold my breath to extinguish any human sound. I roll my body gradually along the wall until my face peeks through a door opening. With my hand wrapped around the handle of my knife, I look inside.

The striped tunic

Only the sound filling empty spaces.

I only hear the sound of vibrating molecules displacing images from the past. And this empty house makes no sound of its own, it seems to breathe, but silently. The world centers on this ruin in the form of sounds. As I lie immobile, I hear the river, or the roaring flow of sweat,

nervous sweat,

pouring out of pores. Not my pores, for I lie wrapped in my wet tunic void of fear. The flow of someone else's sweat, a torrent of fear. I close my eyes and focus on the sound. Human, a human sound, not a river. The tumultuous excretion from human glands flowing and creating a liquid turbulence. The air whistles,

a bird cries,

and leaves touch each other. I get on my feet inside the empty house and wait for the rambunctious moment to end. But the noise does not abate. It lingers in the air, an obscene presence denying the solitude I seek.

—Come inside, whoever you are.

No utterance, no voice responds to my call. But the noise becomes louder, a tidal surge of humanity, a cascade of sweat.

—I can hear you sweating. I know what fear sounds like.

Suddenly, the silhouette of a very tall man grows at the door's threshold, blocking the light from the outside. One of his hands wields a knife, the other hangs limp at the side of his body. I cannot see his face from inside the house, but I can tell he is the source of the river of sweat.

—Why the knife?

—Are you a criminal?

—Put that knife away.

—Are you lost?

—Which of the two do you fear most, a criminal or a lost vagabond?

—You must be a criminal.

—You must be afraid.

The knife fails to bestow the security he misses. That is why he sweats so much, his mind is not settled. He fears me because he does not know me. And if he were to know me, he may still fear me, but with a reason. Senseless fear is an atrocity our minds like to lay on us. The,

bestiality,

of our minds can dominate our most basic human instincts. Motionless at the door, he stands, incapable of slashing my throat. I am not running away from him, he is not yet part of my past.

He enters the room and walks slowly with his back to the wall. The knife, still firm in his right hand, his left hand swinging like a pendulum, a flaccid appendage that makes him vulnerable. Sweat emanates from his entire body, his forehead dripping, his shirt drenched. His perturbed stare, panic mixed with hostility, impales me. I remain in the center of the room, projecting the very image that he fears.

—Don't move. I'll cut you open.

—What happened to your arm?

—Don't move I said.

—I'm not moving. What happened to your arm?

—What do you care?

—I may not care, but you do.

—Who cares about my dead arm? I still have a knife in my good one.

—Do you miss it, your dead arm?

—We are not going there. What are you doing here? What do you want?

—Put that knife away, you don't need it.

—Why were you spying on me?

—You were the one at the door, sniffing me like a mad dog.

I remain standing in the center of the room hearing the sound of his words. They swirl around, the words, bouncing against the stone walls and the dirt ground, words of fear and desperation. I utter words of my own, revelatory words primarily, indecent and caustic. He retorts, he waves the knife at me, his eyes burning in,

> fear,
> exalted by the uncertainty of my motives,
> a claustrophobic sense of inadequacy closing in on him,
> gripping him tightly,
> until he throws it on the ground,
> the knife.

I ignore the fallen weapon, it lies on the ground abandoned, maybe lonely—naked for sure—reflecting the pale light that enters the room, reflecting an air of disposed hostility, or maybe afraid of finding itself alone on the ground, no hand to raise it to domination, a simple blade mounted on wood. Do not look at it. I do not. Do not accept the capitulating gesture. I do not. The knife falls asleep in the middle of the room as the man who accosted me stands with his back to the wall and his face towards me.

—Don't hurt me.

—You had the knife in your hand, you're the one who could have hurt anyone.

—I thought you were after me.

—Why did you think that?

—You hid in this ruin, you pretended to be asleep.

—I was thinking, just as I'm thinking now.

—You waited for me to approach this ruin. You were waiting to kill me.

—I'm only breathing the air that floods this place.

—That air smells bad. You smell like a civet.

—What do you mean?

—You smell like an acrid, putrid creature.

—You smell of fear—shit that is.

Fear blends with the inner gastrointestinal reality of its bearer. An external manifestation of such enmeshment smells like shit. He fears me, otherwise, why would he have thrown away his knife? He must think I have the disposition to harm him. He says I smell like the unctuous cat, the civet. He must be confused. But my odor is not the result of fear, but the result of a denunciation of the regular world. He emanates a non-philosophical essence, a bodily expression, human fear. I emanate bile, or rotten thought, or maimed life, all the result of a forced exodus,

through the river,

leaving behind a collapsing past,

a dying past,

unburied,

far away from this village.

The man continues to perspire, even in the comfortable temperature of this room, a room floating at one thousand meters above sea level. He wears a sad expression on his face, perhaps the expression of a conquered soldier. But we have not battled, we have not taken arms against each other, we have not even discussed the nature of my aplomb or the source of his paranoia.

—What, what?

—You will have to tell me, you came armed.

—Why do you come to this village, why do you hide in this ruin?

—What makes you believe that I'm hiding?

—You're alone and you smell like a dirty cat.

—As I said, you're the one who smells of fear.

The man walks to a corner of the room, his dead arm swinging uncontrollably, and when he gets there, he sits on the ground, grabbing the pathetic appendix out of the way to avoid sitting on it. He appears more relaxed, but a faint cloud of doubt, apprehension, dread even, floats over his head. The empty room contains me, contains his pathetic persona, and at the same time, contains nothing of me, and only an interpretation of his fears. We both exist in this very room, as we both exist in life, or death, but together in this improbable scenario we both breathe.

—What brings you here?

—Nothing brings me here.

—You're here for a reason, you killed somebody.

—I'm looking for a ruin.

—What's so special about a ruin?

—It has a past.

—But everything here is collapsing.

—Yes, this ruin has a past.

—You must be hiding from something.

—No, I'm not hiding, I'm just walking away.

—What are you walking away from?

—My past, it keeps on dying.

—What?

—Nothing.

Only my thoughts and his thoughts occupy the empty room. I sit in silence for several minutes, several hours perhaps, and when a bird flies through the open window, I understand that he needs to go. I get on my feet slowly, shaking my striped tunic free from my body. I stretch my arms as if praying, but no words come out of my mouth for I believe in nothing. I watch as the man gets up on his feet as well. He watches me with great attention and pronounces a few words I cannot understand. He turns his back on me and runs out of the ruin.

The one-armed man

Why did I leave my knife behind? I had complete advantage until I dropped my knife on the floor. He could pick it up and stab me down there by the bend of the path. He may be that kind of person, a monster. I was afraid, yes I was. I am still afraid now. I fear what he plans to do in that abandoned ruin. He may use it as his haunt, a place to return to after doing the unspeakable. I sense his motives. Dark motives, no doubt. But what are they, really? He could tell I fear him. Do I smell like fear? He says I do. Maybe I do.

But he seemed so peaceful, not the rabid monster I expected. He did nothing but stand in the middle of that room, watching me from a distance. He should be desperate from escaping and anxious about me discovering him. He should be coming apart. But I was the one who trembled; I dropped my knife on the floor and ran away. But why did I run away when he did not threaten me, did not attack me, and did not even say a hostile word? Maybe the rancid smell emanating from his body made him seem dark, ominous. Or maybe I found no clear explanations in his words. He spoke of nothing, he exposed nothing. Or maybe Côte d'Ivoire, were instead of bringing peace I brought hell, and hell took my arm from me.

I keep walking down the path until the village comes into full view with its perfect accumulation of medieval houses. Saint George killed the dragon to bring peace to this place. We are always killing monsters. My house waits for me in the lower *quartier* of the village. I can hear the whisper of the stones, I can hear the river applauding my arrival. I climb the common stairs and open the door to a space that feels warm. This room is safe, it does not hold a fugitive, and it does not hold aberrant fears. I add a few pieces of wood to the fireplace and light the tinder. Then I shed all my clothes and sit on the floor beneath my five-pointed red star medal to watch the fire. Naked, exposed to the heat and the smoke, I wonder what his motives are. Is he a criminal? Is he a bandit? Is he a lost prophet? And why does he wear that rancid striped tunic? But a more burning question, why do I fear him?

The striped tunic

No light when the sun goes down. No moon. The only sparkles come from far away, on the other side of the mountain, where a light erupts out of a distant house. They must be honest people; they have no fear of light. I am honest, but I have no light. Not because I fear people finding me, but because there is nothing to burn in this ruin. The walls wear black soot as a cover, telling the story of former occupants. They made fires here, perhaps they killed here. Do we need light to kill? Is killing fostered by the absence of light? What to do without,

light?

kill, light,

light kill,

make light out of life, not death, no.

I step outside the ruin and look for the path. Loose gravel moves under my feet. I need to reach the village at this time without causing turmoil. The path will bring me there, even in this absent night. My steps, the ones that took me through the river, will certainly lead me to the village. Feeling the foliage, stepping over stones, and smelling the smoke of autumn chimneys, I traverse the mountain and reach the edge of the village. The lights greet me but the empty streets speak of rejection,

go away,

denounce,

even when I have not spoken, or told my story to anyone. I move as a ghost would, almost floating, leaving no trace behind. Looking for a source of food or fuel, I keep descending until I reach the main square of the village. A sycamore tree, the required Tabac, and a lot of nothingness at this hour. No moon. No shadows. Nothing, really. I recognize the path that took me to the room with the chirping man. I avoid that path. Instead, I continue to descend through another path that snakes down closer to the river.

The roar.

I can hear the roar.

Out of the roar the face of a young woman materializes. Green eyes, matted hair, earthy, exuding an uneasy luminosity,

hippie,

yes, anticonformist.

For a moment she stares at me, but as soon as I take a step in her direction, she vanishes into the shadows. I try to follow her but there is nothing to follow, she disappears like a morning dream.

Furtive, an image,

white over dark, in a desolate,

 time, in a desolate path.

I stand motionless with my arms raised. Speak, I say to myself, speak now.

—Why do you run away from me? You don't know me.

The roar of the river swallows my words. No response. The night and the closed windows ignore me as well. But a delicate awareness comes over me; I sense she watches me in silence.

—Do I frighten you?

—No.

—Let me see your face.

—No.

A subtle voice born from the shadows. I look around me. I wish I did not. The night seems false, a simulacra. Come forth all of you, the real ones.

—I need food.

—Who are you?

—I need food.

—Where's your house?

—I don't have one.

—Why do you wear that tunic?

—I dress this way.

—Why?

—This is the way I dress.

From behind a portal the silhouette of a thin woman emerges. The white of her eyes radiates light, even in the moonless night. She vaguely approaches me, stopping a few meters in front of me. Fearing she may disappear again, I refrain from moving.

—I can get you some food if you stay where you are.

—And water, bring water.

—I will.

Her figure slides down the path vanishing into the shadows again. The sound of a wooden door closing against stones reaches my ears. She does not live far. But numerous doors open into the path, each door leading to numerous flats in numerous floors, all containing several windows that open into the vastness created by the surrounding mountains, at the bottom of which,

the river roars,

indifferent, carving through the mountain,

gorging.

Then her quick steps advance, no sight of her, only syncopated steps coming from a bend in the path. Then her eyes, the white part of them, cutting a thin sleeve into the black air. Then her silhouette, slender, no more. She stops at a distance and places a basket and a jug on the ground.

—This is for you.

—For me?

—Bread, a piece of meat, some wine.

—Wine…

—Yes, but don't come closer. Wait until I'm gone.

—Where are you going?

—I need to go. I shouldn't be out.
—Wait, what's your name?
—Nadya.

Nadya

He cannot see where I am going. No, he cannot. Poor man, alone and hungry in the middle of the night. He is not from around here, maybe from the lower valley or from the other side of the mountains. And wearing a tunic, my people do not wear that. I hope nobody else finds him, they may think he is dangerous. He is hungry, that is all. And he asked for my name. But I forgot to ask his. Maybe next time. Tomorrow night, maybe.

The door makes a creaking sound when I push it open. My sisters remain asleep. They did not wake last night, or the night before. They sleep that way, abandoned. With tentative steps I make it to my bed where I lie down. Should I close my eyes? No, not yet. What is the purpose? What is the chance that I will fall asleep? Tonight is not different from the other nights—my dreams ignore me.

Some animals come out at night, many cats, swarming termites in the summer, a few people. But I never saw a stranger like him, so lonely, and with such a strange smell, an animal smell. He frightened me, but not enough. I did not run away. That is not what I do, run away. What could he be doing in the middle of the night? I also walk around in the middle of the night but I have my reasons. I wonder what reasons does he have to come out like that, like a hungry animal. He may be fighting for food with the cats, or with the rats. I only wonder.

The first morning light comes through the window and surprises me, still wondering, awake in my bed. When my older sister gets up and starts moving around the house, I close my eyes and pretend to be asleep. She knows that I go out in the middle of the night, but I do not like when she asks questions. And when she comes around to my bed, I keep my eyes shut. She would not ask questions, she does not need to know everything. I do not worry about my little sister, she will not wake up until later. After a full summer of nighttime meandering, this morning routine starts to get old.

The moment comes when I have to enter the day as if I had left the night behind. But the night will follow me through the day. I know that. The morning talk flows as it has to, to what market are we going today, how much cheese are we bringing, who will pack the boxes, how much of the old stuff are we throwing away? My older sister poses these questions and gives the answers as well. They are always the same answers. Except for the place, which changes all the time. But everything else is always the same, every morning, every day.

The night is different; it opens up my world. Because nobody rules the night, I am free to glide through the village mostly unnoticed. The cats, those silent beings of the night, expect me by now, each in their usual corner, licking themselves and waiting to pounce on something. The people I come across do not wait for me as the cats do. They either walk faster, trying to slip away into the night, or sometimes, approach me to propose all sorts of things. My clothes, my hair, makes them say those things to me. I am certain bourgeois girls are not spoken to in the same tone, with the same lewdness. The people that know me, the few that venture into the night, hardly ever say a word to me. Maybe they do not want to be recognized, walking clandestinely from one house to another in this small village.

With the help of a hand truck, we carry box after box of cheese over the stone paths to the decrepit truck parked below the cemetery. We bring comté, Tomme de Savoie, chèvre, young and old, and many others. We descend the winding road to the village of Fontan. From here the road turns and twists along the gorges clad in purple stone until we reach the sad and humid village of Tende. Thursday, we come to Tende on Thursdays. The same spread on the table by the plaza, the same old women with the same straw bags, carrying the same bread sticks while looking at the cheeses with the same stale eyes, looking at my sisters, and sometimes at me, with the same stagnant suspiciousness. Daytime at its most glorious moment.

He wanted food. He waited while I brought food to him. I did not bring cheese to him, my sisters would have noticed, but I brought meat and bread, and I think he loved the wine. Would he come out in the daytime? Would I recognize him if he came to buy cheese from us? The tunic would give him away, and his pungent smell. Many people in these mountains look strange, hippies most of them, but he seemed different, his presence so strong.

The day passes by so slowly. When I doze off my sisters shake me and tell me not to be lazy. Not lazy, I am not lazy. I just need to recover my lost sleep or prepare for the sleep I will lose tonight. Sitting at the table where the display of cheese attracts people and flies, I feel light-headed. At one point, I fall asleep and land with my head on the softest Camembert. My older sister yanks me back up and tells me to go to the fountain and wash my face with cold water. Yes, cold water. I feel the refreshing touch on my skin and hope for renewed energy and enthusiasm. But when I return to the stand, the same old cheeses, the same customers, and my same two sisters are waiting for me. How slow can a day be?

In the early afternoon the market comes to an end. Boxes, vans, and trucks are stuffed with the unwanted, unsold merchandise that will travel back and forth until someone buys it, or until it rots. We return to Saorge and unpack everything. And as soon as my sisters begin preparing the evening meal, I disappear into the village. As in most afternoons, I come to the green grass in front of the monastery where I take a nap under a silent cypress, stealing hours from the day to add them to my errant nights.

During dinner, my older sister laments that no man wants her. I listen to the same story every night and offer no response. She does not want a response; she just needs to hear her own voice proclaiming misery. My little sister also talks about men, boys in her case, but her tone lacks the helplessness of my older sister, her tone is mischievous, playful even. Words come and go between the two of them, dissonant angry words. They never ask what I think about men, they assume I have no interest in having sex. Sometimes I feel my sisters forget I exist. Like in this moment, when I look out the window and contemplate the night falling, my world unfolding, I do not exist for them.

But the night has to come with its darkness. The streetlights fight back but lose the battle against the advancing night. Now all I have to do is wait. Wait until my sisters go to bed and their conversation dies. Restless under the covers, I pretend to be asleep. And as soon as everything becomes still, I rise from my bed and slip out of the house into another moonless night, my wondrous world. The night is my life, darkness falls, the happy night is my sad life.

I follow the path I followed last night coming down like a cat on the roofs. Nobody knows, nobody sees. I turn up in the dark, mute and aglow. One thousand *cigales* applaud my steps. Then I come to the spot where I met the man in the striped tunic last night. He is not here. Some voices approach from the distance. I hide between two buildings and watch as two men walk by smoking and laughing. They sound drunk. Without moving much, I remain hidden for some time, an hour maybe. And slowly, as a miasma rising from the valley, a putrid smell, the smell of the civet, infiltrates the air.

The striped tunic

She will come again tonight. I know she will. And I am certain she expects the same from me. She prefers the night, I know because the way she moved among the shadows, the quiet steps, display the markings of a noctambulant. I am different. Fear leads me into the night, not a fascination with the dark. I venture through this obscure maze to escape the inquisitive eyes of the villagers. Unlike me, she seems to find comfort at this hour,

still, still,

in peace with her solitude.

Let me wait here, the spot where she brought me wine last night. She will arrive. I know she will. Or she might be here already, watching me from behind the shadows. Maybe she is sitting next to me, breathing the same crisp air and listening to my thoughts. I know her name. I will call her name.

—Nadya.

The sound of her name turns circles in the light air before ascending into the night.

—Nadya.

Come forth, without fear, come forth to greet me. But nothing moves and no other sound breaks the silence. I wait, and I wait some more. And after a while, like the night before, a pair of eyes emerges from the thick darkness.

—Are you hungry?

—Yes, Nadya, I'm hungry.

—Did you like the meat last night?

—I liked the wine.

—Of course.

—Who are you?

—I'm Nadya, I already told you that.

—I know your name, but who are you?

—I'm Nadya. How about you, what's your name?

—My name, my name… Why are you here?

—Maybe for the same reason that you're here.

—I'm hungry, Nadya.

—I'm hungry too.

She is hungry, I can tell. No woman will meander at nighttime unless she is hungry for life, or love, or maybe hungry for a sense of self. Nadya comes to me to experience something, fear perhaps.

—Where do you live?

—With my sisters, not too far.

—Do they know you're here?

—Never mind my sisters. Who knows you're here?

—I hope nobody.

—Are you running away from something?

—I'm not sure.

—How's that possible?

—Old sands, a courtyard with orange trees, Atlas roses.

—What do you mean?

Do I really know what I mean? Do I really understand why I traversed the river with a sense of persecution weighing me down, sinking my steps into black pebbles? I know I had to find confinement, and the courtyard with my four flowering orange trees offered the sweetest form of confinement. The courtyard held me. The dry desert air was free to come into the courtyard, climbing down the walls, but I was not free to step outside, or I was free but opted to stay inside. I remember the water singing in the fountain as clearly as I remember the call of the beast. The man, I remember, and the woman, I also remember. She was sensible, but the beast was lodged inside her body. The man was troubled, but are we any different? And I listened to their thoughts without them knowing. They did not want to say much, but they did, with that dissonant expression on their faces. I remember the roses from the high Atlas, they procured hundreds of petals, and the music, that melancholic music, bouncing from wall to wall. A music born from lament, I remember that too. And they despised me, yes they did, they wanted me to tell their truths, but they did not want to listen. In the end, I said what I needed to say, exactly what they could not say to each other. And they listened, in their own way, like birds listening to the wind. They encountered a desperate death, two of them at once, as if death needed company. I can still see them, one next to the other, prostrated on that impossible ground, forming a cuneiform mass in the emptiness of the room. I knew about the tobacco, I knew about the roses, and I knew about the perfume, that fulminant poison. This I remember, clearly, but everything else escapes my memory. Maybe my memory is perfect, but if the events have already died, what is there to remember? Death follows me. I know that. But as I try to remember, my past keeps on dying,

days and nights,

faces I knew and,

the laughter of my friends,

a caress, another, die as well,

well into a misty morning that saw me,

run away, escape the courtyard, head for the river where my steps would,

sink,

deep into black pebbles.

Do I really know? No, I do not. And she will need to understand that the questions she is asking have no answer. I, who embodies an old consciousness, fail to explain to myself the reason for my escape. I crossed the river, yes, and I move through this village as a fugitive. What am I running from?

—Can I get you some food?

—Not now.

—You said you were hungry.

—I'm very hungry.

—I can bring you bread and wine.

—Not know. Come with me.

—Where?

—To the top of the village. Don't be afraid.

—What's there?

—A ruin, an empty ruin.

The debris of an earlier life, walls that refuse to collapse not knowing what they stand for, a place with an anonymous past and an uncertain present, a receptacle that holds me. This she does not know, how could she? But what she seems to sense is my hunger, my animal hunger for food, and my human hunger for tenderness.

In silence, I grab her hand, a warm hand, not the sweaty hand of a frightened person. She does not pull back; she abandons her hand with confidence. I lead her through the dark paths up to the top of the village,

in silence,

incognitos,

ignorant of our motivations. And without asking questions or giving explanations, we reach the ruin that rests in a nocturnal stupor. I keep grabbing on to her hand, afraid that she may vanish into the night.

The chirping man

She makes them run away, the little ratty bastards run away when she walks by, there they go, the cats will catch them, they also need to eat, the cats, but how about me? vermin, that's what they are, vermin

he, he, he again with the tunic, and grabbing her, where's the motherfucker going this late? how does he get to grab her? I've tried and no, no, no, she spat at me, I was only trying to be nice, and she spat at me

up the path they go, wait until they find the colony of cats, fifty or one hundred, not a single mouser though, but the meowing will slow them down, oh, no! they are walking faster, move it, move it, catch up with them, but keep the distance

he pulls her up the path, motherfucker taking the girl away, he didn't show me his money, maybe he'll pay her if she opens her legs, she didn't take my money, she spat at me, yes, yes

he's walking into the forest, this is dark, nothing here but ruins, that's what he's doing, taking her to the ruins, motherfucker! could've done that myself, no, no, no, she said I was filthy, me, ha, ha, ha, filthy, maybe the beard, she doesn't like my beard, filthy she said

and her sisters, do they know she's running around with this insect wrapped in rags? I don't think so, her sisters, the older one specially, no, no, I wouldn't dare, she would hit me if I talk dirty to her, cheese and everything, would love the taste, the cheese that is, but without money, no cheese, no middle sister either

where are they going? into the ruin, nothing there, one dirty place, the bastard could not do better than that, she would go there but not into my place, little flirt didn't like me, no, no, the beard maybe, not the rats, she doesn't know what I chew, must be the beard

he, he, he, can die, dark place, no moon tonight, dark, last year, yes last year, I walked on this path and a fit came over me, I fell hard and lost a tooth, my mouth bloody and the tooth gone, never saw it again, I don't like this path, and so dark now, but I can see from here, sort of, they go in, bastard, he, he, he came from the river, like a rat, wet, and now he's there with the thingy, money, he must have some, money

Nadya

My fingers feel so small inside the broad palm of his hand. A coarse hand, grainy, hands that shape life. And he brings me to the highest point beyond the village, to this abandoned place where the only noise I hear is the distant roar of the river and the slow shuffling of the stars. He must be hiding here. But hiding from what? I should be terrified, I should be letting loose from his hand and seeking safety. But I do not.

The night feels more ample here, heavier, not like the transient dark phase of the earth, but somewhat eternal. I can rest here. With my hand still netted in his, I sit on the ground. A smaller night grows in the belly of the larger night outside.

Worn down by an old tiredness, he lies down next to me. A faint light filters through the window openings delineating his profile, an abrupt profile, like a jagged mountain. His eyes I can barely see, gray, storm-weathered. The scent emanating from his body reminds me of those tomcats that meander the village at night, my silent companions. And he wears this tunic, a sunburned rugged cloth with vertical stripes that were once white. His feet tucked into torn sandals. I have never been close to anyone like this, not in the markets, not in Saorge. Not even the hippies, they do not look this way.

—Why do you bring me here?

—Because you want to be here.

—And how do you know that?

—You didn't resist.

—Should I have screamed?

—No, that would have woken people up.

—Yes, they would protect me.

—But they would destroy your night, your space.

—What about the night?

—I don't know, you tell me.

The night is my personal space, he is right about that. But what right does he have to intrude into my space and demand food? Even if he had not accepted my food, what right does he have to appear in my night space? And then, he takes me by the hand, as if my hand were his country. I do not own the night, but I do own my space within the night, the very space he violated. And, yes, I did not resist, I allowed him to lead me, to bring me to this decrepit farmhouse. I do not understand why I am here, but somehow, the night feels abundant, perpetual.

—I despise the day.

—Why?

—It smells like cheese.

—What kind of cheese?

—Any cheese, it doesn't matter.

—The day has no smell.

—It does for me.

—How about the night?

—White flowers, freedom.

—Freedom has no smell.

—It does for me.

—And what's that like?

—Dreams, the smell of dreams.

—What do your dreams smell like?

My dreams. How would I know what my dreams smell like if I do not really know what my dreams are? I despise the day, yes, I do. And the night seems better, at least more real. But if I were to face a dream, up front, in close quarters, I would not recognize one. And how could I define what a daytime dream smells like? This is confusing to me. I know I wander at night, I know the day feels dead to me, but I clearly ignore what I am doing in the middle of the night holding this man's hand.

—My dreams smell of …

—Yes.

—They're dead. Maybe they smell of death.

—Is that why you come out at night?

—I find it comforting.

—What about the night that comforts you?

—No eyes, no questions, and total acceptance by the cats.

—You want to be invisible.

—So do you.

—I'm not invisible, I'm aware of that. People can see me.

—I wish people did not see me.

—Why?

There is nothing to look at. That is why. I am a little ratty person who amounts to nothing. And what is a mouse to do in daytime but hide? At night, I roam, hoping to be invisible. The nighttime so different from daytime, a time when I simply exist in the form of a middle sister selling coagulated milk. He must know I am desperate for he takes my hand, like I know he is hungry therefore I feed him. Outcasts, we both are.

—Because I don't like them. Or because I sense they don't like me.

—What about you is it that they don't like?

—I'm not sure. I expected you would tell me.

—I'm not them.

—Then, who are you?

He abandons my hand. He lets it fall, discarding it as a dirty rag. Turning his face, he fixes his gaze on me. Yes, his eyes have seen many storms.

—I'm a hungry man.

—Why do you only come out at night, like me?

—Am I different from you?

—Maybe not.

—Then, why do you hide?

—Why do you hide?

The striped tunic

Why do I do anything? Why do I even exist? Or even better, why do I come to this village where the only comfortable space resides in the middle of the night? And I encounter this tender creature, a gentle hippie girl who takes my hand. I take her hand. And that hand, that acceptance, grounds me. The past hides away from me, rather, it dies at a faster rate. And when I take her hand, I dare to let go of the time before,

the dying one,

many steps and many waters behind,

the reason for my escape.

She, who follows me into this ruin, knows I exist as an exile, a runaway, an escapee, or as someone who does not live in this world as most people do. And how is that different from her reality? At nighttime, she roams through the dark streets of the village. Who is she running away from? Why does she have to weave her small self between the shadows? And the strangest thing, why does she accept my hand and follow me to this ruin?

She,

she,

she,

who brought me food and wine,

and then returned the following night to face me,

a stranger.

The night seems to sing for her, full of meaning, challenging, testing the edge of her daytime deadness. For me, the night represents a time of marvel, when those who watch are tired and I am free to explore. The nights before, the ancient ones, gradually lost their luminosity becoming an oppressive burden, with the heavy weight of uncertainty, fueling my urgent need to flee. Those nights saw me prepare my escape, witnesses they were, maybe judges of my actions. I left them behind, and without wanting, I find myself inside this other night grabbing the giving hand of a hippie between my hands. Her chest heaves to an internal rhythm,

fear,

wanting, maybe,

or just the animal need to breathe.

Why do I hide? Do I hide? Are we hiding just now? Or, is this the natural place for two unknowns to come together, away from the others, inside the ruins of a previous life? Is living life behind oneself a form of hiding? Hiding implies persecution. But who follows me?

Who tracks my steps?

The delicate vulnerability of this young woman keeps me from acting on the most brutish desire, a primordial animal instinct residing in my brainstem. I remain docile as I retake her hand and filter the night through my senses. Time becomes immemorial, or maybe the night just keeps on living.

The roar,

not the river,

the roar inside.

This is the time to hold the bridle. This is the moment to drive the chariot into the river. Without words, I lift her from the ground and escort her out of the ruin. I walk ahead of her, retracing our steps back to the village. And feeling every stone on the path, I lead her out of my world,

out of my reach,

into her sovereign night.

—Will you be hungry tomorrow night?

—The animal in me will.

The old sister

She went out again. The idiot thinks I cannot tell. I can tell, yes I can. And all these comings and goings for nothing. No man to speak of. I don't have one either. But I don't go out in the middle of the night like she does. Who cares? I do. No, I really don't. As long as she's awake tomorrow.

She comes. Close, close my eyes. What's the smell? She must have stepped on a dead animal. Horrible! Why do I? Why do I let her? The blood between us, that's all. Could shut the door on her, kick her out. The blood, damn the blood. *La Petite* has my blood but she's no trouble. Does as needed, and happy too.

Not moving, I'm not. Let her think I'm asleep. And she does like before, goes to bed for a few hours saying nothing about her walking around. If she sells it, her cunt, she gives me no part of the money. That'll be the day.

A long day tomorrow. All the way to Grasse, and back again. They don't buy much there. It smells pretty but no cheese moving. Maybe they want to eat roses. Cheese is rotten, some of it. The smell, maybe the smell turns them off. And she'll have to be awake, like we have to be pretty. Not her, she doesn't care. But I do.

My short shirt, tight. The tights, tight. Show crotch. The hair, flow, flow, the air to fluff it. With my smile then, who knows? It may happen. The women don't look, or they do but pretend not. The men, yes, they look. Buy some cheese? Men in Grasse no different from men in Breil, mules, dogs at best. All they do is look or plainly ask for a piece of it. Nothing in between, no courting, the beasts.

And I know she'll nod, keep her eyes open for only a few, then turn all weird and fall asleep on the rug. Men don't look at her, why would they? She all strange and mousy looking. I wonder what she finds at night? There are no men at night. Not normal what she does, I think.

That's what school does. Gives you ideas and then you go around acting strange as if you knew something. She learned something, maybe, but what good comes out? Still selling cheese and no man. And now walking at night, looking for trouble. I don't know what's to learn at night but it isn't good. I don't stop her because she'll run away. She's hard-headed like that. Better to let her be.

She doesn't stop at the bathroom, straight to bed. Covers herself quick and pretends to sleep. Why pretend? She doesn't know I'm awake. No man for her, I'm sure because she didn't go to the bathroom to clean her thing. There's no man. But she does smell weird, rotten.

Bright and early I start packing and she's still asleep. Three hours to Grasse with traffic and all. She looks dead but we need to go. *La Petite* moves fast and we're almost finished packing when she starts coming to the world. She will carry the night with her all day, her eyes look that way. For lunch I throw some meat and bread in a basket and look for wine. No wine. There was wine before, no wine now. Did she drink it? No, she doesn't touch wine.

Cannot do this forever. Do it for *La Petite* but not for her. I know she wouldn't mind going away, she doesn't care about the sister crap. Sometimes I wonder why she stays. Maybe fear. Like, what's the point on trying to sell cheese when half-dead? She has no money and she isn't pretty. Maybe that.

We arrive in Grasse and take our spot. The old woman selling tomatoes is already open and people start to come around. We set the stand, *La Petite* helping more than her. She looks more dead than usual, like her eyes are looking far. I wait and say nothing, just watch her be. Not even the Roquefort cheese covers her smell. She stepped on something, or she's rotting herself. I'll ask her but I know she won't talk. She'll say nothing.

I try to sell the old cheese first, double the price, aged cheese, old, really. A woman wearing a rag on her head says the cheese isn't aged but old from lying around. I thank her for the information and raise her price. She pays. One man comes to look at the three of us, not at the cheese. I ask what he wants and he says nothing. He looks at her and asks if she's sick. Not sick, half-dead. He laughs but buys nothing and walks away. I watch him walk away.

Will die one day, I know, but better not be selling cheese. This I do now, and let them be part of it, both of them. But when that man comes my way there'll be no holding me back. There'll be a house, and room to hang my clothes right, and a dog, yes, I could feed one of my own. *La Petite* could come to visit, but Nadya won't, I know. She'll be out there, at night, still looking for I don't know what. He could be right here in Grasse, my man, not buying cheese but maybe walking by. I look at all of them just in case.

What a day this day. She has fallen asleep twenty times, at least, and no explanation yet. Are you sickly? Nothing, nothing. Did you sleep fine? Like a bell. Want to go in the truck to put your head down? No, no. And I know she lies. She thinks I don't know, but I do. Maybe the next night I just wait for her wired up with the lights on and everything. That'll be a good way to show her. What for? She would walk away, the knucklehead.

We make it to the end. Most stands closed now, we're not last but close. Nadya seems to come alive, closer to the night, I guess. Cheeses aging by the minute and we tuck them into plastic bags and boxes. On the road back to Saorge I ask her what's the matter. Nothing. I knew she'd say that. *La Petite* sings songs and I forget all about the day. No man today, like no man yesterday, or the day before.

The one-armed man

The path climbs up the mountain, dusty now, and I see a good portion until it bends away. When he descends. Will he descend? Yes, he has to come down from that ruin at some point, the criminal, I will see him at a distance, giving me enough time to be ready. Ready for what, I do not know, but I will be ready. From behind this cypress, long, like its shadow, the monastery behind me, I know I could strike first. Only one arm, that is all I need as long as I strike first.

What would the Franciscans say? He was a peaceful man, Francis or Francesco, but he never saw the likes of this stinking creature. Regardless, Francis did not build the monastery; he was dead long before. But it does not hurt to have the presence of his order backing me. I feel bolder, less frightened.

He needs to make his way down in the first part of the day. I imagine he will come down the path no later than noon. But what if he decides to come later, at four, or even at six? No, he has no food and the hunger will bring him out. Unless all he eats are roots and grasses. Then he would roam around the ruin and eat like a cow. His stomach would not resist such a thing. He could catch a bird, or a chamois. Without a gun, I doubt it. Does he have a gun? How can I be sure he does not have a gun?

I can wait. I can wait all day if necessary. My arm does not mind, the dead one, but the other one may grow crazy with anticipation. My eyes can sustain the vigil for most of the day. But what if he comes very late, and I get tired of waiting, would I be quick enough to strike first? I think I have enough time to prepare once I see him around the bend. But if a question burrs into my brain, distracting me, what then? That would be terrible, he could advance and take me down, even kill me.

He wants to kill me, most certainly. He could have killed me yesterday but he did not. I wonder if he really wants to kill me. Maybe he wants to kill me as much as I want to kill him. But I would not want to kill him unless I knew he is determined to kill me first. How could I know that? If I wait for him to strike first, I would be sure that he intends on killing me. But then it could be too late. I need to strike first, even if I am not completely sure of his intentions. If I do not react to his attack in time, he could definitely kill me. I would then be certain—and dead. But if I strike first, and kill him, would that make me a murderer? If I cannot prove that I acted in self-defense my attack would be a murderous one. I am not a murderer; I do not think I am. But how do I know for sure if I had never defended myself from someone who was about to attack me?

What if I simply hide? Instead of confronting him when he descends, I could just let him walk by. That is entirely possible. But who is to guarantee that I will not come across him when he returns to the ruin? He would then think that I am trying to ambush him, to cut his escape. That would provoke him to violence, or maybe he would just run away in another direction. The problem is that he could return to the ruin following a different path. I could wait for him all day behind this cypress, while he makes his way to the ruin rounding the opposite side of the village. He would only do that if he wanted to avoid me. But he does not know I am hiding from him this moment. He could imagine that I would wait for him somewhere after what happened yesterday, but not at this very time, in this very spot next to the monastery. He may believe the monastery is a safe place. Not today, maybe not even when the Franciscans were here. He could not tell what I want to do, but neither can I.

The sweat now. Oh, no! Pouring out of my forehead, cascading over my eyes. If I use my right arm to wipe the sweat off my forehead I would be defenseless. I need the one good arm I have to defend myself. I could shake my head to get rid of the sweat but that would not work well, plus it could give my position away. Perhaps, if I do a very quick gesture, wiping the sweat away in the fraction of a second, I can keep my guard up and be ready for his attack. But I am tense, the sweating will continue. I would need to wipe it off over and over again, and adding those many fractions of a second will amount to complete surrender. I will not let my guard down, not when I am facing such a monster.

What time is it? I cannot hear the bells from here. How long have I been waiting? Nobody comes to the monastery and nobody walks down the path. Could it be that people in the village already know I am here waiting for the putrid monster, knowing there will be blood? I can hear my sweat pouring, but nothing else. This stillness is not normal. People out there could be holding their dogs and watching from a distance until the whole thing is over. But they would not have known he is coming down the path soon. Is he coming down the path soon? I think he is. Perhaps they can see me hiding from the angle in which they stand. If they see me, they would know I anticipate something, a frightening something. Can they see my sweat? Possibly not, but they would notice how I need to wipe my forehead continuously. I cannot wipe my forehead. The sweat will need to drip. But it is so still now, silent, only birds piercing the air with simple songs. So still, yes, but for how long?

The striped tunic

Not one, but one hundred swallows crisscrossing the sky. They have their reasons.

My wings do not arch that far.

Coming here was not like crossing the sky, but more like crossing over myself, or crossing over from a past that must have died by now. For the people in this village I have no history. They never heard the sound of my steps over the river rocks. But when I walk through the village, I hear my steps over rocks that came from the same river and now clad the narrow paths.

Most people turn their faces away from me. No one speaks to me. A child kicking a ball against the side of a church kicks it harder when I walk by. A hand closes a wooden shutter. At the entrance of an épicerie, right in the center of the village, a few men sit on a bench drinking beer. They greet me with indifference, as if they were bored or obligated to do the gesture. Their eyes seem scattered, tracking an unmentionable disaster, maybe tracking misery in the name of a common day. Among them I recognize the bearded man, I remember him clearly, now talking to the man next to him, now drinking out of a beer bottle,

now looking at me,

now smiling,

like a disconnected animal.

Inside the épicerie, rows of food propose experiences I have not had in some time. How long that time? Long enough. The attendant, a poisonous-looking man with a pointed goatee, seems perplexed to see me here, eating with my eyes, salivating through my fingers. He does not ask what I want; instead, he looks at me as if I were some revolting creature, the tunic, perhaps,

my feet.

The bearded man comes into the épicerie and grabs another bottle of beer. I feel his presence, the idiotic smile still hanging from his lips. He does not recognize me, or pretends not to. I wait for him to step outside and join his drinking partners. Then I turn towards the attendant and open my mouth to ask how much is a piece of cheese. No answer.

Stepping outside with the cavern of my mouth empty, I find the row of men still sitting on the hard wood, their eyes lifting, slightly, catching the truth of my thoughts as it drapes over my face,

the commonality of idiocy,

the sense of repudiation for their condition as *marginaux*.

I quicken my step, hoping to dodge their gazes and move past them when the heavy hand of a young man sitting at the edge of the bench lands on my shoulder and makes me turn. His face is broken: unequal eyes, an off-center nose, a mouth turned upside down, like the monsters children draw. He seems to smile. And with impetus, he pushes me in front of the other men sitting at the bench.

—Want a beer?

—Let him be.

—Sit here, come.

—What's with the tunic?

—Let him be.

—Money, got any money?

—Rotten smell.

—Let him be.

—Here, here, drink.

—Sit down.

—Where you come from?

—Go get a beer.

—No money, right?

—Are you alone?

—Stinks.

I stand in front of the mocking row, on the edge of this abyss. All the faces, the face. All the fears, the fear. Exposed, penetrated by their gazes, I feel the urge to talk, use words as swords. And I do.

—Which of you wants to wear my tunic?

—What? No, no.

—Which of you wants me to disrobe and don my tunic on you?

—Oh, no!

—So many of you. I know at least one of you is eager.

—Here, have a beer.

—You need the beer. You also need your friend to hold my shoulder and turn me around. You thought his face would scare me, his nose, his lips. Why do you exploit him? Because he looks deformed?

—You don't like the way I look?

—You look fine to me, but not to your friends, and they seem happy to use you.

—What are you saying?

—I'm saying that your friends take advantage of you.

—Who do you think you are?

—I'm just the reflection of your fear.

—I'm not afraid of you.

—No, you're afraid of yourself.

And with fluid movements, like a night-blooming flower, I grab the bottom edge of my striped tunic and pull it completely over my head. Without a shell I stand,

naked.

My bones seem to poke from inside, holding the transparent skin in place. My body speaks of hunger, of a tortured past, the dead one. Then silence descends on the row of men in front of my flesh.

I extend my arms and offer the tunic to the man with the deformed face. He steps back and returns to the edge of the bench, sits down, and spits on the ground. I turn toward the other men, my arms still holding my tunic like an offering, a cursed offering that none of them is willing to accept. I present them with their own fears, which they despise. They swallow beer and spit, they chew unintelligible words, and they poke each other with their elbows, while their eyes avoid mine.

Donning my tunic, I return to the unity of man and fear. I start walking back to the ruin in the company of my hunger. I take a different path, rounding the village on the opposite side from where I came. The birds are quiet.

The chirping man

he, he, he again with the tunic, coming here looking for food, didn't get any, and showing his balls like that, wouldn't touch that rag of his

stinks, more than me, I think, and gone again in front of my eyes, no money because he didn't get food, coming and going, coming and going, that's all he does, maybe the money is up at the ruin where he went with the thingy, oh, where's she? scared maybe, of him?

the boys are, nobody touched him, all the yes go grab him, yes scare him, but then nobody said a thing when he took off that rag, all scared now, and Fuckface here all bothered, the stench, maybe, no, no, something else

like he knows what we think, standing naked in front of the boys as if nothing, alone like that, he, he, what the fuck, he knows something about the boys, about me, Blood of Christ, no, beer, with the boys, beer

—you scared?

—I'm not touching that civet

—you scared?

—why don't you go get him?

—I've got no reason

no reason, other than getting his money and looking for the thingy, she may still be at the ruin, no, she's with her sisters, doing the cheese thing, if he can touch her why not me?

look at the boys, drinking as if nothing happened, so fucking scared they don't want to talk, and Fuckface drinking faster than anyone, they won't go up to the ruin alone, won't look for him, no, but he'll come again, he needs food, my meaty friends, he'll have them again, I know

—you said you know him?

—don't know him but drank with him

—got cozy with him?

—had a drink, then I got a fit, fell down

—maybe he jumped you when you were passed out

—don't think so

—you kind of smell like him

—better stink than have your face

—can make yours like mine

—drink and be brave

—his balls still tasty in your mouth

—drink and be brave

Fuckface gets up and stands in front of me, so drunk, and ugly, seems all brave now, when it doesn't count, not looking at him, no, better walk away, he'll get drunker and uglier

motherfucker swings at me, I dodge, he almost falls and turns around for another swing, the boys get off the bench and hold him, his mouth spits words, the fear, that's the fear

there was no fear before, but he, he, he came and now we are like this, drunker and fighting, Fuckface here more than any of us, he, he, he coming from nowhere and making us feel weird, like we have to peel that tunic off his body, he did, he did it himself and we choked, Blood of Christ

give me some Blood of Christ because the boys are now leaving, embarrassed I think, or just upset for having to blame Fuckface for their own fears, leave the bench, go leave the bench, it will go nowhere, will be here tomorrow, the beer too

motherfuckers go their own way, paths left and right, not up to the ruin, no, no, but to their dirty houses, the night will hunt them, the rag floating in front of their eyes, they fear him, I do, somewhat, Blood of Christ, fuck me

leave the bench and the boys, walk straight to my room, my little meaty friends will be there, open the door and get into the room, putrid smell, he, he, he smells, the air raunchy, the room sours when I enter, fuck me again, why you? why you? he's here inside my room, leaning against the wall, quiet, no, no, no, keep it to yourself, the tunic

Nadya

My older sister knows people who still live beyond Berghe, up in the hills. They rarely come down. I will need to hike up there if I really want to talk to them. A long walk, but if I start during the night I am certain to get there in the early morning. Maybe they can give me a ride back to Saorge after I talk to them. They need help with their farm, at least that is what they always say. He could go and live with them in exchange for labor. No one ever goes there, no one will ever see him. Would he like that arrangement? I do not know.

I will ask him to come with me to Berghe and talk to the clan. But I need to find him first. He must be somewhere in the village, he must be learning about the people while trying to stay invisible. But before I go around the village, letting people know that I am not with my sisters and fueling all sort of rumors, I must first go up to the ruin to make sure he is not there. He could be sleeping, or he could be completely invisible to me. After all, I have only seen him in the dark, what would he look like under the sun?

The path to the ruin starts next to the Franciscan monastery. They knew, the Franciscans, where to place their ghosts, on a promontory offering a commanding view of the village and the sinners who live and die here. The path then ascends gradually bordering abandoned terraces where someone grew something at some point. And just before reaching Sainte-Croix, at a bend on the path, the walls of the ruin stand in defiance. Daylight makes the decaying stones shine as golden nuggets. I have never seen it under this light, the brilliance of the reflected light hiding its ruinous reality. I prefer the night, when nothing ever looks better than what anything really is.

As I approach the bend in the path, three birds fly above

me chirping loudly. They do not know me, the birds, but they want to talk to me. Why else would they chirp in this desolate mountainside? Or maybe they just want to let him know that someone is coming. Can he talk to the birds? He is not Saint Francis.

My first instinct is to call him from outside the walls. But I do not know his name. Instead, I lean against the frame where a door once blocked the access. Trying to find him, I scan the first room and find it completely empty, as if nobody, not even him, had occupied the place in decades. This is not where I sat on the ground the other night; this is not where he held my hand. An abundance of light enters through the collapsed roof and bounces against the interior walls. So much light deforms my memory. An opening on the wall leads to another desecrated room where ivy climbs from the ground to the sky. No sign of his presence, only an old emptiness.

Could I be wrong? Could I have forgotten where we spoke about the night? No, even if these walls look different now, under the sun, I am certain of the path that brought me here. Yes, his hand led me through the dark night, but my steps carried me all the way. The more I look the less I find, forcing me to realize that he possesses nothing, that he has not altered the emptiness of this ruin. But he leaves a trace, a misty aroma that lingers vigilantly. Clearly animalic, earthy and woody, or something akin to the odor of a civet, this aroma fills the space and confirms that I am not mistaken.

The fragrant particles cross from my nose into my brain forming a clear imprint of his image. I follow his scent down the winding path all the way back to the village. The promise of finding him cancels my silent resentment for meandering the village in daylight. Concentrating in the evanescent trace, I turn corners and walk through plazas until I find myself in front of the épicerie. The bench where the young brutes sit and drink is uncommonly empty. They should be here, collapsing over each other, threatening the world for they in turn feel threatened. But they are not here. I sit on the bench and enjoy this rare moment of peace away from the eyes that sometimes hunt me. As I meditate, a strong wind descends from the mountain blowing leaves, making swallows fly with force, and dispersing the odorous trace. I try to find the lead again but all I smell is the aroma of turmeric, rosemary, and baked bread that emanates from the épicerie.

Where did his presence go? Where was his presence being? I do not know who he is or what brought him here. But I want to hold him. I need to feed him. With so little to remember about him, how could I keep him present? The scent, I must follow his scent and find his presence somewhere in the village. The tomcats would help me, if they knew.

I explore each of the paths that lead away from the épicerie in search of his trace. One smells like mildew, another like burnt wood, yet another like danger. I sit and wait, knowing his presence will come to meet me like it did the first night I fed him. Finally, when the swallows seem to fly at ease, a change in the breeze brings back the animal scent I must follow.

With care not to lose the trace again, I walk slowly into the oldest part of the village where buildings hang over each other and paths barely know if it is day or night. I enter a shadowy path, a tunnel of sorts, surrounded by several wooden doors and a few small wooden windows punctuating the stone building walls.

—Come inside.

—What?

—Come inside.

I follow the voice of the bearded creature I detest and come inside a desecrated room where the scent confirms the presence of the hands that held me. Opposites they are, dirty hands of the bearded creature and his holding hands.

Polyphony

Her face in the tortured light of this filthy room shines,
    the light I need,
and my hand, her hand, comes to me in the daylight.

he, he, he, crazy for the thingy, here inside my room, this moment, like I always wanted, to have her close, to touch her, not touching her now but I'll try, give him Blood of Christ

This is his place, the filthy bastard always trying to get near me, to touch me, to take advantage of an innocent moment, leaning against me with his dirty hands.

She finds me here, somehow, looking for me when I am not looking for her. Just when I intend to learn about this man's fears, she materializes inside this room, so dark. Without time to drink his wine, to drive my questions through him,
    she finds me.

stinky bastard and the thingy, get them both, get Blood of Christ, make him drink, drunk, drunk, make him drunk, get his money, not the tunic, and then she all sweet like that

Why is he here? Why is he standing in the middle of this filthy room talking to this disgusting creature? Does he know him? Should I run away?

Her eyes show fear. This moment, an aberration, may linger in her memory. But hers is not the fear I am after, his and his kind, and those who persecute me.

—Blood of Christ, drink it

Standing there, in front of these two men, holding a glass of wine like a dead bird. This is not my night, it is dark inside this room, but this is not my night.

—drink it, you too, drink it, drink it

I return to my unity, the fear now enveloping my body like a shell, inside is all of me, not different from who I was in the days that died, or when, the past,

the past,

lived a life that escapes me.

—I don't want your wine, like I don't want you touching me.

better wait, he spits the Blood of Christ, motherfucker, I wouldn't touch him, no, no, no, the thingy, yes, wait until he goes away, maybe I can touch her then, but the money, he'll take the money with him, make him drink

This is not her night. She comes to this dark room from daylight, looking for me. She does not fear me. She seems pure that way. In front of her I cannot devour the mind of this creature. My instincts need restraint,

a shackle,

a limit,

fear can wait.

He looks into the glass of wine as if looking into a dead sea. He then sets the glass on the ground. He seems calm now, reflective, unscathed by the sickly air in this dark room. I prefer the real night and the open air in his ruin.

—Blood of Christ, here, here, drink some

—Don't touch her.

—I, I, I touch nothing

—Show me your hands.

—my hands

—Show me your hands.

With a firm grip I grab both of his hands. I interlace my fingers with his and bring his hands in front of his face. I bend them and he kneels down in pain.

—fuck me

—Don't touch her.

—Blood of Christ!

What am I witnessing? He held my hand in a different way. I did not fear him. But the same hands bring this creature to prostration. No sense in daylight, only conflict. I move towards the door away from the battle.

no, no, no, will not touch her now, he may kill me, stinking motherfucker may kill me, and no money yet, nothing, she moving away too, the thingy, for once inside this room and now running away from me, from him, no, from me

The roar of the river reaches my mind. The dull sound of water over water over stones. The same as it was, the same as today. And with the roar, the sense of a dying past that slides numbingly away from me. Her hand gives me a sense of being, his hands a sense of futility. From one hand to another,

being,

in her night a restful water,

in his room a tumultuous monster.

my friends, the meaty ones, run away from him, run away, I eat you, yes, but he'll kill you and not eat you, run away

—Nadya

—Not in the day.

—Nadya

—Tonight, come, I'll feed you.

—The roar Nadya.

—I only hear the river.

1st Middle-Entry

The old sister

One thing is to sneak out at night, like I care, but not coming back and leaving me and *La Petite* to do all the work is something else. I'll make her do all the cleaning, from now on she will. But what could she be doing? Men don't want her. Last few days she's been weirder. Can she be weirder? Yes she can. And now gone, doing I don't know what. I'd go out and find her right now if it wasn't for me having to go to La Brigue. Snotty people there, think they're royalty or something there.

We pack it all, *La Petite* and I, and take the road up to La Brigue. More work for the two of us but we can do it. Soon as we get there I look around for Jules or Julien. I don't know exactly, but I have my eyes on him, him who buys nothing but always comes around. From Paris I think. And the wife with him and him flirting all the same. The only good thing in that stuck-up village—Jules, Julien.

When all is set up, table, tablecloth, fresh cheese up front, old cheese hidden behind, I tell *La Petite* I need to go back to Saorge. Not too many people now, she can do alone. I tell her not to let them handle the cheese, give them a tasting but only a little, count the money twice. She says she knows. Wants to know why I have to go. What else, to look for Nadya. She says makes no difference, all she does is sleep. True. But I sense Nadya isn't right.

She could be anywhere in the village. Maybe she ran into something last night, or got hurt. People will know if they saw her. They know everything, they know the three of us are alone. They don't see much of Nadya because she's with me working, or else sleeping at home. They don't see her in the day. She may see people at night, I think she does, but there can't be that many. Don't know where to go first. Maybe ask at the épicerie, everybody goes there. He buys no cheese from me, the bastard Didier, he gets his cheese elsewhere as if mine wasn't good. Him, with his goatee, runs the place like a bazaar. And all the drunks out there. Shame.

Nadya must be hiding, sure doesn't want to see me. She knows not to miss a day, like I tell her, you must come, look at *La Petite*, she doesn't fuss. But no Nadya today. That worries me, she never not come. Maybe a man? That must be. A man, what else?

I didn't hear her last night. She didn't try to be invisible like she would do. I heard nothing. And I heard nothing this morning. She didn't come. Is not that she can't care for herself, is that I don't know where she is. And here I worry like a mother, I guess I'm like a mother, being the oldest, not that I want to but who else if not me? Like our mother cared for us. Father? Who knows, so many men coming and going and all of us growing up together like bastard puppies. They still do that in Berghe. Don't want that anymore.

This village is small, so many paths, some dark, but most open to the sky. She can't hide, unless she goes to the mountain and that's that. Only a few live there, farms mostly, and I know she hates farming and people who farm. Not schooled enough she says. That's what I mean, give them schooling and they look down on you. She may be hiding from herself. Well girl, I'll find you.

Go everywhere and no Nadya. What about our house? She could be sleeping at the house. After going all night doing what not, she may be resting at the house. Maybe she waited for *La Petite* and I to go away to slip into the house. She's smart like that. I walk up there and get to the door. Don't open the door, just listen. Nothing. Then go in like a thief, quiet, making sure not to trip on boxes and stuff. And at her bed she is, Nadya. All dressed—shoes and all—but sleeping.

What's with this girl? Bet something wrong, the air maybe, because it smells different from this morning. I get close to her and the smell gets bigger, a rotten thing, like an animal when no one cares for it. Her face all sweet, sleeping like an angel, as if seeing something good. What's with this girl? All night out and some of the day too. She then looks like that, cozy. I mean, she skips work and comes back home looking cozy but smelling like a pissed cat.

Not waking her up, what for? She'll say she was here or there and I know that's not true. And me with nothing to do because she's too old to tie down and with her own mind already made up. A woman, girl is a woman. All schooled like she is will sure tell me a story like I'm a fool. No fool here, just worried she doesn't get hurt. Want her to live free, not lost like me growing up. Thing with growing up hippie is you're loose, but you can be lost. I'm going back to La Brigue, let her sleep. Don't know her story. Maybe a man, the mousy girl has a man. I better go back, Jules or Julien may be there and he'll flirt with me. I only have days, no nights to speak of.

The chirping man

fuck, fuck, the thingy and the money gone, had them all, feel weird now, like in the morning with no drink, both here and now gone, fuck me, cannot win, never can

not going after him, no, he seems to know something about me, about all of us, the way he treated Fuckface, he knew what to do, the way he waited for me in my own room, and then somehow pulling the thingy to this very room, something I have never been able to do

he, he, he knows even though he's not from around here, I wonder where from, a river rat who behaves like a king, motherfucker seems to know what we think, like I'm sure he knows I want his money, maybe a treasure hidden somewhere

the boys will help me, if we all come together we can trap him, like the rat he is, and get his money, I know where that ruin is, where I saw him hide with the thingy, we can take him by surprise in the middle of the night, but the boys now fear him, fuck, I fear him too

and that tunic of his, one stinky rag, he takes it off and shoves it in my face, I die, if he doesn't kill me that rag will, motherfucker is scary and stinky, never saw anyone like him, must come from North Africa, but he speaks well, like he knows how to use words, he's a learned bastard, not many like him around here, not even the mayor, that monkey, a drink, yes, another

come out and walk slowly to the épicerie, the bench is empty, the boys must be sleeping, maybe so scared they went drinking somewhere else, I need the boys, with them I dare to follow him, not alone, Didier trimming his goatee and looking after the épicerie as if nothing happens, yes, that goatee makes him like a real goat

—saw him?

—who?

—the man with the striped tunic.

—what about him?

—he came in here, didn't he?

—what about him?

—smells bad.

—so do you.

—fuck you Didier!

—what do you want?

—want to catch him.

—is he an animal?

—you saw him

—yes, I did

—scary, isn't he?

—he doesn't scare me

Didier will sell his soul to the devil, he only cares about making money, makes a lot of money on the boys, all that beer, he would rent his mother, I bet he would, and then acting as if he's above hippies like me and the boys, his mother was an old hippie, and loose too, daddy said she was, he knew her when they lived all together up in Berghe

makes no difference if he's scared or not, but if he says to the boys go get the man with the tunic, they will, kind of a guru or something, he is, and the drugs he puts out help, keeps them coming back, motherfucking guru

get out of this place and walk down to Fontan, the boys may be drinking down there, ashamed, that's what they are, all talk and then nothing, Fuckface the first one, will talk to them and get them greedy, go get his money I'll say, the man came here with money and he is hiding it, go get the money, money gets you beer and dope, beer and dope, beer and dope

seen them do crazy stuff to get money, like fuck that woman from Monaco, yes, Didier said to Fuckface to go and see about that woman, with his goatee pointing at people and telling them what to do, Fuckface comes back saying the woman is missing parts of her body, he did it anyway because she's from Monaco, they have money

they call me an animal, because of my little friends, but I grow them, I don't get them from the gutter, and on a good day, after dope, the boys come and want to taste my little friends, then it doesn't matter, that's how they are, all crazy like that

down the road to Fontan is the tunnel, I hate this tunnel, too long and too dark, I walk quickly to avoid cars coming through at the same time, the lights fuck me up, not many cars come up but once in the middle I cannot go anywhere, wait, wait before going into the tunnel, on the top entrance, and see nothing coming, now I start walking at a fast pace

hundred paces into it and a car shows its lights at the bottom entrance, fuck, keep walking and looking to the side, a dark wall of rocks, hope the car sees me, it does, I think, but drives in the middle of the road as if I'm not here, don't hit me motherfucker

move to the side and keep an eye on the coming lights, don't want to look but it comes towards me, lights will fuck me, try not to look, nowhere to hide, the car goes by fast with headlights glaring, catch the side of my eyes

fuck me

weird taste in the mouth, zigzag lines, body tense up

I've been here, I've been here, the fucking fit, my right arm growing and the mouth too small for my teeth, hell no, where am I going?

zigzag, zigzag

head goes down before the rest of me

The striped tunic

Behind the ruin, towards the mountain, I find a discarded aluminum basin that probably held feedstuff for pigs or sheep. This is perfect for water. Water first, then everything else. The remaining section of the roof tilts towards a gutter, and precisely under its downpour, I place the basin. I drag sufficient fallen rocks to improvise a fire pit inside the walls, a circular arrangement open on the top. Two large slices of purple slate placed flat on top of the rocks serve to make a grill. Roaming around the ruin I find a few pieces of wood to make my first fire,

fire kills,

fire spawns,

life,

and I need life back, not memories of past lives, but life undead.

The first fire glows and warms my body. One fire always leads to another, and this first one promises. I will need tools, I will need materials, I will need some help, and with time, this ruin can be my domain. Stepping outside and surveying the surrounding hills, I find numerous terraces carved into the mountain, now in disrepair after years and years of neglect, but a few houses stand, and their terrain shows workmanship. Not different from where I came from. Where do I come from? Not different from the place I left behind. But what did I really leave behind?

I decide to collect stones and start rebuilding the walls, and the more stones I gather, the more I seem to need. The roof needs new rafters in several places and a new layer of purple slate. The slate is available within the surrounding hills and terraces, the wood needs to be cut and fit into place, the ruin can stop being a ruin. But then, the place will become a place. And thinking these thoughts, I continue gathering stones. This will not resemble the hotel in Marrakech with its red door, the place where I tamed beasts and lost myself to an enchantress. Is that what really happened? Ignore these thoughts, keep on building.

One time,

one time just the other day,

one time, just when I thought I was entering a new world,

the fear of building a place for myself attacked my disposition and made me think this is no different place, you belong to no different world, the deed is done, and you are not to reside here, even if you want.

But when the roar of the river fades away, allowing for my naked thoughts to shine, those thoughts seem false to me. And I realize the sense of belonging arises from false expectations. I realize I entered a world that did not expect me. I understand my existence today depends on how I project myself. All this I understand. But arriving at this village, unannounced, creates tremendous confusion and speculation.

I want certainty. I want to say "this is my world." And looking around at the shambles scattered around me, I see a long path to belonging, a path that can only lead me to a tenuous place,

a leaf trembling,

the air responsible,

the impossibility.

My hands are tools of flesh, and I need iron tools to cut the wood and work the land. I can exchange the use of my hands for the use of tools. So I start exploring in search of possibilities. Following the dirt path, a few hundred meters beyond an abandoned church in the middle of the mountain, I come to a wooden sign nailed to a wooden stake where someone quotes Dostoyevsky, *"La beauté sauvera le monde."*

Further down the path a house stands surrounded by fields of hay. Three mules eat the hay. The muffled sound of powerful jaws churning hay reaches my ears. No other sound, human or otherwise, comes to greet me. Advancing slowly I reach the door to the house and find it slightly open. I pause, consider calling out, but decide to first step into the house. A house like any other, things everywhere, a black and white cat, covered by layers of stupor, sleeps in a corner. No human presence. I then retreat and stand outside of the door as if I had never been inside the house. I approach this house like I approach people, by the time I start asking questions, I have already been inside their heads,

    inside their uncomfortable minds,

    and the sense of exposure, leading to my,

    persecution,

    my fugue,

and the inevitable dying headway of my past. Waiting, then, I stand, in the middle of the silence. After a minute or two, I decide to make my presence known. I project my voice through the open door, *salut.*

Nothing.

The air swirls, the mules chew.

Nothing.

When I turn around and take a few steps away from the door, a figure materializes in front of me. A massive round figure,

    a man as a mountain,

    an albino asteroid,

without hair on his head, eyebrows, eyelids, or face. Skin, only white skin.

His smallish mouth disappears in the immensity of his face, a mouth that can only handle one word at a time. He stares at me with steel eyes and an impassive expression. Neither of us moves. We remain staring at each other until the cat comes out the door and brushes his whiskers hard against his ankles. He picks up the cat and continues to stare at me.

—*Salut.*

—*Salut.*

The acknowledgement of each other changes nothing. With the cat held in his arms, like a baby, the white immensity sustains his gaze, not a hostile one, but a daring gaze inviting me to enter his world at my own peril. I wrap my arms around my body, holding on to my tunic.

—You live here.

—I do.

—I need some tools.

—Yes.

—If I borrow tools from you I could pay you with my labor.

—Yes.

He remains motionless. The cat jumps from his arms and runs back inside the house. The mules chew. The air swirls around him and around me. And noticing a slight fluttering of his left eyelid, detecting a sense of uneasiness, not manifested in any other way, I walk closer to him and stand there in frontal observation. He takes three steps back and continues to look at me as he was doing before. No sign of what he may be thinking.

—I need to work the land.

—Good for the land.

—I also need to rebuild the ruin down the path.

—Good for the ruin.

—Do you have tools for that work?

—Yes.

No further words, just a presence, a white immobility floating over a thin layer of time. I consider walking around his rotund self and head for my ruin, I consider going back into his house and wait for him to follow me there, I consider staying where I am, trying to decipher his gaze. I consider all of this, but what I cannot consider, is that he may simply stand in front of me and observe as I observe him, and be content with that.

—What do you grow in these fields?

—Patience.

—You grow patient or patience?

—Patience.

—The mules seem very patient.

—They eat what I grow.

—You don't seem like a farmer.

—Neither do you.

The stern words emanate from his minuscule mouth with a strange cadence, a rhythm of sorts. Enigmatic in his whiteness, his words reveal nothing. Not the logic of a common man, his logic is not. And the silences… He is an artist of silence.

—Do you grow anything that can be consumed?

—Words.

—Can you really grow words on these fields?

—Yes.

—What do they taste like?

—Bitter, sometimes sweet.

—Do the mules eat words too?

He does not answer, instead, he points at the mules for me to see that in fact they are chewing on words, I presume. His gesture, the index finger extended gently like God in the Sistine Chapel, is a creative gesture. And once his nonverbal articulation ends, he remains in silence. He then lifts his head and points his chin towards the door of the house, urging me to enter. I hesitate, not knowing if he wants me to walk ahead of him or if I should wait for him to lead me there. Noticing my indecision, he keeps the chin elevated, still pointing, while his face expresses nothing. I start walking towards the door while he follows behind me. His elephantoid steps sound like a basso continuo, an overpowering rhythm threatening to crush me. Through the door I enter for the second time. And once inside, he offers me a chair while he collapses on the ground. No chair could support his immensity. Uncomfortable with the silence, I start talking.

—Can you hear the roar of the river?

—Yes.

—Can you hear the roar of the words?

—Yes.

—You're a poet.

—Yes.

The fat poet

And what am I to do when accosted by an intruder other than respond with a pure word. *Yes* is a pure word. So is *no*, although I prefer *yes*. He wants tools. For a noble cause, I suppose. Working the land is a noble cause, rebuilding a ruin could also be a noble cause. The act of working the land can be beautiful. Scaring the surface of the earth and sowing seeds in the wounds. And when the land refuses to give, when it becomes infertile, even that can be extremely beautiful. Working with stones and mortar, cutting wood, primordial tasks that will provide me with beautiful moments. I must welcome him.

But how can he tell I am a poet? What does he see in me? With no company other than a stubborn cat and pensive mules, and then fat as I am, rotund to be precise, a hairless albino. How can these be clues that I attempt to play with words in my dead hours?

As I look at him, sitting inside my house, a circle of words and associations turns over me. Many words, many.

decomposed

putrid   *cabalistic*

amnesic   *innocent*

occult   *symbolic*

wondrous   *dispossessed*

assassin

The circle of words will continue to spiral as long as I stay in silent contemplation. I could grab a few words, the real gems, and work them into a verse. But he would have already killed me by then—if the word *assassin* were more than a conjecture. Strangely, he seems to know something about me. The word *cabalistic* came for that reason, I suppose.

He can use my tools, the breast plough, the hay knife, the pitchfork; I would even lend him the mules. This he does not know yet, or does he? Regardless, if he turns the soil and builds a roof over his head, he would have created something. His vicinity will spurn words. People in the village will talk and accuse him of something. There will be words…

I wait for him to talk. He does not, and that puzzles me, for I expect to be the silent one. At ground level I notice the miserable state of his feet. Torn sandals, the skin of his feet hardened from continuous friction against stone, asphalt, and dirt. Feet that must have covered vast territories. And from them, a pungent aroma impales my nostrils, making me think of the word *civet*, the unctuous cat. The striped animal inside the striped tunic. I have not considered the word *civet* in a very long time. I am happy for the opportunity.

He asked me about the roar of the river. So far from here but still audible. And the word *roar* expands in my mind. A deep cry, a howl, an expression of excitement or anger, a feeling I cannot decipher but he wanted to convey, or maybe share with me. And then he asked about the roar of the words. He knows they roar at me, the words.

We both stay seated, he on the chair and I on the floor, while my cat runs from one corner of the room to another persecuting ghosts. For a moment I fear he will ask more questions. Maybe demand answers. For a moment he appears intent on stabbing my heart. Or so I fear. But in spite of those concerns, the word *sisyphean* comes into my mind. A melancholy of sorts, an endless search for unavailable answers. He comes searching for tools, wanting to work, to move mass against resistance, to build the unbuildable. The essence of revolving failure or eternal duty already in his words. This man is mythical, I can tell. If not, he must be a monster and a desecrator.

Sitting on the floor I ponder the meaning of his visit. *Death* comes to mind, also *rape*, the rape of my silence. His smell brings me to think of *penetrance*, while his dress, the striped tunic, brings me to a place where *sand* reigns supreme. And as I remain in close observation of this man, I realize I know very little about him. The sum of my knowledge amounts to nothing, and *nothingness* is a word I abhor.

The one-armed man

Yes, he must have taken the path on the other side of the village. He won this time. But I am not stopping here, I will find him, and next time, I will be better prepared. Even with my dead arm I can be menacing. Am I really menacing? I am not so sure, but I will appear that way to him. I must instigate fear. But, will he be afraid of a one-armed man? Yes, a hunting rifle held at eye level is a frightening proposition.

Abandoning my post, I head for my house where the hunting rifle leans against a wall in the living room. Can I still shoot after so many years away from the war? Can I wield the rifle with one arm, aim at the target, keep my head and hand steady, and then shoot? All of this with only one arm? Maybe I can. But I never tried shooting again after my arm died. My dead arm, always there. I have searched for another way of thinking about this dead arm. I got a medal for getting wounded in the war, after all. But the same answer emerges every time—a hanging burden.

A box of bullets deep inside the drawer of the bureau provides me with lethal lead. I will send you flying, little ones. The oily barrel seems clean and ready for its duty. The strap allows me to swing the rifle around my body and hang it from my right shoulder, the one attached to my good arm. I am ready.

Retracing my steps, I find the way around the monastery and start heading in the direction of the ruin. The criminal must be crouched inside the ruin, waiting for someone to rout him out. I am not certain what crime he committed, but it must be hideous. And if he is not a criminal but an ascetic, or an escapee from oppression? And if I kill him, would I be lifting him to the level of martyrdom? Unlikely, most unlikely.

He is not from any village in the Roya valley; that is clear. But where does he come from? Does it matter?

After several turns, the path opens up and allows for a clear view of the ruin in the distance. I look for any signs of activity, like smoke, or anyone moving around, and seeing nothing, I continue to advance gradually and with much care. The rifle feels heavy hanging from my right shoulder. At least it does not swing loose like my dead arm. Birds fly in the low sky making all sort of chirping noises. They surely know whether he is inside the ruin or not. Could I be a bird? No, not with this dead arm. How could I fly this way?

At a distance of about one hundred meters I stop and kneel on the ground. If I shoot a warning shot from this position he will know danger is imminent. If he comes out of the ruin to see who is coming, I could shoot him at once and avoid any confrontation. But how could I prove I shot him in self-defense? Him without a gun in his hands and with a bullet in his head. A cold-blooded murderer I would be. He is supposed to be the murderer, not me. His crime is murder. I am not sure, but that is what I think, and I must trust myself.

The path ascends slightly, undulates, and finally leads me to the door of the ruin, the same place where I stood once before. But this time I have a rifle and better knowledge of the fugitive. Is he a fugitive? Yes. What is he running from? He must be running away from something horrendous. Could he be a pilgrim heading for a sanctuary? A person in search of peace? No, I doubt that. Why not? Because I am not a person in search of peace. But how can my reality become his reality? Too many questions in my head confuse me.

After waiting for several minutes and hearing nothing but birds chirping, I venture inside the ruin with my rifle at eye level. Nothing moves, because nothing inside this ruin is capable of moving. A banged-up aluminum basin, stones arranged in different patterns, maybe forming a fire pit, and nothing more. The man in the striped tunic has cleared the ambit, he cannot respond to my intrusion. Searching for any clues confirming he is a formidable murderer, I come across the imprint of a small foot on the ground. This could be an old imprint, but at the same time, this could be the imprint of a victim, a young girl for certain, or maybe a child. He must have killed this child, this girl. Has he really, how do I know? There is no way of knowing, but what if he did, in fact, kill an innocent person?

If he is not inside the ruin, he must be somewhere around here. He needs food and drink. He will find it easier to remain incognito away from the village, walking these back trails. Only a handful of people come this way, hippies all of them. He can live in hiding for a long time. The nearest farm, on the eastern side of the slope, belongs to the fat albino. He may not be a real albino but he is whiter than anyone I have ever seen. Ghastly, and then completely hairless. What could they talk about? The fat albino does not talk much. I wonder if he even reads or speaks in full sentences. I must be careful; the fat albino did not get fat from eating what he grows on his farm. I wonder if he eats people.

As I head east, the sun begins to cast my shadow longer and longer. At this time of the year, the sun exposes angles I hate to consider, oblique, like the nature of this murderer and his fat accomplice. Yes, if they are together, the fat albino is certainly plotting with him. What else could they be doing together but engender evil? But how could they be planning if the albino cannot speak? I never knew the fat albino to be a criminal. But I could be wrong, deadly wrong. If they are together they must be sharing a common cause. Deadly, deadly.

Upon reaching the perimeter of the fat albino's farm, I come across three mules pasturing alone in complete disregard of my presence. They eat in unison, possessed or something. The farmhouse is only partially visible from this position. Moving at a very slow and quiet pace, I advance until I gain a full view of the farmhouse. Nothing moves, a seemingly placid rural picture. They are inside and they probably know I am coming for them. But how could they know I am here and armed? They know, evil always knows. If I shoot from the distance they will probably start shooting at me as well. Two against one, plus they are protected inside the house. I am alone and exposed. Then I will have to handle my rifle with tremendous speed. With only one good arm they will overtake me and kill me. No, I will not shoot right away; I will take them by surprise.

Step by step I make my way closer to the criminals. A few words reach my ears. They belong to the man in the tunic, I can tell. His speech sounds like a monologue, one word after the next, words without response. The fat albino must be agreeing with everything he says. There, there is his complicity, a broad acquiescence with the murderer. When I reach the door I stand like a soldier, armed, quiet, and ready to open fire. But sweat begins to form and drip from my forehead. A torrent of sweat blurs my vision. My right arm keeps a tight hold on the rifle while my left arm, the limp one, is incapable of reaching my forehead.

I must go in, alone, open fire and kill the criminals who are intent on killing me. I think I must go in now. But what if they are just having coffee, not plotting to hurt anyone, talking about the farm, the mules, or the weather? Not possible, why would they be hiding behind walls and talking? Only one of them talking because the other one, the fat albino must be already dead. If I stay outside and they find me, they will kill me for spying on them. If I go in they may kill me, two against one. I am taking my chances. I rush inside.

Polyphony

The same face, the same coward, now with a rifle. He fears I want to harm him

when harm,

to harm,

is not the thought I harbor. A violent entrance at a time when his largeness, right in front of me, has only started to understand my needs.

Violence, *violation*, of my domain. *Intrusion*, maybe the word *rape* applies again. He, with the rifle, who intrudes into my home and disrupts a moment of peace and contemplation. Me, sitting in the center of my space while trying to go beyond *nothingness*.

They do not move, my rifle pointing at them but they do not make a gesture. I can empty the barrel and fill their bodies with lead. But they do not react. The vagabond criminal certainly recognizes me, and just like the other day, he pretends to be calm and kind when I know his real intentions are brutal. The albino, he must be in complicity, sitting there as if presiding over the world.

—Put the rifle down.

—This time I'll kill you.

—I said, put the rifle down.

—*Down*, a relative word.

—What do you mean?

—He said "down," just like I did.

—You're both criminals.

—*Criminals*, an acidic word.

—Yes, both of you.

—What's the crime?

—You're escaping. I know you are. And he's helping you.

—*Nihilism.*

—I'll shoot you.

—What do you fear?

—I'm not afraid of you.

—*Fear*, a piercing word.

The hand tremor makes the rifle unsteady. Sweat pours all over his face making him blink repeatedly. He reminds me of so many others I have confronted, in the desert, later in Marrakech. The same determination to hurt,

to hurt me,

to establish their dominance, a pathetic need to uphold their frail selves. He points the rifle at me, and at the immobile fat man who means no harm.

Maybe they are saints. And if I were to shoot them, the bullets would go through their bodies without causing harm. But if I do not believe in God, how could I believe in saints? This must be fear, just like he says, and that is how they try to control me. The moment I reveal my weakness they will rise and attack me. They will, I know they will.

A rifle and sweat. Three men talking. *Coincidence.* I can balance the word *coincidence* on my fingers. An *i* at the very center, a delectable fulcrum. I at the center of two phenomenal creatures unknown to me until this very moment. Yes, *coincidence.*

He aims at the roof and fires the rifle twice. He is not capable of killing anyone. He thinks he can, but the fear takes a hold of him. The fat man does not move, with his eyes closed he enjoys something privately. This is when I stand and snatch the rifle out of his right hand,

and the sweat,

drips,

running down his face, tears maybe.

My dead arm hanging useless while he disarms me. Could have shot them both. Without the rifle I have no advantage.

Unarmed and confronting two criminals—I have no chances.
I could say a prayer. But I do not believe in God. Do I believe
in God? No, I never did.

The sound of ignited powder. An explosion. But the word
explosion lacks sophistication; brutes use it, easily found in
the newspaper. No, I prefer *cannonade*, or *hullabaloo*, or maybe
just a simple *blast*. I could ask him to fire again so we can all
listen with more care.

—Don't kill me.

—What makes you believe I want to kill you?

—Look at yourself. What else would you do?

—I'm not threatening you.

—*Threat*, a subjective word. *Subjective*, a threatening word.

—And you sitting there and speaking nonsense.

—Words make their own sense. I just mouth them.

—You are trying to confuse me.

—Yes.

—Who are the two of you? Who are you?

His question has merit. Who is this fat albino? I know he
will lend me his tools, but who is he really? I know who I am,
and where I come from, although parts of my past have died.
The real question is who he is. He, who hunts me, armed with
his rifle and displaced anger. But the fear, the fear gets in his
way.

A formidable spectacle. A one-armed fearful assassin
confronting a civet-smelling mystic. I get up from the floor
and stand between the two adversaries. I am the third entity
in this madness, an alternative being, extraneous, yet adroit.
Removing the rifle from the striped tunic's hands, I step aside
and allow the two rivals to gaze at each other. I give them a
word: *anon.*

That must be their secret code. That is how they talk to
each other. They will kill me now; I know they will. Maybe
not with my own rifle but in some other way. The door is still

open. If I make a quick move I could break free. The fat one will not catch me but he has the rifle.

—Why do you follow me?

—You're a criminal.

—What crime have I committed?

—I'm not sure, but it was hideous.

—You're not sure.

—I'm sure, but I don't know.

—You don't know.

—I don't.

—But you're sure.

—Yes, I'm sure you're a monster.

—*Monster*, a misconstrued word.

Quick, oh so quickly, the one-armed man bolts for the door leaving behind a trace of sweat. He rushes through the door with his left arm swaying like a pendulum. And in three or four seconds he disappears down the path. Fear propels him, gives him energy and speed and clouds his reasoning. I know his thoughts are disjointed because his biting words lack logic

or clarity,

or a sharp link with reality,

reality,

the very concept that he twists with self-referential accusations. A criminal, he says, me a criminal, an incompetent incubus perhaps, but not a criminal.

One man flees, running like a damned soul, the other one stands there looking perplexed. I aim the rifle at my cat and he starts batting it with his paws. The word *jazz* comes to my mind. A certain boogie-woogie, a swing of sorts, jiving, improvising connections between these two incongruous selves that came unannounced to my life. There is no peace when fluky accidents barge into my life. However, I welcome the chaos, for it spawns words, and words are my crop and my livelihood. I water them, I cultivate them, I herd them, I feed on them, words. My cat peaks into the barrel of the rifle. I am certain he sees a dark tunnel. If he could speak he would say *rats*.

2nd Middle-Entry

Nadya

Waking up in the middle of the day gives me a sense of gravity. My body feels heavy, as if saddled by criticism. My sister must have found me asleep; I am sure she unloaded terrible words on me. What else can weigh so much? This is daytime, she must be at a nearby plaza selling dead cheese and hoping for the hard hand, or the soft hand of a man. She wants me to be like her, with her limited view of this limited world. She lives for the day while marvel happens at night. I think I despise her.

This is not even our house. Squatting here like the hippies we are. Five years now, maybe even longer. I am sure one day we will be asked to leave, like the pariahs we are. But I am not waiting for that day—the time to go is now. I do not belong here. I feel nothing for her and very little for *La Petite*. Am I being cold? Maybe I am.

I will go to the ruin and join that man. He appeared in the middle of the night, took my hand, and did not hurt me. He also spoke very few words, and that means so much to me. I do not know where he comes from or what happened to him in the past. But he does not know me either. There is nothing to know. When I close my eyes to remember what happened to me in the past, all I see is a blurry mist.

I prepare to step out of this house forever. What I wear suffices. Maybe a piece of meat and bread for the night, maybe some wine. Things to consume—not to treasure. I consider writing a note to my older sister but the purpose fails me. There is nothing to say.

I join the path outside the house and follow it carelessly, meandering through the village. I hear the river, the roar he spoke about. Once I clear the monastery, several hundred meters up the path, after a torturous bend, the ruin arises as it did the day before. Maybe this is my house. Maybe this was always my house. The hands of a stranger first lead me here, but now I come on my own. Who else could belong here? A man who comes from nowhere, or someone like myself, someone who does not belong anywhere. I wonder how the days turn into nights inside this ruin. Would the nights be longer, deeper on this side of the mountain? Would there be cats?

As I enter the ruin a light air descends on me. The space seems diaphanous, immense. I recognize the golden walls, the insistent ivy and the old emptiness. There is nothing here, but at the same time there is so much. I imagine how the hours filter through the open windows and the collapsed roof. Destitute elements: the hours, the air. Bereft people: a man in a striped tunic and myself. That is why we come here, because there is nowhere else to go. Because nothing can claim us.

In a corner of the ruin where the sun fails to penetrate, I deposit the food I brought from my sisters' house. He will need the food tonight as he did the nights before. This time he will not venture out to find me. I will be here, in my house, in this ruin. He may ask where I come from, who am I leaving behind? And I will tell him about my sisters, that I never lived with them, that I only perched there. I will tell him I became a noctambule out of desperation. And we will share the braised lamb and the wine.

I wonder if my sisters will find fragments of my life scattered around the house. Maybe they will not even realize I no longer live there. I wonder how long would it take me to forget them. I can imagine living in the moment, uncertain as to where I lived before. Like in so many nights when I walk around the village in total awe, savoring fresh shadows, innocent of the previous day.

Many hours remain in this day. The light will keep me

company until the shadows return. And I know I need to sleep and wait for his arrival. He may come at any moment. If he finds me asleep, he will then turn around thinking my time has not yet come, that he needs to return at night. He will not wake me up, for he first saw me at night and knows *that* is my territory. Without windows or doors, open as this ruin stands, I feel I can sleep secure. I will leave many hours behind.

Nothing in this ruin resembles a bed. The ground is firm and cold. I could sleep on it for I can sleep on any ground that holds me. A wonderful feeling, to move to another ground, bringing with me nothing but myself. Piled against the wall across the room, a mound of dry straw reveals the empty imprint of a reclining body. He may have lay there himself. And as I get near, the undeniable aroma of the civet confirms this to be his bed. He lays his body on this mound of straw and abandons his own self, his past. I am not different; every time I lie down to sleep I also abandon something.

Settling down, aligning my body with the lengthy indentation on the straw bed, I prepare to let myself go. His aroma penetrates into my consciousness. I feel present, understood. From the margins of this village, from the margins of a clan with no lineage, from the sidelines of my simple life, a meaningless existence, I come to lie down next to his imprint, a presence I barely understand but feel close to my center. This is where I lie now because where I lay before was a mistake. This is where I want my head to rest. This is the time to surrender the day, the night is certain to return. What will come next, I do not know.

The chirping man

bruised and hurt, fucking fit, better get up before another car comes, a car will kill me, not the fits, try to walk fast down the tunnel but the head hurts so much and I see all blurry, blood on my chin, fuck me

outside the tunnel the sun shines, cannot see well, but keep walking all the way to Fontan, my head throbbing, broke something maybe, dirt and blood, make it to the bar, drop to the floor because of pain, one of the boys says I'm dying, motherfucker never seen a dead man, first thing they give me is Cognac, burns, then prop me up on a chair against a corner wall

a big laugh from Fuckface, sees himself in me, banged up, but he stays that way, ugly, not me, I'll get better, he knows that but needs to laugh, he still embarrassed

—went down on your mother?

—I'm not your brother

—what hit you?

—had a fit

—drink up then

—not this shit

ask the barman for Blood of Christ, he puts out a jug of bad wine, the boys still drinking beer, they don't believe, not me either but it does my body good, the more Blood of Christ the fewer fits, will make anyone a believer

—where's the man?

—don't ask if you're scared

—he's got something on you

—he's got something on Fuckface, saw him tremble?

—where's he at?

—up the mountain

—you know him
—like I said, had a drink with him
—he be fucking the albino up there

all talk, the boys, good at nothing but beer and talk, need them to come with me, to the ruin, cannot do it alone, money and the thingy waiting for me up there, the stinker can do me in but not if we all go together, but what if they also want the thingy? they're dogs

need to feel better, put down one glass after another till the throbbing goes away, cannot see well still, slide from the chair and come to rest on the floor, Fuckface kicks me hard on the ribs when the others aren't looking, no pain, Blood of Christ

The old sister

Isaw Nadya sleeping this morning and now nothing. Like I was thinking, come here one day and she'd be gone. After rushing back here to catch her before nighttime. No, she couldn't wait. *La Petite* seems bothered, maybe she thinks something bad happened to her. I tell her to unpack the boxes and put the bad cheese in the refrigerator to give it some life. What got to that girl?

This time is no good because she didn't wait. Gone all night and now during the day too. She thinks she's a grown girl, that's what she thinks, like she could make her mind up or something. Grown girl or not, she's not here. How far can she go? I mean, she's kind of mousy, not a runner. That's why I don't care when she steps out. Nowhere to go. But gone day and night. No, no. Where could she be?

Thing is, I don't want to go asking people. They already talk bad shit about us. As if we were weirder than the rest. I mean, we're just my mother's daughters, nothing else. If it weren't because of that, I'd have had a man already. But I have to find her, even if I have to ask around. Best place to start is Didier. He knows what happens in this village, he has a hand on all things, in your pocket too. He's not as smart as he thinks, looking at you like he's some kind of king or something. People go there because he gets them high. All that money not from selling tomatoes. I think dope, liquor for sure, but I think dope too. Got to see their eyes and their faces, those boys at the bench, high as kites, and all zombie-eyed at the same time.

I get to the épicerie and there's nobody outside at the bench, weird thing. Inside, Didier sitting with his feet up watching me like I'm an insect. I can cut his fucking goatee and throw it to the dogs, his dick, better. He says nothing, just moves his head and makes a face at me. I never come here, never come here.

—Seen Nadya?

—When?

—Today, seen her today?

—Don't you know where she is?

—No, I don't.

—You should, you're her sister.

—Have you seen her?

—I guess not, but I can find her if you want.

—How's that?

—I can send my dogs after her.

—What dogs?

—The boys, I mean.

He means it, because those boys are his dogs. Wagging their tails for dope. He sure would send them after her. I do believe it. If there's something in it for him he would. I hate to ask him about her, but who else? He sees everything and everybody, being here in the middle of the village. Sure he doesn't know where she is. He would've jumped like one of his dogs if he knew. Better to get out of here before he raises his leg to pee on me.

But what did I do for her to leave like that? Take care of her, I mean. Maybe the job, not the best I admit, the cheese stinks, but we get what we need. *La Petite* says nothing, she's happy. It all started with that night thing, the comings and goings. Maybe she's doped too, or there's something powerful in the dark. Can't be the girl has a man. The mousy little thing can't have a man. Me wearing tight pants and making my hair big and can't get one myself. No way. She can't have a man.

But how can she leave us like that? She said nothing, like me and *La Petite* counted for nothing. I don't know, maybe she got bitten by something. Got to find her. How can I not look for her everywhere? She's my mother's daughter too, my little weird sister.

Best thing is to walk every path, there aren't that many anyway, she could be in a corner, maybe down there in the dark passages, *Les diables bleus.* She's capable of falling asleep there, so dark there, I don't like it. I walk along the old fountain, water dripping so happily, before I head deep into the dark. After a few steps into *Les diables bleus,* I feel musty and cold. They say the moist on the walls is the devil's spit. I believe it. I stop walking, steady now, away from the walls. Nobody here, no Nadya, and I get out soon as soon.

She can be anywhere. At the sewer below the old castle, in the tunnel, down by the river, or maybe in Berghe. No, she wouldn't have gone up to Berghe by herself. We come from there but she never goes back. She doesn't like the old ways, dirty she says. The girl is like none I know. All by herself all the time. She doesn't behave normal. Goes around doing things and not talking, not to me, maybe to the cats at night.

She'll come back, who'd want her? I do, but nobody else is crazy about her. She could be like me, show what she's got, not that she's got much but still show it. And she always says no, not wearing that, too tight, not painting her face, and that's how she comes out looking like a wet mouse. She doesn't listen, me her older sister, and she won't listen. *La Petite,* she listens, she's pretty too, like me, kind of. The girl is herself, that's for sure, her very self. I think the world looks different to her. She's not in my world, she's in her own, weird though.

I need to find her. She can sleep all she wants, I don't care. And if she says no more cheese business that's fine with me too. Maybe she took a long walk and got lost. Maybe the day spooked her. Night will sure come soon, she'll come with the night. I need my little mouse.

The fat poet

He who seeps, he who rummages—polar opposites. I like them to be what they are. When the oozing man reaches the bottom of the hill, when his little figure makes a minuscule left turn, his arm swinging madly, still running fast, I feel a sense of ease, and the word *insect* comes to my mind. *In a sect*, an indoctrinated soul who knows very little but fears plenty. He shot the rifle, he actually opened fire, and there lies the proof of his fear. On the other hand, the man in the striped tunic seems to fear nothing. He came to my house, impromptu, to declare a need and a desire. He embodies a brazen soul. And that soul he wears in the form of a garment, a fermented tunic that reeks. To *reek*, what a powerful way to accomplish evidence.

The mules kick the air; they sense when people are out of sorts. I feed them poems, each straw a verse, each grain a word. Eating words makes them astute, perceptive. Their pensive eyes reveal nothing, as if they were ignorant quadrupeds. But they feel the fear, and they feel the audacity. Even when the flies come to molest them, they know the ones that mean it. I call my mules many words; *mistresses* comes to mind, although that is not truthful. *Doppelgängers* may be more accurate, for I eat hay when they eat words.

In front of me, this man who wants to use my tools, who could have killed the one-armed man, this man barely known to me from moments ago, made me, this man, a sort of accomplice. As such, I was accused of being a

criminallacrimalanimal

minimalluminal

lackadaisical

criticallexical

derelictradicalbeast

None of which suits me, for I think of myself only as a poet, and even that is a stretch. Regardless, what came to disturb my musings was this olfactory challenge of a man who had no problem watching how I sit on my own ground in contemplation.

Not knowing what else to do, I step outside and head directly toward the mules. I grab the pitching fork and pile a large amount of hay in front of their muzzle. Verses, paragraphs, words, all at the reach of their jaws. And I see how their eyes brighten as their brains munch on verbal stimulation. If men could eat this way we would not have so many nitwits, or not witty people, which is the same as nincompoops, common poop, excrement.

The striped tunic emerges from the house as if nothing had happened. He walks by my side on the way back to where he came from. An interesting semblance for a man supposed to be a criminal, if indeed that is what he is, something I am not sure about. This does not disturb me; I know his mind is troubled with the past. Upon reaching the first lace in the path, he turns around and fills his eyes with the image of my mules. He seems to take in more than a vision, life perhaps, and I hear him speak.

—We have a deal.

—Yes.

—Can I start tomorrow?

—Yes.

—What's your name?

300

—My name.

—Yes, what's your name?

—You can call me "Yes."

—Yes.

Sufficient for him, it seems, because he turns around and keeps walking away. Could I have used another word as my name? I am not so sure. I could have used *No* but that would have been a narcissistic attempt to appear mysterious, when in reality, I am more open than closed, and clearly more eager to become than to cease. No, not *No*.

At this intersection, between one man and the other, I feel compelled to exist, only for a moment, as a crux, a point where the fear of one man meets the needs of another. Being ample as I am, I contain them both. The one will return to borrow my tools and work my land, the other to accuse and find a screen to project his fears. Creation and destruction will coalesce in this very point. These ancient forces, violent and beautiful, come together in front of my mules and me creating a primal chaos, the true foundation of reality.

The striped tunic

When my feet land on the dirt path, the sound travels and bounces violently against the face of the mountain. The sun hits the same face,

echoless,

like a red glove,

in the late afternoon, without urgency, for the sun has the entire day to travel. And the rhythm of my steps descends on me like a mantra, hovering, numbing. The image of the fat poet sitting on the ground, grounded by his immensity, floats in front of my eyes. He has an ancient soul, I can tell, the kind of soul that fights fear with words. During the time before the time that died, during the past that belongs to the desert, I saw a few souls like his. All vanished now, dust, nothing more.

To survive in this village I need titans, poets and muses. I need to quiet the roar, to bury the non-existing past, I need a reason,

a reasonable,

believable,

reason,

the kind that stands on its own and shines in the dark. She could be that reason, a noctambulant reason. With the audacity to speak to a fugitive of his own making, but a fugitive nonetheless, empty of promises.

As I approach the ruin, the stones burst in the sunny afternoon, making the walls seem eternal. I will house my reason inside these walls. We can all live here, even the titans. Once I bring my steps to a halt, their echo evaporates and the only perceptible sound is the basso continuo of the waters, the fluid that led me to this village. That sound reverberates, ever so softly, ever so present. It travels through my ears and gradually inundates my brain, the roar.

Inside the ruin, the image of Nadya's recumbent body anoints me. She radiates peace, or a comfortable absence of consciousness, breathing quietly, barely perceptibly alive. I do not advance. Why destroy a myth when I need one the most. I simply observe her placidity, how the air swirls around her small body at a slow rate. No beast seems to call her, she owes nothing to world, and I am certain she bears no brunt.

Paralyzed, I prefer to turn into salt. My mind runs backward and forward, finding horrible moments in my dead past when I violated the silence. I stand here,

against my instincts,

arrested,

enduring the misty virginity of the moment. I will not violate this silence this time. I will not destroy the vulnerability inherent in her veiled sleep. Every muscle of my body contracts at once, the rigor nullifying the potential for movement, for annihilation. I claudicate.

Clouds traverse the open segment of sky framed by the standing walls. When daylight disappears, the moon follows the same journey as the clouds. The sun makes an impromptu entry and follows behind the moon.

Once again the clouds.

The cycle repeats itself unceasingly. I do not know for how many minutes, or for how many days. Salt grains stay close to each other, my gesture petrified. Tears would have carved a river on my face but I do not know how to cry. As a statue, I control my impetus, saving myself from myself.

I turn my back on Nadya and step out of the ruin. I think I touched my past, that uncontrollable self I considered utterly dead. But maybe it is only dormant, waiting for the auspicious moment to reemerge, like a virus lodged in my nerves, like the beast that keeps on beasting. Walk away, walk,

away,

walk,

away, from the desert and its sand, from the four orange trees, from people who died for no reason, from my own tunic. And once I reach a comfortable distance, I look back at the ruin and see that it still radiates, unbroken.

To survive in this village I will need to appease those who hunt me and those who despise the fat poet. I will need to disarm the trackers who will sniff for Nadya all the way to the ruin. The world outside the confines of the ruin does not concern me, but the people who hunger to intrude molest me. I know the oppressive openness of the desert and the liberating confinement of a courtyard, and the white magnetism of flowering orange trees. But what is the use in recalling, in resurrecting a past that keeps on dying faster every day? No, I will not look,

back,

behind,

before,

for there is nothing to learn from the hands of an unsung beast. Not the river, the river cannot be a beast, even with its relentless roar, the river is a path like any other dry path, it only cries too often, that is all.

Without realizing the passage of time, or the numerous steps I must have taken, I find myself at the entrance of the épicerie I visited before. The same man I saw then now stands behind a counter covered with crude comestibles comfortably pointing his obscene goatee in my direction. He seems to recognize me because his derisive expression is the same as last time I was here. Standing with certitude, my inaudible presence makes him shift from foot to foot, and visibly troubled, he opens his mouth to speak.

—If you don't see what you want I can always get it for you.

—How would you know if you can satisfy my needs if you haven't tried?

—Just tell me, what would you want?

—Nothing, you're the one who wants something from me.

—You don't seem to have much to offer.

—You're correct about that.

—So, what can I get you?

—Nothing, I said.

—What are you doing in my store then?

—The same as you, breathing.

When he speaks, he moves his head in circles. His goatee making ellipses in the air designed to intimidate and exert control over his interlocutor. He exudes a visceral malefaction, a sense of uneasiness, ancient animal instincts to crucify his prey. And without wanting, he speaks some more.

—You took residence up in the mountain.

—The last time I resided anywhere is now a dead time.

—I mean, you're squatting in a ruin up there.

—No, I'm here right now.

—Yes, you're the one, the boys are afraid of you.

—Afraid?

—Yes, afraid.

—Why would anyone be afraid of me?

—You're not from here.

—Neither are you.

—My mother came here a long time ago.

—A hippie?

—Do you have a problem with hippies?

—No, but maybe you do.

—Maybe I have a problem with people like you.

—Are you afraid?

—Afraid of you?

—No, afraid of yourself.

—Why would I be afraid of myself?

—You shouldn't, but you certainly are.

He arches his back, blows air through his nose, and fixes his dark little eyes on me. I know he wants to bite my head off. The intensity of his stare indicates a disordered mind, or at best, a mind grappling with the concept of control. The bitterness brewing inside him spills all over, drenching his torso and pooling at his feet. He despises me, I can tell, but the longer I hold his stare, the greater the impact I will have on him. I will need to learn how to handle him, like a man who holds a poisonous snake, hissing, spitting venom.

—Why the ruin?

—Why not?

—Does it suit you?

—It suits me very well.

—Who are you planning to kill up there?

—I would only kill you, if you cared to come up.

—You don't really mean that.

—I always mean what I say.

—Is that a threat?

—No, an invitation.

The chirping man

Walk with them, what else, even if the pain says not to walk, I hear the pain but pay no attention, walk with the boys past the train station until we reach the bottom of the village, motherfucker archangel Michael trashing the dragon, like if nothing, guy has guts

boys and dogs behave the same, sniffing each other's asshole, have to hear them bark, they do bark, not much speaking like people, maybe after a few beers but those are barks too, not that I want to say much but I'm not into barking, have to see them pee, they even lift one leg

we reach the bench and the boys throw themselves as if landing on the moon, Fuckface the first to walk inside and talk to Didier, miserable, does more dope than the rest, he kind of hurts, or maybe his face makes him do stupid things, comes out smiling, silly dog he is, beer follows him and the boys cheer like they cheer Zidane or something, motherfucker Fuckface got to get killed, not doing it, not me

drink like the rest of them, like I'm tied to this bench, beer soothes the pain and makes me forget the fits, taste of blood still on my lips, banged something, maybe another tooth fell, fuck me and the fits, and fuck them all, could die here and none of them would care, dogs they are, and if not dogs, something lower, but I need them, now more than before if I want to go up there and get the money and the thingy

the pig, Didier, comes out again with the biggest grin on his face, as if he liked us, motherfucker does not care for nobody, only after money and dope, all he cares about, but he talks to the boys and makes them feel he's their daddy, boys so stupid they believe him, I need him right now to make them come with me up to the ruin take cash and give it to Didier, beer for all, he smiles some more, the drunker the best for him, boys don't think much to begin with, and when drunk they think even less, they drunk all the time so there's not much thinking going on, better that way, I drink my Blood of Christ with them but I think a little more, I do, like right now when I plan to bring them with me and take the man's money, they're pack animals, I may be a sick creature but I run in no pack

beer is long and the boys change their position on the bench, Fuckface always grabbing the middle, he drinks what's left in the glasses, motherfucker cannot have enough, same with dope, he cleans out, see his eyes now, sundowning, creature turns vile in a minute or two

he, he, he was here not long ago because Didier looks weird and talks about the man in the tunic, he spits, the goatee moving around, wonder what went wrong, maybe the smell, does not know about the money, no, no, maybe about the thingy, but I don't know if Didier likes girls, always alone or with the boys, doped often but no girls, wonder about the boys too

here's my moment, all stupid drunk now, more than me that is, pack animals, will make them do what I want, go up there and take it all, careful with Fuckface, careful, wait for them to finish the last round of beer and start talking

—got to get that motherfucker

—who you talking about?

—he with the stinking rag

—want a piece of ass?

—want his money

—he got some?

—motherfucker has plenty

—you cozy with him

—we can go get his money

—where's he at?

—round the monastery, up the mountain

Fuckface stays quiet, he scared so he says nothing, the other boys get excited about money, money is dope, they want dope, Didier pretends not to hear but his goatee points our way, cannot help it

—why don't you go and get him?

—you think so Didier?

—he's not from here and he carries around as if he belongs here.

—where's he from?

—I don't know, but he made fun of you yesterday.

—that was Fuckface

—and you too, he made fun of all of you, he placed his balls right in front of your face.

—no, in front of Fuckface

bolting from the middle of the bench, Fuckface runs into the épicerie and comes out with another beer, puts it down in one swig, motherfucker can drink, eyes looking like glass, his face like a fucking sewer

—go get him, let's go get him

—you all brave now?

—fuck you, let's go get him now

—but what are we going to do?

—we'll teach him something

—and if he gets buck-naked again?

—we'll crush his skull

Fuckface so fierce now, dope, he got some I bet, but that's better for me, the boys listen to him as he were a god or something, ugly motherfucker but no god to me, he trembles like a maniac, so angry with the tunic, yes, the man in the tunic showed him his balls but what about that, Fuckface so sensitive

boys drink a few more beers and push each other on the bench, they dribble saliva and talk, or the words are saliva, I don't know, animals, little beasts they are, not that I'm better but I have a purpose, getting the money and the thingy, now, now, now, this is the time, they crazy drunk and raving mad, for no reason but mad, up the mountain, got to get them up the mountain

—where's he at?

—the ruin past the monastery

—which ruin? many ruins up there.

—no, the one by the path

—he alone?

—motherfucker stinks, no one can get close

—what you give me if I beat him good?

—give you nothing, he did you wrong

boys get up, a pack of animals, they ready to lick and sniff each other, Fuckface, he so angry, raving mad, and dope pumping in his veins, Didier laughing from the door, he likes to see them crazed like this, he brings another round of beers and passes it to the boys, for the road he says, got to get a drink myself, keep the fits away, ask Didier for a beer, he says I got to pay, buy no dope from him so he treats me like that, no money, fuck me

he, he, he will be surprised, sure he's not expecting us, best way, surprise, get him with his hands on the money, the boys so drunk they don't care, Fuckface be happy just to get even, the others will follow, what else, around the monastery boys charge ahead, still hurting I fall behind, taste of blood, and my head about to burst

there, there, I see the place kind of lurking, the air quiet, murky even, we get close and the boys giggle, animals, they smell something, maybe their own pee, the fear I guess, all the arm swinging and silly gestures when they are scared, I know because they giggle like little girls, I track a step or two behind them, they don't mind me, to them I'm sick, hitting my head on the floor and spitting foam, little they know I'll get the money, wait, wait and see

reach the ruin and nobody around, kind of dead, or sad maybe, Fuckface crazy, bugged-eyed and all, first to peek inside but staying outside, motherfucker scared like the dog he is, other boys stay a step behind, top dog likes them there, all very quiet, for being so drunk they really quiet, alcohol and dope swirling making them brain stupid

Fuckface steps inside the ruin alone, boys stay outside guarding, guard dogs, comes out and talks to them, cannot hear what he says, goes back in again, boys look all crazed, foaming at the mouth, nervous, like a storm coming, then the barking starts, the animals trashing around and licking each other, senseless turning and pacing outside the door

a frenzy, a boy bites another, two others bite the biter, can see their teeth, bloody teeth, one boy peeks inside the ruin, gets bitten and dragged outside, the others massacre him, kicks with his feet, scratching, biting, one boy turns against the other, words sound like barking, sniffing and barking, biting, ripping the clothes, one dog vomits against the wall, gets punished by the other dogs, without a top dog they turn meaner, no sense, they bite and bark and show their teeth, the smaller one bleeds from his neck, broken, yips, bitten again on the leg, yips some more till he cannot yip any longer, mean dogs, drugged-up dogs, they human in form, that is all, they worst than animals, seen animals care, motherfuckers care for nothing

Fuckface won't come out, inside the ruin a wailing, a long piercing wailing

Didier

The animals, they are capable of anything. I dare them, I throw them a carrot, and they cannot resist. So little in their heads. Add drugs to the mix and I get what I get, a pack of dogs. Always demanding more drugs and more beer. I am sure if I did not provide what they need, someone else would. But Fuckface seemed particularly vicious today, yes, he can be dangerous when he gets so drunk. And what if they find that strange man who came into the shop, who knows? What if he gets hurt? He probably will. He is not from here so I doubt anyone will miss him. Not good for business though. The mayor will start with his idiotic campaign again, saying I instigate trouble. What does he care? He does not live in Saorge anyway. For him this is a business. We are not different, I guess. What if he makes me get rid of the bench? That bench has been right there on the sidewalk for as long as I can remember. Yes, it is village property, the sidewalk is, so the mayor can have the bench removed. That will cost me. Yes, that will cost me. The mayor and the penitents can blame whatever stupidity the dogs do on my épicerie and on the bench. Black, white, or red penitents. They are all the same. Oh, that will cost me! That is the problem with the dogs. I make money on their vices but they can turn around and bite me.

An animal behaves like a brute, a drugged animal like a beast. And like the beasts they are, the dogs will go after prey. I am certain they will hunt that weird man wearing the striped tunic. They will draw blood. I do not want that blood. The blood will cost me.

I need to go after them. There is no voice of reason in that pack. Drunk as they left they are bound to cause harm. Pack animals, they follow Fuckface, their top-dog, that vicious dog.

If I find them they will listen to me, I think. At the end, I am the one who gets them high. But these dogs can bite the hand that feeds them, the hand that dopes them. A bunch of hippie kids with no sense. We are not the same stock. At least I know where I come from. My mother had a reason to be who she was. These animals have nothing. They live a life that does not belong to them. They think dope and mayhem makes them *marginaux.* Idiotic animals good to milk for money, that is what they are.

Am I going after them? Am I following them up the hill? What a stupid idea—to follow a pack of animals. A revolting pack of hippie idiots, their money dripping from their rabid gums and teeth like saliva. Dirty money. But is there any other kind? No, there is not. So I venture uphill, around the monastery and into the backcountry. If I follow their smell, the trace of their drooling, I am certain to find them. I may be a hound dog, sniffing for money, but I do not run in packs.

These abandoned terraces on the mountainside could produce the best weed. But exposed like they are, the mayor will be the first one to blow the whistle. I am sure he would be happy to grow a little weed himself, but he never will, and I never will as long as he is the mayor. I am not partnering with him, no I will not. He is not from this village, and he considers my kind as filth, even when he owes his post to hippies of all sorts, the new and the old. Fuck the mayor! And fuck him for meddling with my money.

Over the hill, in the distance, a half-collapsed farmhouse stands alone by the side of the path. I recognize the place; some hippies lived there years ago. Nothing remains now, only ruined walls. Initially I take a different path that takes me north towards a farm with pasturing white horses. But an eerie feeling burrs inside my brain and makes me turn around and walk straight towards the ruin.

As I approach, the air turns acrid, a strong smell of shit

overwhelms me. The dogs must be nearby. An unreal silence sits in the open doorways and windows of the ruin. A sudden urge to vomit kicks me at the base of my stomach. I bend over to relieve myself when I hear a light whimper coming from inside the ruin. A melancholic cry oozes and morphs with the decomposed smell. This is not the sound of a dog. A rabid dog barks, it does not moan.

When I step inside the ruin I see a broken, half-naked body. A woman lies on the ground in a posture as unnatural as her moaning. She is hurt. Look at the blood dripping between her legs. I know this woman, Nadya, the sister of the cheese monger. What is she doing in this barren place? She does not seem to realize that I entered the ruin, her moaning continues, like a mantra, clawing life I suppose. The dogs came by, I can sense it, they did their deed and they are now gone. Did they find the man with the striped tunic? I guess they found her instead. The animals had to brutalize her.

I can walk away right now and ignore ever coming here, ever seeing this girl in this condition. Getting engaged in this mess will foster questions and drive clients away. A healthy distance from all of this will serve me better. And if I threaten the dogs with telling about this, they will shit. Or they may sacrifice one of the pack and rat on him. Animals. If Fuckface did this, no one would tell. They fear him, the most rabid of all.

My knee hits the ground next to where Nadya lies and my proximity makes her turn away and moan even louder. Yes, she is the middle of the three sisters. We all come from the same clan, from Berghe, and who knows what really happened among our parents. She could be my sister, or my niece. Better left unknown. I turn her around and grab her hands between mine. She whimpers, no words, nothing intelligible. I pull her skirt down and cover her bare thighs, grab her by the waist, and lift her bent body over my shoulders. Carrying the weight of ignominy I descend to the village. Vicious animals!

The one-armed man

There he goes with a body of evidence on his shoulders. I never knew Didier to be a savior but he never ceases to surprise me. That is the first body, I am certain there will be many more with that criminal meandering through the village. I wonder how that stinking creature killed her. By breaking her neck; that is the kind of murderer he is. A cold monster. But why is Didier walking so slowly? He seems to struggle under the body. She cannot weigh that much. The burden of infamy—that is what weighs him down.

But what if Didier is an accomplice? Like the albino, he could be aligned with that wicked creature. They work together, they kill together. He could be removing the body so the *gendarmes* will not find it. Or maybe they will perform some strange ritual with her body. Satanic, I am sure. I must follow him to see what he will do. Careful, careful, if he sees that I am following him he will change directions to throw me off. Best to leave a safe distance between us, even if I risk losing his tracks. He will not turn around to look at me, but he could hear my steps approaching him. I better slow down and let him move ahead of me. That way he will carry on with his heinous act thinking that nobody knows what he is doing. I know what he is doing. Yes, I know because why else would he be moving a corpse from one place to another as if nothing mattered? More exactly, he pretends like nothing matters because that way, if someone confronts him, he would seem like the guiltless Samaritan he is not.

Didier does not like me. He always looks at me with suspicion, as if I knew something that would somehow incriminate him. I never knew what I was supposed to know. I thought he despised my dead arm but now it all comes clear to me. He must know I am capable of unmasking his true nature, a murderer hiding behind that pretentious goatee. He must have suspected I would follow him, on a day like today, while he would be carrying out his criminal act. He knew all along, and he was right.

Wait, why does he stop at the *lavoir*? Does he want to kill her again? After his partner broke her neck he now wants to drown her. But there is blood dripping from her body. I see it splashed all over the ground and on the side of the *lavoir*. Maybe he wants to cover his trail. The redness will wash away, streaming down the gutter until reaching the river where all traces will disappear. There is no end to his vileness.

And as Didier drops her into the water of the *lavoir*, she swings her arms and legs like a cat. Is she fighting from her death? This is trickery. She is not dead. My god, she is not dead! He may want people to believe he is rescuing her from drowning. He wants to fool everyone. How could that be when I know he is a killer? The murderous brute. But if Didier were the real killer, then the fat poet and the beast with the tunic would be exonerated. Not possible, that is simply not possible.

And now she calms down, she is not fighting him anymore. Standing on her own feet, she walks together with Didier down the path towards the épicerie. If she is completely alive, which she seems to be, at least from this point of view, she will not live much longer because the man in the tunic and the fat poet are certain to be waiting for them inside the épicerie. That is where the satanic ritual will take place. They will kill her once and for all. I may not be completely sure about that but I should call the *gendarme* right now. But he is never in the village. If I go into the épicerie and the ritual is already underway, if they are drinking her blood or brutalizing her, they would either kill me, or make me take part in the horrible atrocity. I cannot, I cannot be forced to join them. I know I can fight them, but without my rifle, my single arm would be useless against the three monsters. They will force me to do things to that woman that I have never dreamt of doing. Have I not dreamt of raping her? These intrusive thoughts again. No, I have not considered raping her. Only so slightly. I have thought of waiting for her in the shadows during one of her nighttime tours, and asking her to touch me. But rape, no, I never wanted to rape her.

They may be aware I am spying on them. Although I never saw the fat poet or the striped tunic go into the épicerie, they have to be there. Evil works in mysterious ways. I better leave before they come out and grab me. I do not want to be forced to do what I dream of doing.

Didier

Better to go into the épicerie now while there is nobody around, the bench is abandoned, and the path leading down from the church is empty. I lay the body on the floor and try to make her feel comfortable. She smiles. Why would she smile when she has been damaged? She smiles. Water, she must drink water. Maybe beer. No, not beer, I am sure the dogs had the smell of beer on their breath. Fuckface was certainly drunk. Fire and alcohol on his breath. Her shirt is torn and I see blood running down her right thigh. Animals. I wish them death, the very animals that fill my coffers.

She looks at me without saying a word. This gentle face I never saw in daytime. Neither in nighttime because that is my time to hide. Her chest heaves. A delicate layer of pale skin rises and then collapses. No tears. Not a single one.

Lifting her from that ruin makes me an accomplice, or a savior, or a *vautour*. I do not want to feast on her flesh, no, that is not what I want to do. She needs to get better and deny that anything happened. No boys, no dogs, just a malady, an indisposition. Without the involvement of the *gendarme*, or the idiot mayor, I am certain she will be ignored and I will be untouched.

She is in pain, I can tell. But that is not my doing, the animals, they messed her up. She is nothing to me as she is nothing to most people in Saorge. How can anyone relate to a noctambulant? And when she wails, I know the village will turn a deaf ear to her plight, to her misery. She comes from hippie stock and the strangeness that goes with that. I have seen numerous *marginaux* attack their own kind as if they wanted to dig the other person's pit. A tribe of boors we are, even when we pretend to care for nature and each other. No need to wait for the barbarians—we are here already.

With cotton rags I dry her blood as best I can while she remains still. Is she urging me? What a disturbed thought, but it entered my mind, it is mine to keep. She seems pleased that I attend to her misery and somehow she relaxes under my touch. I only wonder what memories will she form of this tragedy. Will she remember the faces; will she want to kill them? For how many years do people remember an aggressor? For how many lives do we keep on righting the wrong? But the truth is that she belongs to another sector of this old village and what is wrong with her does not concern me. Or, does it concern me deeply? She lies on the floor of my épicerie, bleeding and broken, impelling my life this very moment.

—Who did this to you?

—I didn't look at them.

—How much does it hurt?

—It hurts.

—Do you want me to call the *Samu*?

—No.

—Why not?

—I don't want my sisters to find out.

—What were you doing in that ruin?

—I don't really know.

Her chin drops when she gives that answer. Is it possible for her not to know? But who am I to judge when I sell drugs and alcohol to the very dogs that abused her? Am I as much an abuser as they are?

—Where's your older sister?

—Somewhere out there selling cheese.

—I can try to find her.

—No, don't.

—What do you want me to do?

—Nothing.

—Nothing?

—Just take me back to the ruin.

—Why?

—It feels right.

—You were abused there.

—Take me back.

I know Fuckface will not return to that place. He is a coward. He only boasts when he is drunk and when he faces weaker creatures. The dogs listen to him because they are a pathetic crowd. Between dope, alcohol, and idiocy, the dogs amount to very little. *Marginaux* among *marginaux*. That is what they are.

—I can drive you to Menton. You can see the doctor there.

—No, you don't need to do that. I want to return to the mountain.

—I just brought you from there.

—I know. Take me back.

So young and so serious. This dry and gentle face has a different take on the world. She fears nothing and hates nothing. Maybe that is why she avoids daytime with its repertoire of brutes and animals. I bet she finds nighttime more comfortable, more real. She knows better. I will carry her up to the ruin. I think she will wait there for that fetid creature, the one who scared Fuckface.

Once again I lift the tiny body and carry her to the ruin just before the abandoned church. I move fast to avoid people seeing me. Enough trouble already. The mayor would have a feast. He wants me out of business just because I make more money than him. He would love to see me involved with criminals. He already thinks I deal drugs, which I do. But that is not important now, she is important, she is important because she makes me do things I would have never done. Look at me, a Samaritan.

The fat poet

Consider the verb. Power accumulated over thousands of mouths, spoken over thousands of years. A universal force compressed within a few letters. When I say, *walk*, not a single man moves but a legion. When I say, *cry*, a diluvium falls. Herding verbs is a dangerous mission reserved only for the steady hand of a poet. What a tragic responsibility.

And he with the striped tunic proposes to work for me. He wants to move mass with his hands, he wants to till the land, and he wants to exchange his work for tools to work some more in his own corner of this mountain. He could have chosen to garner the force of a few verbs instead. But maybe he needs to exercise his body. His mind he exercises, a mystic he is.

Mystic. Is he really sorcerous or supernatural? Can he mediate between our lowly selves and a higher realness? I wonder if he even thinks of himself in those terms? Of course I can ask him, but to ask is such a brutal stockade, a momentous rape, an intrusion propelled by centennial inquiries. I cannot ask him. His answers will be useless, like when I ask my mules about their feelings, they only look at me wondering why do I bother with them. He is not a *mule*, a *mysle*, a *mustic*. A mystery he is.

mysterious mule

mystical mustique

momentous mediator

merde, merde, merde

I wonder in what realms has he lived? What deaths has he endured? No one ascends to these mountains from nowhere. And wearing a dress from the desert and a perfume from hell. I could ask him, but I already accepted I could not. He seems intent in forging his presence, residing even, in a place that was a place before, a ruin, an abandoned farm, ex libris territory. Perhaps he intends to inhabit an old self of his. Is he *libero, exlibraio, exliterati*, is he *terra libre, Librium*? Or is he a simple mound of broken bones?

Consider the noun. Is the noun a name? What is in a name? Does he have a name or does he go by his description? Has his name evolved, morphed, and turned into surprising versions of his original self. Has the act of naming defined him as an individual while killing his potential at the same time? What is his name? If I were to attach a name to what I see I would say *tunic*. More precisely, *striped tunic*. But that is only his surface. How to name his soul? Does he have a soul?

My mules know I am coming for them. Their eyes, usually focused on distant mounds of hay, turn my way and I sense their yearning—they want to go to school. I grab their bridles and start walking downhill towards the monastery. Behind me, the mules walk in silence. Their paucity of speech is not a sign of ignorance, but a sign of natural wisdom. They do not regurgitate words, like most humans, they consume words one blade at a time and then ponder. My mules are not mute, that is a moot issue.

Once in front of the monastery, I tie them to one of the cypresses standing on guard. This place allows them to hear people talk as they walk by. They need to learn words used by the masses. Sometimes, I think they like those words better than the ones I feed them. I saw them chew on the word "awesome" for a very long time. I cried. From this vantage point they can also see the entire village, and more importantly, they can hear the bells. The sound of the bells adds tonality and contrast to the sound of human speech helping them learn faster. There is no better school than this.

Like a caravan of a man, the man in the striped tunic arrives at the front of the monastery, unexpected, an abrupt presence that makes the mules stop chewing at once. I consider *caravan*, another beautiful word with an *a* at its fulcrum and wonder if this man has ever crossed deserts. Has he ever been in the center of a million sands? Does he know

sand   dune   dry   sand   air

striped   sand   tunic

a

sand   air   dune

sand   tunic   dune   striped   sand

intimately enough as to arrive with such determination? He regards me as if I were out of place in this part of the village, away from my farm and my house, lost to the observing eyes of my cat. He knows not, but he seems to know more than he should know. This man spawns words all around him.

—Your mules seem happy to be here.

—Yes.

—But you seem uncomfortable.

—Yes.

—Why do you bring them here?

—They need to come to school.

—The mules?

—Yes.

—What do they learn here?

—Common words.

—Like *croissant*?

—No, like *caravan*.

—I know about caravans.

—I thought you did.

—I know you thought so.

—Yes.

He continues his march forward, bearing left, leaving my mules and I in front of the monastery. Nothing palpable trails him, only a lingering rancid smell and a sense of impending doom that makes me think of the word *infamy*.

The striped tunic

I ascend, and with every step, the thunder of the waters, the tumultuous river, roars,

and roars,

through the middle,

of my brain,

and I wonder if my past is about to reach me in this very mountain, the dead past springing forward from the mouth of a lion to maul me, to drag me back to a time staked by four flowering orange trees. An impossibility, a sentence I reject as I reject wearing something other than my tunic. The river roars, my mind roars, we share the unsought task of carving through the minds of others.

And with every step I come closer to the dilapidated structure holding Nadya inside,

recumbent Nadya,

of the night. She seems to live in that tight space that radiates light between the sea of clouds and the heavy grayness hanging from above, an unbearable space, compromised and dissonant. She seems to belong to a race of others, and that incarnates her beauty.

I approach the somnolent ruin, redolent in the air that glides between the mountain peaks, later descending fast between my legs, around my head, making every flap of my striped tunic vibrate with the expectation of seeing her,

recumbent Nadya,

of my silence,

guarding the ambit until my arrival, fresh from gaining consciousness, emerging from a sleep where dreams do not dare. I do not see her. I see the walls bathed in golden light, or maybe the walls are made of gold and the light only reveals their face. I wonder.

But if light is what we believe in, those who suck from the common udder will find relief, and the more golden the light the better—for the warmth of a golden fleece is inevitably comforting. And my steady approach to the magnificent ruin proves to be a golden one. I see the glow, the reflective quality of myriad sand particles, not the desert, no, that is from my dying past, but the hard wall encasing Nadya. And I walk towards the entrance with some trepidation. She may see through me, like nobody else can, because in front of her I am vulnerable. I know what she will think, the way she may respond to my questions, even the temperature of her emotions. I know all of that without effort. But when she brought me food and wine that first night, she read my yearning. She intuited my vagabond nature, she guessed I came from the desert without realizing she possessed that knowledge.

A new encounter with the sublime night angel who knows about me, even if so little, but enough to disarm me, is about to happen. I know about her fears and motivations, her illusions worn as a solemn mask, her thirst for something other than the day. And the closer I get to the ruin, the stronger the wind blows,
    and a sense of infamy swirls around me like,
    the sound,
    of a fractured night,
    hunting me, leading me,
to the door of the ruin where I stop because the wind stops, to think of images I abhor, deserts I have burnt.

Small, bent over, Nadya's body lies on the floor in the corner of the room. When she hears my steps, she looks in my direction without seeing me. Her eyes, bright green before, now have the color of stagnant water. And she seems to be drowning, or crying. She closes her eyes and remains on the floor like a desecrated temple. When I kneel next to her I

remember the four orange trees dropping their white flowers
in March. I remember the courtyard, the dry desert air, and
the howling of the beast.

—Nadya, Nadya.

—I think I hear the river.

—Nadya.

—The roar is soft, a lullaby.

—What happened to you?

—Nothing happened. Just the day, the day happened to
me.

—You're hurt.

—Give me your hand.

—I know you're hurt.

—Just the day. Give me your hand. Let's wait for nighttime.

I do as she says, my hand grabs her hand, and I hear walls
crumbling around me, a demolition, a vast sadness chanting
in a thousand voices,

hooves over sand,

the slow crawl of a caravan,

oscillating words of dead bodies,

embalmed in Turkish tobacco,

in the fragrance of Atlas roses,

and dry air,

sieving through spaces I thought forever closed. And I hold
her hand knowing she faced something horrendous,

her face,

filled with void, tells me.

Nadya

He kneels next to me and asks questions I cannot answer. What happened to me? I barely know, like I barely know why people hurt each other in daylight. He takes my hand, as I asked him, and I am relieved to feel the coarse dryness of his skin. This man, a stranger, comes to my side selflessly, as opposed to the better-known man who laid his hand on me, his brutish body, his ignorance. I really do not know where he comes from, with his striped tunic and his strong bodily odor, but his presence calms me down and I can hug the ground inside these walls and try to forget the physical insult, the atrocity.

My body feels heavy, leaden, pulled down from beneath the earth, and my head needs to touch the ground, the skin of my forehead and my lips blending with the dirt. I open my mouth and my tongue licks the loose dirt, I chew on it, a mouthful of dirt. This is the soil I come from, the hurt comes from this soil, the brute lives on this soil, and this is the soil where he urinates.

With my eyes closed, I pretend it is nighttime. Even if the air is dry, lacking the humidity of dark hours, I keep my eyes shut and hold on to his hand. The territory of his hand consoles me like it did a few nights ago. I grab him tight, he does not complain. I bring his hand to my mouth and smear it with saliva and dirt. I lick his palm, the back of his hand, his fingers. My tongue paints them the color of earth, I suppose, for my eyes are shut and a conjured night fills my senses. I feel his breath close to my neck, warm, warming, uttering silence. And somehow I sense he knows what happened to me. He seems to realize the atrocity of the day. Without words we talk to each other, I with my earthy tongue, he with his leathery hands, his moist breath, his silence.

We remain close to each other for some time. An hour, a century. I do not know, but as I open my eyes the comfort of darkness surrounds me. The night of my mind wedged inside the night of these walls, the night inside these walls resting under the larger dome of the night outside. He is still sitting next to me on the bare ground. I cannot distinguish the features of his face in the thickness of this night. I bring my hand to his face and palpate the torn landscape. He allows me to feel every edge, every ravine, every mountain, and the boreholes of his vision. And when I touch his lips he begins to talk to me.

—Nadya, can you hear the river?

—The river was always there but I never listened.

—The night was always there but I never looked.

—I hear the river now.

—The river is the road that brought me to this village.

—The night brought me to you.

—Nadya, the night and the river are one.

We stay close to each other. His hand soothes me and I am able to imagine that nothing horrible happened to me. Sometimes we talk, other times we say nothing, if saying nothing is possible. The night feels eternal. If the night and the river are the same, as he says, then the river must be an ocean, an extensive body of water reaching far, like this night that keeps on going. So he must come from far away, oceans away. I can ask him where he comes from, yes, but his answer will shed light into this soft soothing night, shattering its perfection. No, I rather keep the darkness.

—Can you keep a secret?

—Secrets often escape.

—Never tell me where you come from.

—Why preserve the mystery?

—It's not the mystery I want to preserve, it's the night.

—Why preserve the night?

—It's soothing to me.

—You crave the longest night.

—Yes.

—I crave the longest river.

—You said they are the same.

—Yes, deliverance.

I lay down on the ground hoping for eternity. My body feels the earth, the taste still fresh in my mouth, how many flavors of clay? He lies down next to me without touching me. I feel his presence like I feel the world, a breathing world radiating warmth and comfort. For a moment I forget I exist, but then the hurt comes back like an unwanted memory. I try to quiet my mind by listening to the wind, the river. Writhing imperceptibly, like a worm, I bring my body closer to his, still without touching. I form an *S* close to the *S* of his body. I can hear his breath, a basso continuo flowing in and out of his lungs. And the rhythm calms me down.

—You said deliverance.

—I said deliverance.

—Do you need to escape?

—No, I escape nothing.

—Why the longest river then?

—Why the longest night?

I come even closer to him, my skin barely touching his striped tunic. I sense myriad fragrances. Are they coming from the tunic or is it his skin that oozes? I imagine he gathered the spirit of a thousand worlds, all interlaced, forming the strong essence I now perceive. I remain next to him, safeguarding that infinitesimal distance between us. The desire to blend with him invades me but I resist. He seems to respect me for he does not come any closer. Yes, he knows I am hurt.

—Nadya, what's the longest night?

—The one that never ends.

—Are you afraid of dawn?
—No, I'm afraid of people.
—You're not afraid of me, are you?
—You're not people.
—What am I, Nadya?
—All the nights, the night.

The old sister

A whole day and a whole night. She's never been away this long. Maybe she went to Berghe, but she would've told me. She doesn't like it there anyway. How can I go selling cheese if she doesn't show up? I can't send *La Petite* all alone. Where could Nadya be? Not that this village is that big. Maybe she's in someone's home, hiding from me. I will find her.

I stop preparing the cheese packages and tell *La Petite* to stay in the house in case Nadya comes back. If she comes back, she's not to let her go away again. I can trust her, *La Petite*, she's young but serious. Where to start asking? I don't know. Didier already said he could find her but he's not to trust. I could ask at the *Mairie* but they may ask in turn for my permit to sell cheese on the streets which I don't have. I can go around calling her name but people may think there's something wrong. Well, there's something wrong. Yes, I think there's something terribly wrong.

As I walk down the steep path from my doorway, this tall man I've seen before, the one with the limp arm, comes rushing uphill with a mad look on his face. I know him, but I don't know him. He comes straight at me like he wants to harass me. And when I try to pass by him, he moves from side to side blocking the way. I pretend I'm not bothered. Like he could be there all day and I wouldn't care. But then he starts talking and I know there's trouble.

—They're murderers.

—What do you say?

—They want to kill your daughter.

—I don't have a daughter.

—The young girl, the thin pale one.

—Nadya?

—I saw Didier carrying her body. They'll kill her.

—Who're you talking about?

—That monster and the albino.

—Who?

—I saw them conspiring, they want to kill me as well.

—What're you talking about?

—Evil monsters. They would've killed me if I didn't run away. Now they want to rape your daughter.

—I don't have a daughter.

This bugged-eyed man, drenched in sweat, tells me things I don't want to hear. Does he know Nadya? Can he be telling the truth? The truth is that there's trouble somewhere, and Nadya may be part of it. This talk about monsters raping and killing, I don't know, but I don't like it. I try to squeeze between him and the stone wall bordering the path but he leans against me with his limp arm. The arm feels like a dead fish, a big dead eel, even cold. Twisting away I manage to break free and run down the path. He doesn't follow me but his words do.

—Murderers! Savages!

Maybe he knows about Nadya. He looks like a murderer himself. Better to run away from him and try to find her instead. That's what happens in this village. People talk about each other and they end up believing the rumors, even if they're false. Who knows what they say about me? But I don't care now.

Running past the Fontana de Mèdge I see blood on the ground. They don't clean game here anymore. They don't wash clothes either. Could a person get killed here, in the center of the village, in front of everyone? I don't think so. But he said rape. Yes, that's what he said. Maybe I should go back and hear what this man has to say. I don't need to be afraid of him. What's he going to do to me with only one arm? So I turn around and start running up the path trying to find those words again, "murderers, savages." After about one hundred meters I see the man in the distance. But the moment he sees me, he jumps out of the path and tries to hide behind a stone wall. His left arm swings into view but he quickly pulls it back with his other arm to hide completely. He's the one afraid.

As I get closer to him I hear him mumbling something I cannot understand. He peeks from behind the wall and then hides again. I don't stop. I keep on walking towards him, slowly, slowly. What can he do to me? Why would he want to do anything to me? He peeks again and I see his mad eyes, his face dripping sweat. He starts screaming.

—They'll kill her. Rape her... Kill me too... I need to stop them.

—Calm down.

—Apocalypse!

—Calm down.

—You calm down. Evil is at the door. They're plotting to kill me and rape your daughter.

—Where are these people?

—Up in the mountain brewing their malice, drinking blood I'm sure.

He must be talking about Berghe Supérieur and the hippies. He may be afraid of them, like most ignorant people are. Maybe Nadya did go up to Berghe after all. When the man hides once more behind the stone wall, I turn around and walk away. He keeps on screaming but I don't listen.

The chirping man

Blood of Christ, help me, help me forget what the boys did, or make sure nobody thinks about me, I was there but I did nothing, the wailing, yes, but I had nothing to do with it, not even money, no money there, didn't enter the ruin, no money

he, he, he, will come sniffing, looking for Fuckface, he who smells like shit himself, he'll know, and Fuckface now hiding, motherfucker he is, that Fuckface

if he, he, he comes back in here, into this room, like he did before, I'll give him all the meat I have, my little friends, he can have them all, who cares

out of here, yes, out of this room, he may come right now, or who knows when, but he'll come, and he'll grab me by the beard and push my head into the ground, my head hits the ground too often, no more, have to leave

walk, walk, walk, walk more, past the épicerie, not looking that way, walk even faster, out of this village, leave them behind, the boys, my little friends, out for a while, didn't get my hands dirty, did nothing, but he, he, he may not believe a word I say, he'll not talk about the river, no, he'll talk about the girl

maybe go to Berghe, haven't been there in a while, my people, but not anymore, not my fault, with the fits I couldn't work, did no work, got no food, better off catching little friends, but not my fault, the fits happened day after day and my head hitting the ground, no good for work, no good for them, they didn't kick me out but without food I couldn't stay there, now who knows, for a while, maybe stay there for a while, they'll like my beard, so long now

he, he, he won't go there, no way for him to know about

them, or where to find them, clan of people close to the land, he comes from the river, the desert maybe, sure never saw a hippie before, but someone who wears a tunic like that must have seen strange stuff, when he talked about the river, said the roar was loud, but he's not a fish, more like a civet, and with that smell

hike, not climb but hike like a goat all the way to Berghe Supérieur where people live like cats, licking each other, afraid of water and who knows what else, not different from me, except the idea that we're one with the land, silly thoughts, fighting against common people who're not fighting them, fuck me if I did that, and all the way up here now, instead of staying in the village where I've a room of my own, no precipice, no fear of falling and hitting my head against a rock, I hit a rock once, twice maybe, better down there but with that man behind me I better stay up here and say something to these people, the cats, people I left behind once before, no, twice, because the first time I got scared and came back just to fall down hard and almost kill myself

not that they care, hippies, hard working hippies thinking the world could be fair, motherfucking fair it isn't and I know about that, my dented eyebrows, look, hitting hard again and again, I know fair it isn't, like I know a motherfucker

cast a sort of luck for me, now that I come to Berghe, they look but say nothing, they don't remember, but I do, I do very well, the fountain, all pissed in by people at night and cats in the day, nights when nobody knew where nobody was, remember, yes, remember well because this is a short stay, not long, just long enough to let the man in the tunic forget, he, he, he, with the smell, needs to forget or die, or just keep on wandering upriver, I don't need him, but then there's the money, motherfucker

now in Berghe come into the very house I grew up, all dirty, long memories, shit like there's no other shit, with people coming and going and nobody to hold, when the fits got me down, and nobody to hold on to, better now than then, grownup I guess, but still angry about the motherfuckers who went about their business, the land, the animals, me the animal, and then why bother to feed the children when the animals are all grownup and more important, saw a goat drinking my milk, remember that

find the corner, there behind the kitchen, warm at night and maybe some food tossed to the cats, many nights here and now not different, same smell, and safe from other children, now dead most of them, all those drugs and shit, but the place remains warm, no food, but warm, sit on the floor and try to rest waiting for time to go by, waiting for the tunic man, even the *gendarmes*, to forget about me, me, me

clang, clang, clang, a sound, clang, comes to force me to look up, clang, to watch as the hippies gather around me to stare, clang, with their kitchen pots as if waiting to serve me air or something, clang, me standing and saying sorry, or that I grew here and just wanted to see my house, the hippies staring at me as if I had horns, I don't, but the beard, long, they should like it, one looks really hard at me, a woman, she calls my name

hadn't heard my name in years, nobody calls me, the boys only say "you," that's all, and me not wanting to have anything to do with my name, or Berghe, she calls my name again and I just turn my face away, leave this place forever, that I did years ago except that now there's blood and I want no stains, and hearing my name, Blood of Christ, my name

this house echoes like a hoarse mule and I want no part of it, better leave than hear the old name attached to me, piercing me, no, no, no, move thru them, move fast and leave the old house seeking another corner to hide, from the striped tunic, from the old name, but the hippies stare at me, they now surround me giving me no place to go, the woman blocks my way, the others get closer

—look at the old bird!
—came up to work?
—don't think so
—didn't think so either
—what about that beard?
—it grew there
—speak loud, let me hear you
—need to stay here for some days
—still chirping, sounding like the old bird
—did something bad?
—did nothing, just a man after me
—who's the man?
—with a striped tunic and smelling like a civet
—what kind of man is that?
—I don't know
—you don't know old bird?
—no
—well… if you work, you stay
—can't hit my head no more
—if you work hard we have your back, you mind your own head

have to find me some little friends soon before the hunger sets in, never know with the hippies, may see no food until I plough an entire field, not like they tell me what to do either, they just walk away and let me be, I'm free, free to hide and hunger

Didier

An empty bench is what I get for being a guru to the dogs. The moment they smell their own shit, they run away with their tail between their legs. They know they did something horrible and now they hide. Fuckface must have told them not to come out. Last time I saw an empty bench like this was when he fucked that maimed woman from Monaco. The brutes know what is wrong, but they cannot help themselves. Pack animals, that is what they are. I know their nature but how does that help me if the bench remains empty? Nobody buying beer today.

Maybe I should stop living this way and go into politics or something. What is the difference? I know how to lie. Manipulating a pack of dogs is a good school. I can manipulate non-dog people as well. Or I could go away from this village. No, why go away? I could stay right here and become a council member, even run for mayor. Anything but having to depend on selling beer and dope to a pack of animals that will bury me deep in shit one of these days. Maybe that day is today. No, nobody saw me going up to the ruin. Besides, I brought her there because she wanted me to. I did not force her.

People will come asking about her, I know they will. Maybe the very man that cares for her, that strange creature with the tunic. He makes me feel uneasy. He will come, soon he will, trying to find answers. But he is a stranger, so why bother? He is not an old hippie. He will probably take leave just as abruptly as he arrived. Nobody ever stays in this village, unless they really want to. And why would he want to stick around? The girl, maybe. A foolish man he would be. I cannot conceive that creature having tender feelings. Not that I have them myself.

I start refilling the shelves in the épicerie with merchandise that arrived this morning. People always buy the same things. The stack of toilet paper is low. Yes, my neighbor must have come by. The old wench. She either shits a lot or she wipes herself raw. And when the dogs are stationed at the bench, starting early in the morning, the beer bottles fly out the door. Not today, all the bottles are still here. I go outside the épicerie to arrange the vegetable stand by the door when a strong foul smell attacks me. I look through all the vegetables to see if there is something rotten but they look fresh, healthy even. Maybe the meat went bad. But when I turn around and head back into the épicerie, I find him standing there in the middle of the room. The man in the striped tunic, reeking.

I did not see him come. I did not hear him arrive. But here he is, staring at me. I go past him to check on the meat and find it all moist and fresh. But there stands this man and I wonder what will he do. I need to ask.

—What can I get for you?

—There's nothing for you to get.

—What do you want?

—Is not what I want, is what I need.

—What do you need?

—I need to know who the brutes are.

—The brutes?

—Yes, who're the animals in this village?

The boys are animals, dogs they are. But he could also be referring to me. Or maybe he is not sure and needs to poke me to see if I bleed. He seems peaceful in some ominous way, as if he already knew who those animals were and what he will do to them. But then, why would he be invading my presence? I wonder if he knows I found Nadya in that ruin.

—What brutes are you asking about?

—Please, don't be evasive.

—I'm not being evasive.

—Please, don't be defensive.

—What do you want?

—I told you I don't want anything.

His words reach deep inside of me and dislodge my sense of security. I start to feel unwell, at the edge of a precipice. He may see it on my face so I turn away from him to avoid discovery, but the penetrating stench takes a hold of me and the fear starts to mount.

—The boys, are you referring to the boys?

—What boys are those?

—You saw them the other day. You got naked in front of them.

—The drunks who wouldn't accept my tunic?

—They're animals.

—Are you an animal?

—What are you trying to imply?

—I'm simply asking if you're an animal?

He is cutting through me. I do not know where he comes from but people in this village do not talk to me this way, not even the mayor. This is dangerous. I better stop this right now. Two firm steps get me out of the épicerie where I can breathe fresh air. I sit on the empty bench and try to reassemble my confidence. The silhouette of the striped tunic fills the doorframe and I take in what may be my last breath of fresh air before the malaise returns. He then advances and comes to sit next to me on the bench. An empty bench now, sore for being so empty, ready to hold the striped tunic and me in lieu of the boys. A bench supporting what lands on it, what else?

—Have you ever seen the desert?

—No, I never left these mountains.

—Evil grows dry there.

—Dry?

—Yes, it grows dry there. In these mountains, however,

evil is sort of moist.

—How could evil be dry or moist?

—Depends on its source. Here it grows from the waters of the river. You can also find it in the fountains.

—Have you come across any evil?

—You have. You even washed its imprint in the fountain.

—What imprint?

—Your face, your hands, your mind. All were bathed in blood.

—I've no blood on my hands.

—Not anymore, but your mind is drenched in blood.

—What do you know about my mind?

—I *only* know about your mind.

I do not know what he knows, but he certainly knows something. And my confidence crumbles with every second I spend in the presence of this creature. An urge to flee, to simply fly away from this bench and disappear, fills me. Without looking at him for fear of being quartered, I stand and walk away from the bench at a fast pace. I sense his piercing gaze on my back and I can hear his words.

—Where does evil hide?

The fat poet

Can a word contain space inside of itself? The *o* in *hole* suggests a cavernous space exists inside itself, or inside the concept it elicits. Likewise, the *o* in *whole* makes me think of a dome, a round totality, a wonderful space containing everything. But perhaps I think this way because the letter *o* is a circle with walls separating its interior domain from the exterior space. Do people live inside the *o*?

But if I were to consider the word *habitat*, which I am considering this very moment, I see how the letters *a* and *t* create the scaffold of a dwelling, the very structure to house in-habitants. What a wonderful space inside that word.

I sit on the floor, in the center of my living room, while my cat tiptoes around me. He likes to watch when I spin words. Unsolicited, uninvited, the word *rape* descends on me, forcefully entering my consciousness. I quiver. Something in the air. I do not want to consider this word, but I have to. Flat like a knife, this brutal word has no space inside. It creates a rasping sound as it comes out of my lips, the sound of rupture, perhaps the sound of rage, a furious intensity, a storm or disease. And when I pronounce it loudly, my cat hisses back at me and runs out the door.

Not the first time that loose words land on my lap. Yes, falling from the air. I remain still, aware, hoping to channel the word *rape* and comprehend its space, or its flatness. I pause and allow myself enough time to fully consider its nature. But the word *rape* fails to show anything else but its sharp, flat, wicked face. This word can cut.

When I step out of the house looking for my cat, I notice how the grasses, the trees, all the typically green foliage, have turned a burgundy red. Another unsolicited intrusion. I close my eyes to reset my vision, and when I open them again, I see the foliage green once more. The mules seem consumed with their mechanical pasturing while their jaws dribble red saliva, a sort of foam that falls from the side of their mouths tarnishing the ground under their hoofs. The words are bleeding. Can the words really bleed? Yes they can, and I rush to appease my mules, to tell them not to panic, that words are still a good source of carnal and cerebral nutrients.

People say mules are stupid. Not my mules, they extract literature from pasture. But this time the literary sap is the color of good blood, deep, abundant. And I wonder what story are they chewing on? When I approach them they continue their systematic up-and-down jaw motion. Their round eyes stare at me, blinking at intervals, murky and fluid, but clearly wanting to tell me something. My mules have not learned how to talk yet, but their eyes bear on me with eloquence. And this is when the word *disgrace* flattens me to the ground.

Low as I am, breathing the moist air next to the green nubile grass, I understand my mules. Violence, violent-essence, has occurred, and the mules smell it in the air. And when they drench the soil with bloody saliva, they are only churning out what the grasses have inhaled. Air penetrates the million grass blades, and the mules extract and distill their violent-essence. Unwise they are not, my mules, tender revealers they are.

I then hear a chord, dry leaves touching each other, water falling out of a faucet, the earth roiling, or perhaps the sound of what I do not want to see. And this sound beacons me to open my eyes and consider the possibility of violence, the same violence my mules choke on. But in front of me, in this terraced mountain, nothing looks different, or strange, other than a sadness that seems to hang in the air. To stay here and wonder what ruptures this universe is senseless, and a senseless poet I am not. So, with the disposition of a mound of white flesh, I mount the mountain, I penetrate the paths, and I walk wonders, because words arrive for a reason.

I soon find myself walking aimlessly in the heart of the village. Not because I lost my way, but because an overwhelming torrent of words pulls me away from my house. And the more I resist, the stronger the pull of the words, the louder the demand.

imperatore vs senselessness	white flesh vs just flesh
blood vs sap	reason vs un-reason
orbiting vs bearing	demand vs river flow

The bipolar words confront me inside a quadrilateral ensemble of paths and passages, a proof that a man, even more so a poet, is at the mercy of his emotions. I reach the heights of the village and come to the center of Place Caranca where I surrender to my weight, spilling my body on the floor. Here, surrounded by old stones, I try to make sense out of so many words. The irresistible force of the river of words pulls me in the direction of Berghe and I struggle with the idea of hiking up there. Why Berghe? Not so remote but abundant with hippies and un-neutered cats. The words seem to arrive from that direction. A river of words has swept me before but never from Berghe. And feeling the ferocity they pack, I know these words come from Berghe Supérieur.

I embark on this journey and follow the road to Berghe, a road not made of salt, but of the toil of moon seekers. I first descend to Fontan, jump over the river, ignore beehives and clandestine dogs, and gradually begin to ascend, turning and turning, among rocks bathed in blood until I come to a point of physical exhaustion, my largeness catching up with me again. Where are my mules when I need them most? I try to get as much air as I can inside my lungs, but my mouth, being so small, acts like a funnel, limiting the flow, and this makes my white skin turn purple. Saturn, the sixth planet from the sun, an ancient Roman god who ruled the earth during an age of virtue, throws at me a few of his rings composed of small ice particles. The rings circle me and the cold air brings soothing words to my ears. I breathe amply. And for a moment I feel I am floating. Relieved, with saturnine rings around me, I continue to ascend following the stream of words, one of which reverberates above them all:

Fate

The striped tunic

This mountain does not move like sand mountains do, it resists the impetus of wind and rain. People crisscross the mountain inflicting multiple lacerations on its flank. Those scars harden under so many feet. I can follow a path or I can follow a scar. What is the difference? I followed the river when I came to Saorge. Was the river a scar? No, it was a path, the scars, a multitude, I already left behind, some of them hardened by sand and sun, others still open under the waters of the river. And as I hike back to the ruin I feel like opening a new path, like carving a fresh wound through this mountain. What is the use? We are all hurt enough as it is.

Where,

does,

evil,

hide?

Does it really hide? Or is evil as evident and stationary as this mountain? Perhaps all I am doing is walking over the very foe that I am looking for. I never bothered with evil in the desert. Maybe because the sands shifted all the time. A shifting evil? Not possible, there is permanency and consistency in human nature, especially in its dark side.

How could I go searching for the oldest manifestation of evil, man that is, and leave Nadya alone? An evil man already visited her, he could return. In this spiraling world everything keeps on happening again,

everything,

again,

keeps on,

spiraling. And that gives me good enough reason to return to the ruin. Not that I hope to find any answers there, but the questions there are fresh. Is Nadya safe? Would she tell me what the face of evil looks like? Is this village doomed like every other village I have known? Am I still the same man I was before? Is my red past completely dead? I doubt very much that Saorge could offer such answers. Perhaps, at the end, the answers are the same as the answers in the beginning. In that case, why did I set out from Marrakech? Why do I never mention my past to anyone, only to myself? Perhaps all I do is turn my face away from myself. A pathetic way to escape. This village has become acquainted with my face, an image that some interpret as evil. What a projection, I seek evil and people see evil in me. I can throw my face down the river. Yes, I can do that. I can also sit inside the ruin and wait for orange trees to bloom. Corrosive thoughts like these bite me. Not the first time.

I stop carving through the mountain when I arrive at the ruin. Nadya lies on the ground with half-open eyes. Her face, a restful place, even after the hurt. I despise having to ask her again, but I must.

—Who did this to you?

—I don't know.

—What did he look like?

—His face…

—Yes, what about his face?

—An impossibility.

No more questions. Why stir the pain? But her answer denotes a difficult reality. She confronted a face like no other. Maybe a face that should not even exist. I saw such a face, at the bench, among the crowd of drunken men who feared my presence, more precisely, who rejected donning my striped tunic. A young man landed his heavy hand on my shoulder and made me turn his way. An atrocious moment, not because of his distorted features, but because of his distorted wishes. He wanted to destroy me. Yes, he did. Maybe he was angry because of the impossibility of his face. Or maybe he embodies evil. But somehow I felt he wished me out of his life, or out of life altogether.

As a caravan of two, I lead Nadya away from the ruin towards a place unknown to me. A mountainous desert lies ahead, or something worse. Monster clouds behind us, rocks under our feet, Nadya leans back as if she weighed a ton and I tell her to lean on me if she finds it difficult to walk. I hear the roar of the river and wonder where its mouth is. A mouthful of roars, the river swirls at me when I need it least. Night is close but still far, and the discomfort inside Nadya makes her moan.

Two nights,
close on her,
two nights,
one natural, the other brutal.
She follows me,
follows me,
into a promising dusk,
but just as terrible as any other phantasmagoric place. And as we leave the golden ruin behind, I visualize orange blossoms.

—Where are you taking me?
—Into a different night.
—Where's that night?
—I don't know Nadya.
—Is it far?
—Nothing's far.

How far could any night be? We come across nights, relentlessly, we come across nights and glow in measly mornings. Nadya saw a night she never imagined, she saw a different dark. There are many darks, some even sequester all possible light. We need new darks.

Not far from here, up into these mountains, I will find

the source. Evil dark, dark evil, or perhaps the decomposed face of an evil as dark as dark. And without knowing exactly where I am going, I let my senses guide me on the path ahead like I have done in deserts past. And as we descend, the roar of the river grows, it fills the air, it mesmerizes. We come to the banks of the river inside a gorge of red slate. I lift Nadya, drape her over my shoulders, and look for a shallow stretch to part the waters. As I am crossing over, I see my old steps undulating on the water surface. I try to listen for the steps that brought me to this village but I only hear the roar.

—Nadya, can you hear my steps?

—I hear water crashing against rocks.

—No, wet steps, further downriver.

—I hear the roar.

—Yes, the roar.

Once on the opposite bank we continue walking. The river path fades behind, the path ahead is birthing.

Nadya

Once again I follow him. This time under different circumstances, fueled by the need for justice, or maybe clarity. His hand took me to the ruin one night. Today, he takes me somewhere else in the middle of the day. He seems to know where he is going, even when he has never seen this land before. First he carries me over his shoulders, and then he sets me on the ground and pulls me uphill. I do not usually follow anyone in the middle of the night, not even the cats. But this is daytime, and I need to be next to him.

I wonder how he decides in which direction to walk. Does he consciously know where he is going, where he takes me? Somehow, it seems like a guiding force shows him the way. Maybe a stream flows from inside his mind with latitudes and longitudes. He does not doubt; he turns right and left with absolute determination. But I soon recognize this path, my old path, a passage away from the confusion of Berghe, from my own confusion. Those were the days when Antonia came with me to the river. She wanted something else. No, Antonia, do not torture me at this time. I already healed from you.

Under a red *mélèze* we come to rest with our backs on the ground. The mountains never end, they erupt one after another. I wonder if he can see beyond the profile of these mountains, beyond the profile of this day. I wonder so much.

—Do you know where you're going?

—If I knew, I wouldn't be going there.

—I know where this path leads.

—I know you know.

—How can you tell?

—I see it on your face.

—What do you see?

—Longing, a profound longing.

He sees beyond the profile of my own understanding. Why else would he have appeared in the dark of night asking for food and drink? How did he know to take me to the ruin when I wanted to leave my sisters behind? And now he takes me to Berghe Supérieur not knowing about my internal struggle with Antonia and those memories. But there is longing, and he knows that.

On the side of the gorge we left behind, the mountain rises, Saorge barely clinging on the incline. Houses tower over narrow paths. So far away now, another perspective. Why do I live in Saorge? Why do I live in the night? So many nights. I never thought a stranger would take me away from Saorge and lead me back to my old home. Does he know he takes me back in time? For him this is a quest to protect me, or to find some kind of justice. For me, I am not sure. Running barefoot, my mother drunk or stoned, my father, I do not know, an endless reproduction of cats and dogs, and pigs too, eating fried flowers, and the uneasy hand of Antonia. What could a child have done? What did I really do?

On a clearing, as the terrain levels over abandoned terraces, far in the horizon, I see a large mound of white flesh, a pale protuberance over the light green grass. It does not move. I seems to lie there, dead maybe. I have seen dead bodies before but nothing this huge. The recumbent body does not take notice of us or at least does not seem to care as we continue to approach. The flapping of the striped tunic against his legs marks our rhythmic walk. And the closer we get to the bulk, the more it resembles a sitting Buddha. We deviate from the path and walk directly to where this immense person sits placidly on the ground. A round head and body without hair, and white, very white.

Polyphony

*T*wo. Two can walk hand-in-hand, two can talk to each other, and two can be two. I am one, or one and a half, if we consider my size, but still one mind, and that is a disadvantage. But two, a pair, has a lot to offer. Who is she? Ejected, as she seems, she follows the stripes on his tunic.

Once again, I come across the large albino when I least expect it. He seems to intersect my life in anomalous ways. Without his mules he is not a teacher.

The mound unfolds and a man without eyebrows or eyelashes stares at us from a safe distance. I have walked many nights all over Saorge but never seen his light.

The word *troika* shows its face. Not really a Russian word but it sounds like one. Three instead of two, we are three now. *Troika.*

I, who look for simplicity, even distance, need to deal once more with this fat creature who promised to help me. Like Rilke, "I am too alone in the world, and not alone enough."

These two men do not say a word, not yet. They must know each other, or at least, know about each other because they keep their places. No one wants to get close. He with the striped tunic and he with the white skin.

—Who are we? People, or the idea of people? Beings or the spectrum of nothingness?

—Please, do not project your insecurities.

—Last I saw you, you had no woman. Now you have one.

—Yes.

—That's my name.

—I know

—Is it really, Yes?

—Yes it is, my dear.

—Leave her out of this. Why did you leave your mules behind?

—My mules know how to get home after school. But tell me, why did you leave yourself behind?

—I didn't, I'm still in Saorge.

—Are you also going to Berghe Supérieur?

—You seem to know your way.

—No, I'm only following an impulse.

—I'm doing the same thing.

—I know how to get there. I walked this path when I was young.

—I believe you, your old sister taught you well.

—Don't mention my sister.

—Don't mention, "Yes."

—Yes?

—You just mentioned it.

—Never again.

This rotund man lives in the mountains close to the abandoned church. I never came across him but I have heard about him. My sister spoke about him. She does not like him, speaks in weird ways she said. But she does not like most people, only when they buy cheese from her, only then she cares. Not a single hair on his head.

A sensitive man, the albino. Why else would he be on this path if not because he is in pursuit, of a word, many words perhaps. First time I see him alone, without the mules. I decide to approach him, but the closer I get the more difficult to breathe. I sense an absence of air, a vacuum, as if he had consumed all the oxygen orbiting around him. The same happens in the desert, when air is so hot and thinly dispersed that it carries no oxygen. His lips are purple, deep purple.

The unctuous cat, with the iridescent tunic striped in parallel, tinging the air. Gasping, sucking for oxygen, I feel a tingling sensation in my fingers. I look for words. Where is the stream? And the word. What word? The word. The word *primal* enters my mind. An essential need, original, like air itself, beyond human artifact, life maybe, or just language, the language of hurt, coming to me in bands, from the top of this mountain.

The three of us look at each other. The fat man stands and his knees wobble. For a moment I fear he will collapse, hit the ground and roll down the mountain. I move away just in case. But he maintains his balance, and taking a deep breath, he starts walking ahead of us in the direction of Berghe Supérieur. I watch the rotund body maneuvering this familiar path. No hippie was ever this nimble, considering his size.

He walks ahead, a mountain,
a mound,
a being so white,
a white being revealing his thoughts,
words they are, his thoughts,
for me to crack,
or not.
—Why do you go to Berghe?
—An impulse, I already told you.
—My childhood there, you know.
—Keep walking.
—What about the hurt?
—We all do.

Let Yes lead the way. He goes on instinct. I can tell because his body follows no direct line, not even the path in front of him. With Nadya on my side, I let him lead. He seems as motivated as I am to reach that place on top of the mountain. But he is so massive, the path has to stretch wide to let him through.

The inevitable place where I grew up, or grew down, starts to take shape in the horizon beyond the mountain ridge. The albino forms a visor with the palm of his hand to block the sun. He looks far away, or looks far in time, I do not know. He takes small steps, deliberately.

Cagatinga, a phenomenal word I once heard from the lips of a native Cuban. He used it in a loose way, meaning different things all tied by a sense of shitty discomfort. Like hiking up to Berghe Supérieur followed by the likes of these two. I cannot walk faster, slower—yes. But that is my name. *Yes*, myself walking slower and dumping as I ascend. Not a beautiful image but a real description of what I feel this moment.

Walking behind the albino forces me to slow down. Should I walk faster? No, what is the sense in reaching the summit ahead of him. Plus, he seems to know where he is going, better to keep his rhythm. Nadya seems to know where she is going as well. I am the ignorant one, but I know that I must go. I have left so many places before without knowing my way. What is the difference now?

I see the tiled roofs and square houses emerge over the hill, still too far to hear the voices of my old hippie clan. I wonder who remains there, who left, like me, old cats maybe. I have not spent a night in Berghe in so long. I wonder if the shadows still remember me.

The stream of words follows the contour of the mountain. It dives into a ravine just to come back up shooting at high speed. The stream turns around an ancient cypress and follows its elongated shadow away from the sun. I put my hand up and catch another loose word. What a marvel, I grab a naked *anthem* out of the air! I consider the sound of the word as I pronounce it *A-n-t-h-e-m*. I prefer the unpolluted word, without meaning, without the idiocy people attach to their war songs.

—One step of mine for two of yours. A mathematical discrepancy we must accept unless you want to overtake me.

—Why would I take you over?

—You have a presence and a tunic to prove your point.

—I have nothing to prove.

—Then, why do you follow my tracks?

—Nadya needs to go back home.

—Berghe Supérieur isn't my home. It was, but no longer.

—Then because evil resides up there.

—And how do you know that?

—I feel it, like I feel your heft.

—But one does not imply the other.

—Berghe is a heavy place; my childhood was heavy. I needed to run away from Antonia.

—Who's Antonia?

—Who was Antonia?

—A little woman with a different heart. No longer around, I guess.

A caravan of sorts, our figures carve the mountainside at the rhythm of thirst. We lead each other,

Yes,

Nadya,

myself.

This salted self of mine moving away from a desiccated past. Nothing is ever lost, just preserved until water brings it back to life. And the thirst I feel for justice may generate more injustice. Careful, careful.

3rd Middle-Entry

The one-armed man

I am going for them, rout them out. That woman will not dare to save her daughter. That is how evil wins, because people do nothing. Who knows how many more murderers live up there in Berghe. No *gendarme* ever goes to put an end to the rituals, the carnage. They do not want to be eaten. But this is my time, mine. I am going for them.

With the rifle hanging from my shoulder and a knife strapped to my leg I head up to Berghe. Better not use the main road, no, they will likely have someone on guard to blow the whistle. But if I descend from a higher ridge of the mountain, maybe coming around from Casterino, I could ambush them in the middle of their séance. It will take a lot longer to reach Berghe that way, a full day. Even if it takes a week, that is not important, what matters is to take them by surprise. This time I will not miss; I will shoot the monsters between their eyes.

But what if people see me walking around with a rifle? They know I do not hunt anymore. They may talk and, somehow, the monsters could learn that a man is coming their way with a rifle. How else could they exist, untouched, committing so many barbarities, if they do not have a web of informers. Maybe that woman herself is an informer. I told her about her daughter being in danger and she said she had no daughter. She could have been planted there to engage me in conversation. Now they probably know that I know they are in Berghe. They must be waiting for me. Yes, I have to circumvent the major road. But if it takes me longer than a day to reach them they will realize I am approaching from Casterino. I think they know everything.

Maybe I need to surprise them in the middle of the night

when they are immersed in their rituals. The beasts must do their killing at night. Daytime is when they drink and fornicate, I am certain of that. Yes, the excitement of the killing, the taste of blood will make them oblivious. That will be the best moment. And, very likely, they will all be in one place, underground, eating the raw meat of their victims. But how could I aim the rifle in the dark with only one arm? Not only that, but I would need to shoot two or three of them really dead before the rest come after me. Or maybe the monsters will not come after me if they halt to cannibalize their own. I sure hope so.

Following the river, heading north, I come to a point where the river has carved a deep gorge. The path follows the contour of the river as the waters sink into the earth. And down in the precipice, among the purple rocks, I see a creature looking up at me. A rock, no, no…a mouse. A mouse the size of a horse. It has whiskers, round eyes, and a mouth with two prominent teeth. What is this huge mouse doing in the middle of the river? It does not move; it simply stares at me from below. This must be one of their agents; this thing will kill me. I drop to the ground and crawl a few meters out of its sight. The mouse may not see me but I am sure it can sniff me. The mouse can easily climb from the bottom of the gorge, follow my smell, and destroy me with those teeth. Like at the Côte d'Ivoire, the dark forces rounding me. On the ground I push with my feet and pull with my good arm crawling as fast as I can, dragging the rifle, when the sweat starts to get into my eyes. The sweat burns and everything turns blurry. I keep crawling for a while until the skin of my knees, scratched and bleeding, begins to hurt. Then I stop to listen. Nothing. I crouch and lift my head up to look at the mouse. I no longer see it. The rocks are all there but not the mouse. Grabbing this opportunity, I stand and run away, fast, truly fast.

All day I walk, all day, away from the main road, through

the thicket. My dead arm swings out of control accumulating new cuts and abrasions while the blood on my knees begins to dry. The rifle is secure; I hold it really tight. When I try to listen for sounds beyond the visible mountain ridge nothing comes my way. I carry on like this until dusk when I reach a clearing offering a view of the hill below. Finally. There, half a dozen houses, a corral with horses, goats, a few lights. This must be Berghe Supérieur. Yes, I can smell the sulfuric devils down there.

I must wait until dark becomes dark, the time when they will unleash their venomous selves. These are creatures of the night; soon enough they will be in their element. I must remain still, breathing as shallow as I can, revealing nothing. Maybe my thoughts, yes, my thoughts. What if they can hear them? They may come up here and dismember me. I know they want to destroy me even if they have yet to come face to face with me. They really know everything—they do. They could be waiting for me in the pitch of dark. Wait, just wait, still, there, there, breathe slowly, wipe off the sweat, hold the rifle tight, do not think, do not emit brainwaves.

The first few hours pass by. My legs too numb with fear to cry out. Sweat keeps on dripping into my eyes turning the early lights below into splattered stars. I realize the beat of my heart has gone haywire. Fast, slow, syncopated, pounding—everything but uniform. I try to remain calm but the buzzing sound of my thoughts distracts me. If I can hear my thoughts, they will be able to hear them as well. I just hope for the wind not to come shooting down the mountain. And I wait.

Didier

I do not hide, I never do, but I feel better inside my house. That man in his tunic will not follow me, he is looking for evil, he says, and that is not me. No, I am not, even after drugging those idiots. They do not know the difference. But that pestilent man came to my store when I least expected him. And he can certainly return. If he does not find the boys he will be at my store again, I am sure he will. And if he finds Fuckface, the coward would say I sent him up to the ruin. As if I were his master or something. Those dogs are a problem; they will cost me dearly sooner or later.

I will not open the épicerie this afternoon. Why be part of this mayhem? I think I am already part of it. No, nobody saw me carrying the girl. Nobody did. But the stinker said something about blood and the fountain. An "imprint" he said. How could he know? Maybe he just talks that way to intimidate people. He will not intimidate me. Yes, I am inside these four walls but I am not as afraid as I think I am. What could he do? Kill me? Well, yes, but why would he not kill Fuckface instead. Granted, anybody would like to see that dog dead. He pays me money, Fuckface does, money he gets from his parents, good money nonetheless. Pseudo-hippies like him live off the welfare of their families, no principles to go by, just the dirty idea that life is owed to them.

I do not owe my life to anyone. My mother, she did what she could, minimally. In fact, I think she despised me. Why else would she have abandoned me? Enough, I need no more aggravation. As if I did not despise so many, the entire village almost. Easy on yourself, Didier, you are not the bastard they want you to be. Truth is, I make the wheels in this village turn, milking a little profit, but what is a businessman to do?

The doorbell rings. Who wants to buy dope at this hour? The store is closed, that means I am closed for all kinds of business. I let the bell ring several times. They will get bored and move away. But the bell keeps on ringing, demanding my attention. Someone knows I am here. These are the moments when I consider leaving this place once and for all. To hell with the needy bastards. Let them get their fix somewhere else.

I open the door and the face of Fuckface jumps at me. Discombobulated eyes, nose, lips and scars make me cringe. He pushes me to the side and forces his way inside my house. The dog is alone and his rabid expression tells me he is ready to bite. This is how he gets when he needs dope, but he now appears crueler. I wait for him to say something but all he does is breathe deep, in and out, like a hurt beast.

To quell his need, I look for my stash of heroin and offer him some. He would snort the whole thing in a minute. But the dog ignores my offer and continues to pant and dribble. I observe him briefly, I cannot bear looking at his face for too long. And for the first time he appears dejected. Maybe I am so scared of him that I need to humanize him. I do not know.

—Want to snort this?

—No, no more dope.

—Where are the other boys?

—Fuck them.

—Want a beer?

—Fuck you too!

—Easy, easy boy.

—Where's the man with the tunic?

—You go find him.

—He may find me.

—Then what?

—Do you know?

—Do I know what?

—About the girl.

—I don't know anything.

—That man will kill me.

—Why?

—The girl.

I have never seen him like this. His face, that landscape of unnatural features, turns from menacing to uneasy, and I know I am in control again. He will accept my dope, he will. He will eat out of my hand. I take some of the heroin and bring it to my nose, I pretend to snort, make noises, tilt my head back. Twirling my fingers, I dump the powder on the floor without him noticing. A false hit. He will go next, he cannot resist. I know my dog.

—Sure you don't want a hit? This one's on the house.

—You bitch...

—Easy boy. Here have some.

He brings his trembling fingers to that face of his and finds the questionable nose. After a long and deep inhale, Fuckface sits down and waits for the magic to work. I pretend to take another hit in front of him, to egg him on.

—Here's some more my boy.

—Gimme!

Yes, yes, he begins to relax, the intensity of his face melting to the floor. Not a mean dog anymore, a puppy now. Money well spent. I grab a cold beer and sit down next to Fuckface to admire his surrender. This is the problem with the dogs, they go from fast to slow to fast, all the while sinking in their own shit.

He is not totally useless, close to it, but not totally. He can take care of the man in the tunic. Right now he has no reason to do it, plus he is afraid of him. But that can change. Given the right mix of dope and alcohol he will get rabid enough to go and take him down. He is quick to get angry and needs very little to snap. I can trick him into it.

—Feeling good now my boy?

—Good shit, yeah!

—Why are you so afraid of that man?

—Something weird 'bout him.

—Sure, he put his balls in your face. I saw that.

—Fuck off you bitch.

—Easy on me, I'm not the one fucking with you.

—I told him off.

—I saw you walking away from him. That's what you did.

—He stinks.

—You shit your pants, you're the one who stinks.

From the depth of his dopey eyes I see a burst of rage.
There is the seed.

The old sister

When I get to our house, I find *La Petite* waiting for me. She has prepared everything for the day. All the cheeses are packed and ready to bring down to the truck. Today we are going to Tende, colder there. She seems a little sad. Missing her sister, I suppose.

—Where's Nadya?

—I don't know.

I don't really know, but I get a feeling she went up to Berghe. I don't want to go there myself, and she wouldn't have wanted to go back either. But somehow, I think she's there. Wonder what really happened way back because she hates the place so much. We had it sweet, back when we did whatever we wanted. Maybe that girl, Antonia, wonder what really happened there. Shit, nothing's ever clear.

We pack all our boxes, *La Petite* and I, and take on the day as if it were marvelous. I know what's coming: more of the same, the drag. But this may be the day a guy finally digs me. I wish, I only wish. Driving toward Tende in our beaten-up truck, we pass the intersection where the road to Berghe splits off. I try to resist, driving about one kilometer further up the road. Then I give up. I turn around and drive back, coming to a full stop at the intersection. *La Petite* looks at me like I'm crazy or something.

—Where are you going?

—Nowhere.

Where am I going? Nowhere soon, that's for sure. No man, no decent job, and a sister that runs away. This is all a pile of shit, and we're slipping on it. I don't need more of this. I turn the car around and once again continue on the way to Tende leaving the intersection behind.

Maybe the problem is that we're little people. We're nothing like the people I see in Nice, the tourists, spending lots of money. We're going nowhere, that's real, all we do is sell old cheese. How pathetic is that? We're really nothing. Nothing at all. And maybe that's why Jules or Julien doesn't hit on me. He may think I stink like Roquefort cheese. I don't, I really don't, but how would he know that? He never asked my name, he never took me for coffee, and he never looked at me as if he wanted to… Little people we are, that's it, little nothings.

Once in Tende I set up the stand as quick as I can. The other sellers set their stands in the familiar places. Like a dead routine, a habit maybe. Nobody changes anything here. We present the old cheese in a way that looks fresh, and we put labels in French and Italian. Hell must be like this, same shit day after day.

A clear day though, no clouds at all. We'll get lots of customers, I'm sure. After a quick inventory, I determine we have all we need for this crowd. *La Petite* can manage, she's a better seller than me. So I tell her I need to go for about an hour. She doesn't mind, or at least, she doesn't tell me. I put on some lipstick and head for the car. Butt-lipped I go. But nobody stops me along the way, nobody notices. I'm nothing, not even an old nothing.

Drive back to the intersection where the road to Berghe splits off. Make a sharp right and start driving up the narrow road, twisting and turning, one hairpin after another. No other cars occupy the road at this time. This road was good when I wanted to leave Berghe, a quick downhill. Now it takes me back there. Not that I want to go there, but that's where Nadya may be. Stupid girl, Nadya, she may think the good old times were good old times.

Halfway up the mountain I start thinking about the bunch of old hippies. All half-brothers or half-sisters. Everything half-something because nothing was clear back then. Even my mother, the one I should know about, is still an open question. To this day… Shit, to this day. And as the truck climbs up the mountain, I start to hate what I'm doing. These hippies, the new ones, have taken over the place. Not that they're real hippies, I mean, they don't really work the land or make their own cheese. The old ones have adapted, like myself, working odd jobs. This new crowd is big on nothing. Well, big on smoking and drinking, and who knows what else.

I keep on driving until the road reaches a dead end. Right in front of a crumbling building the road dies. I remember as a child thinking this was the end of the world. And I sort of feel that way now. I mean, coming here brings me back to an old end. Fuck this, I'm getting out of here before anyone comes to fuck with me. I decide to turn back and leave at once. Nadya is not here, no, she's not. She wouldn't want to feel even smaller, like a mouse or something. And as long as I can prevent it, I don't want to feel as shitty as I felt back when I lived in this hellhole.

I shift the truck into first gear and let the engine take me away. The road zigzags down the mountain and the truck gathers speed right away. I wheel away, like I did before, when I had enough of the crazy making of this village. But as I glide down the road, I pass by some people, odd people, crowding the roadside. Nadya? I don't think so. No, not the little mouse. I see a strange man dressed in a striped tunic, and a very fat man white as a salamander. The hippies may be starting a circus.

The chirping man

hear them coming, too many steps coming, smells like, dung, smells like he, he, he's close by, cannot be anything else coming, same as down in the village, putrid, more putrid than my little friends in the heat of summer, got to eat them quick in hot days, but he's not alone, the thingy is coming too, yes a fresh twist, hell, hell, they found me

will not show my face, no, let the hippies greet him, he, he, he, and the hippies, they'll talk, who knows, they may think he's the prophet they been waiting for, he dresses like Jesus, give them alcohol they believe anything, wait until he strips bare naked, he did it before, hippies may like that, motherfuckers

run like a rat and duck into a house cellar, see the road from down here, he has to walk right in front, first thing to see will be his feet, torn sandals, the thingy's legs too, not bad, but not yet, not yet, so far only the stink, cannot be long because the air feels heavy, keep my head straight, don't blink too much, last thing I need is a fit, hippies coming and going but no tunic, hear them talk but not the talk he talks, weird, yes he talks weird

hippies won't save me, they'll turn me in, no doubt, they care for nothing, not for me, useless to them, but if I strike him and get his money, they'll like that, I'll keep the thingy

look around the cellar and see a bunch of eyes, fuck, what are these, pairs of eyes, many, cats, no, snakes, hope not, creatures don't move they just look at me, no, no, no, I eat mice but these are bigger, motherfucking hippies growing some kind of creatures down here, better not move now, stay put, he, he, he'll get me if I jump out, still, real still, but one of then moves, blinks an eye, they're coming, fuck no, a hissing sound and a hum

jump out on the road sooner than soon and head for an
alley as my head goes down again, dirt and a thump, no fit,
no seizing, just the pain, the pain and blood, yes, blood again,
fuck me

hippie girl comes around with a smile

—are you hurt?

—I'm not here

-what?

—no hurt, no, nothing

—you're bleeding

—it isn't blood

—I go get somebody

—no, no, I'm not here

get up quick and run some more, hippie girl stays behind,
hurts, head really hurts, better find another hole to hide, came
up to Berghe to hide and now I have to hide some more, like
a rat, hippies don't mind me, but that man, he be looking for
Fuckface but sure thinks I did bad to the thingy, and I can
smell him, close, too close, he, he, he will fuck me good if he
gets me

go back to the house, the old one, where I grew up, many
hippies here doing nothing, smoking and drinking, not aware
the civet is out there, they may think I'm strange or something
because they grimace at me, maybe the blood on my face, they
start talking and using my name, hate to hear that

—old bird got his face smashed

—trim that beard

—bird, you better learn how to walk

—there's a man out there who wants to get me

—listen, he's chirping again

—same pitch, same chirp as before

—I did nothing, Fuckface did

—what're you chirping about bird?

—he never made much sense

—he, he, he… he, he, he…

—get it out bird, chirp it

—Blood of Christ, give me Blood of Christ

burning down my throat, I need that, make the fear go away, around the hippies better than alone, they nudge and jerk me but keep me safe, that man would not come in here to get me, maybe not, but who knows, like he stood in front of the boys and showed them his balls, he may know hippies will throw me out on the street in a whim, motherfuckers

hippies bring out grilled boar, wild beast done on sizzling slate, break it apart with their hands, good for me, taste better than my little friends, hope they throw some my way, like I'm one of them, grew up inside this house, I'm one of them, still, I think

cannot sit here smelling the dripping boar, stretch my hand out, gets slapped, what did I do, try grabbing some meat and get more slapping, no boar for me, hippies keep on eating and I keep on watching, so hungry I don't know what to do

—some meat for me?

—what's the bird saying?

—little piece?

—he wants to eat some

—want to share with us old bird?

—just a little piece

—what did you do today?

—went hiding, this man…

—went hiding?

—same old bird, doesn't wanna work

—the man with the striped tunic is coming to get me

—hear that? someone's coming to get him

—no work, no food, bird

try to be quick, reach over and snatch a piece of meat, run to the corner of the room, sink my teeth in the meat, chew quick and swallow, taste good, so good, two of them come and

pull my hands out of my mouth, force my mouth open, meat
is gone, all gone

a third one comes and grabs my feet, struggle hard to get
loose but hippies are strong, drag me away from the corner
into the middle of the room, wait for the blows, no blows, wait
for kicks, no kicks, held down, that's all

—what're we doing with him?

—throw him out

—I did nothing but he'll kill me

—didn't do what?

—didn't touch her

—what the fuck is he chirping about?

—don't throw me out there

—you wanna eat, go do some work first

—the man with the striped tunic…

—fuck that tunic man and fuck you too bird

out the door, flying, head first to the ground again, deeper
pain this time, lay still until the world settles, see nothing,
hear nothing, but smell something, fuck me

The striped tunic

A rhythm, maybe a shared myth, this village pulsates in ways I have never seen. A certain melancholy the color of dusk, as if the gods never considered it holy,

the village lingers,

grabbing on to the side of the mountain hoping to survive as it tries to bury all who were born here, those who left, like Nadya, and those who never left whose faces I have yet to see. An empty village, or perhaps a village where people are ashamed.

Behind Yes we march into a plaza where overgrown sycamores make a castle of shadows. Like an ivory Buddha, Yes sits in the middle of the plaza in rotund silence with a wide smile on his face. He seems to have arrived. Nadya's hand squeezes my hand and I know a disturbing memory must have entered her mind.

I listen for whispers, loose words, but all I hear is the turning of the earth, when the mass of oceans and dirt spins on its axis, creating wind,

nothing but wind,

a wind without words,

mute.

This mountain is like a vertical desert, seemingly empty but full of beasts. Sooner or later I will hear them speak. I have heard the beasts before, in the past, when nobody knew they existed. And if evil resides in this village, I will find it.

—Nadya, what happened here?

—Many things happened.

—What hurts you most?

—The day hurts me the most.

—What happened during the day?

—They all saw me with René.

—Who was René?

—He grew up here.

—What was there to see?

—They saw who he was not.

—And you, who were you?

— I'm not sure.

Different from mine, Nadya's past has not died yet. Her past seems confusing, fluid, amorphous, made of the slime that makes us sick. She takes to the night because the day hurts, like I keep my body wrapped in this tunic to contain the brutality. We create closed courtyards in our minds instead of opening all doors to the loose winds. I will stop asking her questions. She already gave me her doubts, what more can people give?

By now the clarity of the afternoon has bled away as the sun left to hide between distant mountains. We soon become destitute of light. I grab Nadya's hand and walk towards the light of a gas lamp. A sign of life, or the ceaseless effort to fight the shadows.

A door,
I knock,
I knock again,
nothing.

The false serenity of this village tells me something is brewing behind these walls. People who do not answer doors fear not a robber but an intruder. I approach a different door and knock a few times.

Nothing.

Nothing is an answer, nothingness is a state, and in this village both seem to coexist. Our arrival was not heralded, no, but it was not kept secret either. We simply walked our way into its heart. So we find this village apparently empty when I am certain it has a heart full with people, people who seem to fear us. And what is there to fear? An albino? A skinny young woman? A man in a striped tunic? Where is the threat?

Further down the road I notice the silhouette of a man who rises from the ground and runs across the street, just to fall to the ground again remaining immobile. I stand still and continue watching this figure. Nadya does not seem to be aware of this presence. She points to another shining light.

—Why don't we knock on that other door?

—Wait, Nadya.

—I know there are lots of people here.

—And they know we're here.

—Are you afraid?

—No, they're afraid.

I walk in the direction of the reclining figure. She follows me, Nadya does, maybe my hand, or the trust, or the need to follow. When we get closer, the body on the ground turns around and I recognize the bearded face of the man in Saorge, the one who let me into his house. Same features, now covered by dried dark red blood. A desecrated man, this man has taken a few blows since I saw him last. And his eyes, shifting, even desperate, have seen horror. Maybe I represent the very horror he harbors in his mind, or maybe Nadya reminds him of horrible things.

As we get closer, the man starts to turn and twist on the floor, thrashing arms and legs like half-dead vermin. With a struggle he manages to get on his feet, panting, dripping saliva and mucus, his face emanating a deep fear. And after taking a horrifying look at Nadya and me, the man runs away making some kind of bird-like sound. Down the road the shadows swallow him.

When we return to the plaza we are confronted with the vision of Yes, a contemplative whiteness, reflecting moon rays from his sitting position. A superb peace seems to bathe him, as he seems oblivious to the obscene emptiness of this village. His small mouth pronounces unfastened words that I try to understand. But the words soar and I cannot touch them.

The fat poet

What a lunar delight, to sit high in the mountain and feel lucid words descending on me. These words come clean, unspoiled, even nubile. They ought to originate from the white center of the universe. Here, at this altitude, the words are still new. They have not taken the contaminating path down the mountain. Maybe that is how language started, spoken to us from the heights of Olympus. Homer was closer; he got the freshest words.

A pure word, one unpronounced by people, would have no synonyms. Only when people start mouthing words do they acquire a taste. And once we taste something we are bound to compare it with something else. But a word in its first edition would taste like water, and it would shine a white light.

But if all we have are second-hand words, are we not sentenced to the conventional

convention

    conviction

        con, convict

            no, not convent

                vent…coño?

Who am I to know? I can vent like a bitter poet, but to what end? Better to just sit here for the moment and enjoy the moon rays and the silence. This village is silent indeed. Even the animals are quiet. A quiet that does not last, for the steps of the man in the tunic and the pale woman interrupt my meditation. No peace is eternal.

To preserve the sacredness of the moment, I close my eyes and continue to rotate words through my mind. When I focus on the words they acquire a certain sonority, an auditory presence as if the words were actually spoken out loud. These words create a sort of auditory dome, and inside this dome I remain seated, impervious to the comings and goings of the outside world. This is how I exist in these mountains, this is how I fend off evil, confusion, ignorance, and this is how I choose to live. I have a choice and I have chosen.

The man in the striped tunic walks around me as if trying to decipher my motives. He is wise enough to leave me undisturbed. He seems possessed by his own conundrums, something about good and evil, or maybe the past, the ultimate mélange of good and evil. The pale girl looks deep into the darkening alleys and takes off running after a cat. She is here for a reason, maybe the past as well. *Past*, what a daunting word, dense, short, so easy to pronounce. A word that contains the weight of shame and guilt, the bitterness of resentment, and occasionally, only occasionally, glory. If a saber were to cut our lives in two, we would end with an old self and the unrealized self. The first one we already know, and most likely abhor—that is our past. The second one we fear. Past passes fast, so all we have left is the unrealized self. That is to say, only fear remains.

From inside the word dome I continue to observe the interactions between the man and the pale woman. I see tenderness; I also see her cry. Maybe the cat did not want her company, or maybe the man in the tunic told her a terse word. An ender word, a word for rest, or ten words, ten, a word that ends, a redness, enter, or a tense sense. They do not talk to me; they only talk between themselves. Maybe my word dome looks impregnable from the outside. Words can create a shell around people.

The man stands in front of me and starts talking. I hear everything he says but do not understand what he means. I recognize a few untied words, like *beast, roses, desert*, I think he says something about *death*. I try to listen to his discourse but the stream of words I have been following floods my ears, turning his speech into a confusing gibberish. I look for logical sense but find no associations, no meaning. It seems like his sentences jump tracks, becoming completely derailed. I then raise my right hand and say, *yes*. He seems to understand for he stops talking.

The man turns away from me and sits with the young woman on a nearby bench. From this angle they look like lovers, the closeness, the warmth. An unlikely couple as far as their appearances are concerned. But in their disparity they seem to understand each other. One speaks and the other one listens, an interaction creating a sinusoidal wave of language. They seem to build a word dome completely separate from mine. I wonder what words they use with each other. I wonder if they recognize the miracle. I also speak to my mules but that is different. I have never spoken to a woman like that. I can imagine the words they use. I think I can.

Darkness is now complete. Only the moon is alive, no other lights endure. And the stream of words that lead me to this village continues to flow thru me. They come in bands, changing their length, meaning, cadence, and origin. They also come in different languages. I need to hoard them, I need to savor as many as I can. Some taste like dew, others like tragedy, two short ones like burnt sugar. I mouth them all, I chew them all, and I pronounce them delicately. The more words I let into my mind, the more words I pronounce, the deeper my intoxication. My head begins to spin and the words start to irradiate bright colors. I see obsidian blues, aquamarine, fire brick, impossible pinks. And when the white moon rays converge with the colors of the words, the horizon bursts in life and meaning. Yes, this is Yes, yes, I exist. The logos becomes flesh.

The one-armed man

The bright moon conspires against me. With no clouds in the sky, the moon has all night to shine on me. Look at my rifle, the silver barrel reflecting a gray light certain to alert the monsters. I wish this were a different night. But the criminals will not let up, full moon or otherwise. They are probably happy to see the bright moon rays, the lunatics. I will come down the mountain and take them by surprise, even if I have to crawl under shrubs to dodge the light. What matters is to stop the carnage.

I notice a different source of light in the center of the village. A strange round object, immobile, shines a white light. A sort of second moon, this object reflects the moon rays that fall from above. The hippies know all sorts of tricks, necromantic foes. They must know I am coming for them, why else rig this second moon? Maybe they want to blind me, or maybe they want to see my every move coming down the mountain. Beasts, criminals, cowards!

I begin to descend at a very slow pace, half crawling, hiding under the shadows of red *mélèze* trees, my rifle strapped to my back, my right hand clearing the way, and my dead arm just hanging. I hate this arm. I will cut it off and feed it to the dogs one day. After one hundred meters I stop and try to listen for any sounds. People will squeal when tortured. I hear nothing. They are probably waiting to deal with me first, the dismembering, before continuing with their ritual.

As the slope ends, I come to the edge of a clearing, and on the other side of it I see the first few houses. All of them dark harboring dark evil, I am sure. If I stay close to the ground and crawl, it will take me about 10 minutes to cross the clearing. Too long to be exposed like that. They may spot me from their hiding places and shoot me at once. If I were to make a mad dash and run as fast as I could, they would likely see the bouncing reflections of the rifle and also shoot me at once. I could also wait for a cloud to block the moon rays, but the sky is impossibly clear. They probably sacrificed people to their devil to get a clear sky like that.

I need to think. This is a crucial moment. And as I rehearse numerous strategies in my mind, the sweat accumulates on my forehead, and now it begins to drip. I wipe it off with my sleeve but it keeps on pouring out of my pores. Maybe they will hear me sweat, diabolical monsters they are. I am not holding back now. I would rather die in the assault, taking them head to head. I am not the coward. I am going in.

Run, run, run… I cast diagonal shadows ahead of me. No shots yet. Fast, faster. The rifle weighing me down. I hit something with my foot and stumble down to the ground. They will shoot me now. Get up quick, get up, the bullets are coming. I lean on the rifle to get back on my feet. Faster, run faster. As I get close to the end of the clearing I throw myself on the ground and seek cover under a crumbling shed. Suffocated, I try to get air. I need air. But stay quiet, silent, shorten the breaths, they may hear me. Sweating even more. Stop the sweat. Do not think. They may hear the thoughts. The murderers can hear me. Yes they can.

I see no blood on me. They did not hit me. I did not hear them shoot. I fooled them. No I did not. Now they know exactly where I am. They are probably waiting for me to get closer. Then they will jump all over me, the massacre. I must calm down, calm down, and continue moving forward. Use the shadows. But the moon does not let go of me. This is the night they needed, with a full moon they can kill more.

Following the perimeter of the dark houses I move slowly, looking for signs of brutality. I see nobody, no lights either. They must be gathered enjoying their séance in some basement, possibly drinking blood and eating human flesh, the beasts. I stay close to the walls, stopping every ten steps to listen for their chants. As I turn a corner I come to what seems like a central plaza, dark houses surrounding a few trees and benches. And in the center of the plaza I see that horrendous fat albino I should have killed down in Saorge. He seems to be just sitting on the ground soaking the moon rays. His skin inhumanly white. He must be a decoy, a way to lure me into their hands. From this vantage point I can take him down with my rifle. No, no… that is surely what they want. He may not even be real; he may be a projection, a vision. Maybe the moon is playing tricks on me. Better not shoot him.

I crawl from one shadow to the next trying to get closer to this vision. The closer I get the more intense his radiance. The burning bush he is not. More like a devil, an incubus, Son of Satan, Beelzebub. And he does not move. He only moves his lips, as if praying, the sorcerer. Do not believe. Do not believe what you see. Do not believe what you hear. A series of words come out of his mouth in a low monotonous tone, conjuring something, or just trying to bewitch me. An onslaught of words.

Nadya

ow sad to see this village again, empty. More memories than people live here. Or maybe there are more people in my memories than in my life nowadays. All those who left, René, Antonia, even my older sister, I cannot see or do not want to see anymore. Maybe this is what happens when people get old. But I am not old yet.

He keeps holding my hand and I like the warmth. I would not have come all the way back here without such warmth. There is something about it. A sense of safety, as if nothing could hurt me. I squeeze his hand tightly, like this, yes. I will not be hurt anymore, not if he holds my hand. I love the dark of nighttime even more.

But I know he comes here looking for the bastard who hurt me. I wish never to see that face again, but if he finds him, I will have to look into those eyes again. A deeply hateful stare. Horror, that is all. I wonder if René or Antonia ever felt this way. Outcasts they were, not different from me. They must have been abused, what else can we expect when outcasts get out into the world? I thought leaving this place was a good idea, but existing as an outcast somewhere else is not any better. I do not hate my life, but I hate when my life gets wounded.

So many houses and so many doors. And everything closed. This was a lively place before, I remember. Not sad like it seems now. We used to run around, ignorant of the rampant confusion. Who was who? Who was whose son or daughter? Why did we play games we should not have played? Why did René cry more than me when they found us naked? Why did Antonia want to touch me? I wanted to be happy but I ended up confused and without anyone to ask. I could not count on my older sister. What else could I have done? Run away. That was it. Run away.

I feel like losing myself in the shadows, bolting into the night. But in this bright night the shadows are scarce. This is not my typical night. Night it is, but not as obscuring. And if I were to let go of his hand I know I would feel small. Last time I let go I ended up hurt. No more hurt for me. So I grab on to his hand and lead him through the paths I remember. We walk away from the plaza in no particular direction. My memory of this place is faulty and a path I recognize quickly turns into unknown territory. I think I know where I walked before, or maybe I walked without knowing, who knows?

On the far end of the village we come to a house with lights shining through the windows. The only sign so far that someone lives in this place. From the distance we do not hear much, but as we get closer, the voices begin to fill the bright night. At this point he walks ahead of me. I follow. I wonder why all the other houses are dark. Why is everyone together in one place? I remember times when we were all together, and the chaos that went along with that. But it was always at the plaza, or out in the fields, not inside houses.

We get to the door and stand there without knocking or making any other sound. He seems to listen for the pitch of every voice. Many people talking at the same time, hard to tell what they are saying. The voices have a familiar sound but I cannot identify who they are. I was never a listener, of people that is. He then straightens his body assuming a posture of complete serenity. Under the moon rays his weathered face assumes a relaxed expression. I hear his breath slowing down and settling into a rhythmic flow, like the purring of a cat. A certain light he radiates, an untouchable light. And as if performing an ancient ritual, with slow and determined movements, he takes off his striped tunic, folds it delicately and hands it to me. He pushes the door open, and in broad nakedness, walks inside the house where the voices are coming from.

I fear the hippies will kill him. Why are they gathered inside this house? I try to listen but all I hear is silence, a dead silence. All the voices died inside the house. Maybe I should go in there to help him; I am an ex-hippie after all. But I doubt they will remember me. Like I do not remember them. Only the troubling moments with René, with Antonia, and when my older sister was found in bed with an older man, someone's father, I remember those moments but nothing else. What a miserable feeling, to remember only what I should forget.

At this moment the lights continue to shine and the silence continues to reign. He came up to Berghe because of me, he disrobed because of me, and he went in there to confront this hippie group because of me. And all I did was give him food and wine, and my hand. I wonder what I mean to him. Me, so little, so nothing. Does he need me? Does he really need my hand?

Waiting in this clear night makes me feel exposed. Standing here in anticipation of something horrible. What is the point of me being here? I am holding his tunic, yes, and I hold it as if I were holding him. That is what I am doing; I am holding his shell. He left it behind and he went in the house without it. Maybe he needs to confront evil in his bare skin. Where did he learn to fight this way?

The lights continue to shine through the windows. I try to listen for the voices but the house remains completely quiet. The only thing I hear is the wind. Time begins to turn into an anomalous mass. Have I waited for a few hours or a few days? Maybe I was born in this house a few minutes ago and I am just a baby. If I went into the house both of my parents would be there. I could tell who my mother is, the one with the pool of blood between her legs. But how could I tell who my father is, the one with the ample smile or the one who is not here at

all? I could just push the door open and walk into the middle
of the mêlée. But I do not. Sometimes it is better not to know.
I decide to avoid the confrontation with my uncertain past.
I will stay outside this house; I will not enter the quagmire.
Out in the open, the moon rays spread an obligatory light that
blinds me. No, this is definitely not my kind of night. I like
them dark, dark as dark can be. What good is a night without
its darkness?

The door opens suddenly and out comes this man who I
am trying to understand. He takes his striped tunic from my
arms and dons it in the same ritualistic way in which he took
it off before entering the house.

—What happened in there?

—You were born.

—How can that be possible?

—Look at yourself; you're like a newborn baby.

—I think I'm old; I even have memories of this place.

—No, you were just born.

—I don't feel that new.

—Maybe the moon, the white light.

—Yes, the white light destroys my night.

—A young moon casts shadows; you can still find darkness
in this light. You're made of both, darkness and light.

—And what're you made off?

—Consciousness.

—Is that why they didn't kill you?

—No, they couldn't find a reason to kill me.

—Did they even touch you?

—Not a single one of them.

—So, nothing has really happened.

—Many things have happened. I found out where evil is.

—Where is it?

—At the end of the night, Nadya.

Didier

So bright this night. Fuckface will have no problem finding that smelly man if he sets his snout to it. Or maybe that man will find Fuckface first. Either way I win, at least one of them will be killed. I really do not need people like them, pissing around my shop and making me worry. It will be great if they take care of each other. Fuckface is the one to do it because the other dogs are a bunch of cowards. Cowards... that is what they are. I think another top dog would be better for me. A more docile one, stupid like Fuckface, but not as brutish and impulsive. If he were gone, another dog would be at the top at once.

And what if Fuckface finds that civet but Nadya happens to be there with him? If Fuckface gets to kill that man he will get all rabid and try to rape Nadya again. This is horrible but I cannot control what happens. You deal with beasts and this is what you get. The poor girl should be with that wench sister of hers. She should not be meandering the village at night or opening her trap to strangers. But what is she to know? Confused like she seems. And if someone gets killed I will be the first one to get drilled by the *gendarmes*.

That house where the sisters live does not belong to them. Squatters they are. I do not really know which house it is but the smell of cheese will tell me. Nadya could be there. I hope she is. I traverse the two main paths at the bottom of the village, the pit of the village, where I have heard they live. Down by where the *lavoir* water drains into the river, next to a sickly looking garden, I come near a house with the strong smell of Roquefort. Three or four cats are sitting by the door taking a moon bath.

I knock hard on the door. I knock again. The door opens and the face of a young girl pokes out. The cats take advantage and run swiftly inside the house. The face vanishes quickly, leaving the door halfway open. No, do not go inside. Do not intrude into their lives. I wait to see if anyone else would come to the door. I wait some more. A conversation grows inside the house. And suddenly at the door's threshold, I see the face of Nadya's older sister. She stares at me with disdain, as if I were a filthy creature. She has no sense of politeness. After all, she knows about me as much as I know about her—not much. She probably thinks I despise her. And if that is how she thinks, she would be absolutely correct, as I indeed loathe the woman. That is the least I can do. I could also hate her, but I do not love her enough for that.

—Is Nadya in the house?

—No, she's not. Why do you ask?

—I think she's in trouble.

—Why do you say that?

—People, things I see.

—There's nothing to see around here. Get lost.

—Where is she?

—You told me yesterday you knew how to find her.

—I'm not sure I could find her.

—She's fine wherever she is. Fuck off now.

The door closes with a loud thump. What else should I expect? I barely know any of these women. The few times I said something to Nadya, strange daylight moments, but she ran away from me. I could fool myself thinking she does that only in daylight. I am sure her quick rejection happens day and night. Day and night can make for a long period.

Someone could have seen me when I brought Nadya to the épicerie, or when I carried her back to that ruin in the mountain. Maybe someone saw me at the *lavoir*. If the *gendarmes* come to question me I will be doomed. I cannot let this unravel. I could go around looking for Nadya all night and find nothing. Better to use this night to cover everything up.

Trying to be as quiet as possible I go back and open the épicerie. I grab a couple rags, a scrubbing brush, and some detergent. I then walk in the direction of the Fontane de Mèdge making sure the shadows cover me. So bright this night, so hard to find good shadows. As I approach the *lavoir* I hear the water running, continuously running, from the source in the mountains to the interconnected *lavoirs* in the village, and then down to the river below. Water runs through the heart of this village, cold water. And once at the *lavoir*, I see how still and peaceful the water rests in the basin, reflecting a pristine moon, reflecting my face.

The ground is splattered with dark spots. Blood, I think. Hard to tell because none are red anymore. The ones that look like a granular crust must be dry blood, the purple ones. I kneel on the ground, wet my index finger with saliva, and scratch a deep purple spot. I lick my finger. The taste of blood, I think. Blood will cost me. With both of my hands I scoop water from the basin and wet the evidence. I pour detergent and start to scrub as hard as I can. Scrub hard, harder. Nothing should remain. I do not want her stains. Let Fuckface be the stained one, let him pay the consequences. He is the vicious dog, not me. And he will likely spill more blood, the animal. Pour more water, rinse the blood away, scrub, pour more water, more.

The water in the basin is no longer still. The moon rays get reflected in scandalous ways creating a broken light that falls over me. And when I look in the basin I no longer see my face, but my disfigurement.

The old sister

That devil knocking on my door this late at night. Fuck off, yes, fuck off, that's what he needs to do. And then asking about Nadya. He's trying to tease me. He sure knows I've no idea where she is. He wants to get me mad so he can laugh at me and tell all those idiots that kiss his ass how ugly I look when mad. But he's not getting that. He can go back up to his filthy shop and get drunk with the other losers. I don't need his shit.

Thing is, he's right there in the middle of the village where everyone goes by. Maybe he does know about the little mouse. And he said that she could be in trouble. I mean, what kind of trouble? That girl knows how to take care of herself, walking all alone at night as she does. But he didn't have to come all the way down here just to get me upset. I've never seen him down this way before. He sure thinks this is the armpit of the village.

But why does he give a shit about Nadya? I thought he didn't care about anybody. Never heard anyone say anything good about him, ever. Always looking at you like you're an insect or something. And he wouldn't buy my cheese because he thinks it's rotten. Like I said, get away or he'll pee on you. So, why does he bother to come here? Unless he's got a big urge to pee on me.

He sure did me a number because I can't sleep this way. All this crap in my head and worrying more by the minute. Where could the little mouse be? In Berghe? I didn't look around much this afternoon. Hate that place. Well, I didn't look at all. She could've gone there for real. She could've met a hippie who dragged her back up there. The little mouse with a man before I get my own man. Can't believe it. And that idiot

Jules or fucking Julien, whatever his name is, not talking to me. I hate this. Better go back up to Berghe again now that *La Petite* is asleep. I could bring Nadya back with me before sunrise, if I find her. Little mouse from hell.

Crank on this old truck and the noise wakes two slumbering cats that run for cover. Shift into first gear and off I go. Don't like driving these curvy roads at night but it is clear enough. Look at that moon. What a big cheese that is. Going down the road to Fontan is easy, but driving up to Berghe, doing those hairpin turns, shit. One good reason to never go back there, among many others, like having to get up at dawn to go work in the fields. Never doing that again. That's what I'm saying, the little mouse wouldn't want to return to Berghe. A man, yes, what else would take her there?

Drive by the spot where I saw those two circus men earlier but no one's there by the roadside. Not sure if they were coming or going, but if they went up I'll recognize them. Maybe that's what Didier meant, those could be nasty people or something. They sure were not hippies. And what harm could those people do anyway? Everyone in Berghe is so ready to fuck someone up if they have to. I don't know, but I better get up there quick.

Get to the end of the road in Berghe. Park the truck right there blocking the turn around. Not that many people come here, not at this time. Look around and see nobody. This place seems deader than before. Not a single window with light. Maybe they changed their ways, the hippies, they used to carry on until the late hours, the mêlée, the craziness, but not anymore it seems. With the bright moon I can see like daylight, and the place just looks like before, except for the lack of people.

What can Nadya want from this dead place? Girl has all she wants with *La Petite* and me: a house, well not our house but just the same, a job, all the food she needs, good cheese, actually best cheese ever, not the rotten rubbish we drag around but the good one we keep home. I admit, not the best life to meet a man, but that hasn't driven me crazy yet, so why should she get desperate? I don't think I'm desperate, not really. Girl thinks she's smarter than me. Well, she is but not by that much. I'm older, I know better.

From a ditch between two houses I hear animal noises and see a bunch of legs and arms whipping hard. A big cockroach? No, no, it sounds like a bird. A tweet or something. Wonder what the hippies are growing these days. Get a little closer and see a man on the ground. Shit, he looks bad, like smashed or trampled. A big beard, blood all over, a beaten man. He sees me coming closer and tries to crawl away. Nowhere to go. Stuck in the ditch he turns his face to me. I might've seen him in Saorge. I stop moving and he stops thrashing. Catch his stare straight. Yes, life has fucked him up.

—you're the sister

—What you say?

—didn't touch her, not me

—Touch who?

—Fuckface did, I didn't

—Go slow, go slow.

—did you smell him?

—Who're you talking about?

—that man with the tunic

So weird his voice, I can't tell what he says. Like some kind of bird talk. Yes, I've seen him hanging with the drunks at the bench. Didier's crowd. But what's he doing up here? And looking so hurt. Never seen a man like this, so bloody and beaten to the ground. He won't get up, he stays on the ground looking around him as if waiting for something.

—got any food?

—No.

—you're the sister, yes you are

—Are you talking about Nadya?

—didn't touch the thingy

—I'm trying to find my sister

—not me, not me, Fuckface did

—Have you seen my sister?

—don't hurt me

—Listen, can you make any sense?

—Fuckface, Fuckface, I swear

Don't really know what this devil is saying. Even if he saw Nadya he couldn't tell me. She must be somewhere around here. I feel it. Better move away from this man before the same thing happens to me. Don't want to get beaten like that. But when I try to step back, he lurches at me and grabs me by the leg. Greasy hands. I kick him to let myself free, he rolls back.

—Get away, you fucker.

—thingy got hurt

—I'll hurt you if you touch me again.

—wasn't me

—For God's sake, what're you trying to say?

—he, he, he'll kill me

This time I move faster out of his reach. Who knows what happened to this man? Maybe that's what Didier said, people getting hurt around here. Better find Nadya soon. A small village this is, won't take me long to find her if she's here. I get out of the ditch and go to the center plaza to start looking there. And as I get closer I see a large hump, a man or something, yes, that white thing I saw by the side of the road, now sitting there in the middle of the plaza talking out loud.

The chirping man

Should have grabbed her even tighter, now she's gone, and if she finds the stinker she'll tell him where I am, she'll say I'm half dead, not so, just a little hurt, and that won't keep him away, he'd like to see me fully dead, fuck me

try to get up and run away but everything hurts, the head, like a big balloon, the legs bending, push off the ground with one hand and the world spins, without Blood of Christ, the world spinning without Blood of Christ, no food, maybe that's the problem, or the fear, try to kneel, better this way, easy, easy, spinning a little less

hear steps, catch the smell, he's coming for me, get back to the ground and roll sideways away from the moonlight, steps get closer, louder, and the smell, shit, he'll get me, stay quiet, try not to breathe, tuck my head in between my knees, I don't exist, gone, I'm gone, skip me, walk by me, go get Fuckface, he did it, I know he did it, the dog

hear them talk, the thingy, yes, like to hear her talk, wish I would only hear her but the stinker is also talking, they're here, fuck me, she knows it wasn't me, but my face now all bloody, how could she tell when all she saw was fear, face of fear, Fuckface, my face

so many words, talk, talk, talk, he'll kill me with words, cover my ears and still hear them, right now, over me, next to me, soon the blow, get killed by a blow to the head, or the words banging on me, words are hurting, press hard with my knees, squeeze my head, balloon head, keep those words away, but no, they get louder, drilling me, this hurts

weird taste in the mouth again, the zigzag lines, and my body tensing up, hell no, the teeth growing, in two seconds, it will all go dark in two seconds, here we go again, fucking fit, he'll see me kicking and pulling, keep tight, wrap the arms around the knees, zigzag, zigzag, the smell, metal in my mouth, the stomach rising, I've been here, fuck me, bite the ground

The fat poet

Consider the weight of a single word. For example, if *lead* were to be the last word in a sentence, it would pull the sentence down.

Open
   your
      chest
        to
          my
            bullets,
              learn
                to
                  lust
                    for
                      lead.

Am I worth my weight in words? Bearing in mind the largeness of my body, the sheer weight of my bones, muscles and fat, I would have to be a modern Shakespeare. Sitting in the vacuum of this night uttering one word after another, am I worthy of my words? Or am I a weightless sham, a vacuous bard? I could use light words to float my verses. Would that make me a better poet? No. But what if I considered, not the weight, but the impact of a word, how strong a word hits the brain? Well, force = mass x acceleration. And mass is nothing but weight. I am back to weight.

I then concentrate in directing my entire weight down to the center of the earth while looking up at the sunny moon. The stream of words continues its relentless flow indicating I must be on the verge of greatness, on the verge of writing one verse worth my weight. And as words flow close enough, they touch me with their personal tone. A soft ripple, a sound wave that enters through my ears and circulates inside of me. I absorb each word, I integrate them into my unconscious, and my brain gets intoxicated with their plenitude. If my mules could see me now! They would understand why I feed them words. They cannot hear them as I do, but they can grind them with their jaws and drain their meaning, my mind being nothing superior to that of a connoisseur of grasses.

Shifting from the realm of weight into the realm of musical notes allows me to forget about my body and concentrate on the minute vibration that each word produces. I extend my open palm to the sky and wait for the first word to land on it. And almost at once, the word *serene* comes to lie peacefully. The fingers of my mind start playing the word, stroking each of its fibers, plucking deep into its core. And the variations resonate in the lunar night.

serene

essere

ser

René

Reneé

qui es-tu?

I do not know who you are *Reneé,* but this village owes you a canticle. Because the words come from everywhere and everywhere they go. Always resonant, composing brilliant melodies sometimes, other times grotesque. And as the wind blows, another word lands on my hand. This time I hear the oppositional timbre of *antonym.* My mind prepares for a confrontation, but I play the word nonetheless.

antonym

anonym

Antonia

non

nay

Nadya

This last word, a name, has a special sonority, demure, yet spacious, with an undeniable presence. Who are all of you? Why do you want to sing? The wind then stirs the flow of words and they start to land on my hand in duplets, triplets, quadruplets, even quintuplets, making for a polyphony of past and present melodies.

Listening to the words, listening to the songs, listening to the inherent vibrations in every syllable, I come to conceive the literary world as a musical creation where every effort to mesmerize with text, every attempt to excel in prose or verse, is nothing other than a venture into musical composition. And if I were to sing a *vida*, or if I were to write a sonnet, I would be doing one and the same thing. And if I were to write a novel, or if I were to compose a symphony, my writing hand and my musical mind would be in unison. I open my mind to the world of sounds, to the world of words, to their communion. And I am happy.

Lunate crown, the words are, lovely-haired trace of the benevolent goddess. When Selene crosses the sky, riding sidesaddle on an ox, with her horns and torch, she engenders a wake of words, brilliant words, as luminous as her crescent self. To say words are stars would be false. Dust they are. Or diminutive fragments that fall from above. The strong winds play havoc with them, twisting and pulling them, creating the stream that brought me here. Go find him, Selene, and feast on his flesh, your Endymion, while he sleeps an abandoned sleep, like everyone in this village.

I feel the immensity of my weight attaching me to this desolate plaza. Without a desire to go anywhere else, I accept my reality. And as I look for reasons to stand up and leave this village behind, I find none, not at this moment, not when the words are still flowing. Who knows if the man in the striped tunic and the pale girl want to stay in this village? They seem content with each other, but do they share words, do they feast in the flesh of language? I watch as they get close to me, walk around me, circumnavigating the continent of I. The girl touches my knee with a certain degree of trepidation. I wonder if she thinks I am dead. The man in the striped tunic remains stoic, thinking it seems, or maybe just remembering. They do not speak to me. A situation I appreciate, for I am surrounded by so many other words I have yet to entertain.

The mountain range towards the east, jagged, grows a thin sliver of yellowish light on its back. Selene looks behind her as if pressured. She has not completed her journey, not yet. I rush to taste more words, I swallow a bunch, chew on some of them, and spit out a handful as if blowing a horn. Silver dying and gold rising, the never-ending cycle, the regeneration of hope, love, fear, and the human attempt to make all of it verbal. As for myself, I have yet to finish my own journey. Language is eternal, that is why I am a poet.

The man in the striped tunic pirouettes away from me, the pale woman holds his hand, and they whisper to each other, they share their breaths, secrets maybe, or painful words. I want to join them. I want to feel I belong to them. My mules belong to me, and I belong to my mules. But they have not yet reached the level of emotional language, when a word, or just a mere syllable, contains the entire meaning of the universe. My mules are advanced students, more astute than the vast majority of people in the village, but they do not know when to cry. And this man and this woman know when to drop their tears.

The pale woman presses her body against the man. I wonder how her skin reacts to the harshness of the garment. If a word were to describe that shell it would be aromatic or textured or maybe deadened, like the discarded skin of a large reptile. But the marvel of their togetherness rises in the clarity of the moon. They could not kill the night even if they wanted, but they could easily generate a stream of words of their own.

And as I retain my position, unleashing my weight on this unbiased ground, as I continue to taste the words that circle me, as I consider the numerous iterations of verbs, adjectives, nouns, proverbs, articles, tears, lies, loneliness, perverted memories, and images of myself as a Buddha, as a white whale on dry land, a leviathan of the mountain, a morose mound of white flesh soiling itself in the center of this plaza, I come to terms with my limitations. I live for language, but language does not live for me.

The striped tunic

What is the precise end of the night? Is it when the first breath of light bursts in the horizon, east from west? Or when the last shadow capitulates, overwhelmed and weakened by the advancing glow? Aurora, cover your body, do not show me your breasts. I refuse to cross that,

line,

this night must last,

a long time,

longer than ever,

saving her,

saving me.

An uneasy sense of impending doom penetrates through my pores. I know this feeling, so prevalent in the desert, where the vast emptiness proposes a million deaths but there is no one around to kill you. In moments like this the beast howls the loudest. But all I can see or hear around me is Nadya, small Nadya, and Yes, sitting in meditation and chanting words. Beyond them there is nothing, or the impression of nothingness, which fuels the sense of doom and serves as an echo chamber for the howling.

Uneasy feelings do not threaten me. I let them enter my mind and stay for a while. I sometimes reason with them, other times I completely ignore them, but most often I watch them in silence until they get bored and decide to leave. I win every time. However, when the beast howls or when the river roars, I pay attention. The river is far from here and its roar cannot climb this high in the mountains. But the howling exists anytime people surround me, for it is from within deviant minds that it originates.

I remember walking north in the desert, or west, but

always trying to reach that point where all things and souls coalesce. That place where nothing existed until trade, human and otherwise, brought upon a new reality.

I remember I had a name,

but I do not want to remember what that name was.

The mind knows how to protect itself.

With Nadya holding my hand, I walk closer to where Yes is sitting. His bald head and hairless face reflect the totality of the moon, making him a geminate moon, as white, as brilliant. His smallish mouth does not stop articulating words, a litany, maybe a mantra. He seems completely unaware of our presence. Such is his level of concentration, consumption, or perhaps ecstasy. I try to listen to the words but they defy my comprehension. A language without modern meaning, a proto-language, an original consciousness as ancient as the first man. His large body seems bloated, sourcing all the words in the world.

A series of steps, a shuffling, and a forceful breathing suddenly break the uniformity of the chant. I look everywhere, but the receding shadows still cover the surrounding houses. The hippies are indoors, Nadya is next to me; only evil could be lurking around. I remain steady, listening to the stream of words Yes unleashes while holding Nadya's hand. Once again the sound of feet, something dragging on the ground, and the liquid sound of sweat oozing from someone's body. Nadya does not seem to hear anything, her face tranquil. But I know when another mind enters into my realm, especially a troubled mind.

Letting go of Nadya's hand I turn around and prepare to face the forthcoming consciousness. But there is nothing visible, only the sound of feet and sweat and the sense of a presence. Wait, just wait, everything becomes manifest. And for the fraction of a second, a loose moon ray bounces against a shiny metal surface. A dark cylinder, the cannon of a rifle, probably covered in sweat. I resist my urge to confront, to disarm. I just hide inside my mind in anticipation. The moon grows to an impossible size as it begins to search for a place to rest over the silhouette of the jagged mountains.

From under the overhang of an old house, the figure of a tall man emerges. I recognize him, the limp arm hanging against the side of his body, a rifle barely propped up and pointing in my direction, the fearful expression. This man who wants me dead for no other reason than his need to silence his derailed mind, a mind fractured, vitiated by generations of disordered thoughts. As he starts to walk toward me, I appreciate the vastness of his fear. His feet shake slightly before he plants them urgently on the ground. He holds the rifle with such force that the tip of his fingers and the nail beds turn white. And then there is the sweat, a river of sweat, streaming down from his forehead. And for a moment I wonder if he is crying.

Polyphony

lift my head and see the low moon, staying white even as it goes down to the ground, unlike me, I'm bloody, where's my Blood of Christ, need you now, better drink now before the rancid man comes

Wonder what he's saying. He looks like a globe or something. This can't be the man my little sister is after. Granted she's strange, the little mouse, but not strange enough to come up to Berghe for this man, or elephant.

Some words seem to shine more than others. Is their radiance a result of their sound or their inherent meaning? If, for example, I consider the word *caprice,* a certain brassy light invades my conscience matching the word's harmonious sound. However, when I consider the word *moon,* a silvery glow comes to meet me even when the actual sound of the word is anything but silvery, to the contrary, it sounds deep, even obtuse. And as the moon retreats in this dying night, I wonder if I will miss its glow, or would I be missing its meaning?

This immense albino talks nonsense to bait me, to pull me into the center of this plaza where I will be fulminated by his kind. I point my rifle at his large body. I cannot miss. I will get only one shot. My eyes so blurry with this damned sweat. I cannot wipe my face now. I cannot lower the rifle.

—Are you sure you want to shoot that rifle?

—Beelzebub!

—In your mind I am.

—Monsters, all of you.

—You're the one with the rifle.

—Son of Satan!

—Why are you crying?

—I'm not crying.

—Why are you so afraid?

—I'll kill you too.

—Put that rifle down.

—Incubus!

Why is my old sister looking for me? I try to leave her behind, together with everything the day represents. I am done selling cheese, I am done being the weird sister, and I am done with day life and all the people who profess to it. I need to go away and find my own night. But she follows me, to this original place that only breeds confusion and a sense of strangeness.

hear their voices, motherfuckers gathering at the plaza, all of them, he, he, he among them, the end of me, better stay low, close to the ground, invisible, but look at the moon, look at the man that looks like the moon, fat, and that rifle pointing at him, and the thingy, pretty, pretty, but no hippies around, motherfuckers, grab the ground, low, stay low, no more hurt

I am not my cat. I cannot bat the rifle pointing at me with my paws and expect life to continue. But what if the rifle had a voice? Not the thunderous blast of gunpowder and excrement, but an articulated utterance, like the human voice. A loud voice, I would assume, even convincing. A doubtful proposition that is. But if a bullet were to speak, would it speak in French, or Spanish, or perhaps in a language of its own. A fast, leaden, often destructive language, the language of ignorant brutes. I better not hear. Give me simple words instead, silent ones, the ones humans and educated mules know how to wield.

Look at her, next to that strange man with that filthy tunic. Is this what she wants? All those nights running around the village to end up with that misfit? I know I don't have a man, but I would never settle for a freak like that. And all that schooling for nothing. What a waste. She's got to be confused, or drugged, or maybe she's hurt like Didier said. But she doesn't look my way, keeping her eyes set on that striped tunic. She could be under a spell or something.

—What will happen to you after you pull that trigger?

—I'll shoot you and throw you in a bottomless pit.

—No, you won't dare.

—I'll stop your bloody rituals.

—Where's the blood? I don't see any around here?

—Inside those houses, where the devils are.

—People sleep inside those houses. Don't you hear their silence?

—I hear their screams.

—The screams are inside your mind.

the thingy so pretty, and look at the old sister, nothing like her, no, no, she's beaten like me, wonder if she knows about the rape, maybe she came here to take her back home, but he, he, he'll not let her go, if the sister sees me she'll scream, he'll kill me then, hug the ground now

This night is ending. The morning glow is creeping up from behind the mountains. And the day brings misery again. I want my nights back. This man, holding the rifle with only one arm and pointing at Yes looks crazy. There is something wrong with him. I am afraid someone will get hurt. I got badly hurt yesterday. It cannot be me again. I hope not.

They are surrounding me. They are looking at me. Even the mother of that young woman, and the young woman herself. They turned her into a she-devil. They are all in this together. This is hell. Evil has spread. Armageddon! The end of days is here.

Words pronounced in total darkness imply certain complicity, their existence depending on validation by another consciousness. The same happens when we talk to ourselves, that moment when our consciousness validates our very existence. We are the words we say to each other. And when there is no other, to our own selves. This is why I teach my mules to think out loud. And when the morning comes, this miracle unfolding in front of me, words fly like frenetic butterflies flashing their colors. Words infused by light for all to see. They flutter, land on white paper, on the tongues of children, on the grasses that feed my mules. I hear the words. I see them. And at this moment I hear the word *blast*, resounding like thunder. And I see the word *red* dripping out of my rotund belly. And I know I exist because of language, and will continue to exist because of the words I leave behind.

—You're next, Beelzebub.

—You're not done crying.

—I'm not crying.

—Maybe it's the river in you.

With force, I tackle him down to the floor, wrap my hands around his neck, and tighten them, hard, harder. I have not touched a man in a very long time. And I do not want to touch this man now, but I have to destroy this ignoble life form. This is not the desert, but these are the same hands I used in the desert when I had to right wrongs. But that is part of my past, and that past is mostly dead. The now saddens me,

the death of the poet saddens me,

the words,

who will usher the words,

Yes?

So bright this morning. So horrible. Everything seems unreal. Maybe that is what happens, light revealing real darkness. And as he steps back, leaving that disturbed man lying still on the ground, I grab on to his striped tunic and hold him tight, hoping for an unquenchable night.

And she, holding on to that strange man. What has she gotten herself into? Two people dead. I don't fucking know. Maybe I don't want to know. Nothing changes is this fucking place. Shit's always coming down. Best thing is to leave now.

Like I'm running for that truck and getting my ass somewhere else. But if I leave her, my little mouse. Fuck, I don't know anymore. All I know is I don't know who she really is, my little mouse. Maybe she's not mine as I think. Maybe she never was. Out of here.

he, he, he did that, knew he was dangerous, and that poor white man bleeding on the ground, better look for cover, I may be next, the hippies will take me in, they may throw me around some, but they remember my name, I need Blood of Christ

CODETTA

Didier

Better not leave anything to chance. Chance will destroy me. And with Fuckface roaming around, chances are things will get worse. I am who I am because I take matters into my own hands. There is no sense in waiting. This morning is clear and the air is calm, I will find Fuckface, even if I have to search the whole village to find his trace. The animal is not that smart, he must be peeing against a tree somewhere nearby, waiting for the rest of the pack to get high.

If I open the épicerie the other dogs will soon come to buy beer and sit at the bench. They may know where he is. But if he comes to join them, he will get high and start talking and saying stupid things that may get me into trouble. I will not be able to pull him away from the pack. No, I need to get to him when he is alone, before everything begins to unravel.

Without turning on the lights, I go inside the épicerie and unlock the drawer under the cash register. There it is. The barrel is full. One thing is to have a gun ready to fire; another thing is to fire it. The gun feels heavy. I can deal with it, I am sure. Before stepping out of the épicerie, I look in all directions. The bench is empty, so is the path coming down from the church except for a cat or two. I quickly move away from the door and take the path leading down to the lower part of the village where Fuckface squats like the dog he is. Too early for him to be anywhere else, plus where would he get any dope at this time? I hope he is not with the pack.

A dark passage leads to a landing open to the southern light. A sharp turn to the right, down a few steps, and I see the door to the room where he squats. I move slowly and come close to the door where I stand in silence, listening. I hear a moaning, a whimper maybe, coming from behind the wooden door. It sounds like Fuckface. I cannot understand the words, the dissonant slow bark, the drool. But the tone is his. I have no doubts. Outside the door I remain, trying to get a real sense of the weight of the gun.

All in one motion, I kick the door open and step into a small room holding the gun in front of me at eye level. I find Fuckface on his knees, rocking back and forth like a hurt child. He looks up at me and I see his face, that desecrated territory, covered in tears and snot, everything dripping. He must be coming down from dope, or maybe he is sad. No, he is a damned dog, there is no sadness here. What a world he lives in! Who can blame him, with that face?

Keeping a safe distance I walk behind Fuckface who remains kneeling on the ground. I lower the gun and touch the back of his neck with the barrel. Pressing hard against his neck I force him to bend over his knees and face the ground. His knees bent, his body bent over his knees, his head bent over his body. The prostrated dog dissolves himself, oozing, dripping. And his whimpering continues, louder now.

—Need some dope?

—nnnn

—Kick it, kick it.

—nnrnnrn

—You haven't found that stinker, have you?

—nrnnnr

—How about that girl. You had to rape her. You had to.

—arh, arh

—Was it fun?

—nrnnrn

—Stupid animal.

—uhhn, uhhhn

All I have to do is pull the trigger. He will not feel it. Put an end to his misery, that is what I should do. What do I care? Do I care? No, not for a second. Does he even know that I do not care? Look at him, bent over like a child, and whimpering. The beauty of the gun is that it can bring an end to this moment. I can get him and all his mange and boiling bile out of my life. His body will rot before anyone would care to look for him. A dead dog is a dog, but dead.

He falls on his side and for a moment I fear he will get up from the ground and attack me. But he does not. He just looks at me, immobile, dejected, forcing me to sustain my attention on his face longer than I ever had. For the first time I see him as something other than a dog, a person, maybe. And from under the film of gook that covers his disastrous face, I recognize the angle of his jaw, the downward slant of his eyes, and the crooked nose—a revolting familiar air. This is horrible. This is worse than horrible. Fuck you Fuckface. And fuck all of you, your kind, your fucked-up origin, my mother for having had you, and all who played the game of confusion, fuck all of you, fuck all of me. The brutal genetic mandate does not allow for changes. It all passes down, from one disturbed generation to the next. Except my face, the pretty one, goatee and all, coming from the same hippie stock, did not get spoiled, to the contrary, remains a truly composed face.

I kick Fuckface on his flank as hard as I can. I continue kicking him, again and again again, until he rolls all over the ground. He moans, but not a word, the dog has no words. What can the animal say? I hope he will leave this village on four legs, licking his wounds, the tail between his legs. He will find another master, the dog.

I stick the gun barrel inside his mouth. What an unbearable steel taste this must be. No gunpowder, no smoke taste yet. Just a hard, clean, irrevocable metal taste. And his face bursts into pieces when I pull the trigger. Am I not another dog from the same seed? Am I not as rabid? My face is not vandalized, but what have I become?

Nadya

People behave in animal ways. Not my cats, those who come to greet me at night behave the way people should, they mean what they say with their eyes, they do not know how to lie, and they are not possessive. There is no pretending at night, there is no covering your eyes from the sun, and the shadows are real, dark is dark, and what you do not see is not really hiding from you. The day inflicts blood and confusion. I do not want it. I do not need it.

I wrap a loose end of his striped tunic around my head to keep the light from reaching me. I make a beautiful cocoon, symmetrical, all tightly wrapped in an oval shape. I welcome life inside the close-knitted fabric of his tunic with the strong body aroma and the essence of places far from here. This is how I build a long night, a continuous night, a bridge to carry me from dawn to dusk. This is what I need. Not the day. I do not belong to the day, like I no longer belong to Berghe, like I do not belong to the life my sister has created for me.

We walk down the mountain. Sometimes we run, or skip over the hard rocks shaping the path. We seem to be alone because I only hear our steps. Nothing other than our feet stomping over the path. And as we descend from Berghe Supérieur, I do not dare to look at the day. I keep my head wrapped in his tunic while his arm tucks me close to his body. For a moment I fear the blood dripping out from the albino follows us like a fluid serpent, hissing. But that is not possible. My own blood did not follow me after that beast violated my body. We are nothing to the world. We are all detached from our own blood.

The river now. At the bottom of the gorge this river stands, vibrating, demarking the limit of my night realm. And the water, cascading, licking my feet, cold water. Before I dare to part the waters, I find myself floating. He lifts my body and makes me float over the water, keeping us in motion, flowing across the current. This river is familiar to him, he spoke about it before, about his steps in this river, about the roar, and I wonder. What brought him here? What other rivers has he crossed? I could ask but he will answer with words. Words do not serve me now, only touch does, and the hope of impending darkness.

Without rest, we start walking up the mountain in the direction of the ruin, the ruin with the golden walls in daylight. I fear entering that place again, I fear falling asleep inside those walls. And somehow he seems to know what I think for he takes a completely different path. Veering east we gain distance from the ruin and the village, moving deep into the valley where grasses grow. He must sense my pain without me saying anything. I think he reads my silence, I think he feels my thoughts. I could talk to him, but why waste those precious words when I can save them for something magical?

The smell of green grass, humid green grass, rises from the ground and penetrates the fabric of the striped tunic. I breathe deeply and enjoy the freshness. This must be a new territory. Sticking my head outside the cocoon I see a landscape I must have ignored. My night walks have never brought me in this direction. The slant of the mountains is the same but the grass is taller and greener. And as we round the crest of a soft hill we come to a sign that reads, "*La beauté sauvera le monde.*" I want to believe that. Further down the path I see the distant silhouette of three mules feasting on the green abundance.

He grabs my hand and leads me to where the mules are grazing. They do not retreat, the mules. Instead, they look at us with those large eyes, inquisitive humanoid eyes, as if waiting for us to say something. They sink their muzzles in the grass, savor the fresh grass, then lift their heads again to continue looking at us. Maybe they want to converse, or maybe they are just thinking mule thoughts. But their poise and gracefulness makes me believe these creatures know more than the typical beast. I have seen many beasts, abusive men that hurt me, with rabid eyes and full of ignorance. The mules do not look at me in that way.

Not far from where the mules graze, a farmhouse stands with its doors and windows open to the vagrant day. He brings me there with such determination, another place known to him, I guess. And without hesitation, he enters through the door with my hand in tow. The pulchritude of the house impresses me, the openness. He lets go of my hand and comes to the center of the room where he sits on the ground, crossing his legs, keeping his tunic close to his body. I follow his lead and sit next to him. Then something magical happens. The world slows down. The mountain air, flowing freely through the open door and windows, makes pirouettes inside the house. And in this slow moment I fear nothing.

—Why do you bring me here?

—Because of the words.

—What words?

—The ones we have yet to pronounce.

—Do you know what those words are?

—No, but Yes did.

—Yes.

—Yes did, he did.

I feel calm in anticipation of those words. Words mean the world when the world means little to me, which is all I can say.

The striped tunic

The cat walks through the door carrying a dead serpent in his mouth. He meows loudly. After trying out different corners of the room, he decides to drop the corpse in front of me. He meows some more, runs back to the door, and exits without looking back.

Is that cat a monster?

Is he cruel?

The cat kills. How often? I do not know.

I have killed more than once.

Am I a monster?

Am I cruel?

From the beginning of my journey, from the days when the sands burned and the dry wind took away my past, from that moment, I knew I would have no end and no beginning, from that moment I started the end of my genesis.

In the beginning there was nothing,

and nothing remains at the end.

I could not help Yes, bloated with words and slain. I killed a man with a dead arm. And I have destroyed so many lives in the desert. For whom am I leaving those serpent corpses?

Nadya,

breathe,

breathe again Nadya,

take my hand but do not hold onto it.

If I were to remain in this house she would soon be dead. But if I were to leave her alone she would be preyed upon. The beasts never rest.

So when she succumbs to the day, when she rests her head on the ground and falls asleep, waiting to wake up to the longest night, I come around to hear her breath,

her life,
recumbent Nadya,
of my inevitable silence.

I do not say a word. I do not give flesh to my thoughts. Let the dry air come into this house and take my thoughts away. All I have to give is my absence and a cover for her life. So I part with my striped tunic and lay it carefully on top of Nadya, infinite Nadya.

I begin once again,
naked.
I begin to walk away,
to where the roar comes from.
I begin to descend to the gorge,
to the river.
I begin to enter the waters,
to the deepest part of my past.
I begin to enter,
the roar,
of the river.

The Spiral Of Words

"Words are symbols for shared memories."
—Jorge Luis Borges

Part I
The Writer

He walked often. He walked because new words did not find him and the spent ones stuck to his skin. So he often walked. And the path became a river, and the waters burned. And every step was nothing but a dream. So he plunged... deeply.

Sometimes walking really meant propelling himself forward by the elliptical cadence of hips, knees, ankles, and toes. Other times it meant staying firmly grounded but letting his mind drift ahead rhythmically, one thought after the other, in a march towards the unknown, towards those oblique words that had yet to own him. That kind of walk was dangerous.

By this time the air had awoken, and the sun was assailing the beach. He had already reached the Pointe de Rauba-Capeù, and when he turned around to take in the view, he realized his thoughts had walked past him and were playing by themselves. He shook his head, sat down on the stone parapet, and listened to the waves crest over and throw themselves against the rocks. If the sea did not have to return to where it came from, neither did he. So he just sat there and watched as the wave of humans emerged from La Prom' and passed by him, some walking, some running, all dreaming, of course, all apparently going somewhere. Even the seagulls were fluttering up and down in a sort of a frenzy as if the air was burning them.

In front of him, the vast sea lay almost supple. Except for a few white crests frolicking in the horizon, the sea was essentially unmoved by his personal need for moving. And perhaps that was the reason for his need to see the sea, to see the sea eternal, always occupying the same space while violent currents flowed within its body. He looked up and focused on the line where the blue of the sea met the blue of the sky and wondered how long would it take him to get there. If he were to walk on water, would he ever reach that mythical juncture?

Or would the line move away from him with every watery step? He looked hard and tried to sustain his gaze, but the intense solar reflection felt like a silver sword, blinding him. So he closed his eyes and followed the steps of his mind.

How is today different from any other day? Who cares if I finish my novel today? How many pages should I write? For how long should I walk? How many steps should I take? I can walk the beach from end to end, and then what? Yes, I can climb the chateau hill and leave the beach behind. But then I'll see the beach at the foot of the mountain, like a recumbent half moon, and I know I'll feel the need to walk on its edge. The edge pulls me, that edge formed by the white foam. Sometimes the edge of a sidewalk drags me along, sometimes the edge between light and darkness. Between the known and the unknown, there's an edge, and it also pulls me along… Look at the people coming and going down La Prom'. I wonder what motivates them. Maybe the desire to feel the open space. Maybe no desire at all, just a habit. Too many minds out there, who knows what they're thinking? Who cares, when I start walking, everything changes and I forget why I started.

After a few minutes of contemplation, he got to his feet and started retreating to the other end of the beach where the sun was on its way down, splashing red everywhere. He did not live on the west side of town, but finding himself far out there would force him to walk back to the old port where he rented a small flat behind a flaming red façade. And then the dusk grew immense. A million lights on the buildings lining La Prom' began to form yet another edge leading him along. And at that unexpected moment, a woman wearing a pair of tight running shorts and a loose shirt joined his rhythmic walk at an uncomfortably close distance. He did not know this woman. He kept walking at the same pace and pretended to ignore her. And they walked side-by-side for about a hundred meters until he stopped his march abruptly. She also stopped. They examined each other. He felt her uneasy eyes scanning him. Then he asked her what was she trying to do. And she answered that she was not trying to do anything. The little lights from the buildings cast a strange brilliance on her. He stepped back and tried to capture her full nature. But her nature was not evident; she had an elusive nature. She then started to walk away from him at a brisk pace, and he clearly noticed three red stars tattooed on her right ankle. He followed her down the boulevard for a while until she descended to the pebbles on the beach and ran into the incoming sea without taking off her clothes. At a healthy pace, she swam into the body of the sea until the waves swallowed her completely. And that was all he saw of her.

He sat on one of the blue chairs that lined the beachfront and continued to scan the sea. Nothing splashed, nothing moved. For a moment he feared the woman had drowned, but that preoccupation did not last too long. If she took to swimming, she must have known how to swim, he thought. He looked up to the sky and found it becoming, that is, he found it dark enough, yet luminous. Once again on his feet, he continued his journey back to the old port. But his steps felt heavy as if he was dragging something. Did that woman drown? Was he carrying her dead body?

Once he reached the old port and sat in an Irish pub, he ordered the first pint of beer and set his eyes on the lazy boats. While absorbing the refracted and devilish light bouncing from the brightly painted hulls, his preoccupations began to melt away. He had completed his walk, traversed the terrain, and interacted with others from whom he managed to detach. Alone he was, or solitary, or simply free from human encumbrances. He was a single entity, a creature of the land of one, an essential element free to extend his travels unburdened. He was all to himself. And there lay the tragedy, the frailty—the strangeness.

The second pint of beer reminded him that in two days he

was supposed to travel west. West and south to be precise, to the conflicted capital of Portugal and its haunting river. And he knew the trip was not mandatory, although it felt like a primordial need. He had promised himself to explore living and writing at the edge of Iberia with the great Atlantic Ocean at his back. He wanted to write prose on the verge, on the verge of meaning, on the verge of gravity, on the verge of nothingness. He wanted to write dangerously. The great explorers had left the shores of Iberia behind and leapt into the unknown. Likewise, he was looking to catapult his prose out into the tumultuous ocean, hoping to reach a new shore. And while considering what that prose would sound like, he managed to forget about the woman who went swimming.

And as he dreamt of his future discoveries, an intense chill cut through him when the body of a woman, the same woman he saw swimming into the sea, stood in front of him, blocking his view of the sailboats in the old port. He closed his eyes and pretended her presence did not bother him. But when he opened his eyes again, there she was, in her entirety, wearing the same attire, wet now, and somewhat wanting. He took a good swig from his pint and laid on her the thickest gaze possible. But the woman did not move; she just stood still and returned his gaze with the intensity of a jackal.

She asked him what his name was and he said, Calixto. But that was not his real name. That was his pen name. The real one, the one given to him at the baptismal fountain, he did not share with her. In reality, his real name was not known by anyone who knew him.

She sat next to him and ordered a pint. She also looked out to the sailboats, perhaps in an attempt to identify with his interests, when most likely she had no particular affinity for sailing. But when the waitress brought her a sweaty pint to the table, she raised it and toasted to the brave sailors and the muses that hide under the surface of the sea which she just came from visiting. And the fact that water was dripping all over the table from her long hair and wet clothes did not seem to bother her. She raised her pint again and proclaimed that her name was Lulu and that she knew about the sea and its inhabitants. She then said that nothing new ever emerged from the dry surface of the land, that the sea was the true incubator of life and creativity, that all things worthwhile originated from its depths, and that if he wanted to write anything worthwhile he needed to take to the sea. He listened to her attentively, and after those comments, he took another good swig from his pint. They remained silent, although they finished their respective pints right in front of each other.

I wonder if I know this woman. Not her physical self—I've never seen her before—but her soul. There's a familiar gravity to her gestures and her confident manner. Maybe I've written about her. She could have been a character. No, I don't think so, she never got into one of my novels. But how could she know I want to write something worthwhile? Perhaps she is known to one of my characters, in which case, I may know something about her. But my characters don't share everything with me. Sometimes they lie. That happens when I lose control, and they run ahead of me, ahead of the story. I really don't know what the characters do when they jump outside of the story. Nevertheless, I think I've come across this intrepid soul before.

On the horizon, numerous white sails crisscrossed the unending blue, signaling the near end of the afternoon regatta. He focused on the action far away, away from Lulu, away from his rumination. Everything that had to happen would happen far away. And today was clearly not different from any other day, so he tried to disconnect from the moment and think of the upcoming trip to Lisbon. He could touch the brume climbing up from the banks of the Tejo, flooding the Praça do

Comércio and the old streets nearby, confusing the seagulls. And at once, mounting an attack he did not expect, reality interrupted his daydreaming. Lulu got up from her chair, left a few euros on the table, made her way down the quay of the old port, and kept on walking until she disappeared onto a side street. And that was all he saw of her and the three red stars tattooed on her ankle.

*****

The next day, early in the morning, Calixto considered walking along the same route as in the previous day. Probably because he hoped to see Lulu again. But deep in his mind, he knew things usually did not repeat themselves. If he were to replicate the actions of the previous day, everything would turn out completely different. For that reason, he discarded the idea of walking along the beach. He wanted to allow for the possibility of running into Lulu—by chance. He did not trust chance at an intellectual level, but viscerally, he surrendered to it.

There was the chateau hill with a system of paths circling around it, bringing people from the street level all the way up to the top of the hill. There was also the confusing maze of streets in the old town. Together, those two sets of convoluted paths allowed him to walk in concentric circles for as long as he wanted without getting anywhere. But the problem with those routes was precisely that, the getting nowhere. Calixto rejected the absence of a destination on the principle that walking was more than just walking; there had to be some kind of displacement. If physical displacement did not happen, at least there had to be a displacement of the mind. So walking in circles around the chateau hill would clearly set his mind in motion, or in search of Lulu, or perhaps in search of the vagaries of chance.

Soon after breakfast, he emerged from the red façade looking firmly ahead. He set out at a comfortable pace, ignoring the faces of a multitude of people walking along, around, or against him. The air felt thin enough to encourage a faster pace, but he did not hurry. What needed to move fast were his thoughts, and they were indeed racing. Leaving the old port behind, he took the path at the bottom of the hill and started his ascent. After completing two full circles, just as the path became steeper, he saw the silhouette of a woman walking ahead of him and turning left at a bifurcation. He stopped walking at once. The resemblance between this unexpected silhouette and that of Lulu was remarkable, and he immediately knew he needed to make up his mind. Should he turn and follow the vanishing figure or should he keep on walking straight ahead?

Could it be her? Could it really be her? She looks very similar to Lulu, but from this point, I can't tell for sure. If I turn left at the bifurcation and walk faster, I'll catch up with this woman. I'll then find out if it's really her. But then, this won't be a chance encounter because I'm pursuing her. I'm supposed to find her by chance, not by design. But perhaps it was by chance that I saw her turn left at the bifurcation. If it's really her, the chance event already took place the moment she crossed my path before turning one way or the other. But there's no way for me to know for sure. So, what already happened clarifies nothing. If at the bifurcation I turn right instead of left and then find her at a later time, that would be a chance encounter. Or maybe everything is exactly the opposite of what I think it is, a perverse antithesis of my expectations. And of course, there's the rare possibility, that one dictated by chance, that I won't find her at all.

When he reached the forking he took a long look down the path veering left. He could see far enough to realize that although crowded with people, the path offered nothing for him. So he turned right and took his chances. At a faster pace he walked, hoping to gain on the possibility of an encounter. After a few meters, the gradual incline of the terrain brought him to a new height from where he could see the shore stretching west. There, he paused to admire the parallel edges of sea, sand, people, promenade, and buildings clinging to each other—all inseparable. Resisting the urge to linger there and dream of a distant shore, he continued climbing and hoping. He passed by hundreds of agave plants, rows of pine trees, beggars, lovers, children, and dogs without stopping or paying much attention to any of that, only fantasizing about that furtive silhouette. He pushed forward until reaching the top of the hill. There he stopped. He caught his breath. And not seeing Lulu or any other image that could resemble hers, he wept a little. Once again, he found himself alone. Chance evaded him, more precisely, his expectations of the miracles of chance were shattered. Even though he was at the highest point of the village, he felt as if he had descended into a deep hole. He lifted his head and looked forward. The coiling path that would take him back to where he started from awaited his descent. And there he stood, almost paralyzed, when the floodgates of his mind opened.

A while back, in a place where the hills were covered by moss, my steps fell silent. And silence is what I need, now when the voices of those who walked ahead are calling me. I hear the poets saying there's no path, that we make our path as we walk. I hear my characters, the brave ones who dare to exist outside my realm, calling me. I hear the inner voice hammering hard, propelling me to move on. But now I yearn for silence to mourn the loss of Lulu, a person I barely know. Or perhaps I mourn the loss of her image, that image that walks away from me. I also need to mourn the loss of chance. For all of these losses I need silence, but I see no moss to quiet everything down. So I'll circle down the hill to the edge of the old town. I'll walk through the maze of twisting streets, plazas, and churches. I'll retreat behind the red facade of my flat. I'll close the windows. And once silence finally rains on me, I'll try to forget that walkers bury their hopes under the dust of forsaken towns.

The rest of the day disappointed him deeply. With no more walking to do, he resigned to prepare for the trip to Lisbon the next morning. A new shore would provide a new vision of life, and perhaps, new prose. Words would be born in new ways, he hoped. But his enthusiasm was obliterated by the sense of loss he had experienced that morning. So he decided to try to forget everything that happened in the last two days by finishing packing and reading a few passages from Clarice Lispector's Água Viva. He floated in the words for a few minutes. The water was cold, and so was his memory of Lulu, or the image of Lulu.

*****

On the way to Lisbon, Calixto considered leaving behind anything that could potentially drag him down. He inspected his suitcase, carefully evaluating every item with a draconian eye. But the content of the suitcase was minimal, so he found no reason to castigate himself. His mind, however, contained a more complex inventory: many doubts, including profound insecurity and a significant amount of self-pity. Those thoughts slowed him down that fine morning. Had he not rushed out of his flat, he would have missed his flight to Lisbon. Aware of the time constraints, he called a taxi, grabbed on to his copy of Àgua Viva, and ventured into the conflicted unknown.

Lisbon was not new to him; he had already tasted its delicacies; he had already abused its offerings. But living in

Lisbon as a writer was completely different. The Tejo made its presence felt season after season; it lived the life of a redolent corpse. And even if he wanted to ignore the Tejo's influence, the river infiltrated the very fiber of every living cell in Lisbon. And he was prepared for the abuse, for no extraneous forces ever made a dent on him. Or so he thought on that fine afternoon when he finally descended into the streets of Old Lisbon.

Without a clear destination, he ventured into the heart of the city singing a private song. He wanted to open his mind and heart to everything the old city had to offer. He wandered freely, unbound, taking in the weeping colors of the old façades, the acrid smell of people and buildings, and the tired afternoon miasma. But his enthusiasm was hindered by the water molecules and their maleficent agenda. Those moist molecules ascended directly from the superficial layers of the Tejo, high into the middle winds that caressed the myriad town hills, extending themselves supremely until they finally landed with aplomb on anything human, animal, mineral, or vegetal, injecting moisture into everything they touched. And as a consequence, a strange sweat grew from every surface. Even as he avoided touching anything, he could smell the moisture, and that disturbed him.

At the Praça do Rossio, he found a chair and a table from where he could write on his laptop and watch the human intercourse. People transacted, lied, exploited, exalted, exhausted, and loved each other. People behaved as people behave. And somehow he knew that this would help his writing, for the visceral exchange between people cannot be invented. As a writer of challenging prose, the raw interactions between human beings had to be recreated, not softened or diluted but rendered as true with whiskers and tails.

The human river poured down in front of him. People of various colors invaded the plaza at a frenetic pace, suggesting

They soon found a café with a terrace on the sidewalk overlooking people and cats. Calixto sat far enough from her not to appear threatening but close enough to feel her intriguing presence. She asked for a coffee, but he did not follow his own suggestion and asked for a glass of Alentejo. Once she took the cup of coffee and brought it to her lips, he clearly saw three words tattooed on the inner side of her right forearm. They were written in a beautiful typeface with elegant twirling serifs. But he could not recognize the language nor could he decipher the meaning of the words. And when she took another sip from her cup, the words danced in front of him, begging for interpretation. Considering that she did not want to be asked if she was a writer, he concluded that asking what the words meant would be equally forbidden. So he did not ask anything at all. She clearly noticed that he was looking directly at her tattoo, and as if instigating his curiosity, did not bother to cover it.

After taking another piece of the baguette, dipping it in her coffee with delicacy, and savoring it thoroughly, she asked him what was the true nature of a lie. He was not prepared for that question. He fumbled. A lie was a lie. A lie was something with no foundation in the truth. A lie was a pretense. But then he said a lie was anything we say at any moment in any place. This sent him on a line of thought he wanted to avoid. But he continued and told her lying was not different from telling the truth. She reflected on this answer and asked him if he was lying to her that very moment. He said he was, indeed. Again she did not flinch.

She says nothing. I tell her that my words are false and she says nothing. Maybe her words are false as well. How can I tell? I really don't lie, I just write the things that come to my mind, often unadulterated, but ultimately honest. Honest in the sense that I don't fabricate on purpose. Yes, what I write isn't necessarily

the world was coming to an end. But there was no end nearby; to the contrary, the world was blossoming. And in his mind, the words were brewing. He abandoned all preconceptions and launched himself into the creative process. Without a predetermined path or a preconceived plot, he ventured into the unknown, peering down into the abyss, and then tried to release the river of words.

Soon into the writing process, before the prose had a chance to twist and turn, he came across the image of Lulu. His fingers froze. He stopped writing at once. A woman had crossed the plaza from corner to corner bearing an uncanny resemblance to Lulu. He looked at the woman and wondered if that could be her, in Lisbon, walking right in front of him. He considered the absurdity of that thought. And after convincing himself that she was nowhere in that plaza, he tried to start writing again.

*****

Calixto wrote lies mainly, not because he wanted to deceive anyone, far from the truth, but because he thought that reality was as much a lie as any good fiction. He absorbed reality as it undressed in front of him. He took it all deep inside his mind and body. But somehow he found reality questionable, not entirely truth-worthy, even when it screamed and flapped its arms. He was suspicious of the way life needed to convince us of its force, of its existence. And with a certain disdain for anything real, he wrote prose that took flight, a flight as real as any presumptive reality.

Once he wrote the first sentence that afternoon, a sentence that had no reason to exist other than its sudden appearance on the blank computer screen, a sentence that read, *there is no path, you forge the path as you go,* that very moment he decided to stand up and merge with the flow of people traversing the plaza. First, he walked among the crowd with no clear direction. But as soon as he got a glimpse of the various medieval streets radiating away from the plaza, he turned left and walked onto one of them. He did not know where he was going, but the street felt so welcoming that he could not help but to smile and hop like a child. Not expecting anything, not succumbing to a prescribed order, his senses were free to register life anew. He heard words, music, and mopeds sounding like frenetic mosquitoes. He saw shadows, light reflected from store windows, colors copulating. He felt the dampness in the air. And then he was surprised by the aroma of freshly baked bread. He followed the olfactory invitation inside a bakery where people were queuing to purchase their daily loaf.

This must be the smell of life. I don't know how else to describe this sensation. So simple, yet so deeply rooted inside my brain. Bread can keep me alive, or maybe I'm alive so I can eat bread. So powerful, so elemental. And it doesn't matter where I am, what city, what continent. This smell burs inside of me and reaches the core of my existence. More compelling than bliss, more potent than fear. I think of bread as the primordial substance. The man makes bread so he can continue to be a man who eats bread. Circular, never-ending…

Inside the bakery, standing in line to grab a piece of life, the person immediately behind him, a woman unknown to him until that moment, asked him if he was a writer. He admitted he was a writer and ignored the uncanniness of the question. This he did because he was under the succulent influence of the aromas swirling inside the shop. He could not grasp the strangeness of the situation. But once outside, before he had the opportunity to taste a piece of the baguette he had just purchased, the woman approached him again and asked him what kind of writer he was. Looking at her, appreciating her angular features, noticing that she also held a baguette under her arm, he told her that he was a writer of lies. She did not flinch. She continued looking at him with an unfamiliar face. And after digging into the well of recent and remote memories, he concluded he had never seen or spoken to this woman before. But somehow she knew, or at least sensed, something about him that was true. And that capability to elucidate the unknown disarmed him. They both stood there on the sidewalk, each holding their respective baguettes, unsure of what to say or where to go next.

The impasse did not last long, for they both started walking down the street in the same direction, side-by-side, occupying the entire width of the sidewalk. People who came up the sidewalk needed to step into the street to pass by them, while those coming from behind found their path blocked. And this continued for a few blocks until they reached the formidable banks of the Tejo where they were swallowed by its miasmatic breath. Still intrigued, Calixto cut the curtain of fog with his words. He told her that he wrote about lies not because he feared the truth, but because he did not really know what the truth was. She listened to him attentively and then she broke off the tip of the baguette and proceeded to savor the crunch of life. After thinking about his declaration and chewing on the bread, she told him that the bread was excellent and that she had no interest in the veracity of things either. She then asked him what led him to be a writer. And this he did not answer. Instead, he considered asking how did she know he was a writer in the first place. But concerned about the potential answer she would give him, he decided to abort that question completely. Alternatively, he asked if she would join him for a cup of coffee. She said that she would love to join him as long as he would not ask her if she was a writer herself. He agreed, and he wondered.

the world was coming to an end. But there was no end nearby; to the contrary, the world was blossoming. And in his mind, the words were brewing. He abandoned all preconceptions and launched himself into the creative process. Without a predetermined path or a preconceived plot, he ventured into the unknown, peering down into the abyss, and then tried to release the river of words.

Soon into the writing process, before the prose had a chance to twist and turn, he came across the image of Lulu. His fingers froze. He stopped writing at once. A woman had crossed the plaza from corner to corner bearing an uncanny resemblance to Lulu. He looked at the woman and wondered if that could be her, in Lisbon, walking right in front of him. He considered the absurdity of that thought. And after convincing himself that she was nowhere in that plaza, he tried to start writing again.

*****

Calixto wrote lies mainly, not because he wanted to deceive anyone, far from the truth, but because he thought that reality was as much a lie as any good fiction. He absorbed reality as it undressed in front of him. He took it all deep inside his mind and body. But somehow he found reality questionable, not entirely truth-worthy, even when it screamed and flapped its arms. He was suspicious of the way life needed to convince us of its force, of its existence. And with a certain disdain for anything real, he wrote prose that took flight, a flight as real as any presumptive reality.

Once he wrote the first sentence that afternoon, a sentence that had no reason to exist other than its sudden appearance on the blank computer screen, a sentence that read, *there is no path, you forge the path as you go*, that very moment he decided to stand up and merge with the flow of people traversing the plaza. First, he walked among the crowd with no clear direction. But as soon as he got a glimpse of the various medieval streets radiating away from the plaza, he turned left and walked onto one of them. He did not know where he was going, but the street felt so welcoming that he could not help but to smile and hop like a child. Not expecting anything, not succumbing to a prescribed order, his senses were free to register life anew. He heard words, music, and mopeds sounding like frenetic mosquitoes. He saw shadows, light reflected from store windows, colors copulating. He felt the dampness in the air. And then he was surprised by the aroma of freshly baked bread. He followed the olfactory invitation inside a bakery where people were queuing to purchase their daily loaf.

This must be the smell of life. I don't know how else to describe this sensation. So simple, yet so deeply rooted inside my brain. Bread can keep me alive, or maybe I'm alive so I can eat bread. So powerful, so elemental. And it doesn't matter where I am, what city, what continent. This smell burs inside of me and reaches the core of my existence. More compelling than bliss, more potent than fear. I think of bread as the primordial substance. The man makes bread so he can continue to be a man who eats bread. Circular, never-ending...

Inside the bakery, standing in line to grab a piece of life, the person immediately behind him, a woman unknown to him until that moment, asked him if he was a writer. He admitted he was a writer and ignored the uncanniness of the question. This he did because he was under the succulent influence of the aromas swirling inside the shop. He could not grasp the strangeness of the situation. But once outside, before he had the opportunity to taste a piece of the baguette he had just purchased, the woman approached him again and asked him what kind of writer he was. Looking at her, appreciating her angular features, noticing that she also held a baguette under her arm, he told her that he was a writer of lies. She did not flinch. She continued looking at him with an unfamiliar face. And after digging into the well of recent and remote memories, he concluded he had never seen or spoken to this woman before. But somehow she knew, or at least sensed, something about him that was true. And that capability to elucidate the unknown disarmed him. They both stood there on the sidewalk, each holding their respective baguettes, unsure of what to say or where to go next.

The impasse did not last long, for they both started walking down the street in the same direction, side-by-side, occupying the entire width of the sidewalk. People who came up the sidewalk needed to step into the street to pass by them, while those coming from behind found their path blocked. And this continued for a few blocks until they reached the formidable banks of the Tejo where they were swallowed by its miasmatic breath. Still intrigued, Calixto cut the curtain of fog with his words. He told her that he wrote about lies not because he feared the truth, but because he did not really know what the truth was. She listened to him attentively and then she broke off the tip of the baguette and proceeded to savor the crunch of life. After thinking about his declaration and chewing on the bread, she told him that the bread was excellent and that she had no interest in the veracity of things either. She then asked him what led him to be a writer. And this he did not answer. Instead, he considered asking how did she know he was a writer in the first place. But concerned about the potential answer she would give him, he decided to abort that question completely. Alternatively, he asked if she would join him for a cup of coffee. She said that she would love to join him as long as he would not ask her if she was a writer herself. He agreed, and he wondered.

They soon found a café with a terrace on the sidewalk overlooking people and cats. Calixto sat far enough from her not to appear threatening but close enough to feel her intriguing presence. She asked for a coffee, but he did not follow his own suggestion and asked for a glass of Alentejo. Once she took the cup of coffee and brought it to her lips, he clearly saw three words tattooed on the inner side of her right forearm. They were written in a beautiful typeface with elegant twirling serifs. But he could not recognize the language nor could he decipher the meaning of the words. And when she took another sip from her cup, the words danced in front of him, begging for interpretation. Considering that she did not want to be asked if she was a writer, he concluded that asking what the words meant would be equally forbidden. So he did not ask anything at all. She clearly noticed that he was looking directly at her tattoo, and as if instigating his curiosity, did not bother to cover it.

After taking another piece of the baguette, dipping it in her coffee with delicacy, and savoring it thoroughly, she asked him what was the true nature of a lie. He was not prepared for that question. He fumbled. A lie was a lie. A lie was something with no foundation in the truth. A lie was a pretense. But then he said a lie was anything we say at any moment in any place. This sent him on a line of thought he wanted to avoid. But he continued and told her lying was not different from telling the truth. She reflected on this answer and asked him if he was lying to her that very moment. He said he was, indeed. Again she did not flinch.

She says nothing. I tell her that my words are false and she says nothing. Maybe her words are false as well. How can I tell? I really don't lie, I just write the things that come to my mind, often unadulterated, but ultimately honest. Honest in the sense that I don't fabricate on purpose. Yes, what I write isn't necessarily bound to anything tangible. But isn't that the nature of fiction? She was the one asking if I was a writer. Can she smell the lies? Possibly not, because I was the one volunteering that what I write are lies. She didn't say that, I did. But why would she preclude me from asking her if she is herself a writer? Could it be that she doesn't want to lie to me? Maybe one liar is more than enough. There's danger in repetition whether we're telling the truth or not. She may sense that. And then her arm is branded with words I cannot decipher. I could ask her what those words mean. But what if she plainly lies to me? Would it make a difference? The truth is that she knows something about me and I only know that I know nothing about her. Only that she likes bread, that seems to be true.

The next gesture took him by surprise. Without asking for approval, permission, or anything, she reached for his baguette and took a piece of it, dipped it in her coffee, and swallowed it at once. She was pensive for a few seconds and then told him that his baguette was just as tasty as hers. In her face he found no trace of concern, not a line of preoccupation, it was placid, still, like the waters of a lake in the morning. Tempted as he was to respond, he could not find what to say to her, so he had some of his wine, stood up momentarily, and then sat down again and acted as if nothing had happened. Calixto knew that something was happening, but he could not put his finger on what it was.

She then called the waitress and asked for a glass of Alentejo as well. Once served, she raised the glass and toasted to the vagaries of life. When Calixto asked her what vagaries she was referring to, she said that none were coming her way lately and that she was hoping for that to change. She went on to explain that their encounter at the bakery was not unpredictable enough, that she had expected it would happen like that. Not convinced, he questioned her if in reality she already knew about their encounter or was she just trying to explain her peculiar behavior. She took a while to respond, the faintest of lines crossed her forehead, and she slightly tilted her head as if perplexed almost. With a tone, impassive and inscrutable, she said her behaviors were not peculiar, that to him perhaps they were, but not so to the universe. This exchange led to a silence that hung from a low cloud.

The afternoon continued its relentless advance. Fearing that the hours would engulf him in the company of this puzzling woman, and also fearing that she would not reveal much, he felt compelled to press for answers. He jumped into the abyss of the unknown and asked about the meaning of the words tattooed on her forearm. He knew he was taking a risk, but could not appreciate its magnitude. After listening to his question, she looked at the words and contemplated them with tenderness, as if they revealed a sweet memory. She then pronounced each word in a soft voice, almost caressing each syllable. When she finished speaking she stared at him, and he saw, once again, the still waters of a morning lake. But still, he did not understand what the words meant. The language sounded completely foreign to him, a beautiful sound he had never heard before. And when he asked her what did the words really mean, she said that the meaning rested in the words themselves and that she had just spoken them to him.

First Lulu, then this woman whose name I don't even know. These encounters taking place in two different cities, back to back, within days of each other. Is this chance? She may simply disappear, vanish into the brume. Or she could sit across from me, as she does now, and speak in a language I don't understand. The words have their intrinsic music but no meaning to me. Perhaps her appearance demonstrates there's no inherent meaning to those words, that the sound and emotion they elicit is all there's to have. I'm not ready to accept that notion, not when my life still

Then the lightning, a white so fast but so decisive, turning the afternoon into a theater with a torn curtain, a deep rip down to the edge of the waters, and a river that flowed quick and away. They both marveled at the spectacle. The sound followed, call it thunder, but to them, it was more a like a roar. The words had no chance against the roar. He knew not to challenge the might. She, instead, kept on talking. Her words did not reach his ears, drowned they were by the thunderous roar. But the silent elliptical movement of her lips caught his eyes. Calixto could not decipher what she was saying. But the movement, the act of uttering, the giving birth to that unknown language, made him grab the seat of his chair and contain himself from embracing her, or from running away from her. The lightning continued, completely unaware of what both of them were thinking or wanting.

Then the rain, enormous, as if the river had fallen from the sky. They got up from the table, grabbed their respective half-eaten baguettes, and moved inside the café seeking shelter. But what shelter could they find when the wheels of the mind had already started to turn? The cramped space inside the café forced them to breach the tenuous line of the impersonal. Convinced that she knew a world about him, Calixto was surprised when she asked his name. This time her words were clear and direct. But when he tried to answer, he fumbled the words and failed to say his name. A faint smile grew on her face, a peaceful smile. She then turned away from him and began to contemplate the falling rain. He feared she would simply vanish and be one with the water. But he also feared she would not vanish at all, in which case, he would have to reveal to this person more about himself when she was not revealing anything about herself. He lied, while she was still looking out at the rain, when she could not scrutinize his face, he told her his name was "Calixto." She remained quiet for a moment, a moment that dragged for a century, before speaking to the rain and saying that "Calixto" was not his real name.

Calixto did not mind shifting paradigms. He accepted darkness at noon. He even welcomed the world upside down. But, most often, he was the author of the chaos in his life. The sweet taste of the unknown suited him well, as long as there was a safety net underneath it all. So what he could not bear that moment was the certainty of the uncertain woman. She seemed unperturbed and placid, inquisitive and yet accepting. And somehow, somehow she knew something about him. He then remembered the first sentence he had written earlier at the plaza: *there is no path, you forge the path as you go.* So he stood up from the chair and started walking away from this woman he could not unriddle, his baguette getting completely soaked under his arm under the relentless rain.

*****

After walking aimlessly for several hours, Calixto finally reached the hotel room he had secured upon his arrival in Lisbon. It was 10 pm. That was a good time to continue writing and expanding on that first sentence he wrote at Praça do Rossio. The night was young, but young only in the sense of time, for nights have existed forever so nothing about a night could really be nubile. However, the immediacy of his need was truly nubile. And his need walked along two parallel paths: a strong desire to create meaningful prose on one side; and just next to this noble need, a nagging urge to find out about this woman who shared with him a baguette and the rain. Anyone could have been conflicted when deciding which path to choose, but he knew not to take sides, he simply thought hard about the fleeting images of the woman while he typed a few loose sentences in his computer. He managed to do just that for a few minutes, he then walked over to the small kitchenette in the hotel room and poured himself a glass of Alentejo. Back at the computer, he read the sentence he had just written. Ashamed of the baseness of the language and the poverty of the images, he closed his computer and walked over to the window to look outside. The view was magnificent, open and dark, even vulnerable. And he looked into the night like a hunter. But the night basically ignored him. Like any other night, this one continued to deepen its shades of gray, to relax its grip on common anxiety, and to gather the first droplets of hue.

Two women had brutally intersected his life while he was simply being, or walking, or just having a piece of bread. All within the last few days. He considered the inherent anomaly of these two encounters, and before accepting them as fate, or even luck, he resolved to integrate the bizarre events into his writing. Not an easy task since all he had accomplished during the day was to write a single sentence. He considered how to best represent the oddity of both encounters. Lulu cast a spell, an image, a presence that still surrounded him. The woman at the bakery had no name, but somehow, she knew what his name was not and that he was a writer. And without saying much, that woman sent him into the rain and left him wondering what had just happened. That was powerful, he thought. And after searching for the right words and the right sentence structure, after writing and re-writing a few sentences in his mind, he felt defeated. So he abandoned the idea of writing anything at all.

He took to the night, the night that had no regard for him. He opened it like a moon ray would open any night. He pierced its layers. He walked into the vast space between the dark pavement and the dark sky. And as he walked into that emptiness, his steps felt equivocal, the ground moved, his legs failed to support his body erect. So he fell down, on his knees first, on his side next, and finally on the ground. There he lay, over the dark pavement under the dark sky, wondering what had brought him down; but more precisely, or even more intimately, how to write anything from this position?

Having had those thoughts before, he knew to ignore them. He eventually managed to stand up, like the capable man he was, and to start walking towards the river. If the night would yield to his needs, it would likely do so by the river. Once he regarded the expansive body of the Tejo, he realized it shared the same dark shades as the pavement and the sky. Relief was nowhere to be found there. And this is when he, once again, engaged in walking. He walked. He followed a circular path that spiraled away from the river, larger and larger with each turn. He kept a steady pace and tried to forget all that took place during the day. He walked ahead, always bearing left and keeping his head high. And this is all he did until the early morning came to greet him. He did not applaud when the sun showed its face. He felt tired, and not more enlightened than the day before. Walking the entire night had not provided any rewards. He did not get any revelations. He was simply spent.

But once he looked around and recognized the neighborhood, once he identified the color on the façades, and once he was assaulted by the aroma of freshly baked bread, an assault he recognized and cherished, he knew where to direct his steps. He followed his olfactory senses until he came to the same bakery he had visited the day before. There he stood in line hoping for a piece of heaven, but also hoping for a fresh acquaintance with the woman who knew what his name was not. When his turn came up, he said to the attendant that he was not ready to order and asked her to take care of the person behind him in the line. He used this newly acquired time to look around wishing to find the mysterious woman again. But nobody in the line, or around the bakery resembled the woman from the previous day. This he found disconcerting, for he expected the inquisitive woman to visit the bakery every single day.

Although his expectations had come into question, he remained in line and accepted his turn once it presented again. He asked for a baguette. The attendant acknowledged his request and said that it was good to see him again, that they did not often get writers as customers. He smiled, took his baguette, and quickly left the store. Once on the street, he stood still with his baguette under his arm. That was when he started breathing hard and fast. How could this woman, a young employee at a bakery, know that he was a writer? How was it possible that random people in Lisbon had knowledge of his profession? Clearly, the mysterious woman from the previous day must have spoken to the attendant, conveying his personal information. But he could not be certain that those two people had spoken to each other or shared any information about his writing. Why would that be relevant?

He stepped aside from the sidewalk to allow the flow of pedestrians to proceed with their morning routine. But as he stood in front of the adjacent storefront, he could not help but gaze at his own image reflected in the window. There he was, in all his reality, the very image of himself. He took a long time scrutinizing every angle in his face; he tried different facial expressions, some grotesque, others more affable. He moved forward and backward to study different details of his body. When two women came close to him on the sidewalk, he stopped all strange contorting in order to appear normal. But once they walked away, he continued with his private performance. After a while, he concluded that his appearance could not actually reveal that he was a writer. So, if the attendant at the bakery had that impression, it had to have been communicated by the strange woman he met the previous day, whose name he did not know, but to whom he admitted that he was, indeed, a writer.

Tired as he was, missing sleep, missing a sense of certainty, he decided to return to his hotel room in search of rest and restoration. Restoration of a sense of order for what he had considered to be obviously clear, like the lack of revealing details in his appearance, had all of a sudden come into question. Once he found himself in the safety of his hotel room, he considered writing the next few sentences of his book. But what he feared most, what he hoped never to face again, resurfaced all at once. He found himself watching himself as a writer while writing. This, an image he did not appreciate, so intimate, so uncomfortable.

So he worked fast to concoct a few sentences he doubted would ever make it into his next book. Not because the sentences were flawed, but because they were constructed under pressure. Instead of writing for the sense of discovery, he was writing out of fear. Not writing would certainly usher a heavy emptiness, or perhaps destroy the images of the two women he had now carried in his head for the last few days. In either case, the sense of writing under pressure overwhelmed the simple sense of pleasure, so he stopped at once. He took a piece of the baguette and savored the beauty of its construction. He then had another piece.

*****

In the early morning, Calixto was completely immersed in the sound of silence. A sound composed of nothing except minimal sprinkles of bird songs. The birds cared not for the silence but for their sex appeal and procreation success. So they sang energetically in the late morning. They were sparrows after all.

As soon as a deviant ray of sunlight penetrated through the window, biting a chunk of his leg, he opened his eyes and realized the day was upon him. And this day made its presence known immediately, for it brought forward all the possible words a language could contain, and at the same time, it presented all the limitations a mind could encounter when forging such a language. He felt the pressure. With conviction, he sat on his bed and held his body still for a few minutes. And only when he believed the world would open up to him, only when he sensed the words would be at his reach, he then got out of bed to listen to the singing sparrows.

After listening to a few melodic phrases, the urge to walk began to infiltrate his consciousness, leaving very little room for any other concern. He resisted the urge. He wanted to enjoy the simple pleasure of writing freely, writing unencumbered in the morning hours, writing with a background of bird songs. But in a matter of minute, he found himself walking down the street in front of his hotel with no clear idea as to were to go. He could still hear the birds that comforted him, but he knew that writing had died for the morning, or maybe for the entire day. Freedom and surprise would need to emerge from the act of walking. So he embraced that thought and continued his march. One crossroad followed another; some stores were bursting with people while others were desolate, people and dogs, but nothing that would ignite his curiosity. That was when he made a right turn onto a narrow street that climbed at a puzzling steep angle. The allure of following the tight corridor to a sort of heaven above drove him forward. He climbed fast, skipping steps. And after about a hundred meters, he reached a clearing that opened up in front of him, a truly profound openness.

The midday sun fell hard on his hat. Calixto stood as straight as he could to prevent the burning rays from touching his body. The slightest movement or leaning would have exposed him. But standing was not walking, and that presented the biggest challenge. He considered waiting around for an hour or two before taking the next step. The sun would have moved a few degrees west allowing him to angle his hat and walk under the precarious shade. He decided to wait. To amuse himself as he waited, he tried to remember word by word the last paragraph he wrote before leaving Nice. He could not remember the words. He remembered the concepts and the tone of the sentences, but not the words. If the words did not remain in his memory, did they matter? He recognized the nefarious self-doubt at once. So, enduring the burning rays that attacked his body in motion, he set out to continue his walk, away from self-doubting thoughts, and toward the edge of the Tejo.

The river surprised him. He looked at it expecting a deep gray frown. But the river did precisely the opposite; it smiled at him. He waited for the river to flow, to take its course, to serpent at a continuous speed out to the ocean. And the river did just that. But when he regarded the visible expression of the river, when he saw the wind-induced ripples, the undulating wake of sailboats, the surface wounds inflicted by white birds, he was again surprised to find a lingering smile. Accepting the message, if there was any message in that vision, he turned away from the river. And without doubt in his mind, he started looking at people's faces expecting to find a legion of smiles. He found a few, not necessarily directed at him, but encouraging enough. That ignited his forward march once again. Across the Praça do Comércio he walked, this time displaying a smile of his own, inevitably eliciting further smiles from those he came across.

At a comfortable rhythm he traversed streets, he crossed a few plazas. A diagonal smile hung from his lips while he forged ahead following nothing but his instincts, or perhaps his olfactory sense fetched the smell of old leather and dust. And thereupon he arrived at the door of an old bookstore with a sign that read "Livraria Mundo." He stepped inside, careful not to alter the generations of dust covering the books on the display window. A young woman, sporting a colorful tattoo of a salamander on her neck, sat behind the sales counter reading a book. She looked up when he entered the store; the salamander did not move at all. Looking around he identified books from authors he recognized, and there were others he had never heard about, but they were lying around in no particular order. Walking through the empty store felt as if violating a private sanctuary, so after a few minutes he stopped meandering and asked the tattooed attendant if she could recommend a book for him. She first ignored him, but when he repeated his request in sketchy Portuguese, she looked at him and smiled but did not give an answer.

Erratic behaviors did not dissuade him from interacting with people, often random people, for he considered anything unusual the stuff of novels. So after browsing around for a little while longer, he returned to the sales desk and asked the attendant if she had a book about bread. This time the woman looked at him, caressed the salamander on her neck with the tip of her fingers, and once again said nothing. Bewildered, he remained standing in front of her and retained her gaze for a few seconds. The attendant bit her lower lip softly, caressed the salamander one more time, and turned her gaze down to the book she was reading. A deep silence took hold. Calixto then asked her what she was reading, but this time she did not even look up at him nor did she respond. He then turned around and headed for the exit. But just before stepping out on the street, he paused, he reconsidered the purpose of his walk, and convinced about the hidden liaisons operating in the universe, he returned to the sales desk. The young woman closed her book and stood up, the salamander calmly resting vertically between her chin and her collar bone. He asked again if she had a book about bread. The young woman nodded affirmatively and left the sales desk to enter into what seemed like a back-store office. She returned with a basket containing a couple of bread rolls which she placed on the sales desk right in front of him.

Calixto picked up one of the rolls and ate a piece of it. Instantly, he remembered the nameless woman he had met at the bakery, who knew he was a writer, and wondered if the tattooed woman who now offered him bread knew as much about him. After eating about half of the roll, he told the attendant that the bread was excellent but that he had asked for a book about bread, not for bread itself. She finally spoke with an accent that sounded Eastern European and said that real bread was better than a book about bread. Not wanting to enter into a discussion about the signified versus the signifier, he finished eating the roll and almost agreed with her by saying that bread was the essence of life, but that life without books had no essence. She pondered his words, had a little piece of bread herself, and told him that he must be a writer, probably a novelist. He felt disarmed, revealed. He did not have a tattoo on his forehead that read "writer." He had not mentioned any specific authors. Maybe the titles of the books he perused gave him away. It could not have been the bread. Or was it?

Not wanting to confirm or deny her assertion, he attempted to turn the situation around by telling her that salamanders used to roam around freely all over the Carpathian Mountains before they were decimated by wars and bad weather. He guessed she would be a native of one of the many countries straddled by the fabled mountain range. When the attendant heard him mention the Carpathians, she touched the tattoo on her neck with the tips of her fingers, and the salamander appeared to twitch slightly. For an instant, he thought the salamander had stuck its tongue out to lick her fingers. But he soon dismissed the image and focused on her soft smile instead of the reptile. She appeared to be daydreaming or remembering something sweet. She then said in her peculiar accent that reptiles were found only in the lower altitudes and foothills of the Carpathians, that she came from the small village of Rakhiv, high up in Ukraine, where wolves were more common than salamanders. Then she added that he should visit Rakhiv, where he would find a lot to write about in his novels. This meant she did not speculate when suggesting he was a writer, she was certain he was one, and that thought disturbed him.

Calixto could not help but consider the inherent importance of the number 3. He found it mysterious, metaphysical, and magical. From time to time in the history of the world various numbers, chiefly those from 1 to 12, have been regarded as possessing mythical significance, but there can be no doubt that in the extent, variety, and frequency of its use the number 3 far surpasses all the rest. Aristotle's *Rhetoric* consisted of 3 books; the original Hydra had three heads, the *Dies Irae* is composed of 3x3x3 stanzas, each consisting of 3 verses and a triple rhyme, there were Three Graces, goddesses of such things as charm, beauty, and creativity, the scepter of Neptune was a trident. But more relevant to his immediate reality, three different women have inadvertently crossed his path and rattled his sense of self, purpose, and direction.

Unsure as to the meaning of anything at this point, he confessed to the attendant that he was indeed a writer and asked her if her name was Lulu. She smiled again, shook her head, and said nothing. Then she stepped around the sales counter and walked toward the shelf that contained newly released fiction from all over the world. With a gentle gesture, she pointed at various books without signaling one in particular. Then she asked him to identify his own novels. The chances that any of his books could be found in that bookstore were practically nonexistent, so he did not even try to look for them. When she saw he did not try, she asked him if he was afraid to actually find one of his books in the store. He was not afraid, and he told her so. With the same irresistible smile, she said her name was Lyubochka and that he should consider writing a book about her name. He hesitated, not entirely certain he wanted to unravel the mysterious and captivating presence she exuded, but driven to know more, he asked her for the meaning of her name. She said, *love*... Perhaps *love*.

At this point, Calixto knew his reality was under siege. Remaining at the store would have created situations capable of derailing his resolve to write. He realized Lyubochka had ignited his interest, that she had the capacity to distract him today and many more days to come. But he also understood that she was not different from the other two women that had recently captured his attention. They had materialized from nowhere, they had interacted with him, and they had departed leaving him baffled. Lyubochka, however, was still in front of him and had not vanished as the others had done. And maybe that made her irresistibly dangerous.

Calixto said that *love* was meaningful, that more people in the world should understand *love*, or experience it fully, or maybe make it the center of their lives. And he said all of this while walking towards the door, away from her, somewhat afraid he would believe exactly what he was saying. But before he managed to step out on the street, Lyubochka grabbed the remaining piece of bread and offered it to him. He could not resist. Life was bread and bread was life. So he tasted the product of the earth and sat at the steps of the store, half of his body leaning forward into the street, away from Lyubochka, and the other half wanting to stay behind to learn more about her.

But the urge to walk reverberating from within mounted a phenomenal attack on his immediate reality and dislodged him from the steps where his mind was indulging on everything Lyubochka. And he accepted the power of that inner drive, the destabilizing force it represented, the might it possessed. So he stood up, looked one more time at the salamander guarding Lyubochka's neck, and started to make his way down the street. She asked him if he was leaving for the day or leaving forever. He stopped, the road continued at a steep angle down toward the river that had delivered him with a smile earlier that day. He wanted to say he would come back at another time, that he needed to see her again. But he did not manage to promise anything; he only said that *love* had a meaning, a meaning that he could not yet understand.

*****

On his way back to the hotel, Calixto avoided bookstores and bakeries. On one occasion, after changing his course by two blocks just to bypass what seemed to be a bakery from a distance, he landed on a side street right in front of a small bookstore with foreign titles on display. He felt the temptation to go into the store and start browsing. But out of fear of the potential scenarios that could be unleashed, he turned around and headed in a new direction, away from the bookstore — changing his path while walking was not unusual for him. After all, his walks were predictably unpredictable. But making a change out of fear did not settle well with him. Any force, external or internal, could dictate the direction of his walks, except for the force of fear. Fear foretold disagreeable events that had yet to happen. Why endure the emotional turmoil of something that has not impacted our lives thus far? With that thought in mind, he changed his path once more, he backtracked and walked right into the small bookstore. Life would not be worth anything without facing fear and surprise, he thought.

This time he did not ask for any books, he did not look for bread, and he did not expect to meet any mysterious attendant. But reality was ready to usher the unexpected. And it did. On top of a reading table, in a pile of commercial novels, he identified one of his own books translated into Spanish. He was very proud of the Spanish translation but did not appreciate seeing his novel mixed with inane books ready for easy consumption. He felt wounded. Not finding a salesperson around, he rung the little bell on the sales desk several times. After a few minutes, an old man came up through a spiral staircase that possibly led to a cellar, and asked him if he was in need of help. Calixto was not in need of any help; he just needed to express his indignation. An indignation that had no bearing on the man that just emerged from the cellar, but perhaps on the natural order of things: finding his book piled among a divergent crowd. The old man, looking above the rim of his glasses, asked him if he had found what he came looking for.

To this question, Calixto could only answer that he did not really know what he was looking for, that he felt the drive to come into the store because the alternative was to yield to esoteric fears. Here the old man nodded, he seemed to understand his level of distress. Taking small steps, the old man moved towards Calixto and placed himself in front of the reading table displaying science fiction, romance, and detective novels. Feeling an uncomfortable pressure from the old man, Calixto took turns between looking at the books and looking sideways and upward at that carved face the old man presented. He then picked up the Spanish translation of his book entitled "*No Somos Pero Somos.*" He showed it to the old man and asked him if he had read it. Very quickly the old man responded that he had not read the book, that he could not read it as other people could. Not understanding what the old man meant, Calixto felt compelled to clarify that he was the author of the book. The old man took this information very seriously. He grabbed the book and paused to read the title again. He then started to turn one page after the other as if trying to find an important phrase or word. The old man closed the book and held it tight against his chest. He then looked straight into Calixto's eyes and said that he was very sorry for him, that if he could, he would take him as his son.

At that moment the afternoon light had changed in quality; it reflected the harshness of expectations while the building walls across the street emitted a hue akin to tired human flesh. This did not pass unaccounted, for the old man said the afternoon was testing. And it was, indeed. Calixto took the book from the old man's hands and told him that nothing was, but that everything was. He told him that he could be a son to no father, that he was happy to see his book on the table yet not seeing the book would have also been glorious. The old man listened attentively, his eyes on the book, probably not believing what he was hearing. And at this point, the old man grabbed the book again, tossed it away from sight, and pulled two chairs from the reading table. He placed one chair in front of the other. He then sat on one of them and invited Calixto to sit on the other one. He did.

The old man started talking about the brutal times of Salazar when good books could not be sold openly when everything was censored. That was when he started selling books in translation because their "subversive" nature was not easily identified by the thugs who came around to inspect his inventory. Books in Spanish were still a risk, and so were those in French. But he could get away with almost anything written in German or English. The problem was not only obtaining such books but that once he had them, most of his clients in the resistance did not understand those languages. So he felt suffocated, the regime cutting off the source of illuminated words and critical thinking. He said that he started selling books that looked like real bibles. The cover and the first few pages in Portuguese, but experimental fiction in the core of the volumes. That was thanks to the artistry of an atheist bookbinder in Lisbon who delighted himself more by ripping the bible pages apart than by inserting the new experimental work. It was the sweet sense of desecration that emboldened him. He also spoke about the recent recession when nobody had any money for anything, let alone for buying books. He had to survive by selling newspapers that were reporting on the catastrophic financial situation of the country, which resulted in people feeling more anxious, which lead them to spend less every day and hurting his business more. So he stopped selling newspapers. And then he started talking about the importance of fiction in people's lives, how he enjoyed selling aesthetically adventurous literature. He spoke about how happy he was not to have to mask good literature as bibles anymore, that he could openly promote challenging, innovative works of high quality and exceptional ambition, how he hoped that the books he sold could, perhaps, alter people's perception of the world. He then quoted Clarice Lispector saying, *In order to write I must place myself in the void. In this void where I exist intuitively. But it's a terribly dangerous void: its where I wring out blood.* And then he asked Calixto if he ever felt that way.

After giving thoughtful consideration to everything the old man had said, and after reflecting on what he had done since arriving in Lisbon, Calixto admitted that, yes indeed, he was in a dangerous void. A void created by his need to walk, always leaving behind the known spaces to venture into the unknown. And in this frenetic need to move forward, he often wondered if valuable thoughts, experiences, or opportunities were continuously left behind, aborted, or simply ignored. That was not a comfortable thought for it implied careless waste and inefficiency. But a sense of void, as explained by Clarice Lispector, was not to be disregarded, to the contrary, the old man was squarely on the mark when he presented him with such a challenge. So admitting he was in the depths of a void felt like a relief, but not for too long, because the old man gave him no rest and immediately asked how was he going to remedy his situation. Calixto had not resolved what the next steps would be. He really did not know how to fill any void. In lieu of an answer, he spoke about an upcoming trip to a place he was not sure existed, but that if it did, his void would not be that empty after all. A critical smirk hung from the old man's lips when he heard this statement. He then took another good look at Calixto and said he was, undoubtedly, a writer.

Once again, the confrontation with his profession assaulted him. Not that Calixto aspired for anonymity, he actually revealed to the old man he was a writer, not that he wanted to hide from the judgmental eyes of readers or critics, nor was he avoiding the social responsibilities of a contemporary writer, nor was he attempting to deceive his interlocutors; but to be regarded as a genuine writer at once, based on minimal interaction, made him feel exposed. And he did what he could to maintain a neutral expression when facing the old man. He took a deep breath and gazed deeply into the old man's eyes, hoping to reveal what he really was: a conflicted writer and a walker in a dangerous void.

Without moving from his chair, the old man stretched his hand and grabbed a book from a low shelf next to him. He blew away the white dust that had accumulated on top of the book. He opened the book and read the following passage: *In order to write a single line, one must see a great many cities, people and things, have an understanding of animals, sense how it is to be a bird in flight, and know the manner in which the little flowers open every morning. In one's mind, there must be regions unknown, meetings unexpected and long-anticipated partings, to which one can cast back one's thoughts...* The old man closed the book. And with the most untroubled expression, he stared at Calixto for what seemed like a lunar year. The void deepened, and from its depths, Calixto managed to ask who was that writer who seemed to know his soul. The old man handed him the book. It was a very worn copy of Rilke's *The Notebooks of Malte Laurids Brigge*, a book Calixto had read many years ago with delight and had felt transmuted by its existential disquiet.

This man, this bookworm, seems to know me. How else could he have selected that passage? I must be transparent; he just read through me. Or maybe he has read some of my books and knows what haunts me. He sells books, he knows all writers confront turbulence. Every writer faces it in his or her own particular way, but turbulence nonetheless. Could the experience of writing be universal? Perhaps... But not the experience of walking. Everyone walks, but not everyone needs to walk. And certainly, not everyone needs to write and walk. That cannot be a universal necessity. I'm drawn to writing while I have an urge to walk. These two are different forces, and they impact me in different ways. I doubt other people feel it this way. However, this old man intuits that there is something, a force, a need, something, compelling me to do just that. But the more I think about him, the more I suspect he's also a writer. Or maybe we're all writers, all of us, the entire human species. We survive on words, don't we?

Calixto could not tolerate sitting in front of the old man much longer. Although he wanted to learn more about this person, about his ideas, about his experiences with other writers, and about his intuitive capacity, the urge to walk away impaled him. He stood up and headed towards the door. But before leaving behind the old man, Calixto told him that he wanted to come back at another time to sit in front of him again. The old man agreed, waved him goodbye, and told him to be careful with the sirens.

Gliding over century-old paving stones, Calixto made his way back to Praça do Rossio where he hoped to tap into the writing vein once more. He found the same café where he had written that one sentence. This time, however, he was determined to go deeper. Without a pen, notebook, or laptop; empty-handed as he was, Calixto went for the open sea. He swam into the turbulent waters of thoughts and recent events in search of the next phrase. Almost immediately he came across the images of Lulu, then the unnamed woman with whom he shared a baguette, then Lyubochka, and finally the old man in the bookstore. These were a great many people as suggested by Rilke, and he had certainly seen a great many cities. But in spite of having seen plenty, he was at a loss for that next single line. A sense of discomfort and uneasiness pounced on him. Calixto ordered a glass of ruby port hoping to soothe the pain. When the waiter brought him the dark-colored balsam, he did not allow him to place the glass on the table. Instead, he took it from the waiter's hands and drank half of it at once. He was not attempting to drown his consciousness; he only wanted to feel a little less. Emboldened, he swam deeper into his thoughts.

Calixto reminded himself that coming to Lisbon was an attempt to write prose on the verge, that he wanted to write dangerously. So he understood there was no need to fear fortuitous encounters with strangers. To the contrary, those were the pearls of his journey. Those accidents were the raw material for equally accidental prose. He had met those iconoclasts while randomly walking through the streets. This realization soothed him as much as the ruby port. And as the sense of discomfort loosened its grip, Calixto allowed himself to observe the unknown walkers that came to the Praça do Rossio. Some entered the plaza from around a corner, crossed it diagonally, and disappeared in haste. Others entered the space and felt compelled to turn in circles around the fountains. There were those who seemed to walk erratically. Yet there were those who came and stayed in the plaza for a while, only leaving after an internal force pushed them out.

But to some extent, the immense mass of walkers must have been affected by the black and white pattern of the floor in the plaza. That was the grid that bound their feet. And Calixto firmly believed that all of those walkers could tell a story about their walk in the plaza. Walking was movement, movement was life, and inevitably, life led to fiction.

The sun started to soften, the air started to divagate, and Calixto's thought process found a quiet moment. He regarded the river of people traversing the plaza and felt satisfied. A multitude of minds had no other purpose but to imagine. And imagination had the power to render the world anew, to uncover the unseen. And in the process of uncovering, risks would be taken; maybe language would be forged. And the forging of new language meant we had a future, in the words, in the inventiveness of the minds that write, and think.

*****

The morning did not wait for Calixto. By the time he managed to get dressed and step out the door, bread had been consumed all over Lisbon and sentences had been written by innumerable writers. He was unsure how that happened, but it had. And he knew because the air was impregnated with the smell of fresh baguettes and the sound of fresh words. Both were essential elements for him, for his life, so in that particular morning, he felt completely alive. He then started walking with the idea of creating a large spiral with his trajectory. To accomplish this, he only turned to the right while covering increasing distances before making a new turn. He wanted to avoid the constancy of a circle's diameter and the repetition that such constancy entailed. He wanted to experience a rotational force, ever growing, bringing him forward, but at the same time remaining linked to the essential elements at its center. He did not want to lose the sound of the words or the smell of fresh bread; he wanted to stretch their limits.

Calixto accepted the possibility of a chance encounter with any of the people he had met since arriving in Lisbon. That thought made him smile. So as he started to walk and turn, and to turn and walk, he scrutinized the faces of people he came across on streets and sidewalks, expecting a familiar face. There were many profiles that could have been confused with those of Lulu or Lyubochka, but none turned out to be the real Lulu or Lyubochka. About a block ahead, a man carrying a book under his arm waved at him. Calixto accelerated his pace to catch up with that man, but by the time he reached the corner, the man had already disappeared behind a massive wooden door. He wondered if that man could have been the owner of the bookstore. But all he saw was a gesture and none of his face so that man could have been anybody waving goodbye to anybody else on the street.

The streets in Lisbon had the mischievous habit of ascending and descending at will. Often, Calixto's need to turn right would force him to hike numerous steps just to encounter a fretful freefall on the next right turn. Nevertheless, the hilly terrain did not keep him from pursuing his goal.

He walked assertively until the inevitable happened. The last turn he made brought him face to face with the nameless woman he had met two days before. They both stopped walking and regarded each other. She started talking and said the vagaries of life were finally coming her way but that she was not clear if that was a good omen. Then she bluntly asked him where he was heading. Calixto took a few seconds to respond, unclear if he wanted to say that he was heading nowhere, that he was merely walking in circles, ever-growing, but circles nonetheless. He also considered saying he was on his way to buying bread. That would have been a paltry lie. Although he considered heading for a bakery at another time in the near future, he was not heading for one that very moment. Once he made up his mind, Calixto explained that he was trying to trace a large spiral by walking in circles of increasing diameter. The woman did not seem surprised, and with her index finger, she traced a spiral in the air just in front of Calixto's face. She mentioned that spirals required a point of axis and asked him what important element was he turning and turning around. Once more, Calixto feared the incisive nature of this woman's questions, her ability to unearth vital information without revealing much of herself. He did not respond. Instead, he invited her to walk along with him. She agreed, and both marched ahead in silence. And just after the first right turn she started to sing a soft melody in a language Calixto could not understand. He was almost certain it was the same language as the words tattooed on her arm. The melody enlaced Calixto's mind, creating a spiral of its own, and for a moment he felt disoriented. When they reached the end of a long block, Calixto, dizzy as he was, attempted to turn left. She held his arm and directed him towards the right instead. She told him that the very important element at the center of the spiral had to be on the right side. When he asked her if she was referring to the aroma of freshly baked bread, she said that she was actually referring to the sound of fresh words.

Is it possible for this woman to know the real importance of words in my life? Bread is just as important, but given both options, she chooses the sound of fresh words. Exactly as I would've done. Just the other day we spoke to each other, but I didn't use words in ways that revealed how much they matter to me. But maybe I did so without knowing. I seem to talk without talking, to share ideas without a clear discourse. And at this very moment, we could be discussing how afraid I'm to say anything to her, how much I fear to become transparent. Even if I'm now silent, we could have spoken to each other at another time, in another place. Then she would know plenty about me. But would it really matter if everything about ourselves had been said before? If that were the case, the words we utter at this very moment would lack freshness; they would be stale and flat. And that's not how it feels. I feel as if we're about to say something surprising to each other, something that would reveal a vast unknown.

After walking for several blocks, making several right turns, and after struggling in his mind with a multitude of questions, Calixto reached a district where the walls of the decrepit buildings stood straight and showed no signs of shame. He did not intend to reach any particular place in this vertical city; he just followed his preconceived trajectory. Not knowing where he was in the large scheme of the spiral, he suddenly stopped walking and asked the woman if she wanted to sit down for a coffee or a glass of wine and talk about things they have not talked about. She agreed, and they sat at an outside terrace completely exposed to the wind, the sun, and the words of the walking crowd. Calixto asked for a glass of Alentejo, and the woman said she wanted the same thing. And this acquiescence disturbed him, for he expected resistance or at least divergence. But he did not allow the sense of distrust to take over, he reigned in all doubtful thoughts and had some of the wine. She did as he had done and both stayed silent for a while, listening to the incessant steps of the crowd that paraded right in front of them. Without a prelude, she asked him if he was proud of the books he had written. This question struck Calixto like a freight train running through the middle of his head. Not only had he not discussed with her the books he had written, but the concept of pride was foreign to him. He wrote because he needed to write, no pride sought, no glory expected. But the fact that she would pose this question so openly and straight disarmed him. There was no answer, and he said so. He drank from his glass, and she emulated him. And trying to avoid further uneasy subjects, Calixto calculated what to ask her in return. He could not contain himself and ventured to ask what her name was. She paused and played with her hair, she bit the nail of her index finger, and looking at him directly she said her name was Leda. She immediately became quiet, silent, and looked away from him. It seemed like she was trying to escape the world. It looked as if she needed to glide away from all contact, physical or mental. She simply stopped existing in front of Calixto and butterflied away. But Calixto could not let her go; he grounded her with another question. He asked if she really considered words essential to her existence, and if so, how did she usually engage with words in her own life. Leda smiled and drank some wine from her glass. Then she looked at her tattoo, those words unknown to Calixto, perhaps looking for an answer in them. And she went on to pronounce the words softly as if layering them one by one, as if those words explained everything about her and about her life. Calixto listened. He felt the words again, the emotion in the words.

Neptune and his trident. The mythical number. Three women, three encounters, three tattoos, and three names that start with the letter "L." This cannot be the product of chance; the world is not that harmless... wicked it is. But what makes it even more disquieting is the fact that the three women intuited that I'm a writer. Could I have precipitated those encounters? Perhaps I inadvertently created the conditions for them to take place. But if that were the case, the number 3 has to be secretly operating inside my mind, subconsciously directing my steps, fabricating falsely fortuitous events. I could consider that probability, but I wouldn't like it if it were true. Chance is beautiful, even dangerous. I need chance in my life. Otherwise, what would be the purpose of walking?

Trying to recapture the sense of serendipity, Calixto attempted to decipher the meaning of the words indelibly imprinted on Leda's forearm. He ventured into the unknown once more. He said the words meant "Love Your Dreams." To this conjecture, she simply responded with a faint smile that did not confirm nor reject the accuracy of Calixto's guess. And her expression, neutral, would not reveal if Calixto had even approached the themes embedded in the three words. For a moment Calixto considered guessing again, but he stopped himself. He had proposed one meaning, that was sufficient. A second guess would not clarify anything. So he accepted the vagueness of the situation as a clear confirmation that not everything is manipulated by his subconscious mind. Encouraged, Calixto allowed for time to grow on its own, for silence to decide what to do with itself, and for Leda to speak whenever she wanted. He would not pursue any further answers at that moment.

Leda leaned back in her chair and assumed a comfortable position, welcoming the wind and the sun. She asked Calixto if he felt like writing that very moment. He would have loved to say he did, but that would have been another lie. And he feared that she would see through that lie. So Calixto admitted that writing was not an urgent need, that perhaps knowing was more imminent. Leda did not ask him what it was he wanted to know about, as he had expected. Instead, she mentioned that writing should be everyone's need. But before Calixto had time to agree with that statement, she asked him if the center of his spiral felt closer to him that moment. Calixto had forgotten about the smell of freshly baked bread and the sound of fresh words. In her presence, those concerns had disappeared. Perplexed by this realization, he felt a sense of vertigo, as if the very spiral he had conjured was pulling him down into a deep void. He closed his eyes and held on tightly to the wine glass. He waited a few seconds, maybe longer, for the world to feel stable again. Once he felt the ground firm enough, he opened his eyes and found Leda looking directly at him, her expression placid. She asked him if closing his eyes let him walk far into his inner journey. Calixto was not sure how far he had walked, or whether he had walked at all. He may have fallen fathoms into a deep fear, and that kind of emotional journey did not happen in real space. But not ready to admit any sense of uneasiness, he said he had not walked a single centimeter.

The wind started to blow harder. The umbrellas shading the tables rattled. Someone's hat went flying by and disappeared down the street. Calixto was not afraid of the umbrellas or flying objects, but he was afraid the wind would steal his words and never bring them back. And at this moment he needed every single word, so he made sure to keep his mouth closed. He looked at Leda from within his silence, and this must have emphasized the appearance of anguish because Leda asked him if everything was fine. Exposed and vulnerable as he felt, Calixto pretended to be at peace by gazing over the rooftops of the old buildings far out to the magnificently calm Tejo. The river, with silver scars on its back, walked its undulating walk out to the ocean. This vision served to calm Calixto, who stood up and announced he was ready to continue walking and making right turns. Leda said she understood his need, and without further explanations, she got up from the table and followed the wind down the street leaving Calixto standing alone.

*****

As the spiral expanded, the forces at its center began to lose their power. Calixto felt this weakening and stopped walking. He did not want to fall off the spiral for fear of coming unhinged. He considered simply backtracking, circling in the opposite direction towards the point where he had started from. But that would oblige him to walk over the same streets, repeating the walking experience in reverse. That would not elicit fresh words, and he needed them. So he decided to walk in a straight line toward the center of the spiral, skipping over concentric rings, following the centripetal force.

Calixto had not gone too far in his new trajectory when he found himself once more in front of Livraria Mundo. Arriving at that location unexpectedly made him hesitate. He had not planned to be there, but there he was. So he walked inside the old bookstore, hoping to find Lyubochka and her salamander at the sales counter. And that was exactly what he found. This time Lyubochka did not ignore him; to the contrary, she looked directly at him from the moment he went through the door. And before Calixto managed to say anything, she asked him if he had already written about love. Calixto wanted to say he had written volumes and volumes about love since they met the previous day, that he had learned all about her home village in Ukraine, that he had even baked bread. But that was not possible, and she intuited that, for when he did

469

not answer her question, she looked down to her lap and continued reading her book. Calixto felt the weight of the disappointment.

I know about the ancient salamander, the lizard who lives in the fire. It comes out of the fire and extinguishes it. And as quiet as she is, she is just as fiery. What does she expect from me? Or is it me who expects something from myself and she only reminds me of my own expectations? Could she be made of fire? Who knows? All I know is that in her presence I feel uncomfortable. No, not in her presence… in her silence. Her silence cuts through me. The fire of coal is silent, but just as consuming. And she expects me to write about love. Perhaps not about love but about her. But I don't know one nor the other. This is how I fail, by not distinguishing between fire and fear, between love and the object of love. And she knows I should write about that, somehow she knows. But where should I write about love? With the immensity of the Atlantic Ocean on my back? That's what I thought before departing from Nice, that's what brought me to Lisbon. But what brought me to her, to the fire of her expectations? Was it the randomness of my walks? Perhaps my walks are not random at all. And if they were not random, what are the unseen forces pulling on me?

Calixto respected her silence. He wanted to ask her about the book she was reading but thought that would not be prudent. Not when he just failed to respond to her question. He moved about the store and pretended to be looking for a particular book. He shuffled a few titles, read a few random passages, and eventually found a section containing several books by Clarice Lispector. Here he stopped and inspected the copies. They were all in Portuguese. He looked up to Lyubochka who was still immersed in her reading and interrupted her by asking if there were any books by Lispector in English or French. Lyubochka emerged from her reading as if from a dream. She then lifted the book she was reading for Calixto to see. It was a copy of *The Passion According to G.H.* in English translation. Calixto held his breath. He could not comprehend how Lyubochka happened to be reading the very book he would have liked to have found. He proceeded carefully and mentioned that it was precisely that book, *The Passion According to G.H.*, that he was looking for. While caressing the fiery salamander, Lyubochka said that she was happy he found the book he came looking for. And when Calixto asked if he could actually buy that copy, she said he could not buy it because she had not finished reading it yet. And just as simple as that, Lyubochka looked down and continued reading the book.

Unclear as to whose expectations he was not meeting, Calixto considered escaping from the bookstore and continuing his walk down toward the center of the spiral. But the drive to move ahead yielded to the need to solve the intrigue Lyubochka presented. He walked to the sales desk and stood firmly in front of her. There he remained for a few moments, waiting for Lyubochka to acknowledge him. When she eventually stopped reading and looked up at him, he felt a sense of vertigo. In spite of his fear for what might ensue, Calixto persisted in being there, standing, sustaining his equilibrium. Lyubochka started talking and said that somehow the book mirrored him. And she proceeded to quote a phrase she had just read: *"We are creatures that must plunge into the depth in order to breathe there."* Calixto tried to decode what Lispector would have meant by those words. But he was more interested in knowing why Lyubochka thought they had anything to do with him. So he asked her. And he did not get an answer. Instead, Lyubochka went back to reading the book and completely ignored him once more. There were times when Calixto found no words to continue writing. There were other times when he did not find a clear path to follow in his walks. And yet there were other times when he was not clear as to what the universe was preparing for him. This was one of those times.

The only way to comprehend the universe was through words, and Calixto knew that. Nothing could exist in full plenitude until addressed by words. So Calixto turned around and searched the bookshelves for a dictionary. He wanted a sizable volume with the largest number of words. The Cambridge English-Portuguese dictionary caught his attention with its imposing shield, where four lions were flanked by a white cross. He grabbed the dictionary and let the full weight of all the words contained within it fall on the sales desk. The loud thump did not disturb Lyubochka who remained immersed in Lispector's strange and hypnotic prose. Calixto then reached across the desk and took a solitary pen sleeping next to the cash register.

The gesture did not bother Lyubochka a bit. He opened the dictionary and started writing on the white interior of the back cover. He wrote fast, desperately. When he had covered about half of the back cover with his meticulous calligraphy, Lyubochka detached herself from her book and asked him if he was finally writing about love. Calixto stopped in the middle of a sentence and said that he was using words to find the way to the words that might help him understand this moment. That if all the words were contained in this dictionary, a combination of the right ones would certainly shed light on what was about to happen. Lyubochka took a deep breath and seemed pensive. She took the dictionary and turned it in her direction to read what Calixto had written so meticulously. Her expression could not have changed less as she read the text. After returning the dictionary to Calixto, she said that she could not understand the spirit of the characters. She then asked him if he thought the text was capable of breathing.

Words are life. I naturally expect my writing to breathe. But perhaps she's asking something completely different. She wants me to write about love, and love is the meaning of her name. She may be looking for an image of herself in the writing. Or perhaps a living, breathing equivalent of herself. If she's reading Lispector, there must be an existential yearning beating inside of her. Her placid expression could be a mask covering a deep, brutal mystical crisis. Maybe she's the one that must plunge into the depth and breathe there. Regardless, she instigates in me a sense of imbalance, an uneasy feeling that makes me doubt. Yes, I know I need to write books. But that's not where the answer is — not the answer to why an abyss forms in front of me at this moment. I need to write to understand. I need the words to shine their light and lead me to the center of the spiral. They're all there, in the dictionary, the words. A million points of light contained between the covers of that one book. So if the words are not clear to her, if she cannot hear their breath, then I've failed to find the correct ones.

Resolved, Calixto carefully scripted two more sentences on the dictionary's back cover and showed them to Lyubochka. He was certain the words had all the necessary space to breathe. He really meant what the words implied, especially the word "blue." This time Lyubochka broke the surface of the mountain lake and offered him an ample smile. The smile fastened itself to the thin air inside the bookstore and hung there for Calixto to admire. Her response was swift and acute. She said the ocean was there for all to find, that if he traveled west to Adraga, he was certain to find the ocean, a large one, capable of sourcing all the words he needed. She added that water was the essence of all living creatures, including the seagulls, and that to carry an ocean on his back was certainly an advantage if he could tolerate the magnanimous imposition. Calixto did not expect such an apprehending answer. He marveled at the insight Lyubochka revealed. But he felt disappointed that she had not reflected on the color blue, a reference he clearly made on those two sentences. Maybe he left very little room around the word "blue" for Lyubochka to comment. When he imagined writing with the enormous ocean on his back, he imagined an aqueous universe, diaphanous, transparent, and exquisitely blue.

Lyubochka left the sales desk in a rush and went looking for a map of Lisbon. She moved the dictionary to the edge of the desk, without closing it, and opened the map right in front of Calixto. The city, the neighborhoods, and the hills were all there for Calixto to regard. He took some time to become acquainted with the relationship between land and sea. He marveled at the proximity of the ocean and wondered what happened to the waters of the Tejo when they entered the body of the ocean. Did the river waters understand what was happening to them, did they know they were being absorbed? He thought about language and how words from one language had been absorbed by another language throughout the history of the world, over and over again. He wondered if, in the end, the ocean contained all the waters of all the rivers in the world. Likewise, he wondered if one universal language would contain all other languages of the world. But not wanting to destroy the grace of the moment with unbecoming questions, he went back to the color "blue." Calixto pointed to the shores of the Atlantic Ocean on the map and asked Lyubochka if the waters along the shore were blue. She looked at him with the sagacity that had perturbed him earlier and said the ocean had no color of its own, that it only reflected the color of the sky.

Calixto understood what she meant: the essential relativity of all perceptions. And that led him to consider that his need for words was a personal conundrum that would continue to exist in spite of the extensive walking he had done. He also accepted that chance was playing a crafty game on him. But above all, he confronted the possibility that what he considered essential, what he considered utterly obvious, could be questioned. In his genuine depths, Calixto wanted to find the color blue, but such a color would only come forward as a reflection of his own self. So, exposing his vulnerabilities, he asked Lyubochka if she thought the ocean flanking the west of Lisbon would be kind to him. She said he had nothing to fear, that the ocean was simply there.

*****

The path to Adraga was paved with uncertainty. Calixto would need to walk at least nine hours to face the ocean at its rawest. He knew there was no other path, and he needed to forge the path alone. The words of Lyubochka continued to resonate in his mind. The ocean was simply there, there it was. And carrying only the most bare essentials, he ventured west of Lisbon. He imagined what the ocean would look like upon his arrival at Adraga. There would be the color blue, the expansiveness. But he also knew that standing at the shore of the ocean would not be different from standing at the shore of the sea. The blue body of the Mediterranean would resemble the Atlantic Ocean. But perhaps what resided in the horizon beyond the line between the two blues was completely different. That was not a tangible element; it only existed in the realm of the mind. For Calixto, beyond had yet to happen. He was searching for a vision of beauty, and a new language, the one he knew had to exist.

Along the long road to Adraga, Calixto saw people engaged in needs so different from his own. Children went to school, office workers went into their tombs, and dogs looked for inviting posts. The world turned in so many different ways. Those realities meant nothing to him at that point, he knew they had a place in the world, and he also knew they would continue to exist independent of him. So he carried forward, walking at a pace that would bring him to the ocean in the late afternoon. But what he could not have predicted was to come across the image of a woman who resembled Lulu walking toward him. Upon such sighting, he went under an awning on the side of the street and remained motionless. From that vantage point he observed the figure of Lulu, or someone who looked like her, move past him and disappear through a side street. He had encountered a similar image while sitting at Praça do Rossio, and now he wondered if this was the same image or a similar sensation. He was not prepared to make the distinction between a real image or a sensation, so he treated the experience as if it was the very image of Lulu. But by the time he decided to follow her, the image, or the sensation, whatever that was, had already vanished.

Undeterred, Calixto continued his long walk. He tried to follow long, uninterrupted lines; he avoided turning right or left; he kept his gaze ahead and followed the distant smell of salty water. Ahead of him was the ocean, and perhaps, the words he needed. And the pull of those words was so hard that Calixto did not realize the passage of time, the passage of distance. He walked, and he walked some more. And by the time the sun was calming itself down, Calixto had arrived at a promontory from where he could see the horizon opening up in front of him. He regarded the blue, the expansiveness. He readied himself for a new language.

Calixto approached the ocean. He felt its cold and raw nature, and its yearning to extend itself out west, far beyond where he had ever ventured. The roar of the ocean was magnanimous, and Calixto knew that words could be sourced from that immense volume of sound. So there he stood, at the shore, tired from walking all day, but ecstatic to be in the presence of such magnificence. He closed his eyes and took a deep breath. The salty air flooded his lungs, and his mind felt as if he was part of something larger than himself. He felt a sense of belonging as if all beings were connected to each other by means of the waters circling the world. And that oceanic sense of connectedness gave him hope. Perhaps his random encounters with men and women along his extended walks had a sense and a meaning after all.

Soon the sun turned red, and Calixto started walking back to the nearby village of Almoçageme to find a place to sleep. It was a short stretch but the long day started to weigh him down. Had the ocean not infused him with new energy, he would have collapsed on the sandy beach. Once he reached the village, Calixto came across a *quinta* that seemed welcoming. He went inside and asked the host if they had a quiet room with an open view. The host said he had the perfect room for him on the top floor, overlooking the horizon, with a distant view of the ocean. Calixto accompanied the host to take a look at the room and found it utterly appropriate for his needs. He then agreed to stay there for five days, perfectly knowing that five days would not be enough to accomplish much in terms of language. Once the host left, he collapsed on the bed and abandoned himself to recumbent relaxation. The morning would arise with a brand new offering, or so Calixto expected. But somehow, the hours between night and morning needed to be endured. The night arrived at once and swallowed him complete. But as soon as he went into REM sleep, his dreams took flight. He saw himself standing in front of a large crowd in an amphitheater, dressed like an ancient actor, delivering phrases by Euripides: "Some shrewd and intelligent man invented fear of the gods for mortals, so the wicked would have something to fear… concealing the truth with a false account." He heard the crowd applaud. He then declared other phrases, elucidating, even brilliant, and he felt understood. His capacity to transmit his thought process by means of words made him feel accomplished in his dreams. But when the night came to an end, in the impossible morning hours, the most despicable moment of the sleep cycle, Calixto woke up feeling as if he was betrayed. He had spoken the words of the heroes in his dreams, but the erratic day showed a burning face certain to challenge him, to reverse his accomplishment.

Calixto left behind his bed and his doubts and went to open the window in his room. The light rushed to meet him, a blue light. And far beyond the hills, a sliver of ocean saluted him. He felt a sense of belonging as if he was where he needed to be at this very moment in his life. And knowing that such a feeling could easily prove temporary, he prepared himself to walk to the beach to confront the ocean, the words, and the unknown.

At the breakfast room, the host asked Calixto if he wanted a basket of croissants. He said he preferred bread, any kind of bread as long as it was fresh. The host then asked him if he wanted coffee or tea. Calixto said he preferred a good glass of Douro. The host said he understood and brought him the glass of wine. He then asked Calixto what had brought him to Adraga. Calixto pondered for a while, he knew the essential forces that brought him there, but he had doubts about those other forces that lay buried deep in his unconscious mind. Those were the forces he feared the most. But after a moment of consideration, he said that words had brought him there. The host looked at him and made a grimace that he could not decipher. Calixto could have said that the ocean brought him there. But in reality, the ocean was what he found after getting there. The words, or the search for words, was the true force behind his long walk from Lisbon. But explaining this to the host was not what he intended. So he simply drank the wine, all at once, and took to the road to follow the salty air.

Calixto approached the ocean slowly. He saw how the

horizon grew blue in front of him. He noticed how the sound of the waves overtook all other sounds. He observed how the limit of his visual field expanded until vanishing completely. And far away he saw that line between the two blues, the line he could not reach unless he walked on water. From that spot, he walked down the beach until finding a rock where he could sit down and begin the labor of words. He was exactly where he wanted to be, so he dove into the language.

Sometimes, words came to Calixto as blue words, perhaps wet and salty. Other times words bounced on the surface of the ocean, traveling from wave crest to wave crest, finally arriving at him entirely dry. Other words just floated in the air, at the whim of the winds, erratic in their behavior. Calixto appreciated the unpredictable words, but at the same time, he needed certain consistency. Capturing the various words proved a challenging task. He tried to compose sentences that contained an elegant mixture of the various word sources, but he failed. When he wanted salty words, they were not available. When he needed a dry word, a wet one would land on his lap. When he aimed at channeling the whimsical nature of the windy words, they flew around him in spirals making it impossible for him to grab a single one. He then waited for the silvery words, those that grew from the underside of the waves when caught by the oblique sunlight. Those words traveled faster than any other words; they were fleeing the pressure between water and light; they were blinding. Calixto caught a couple of those silvery words and felt lucky. He waited and held onto some of the wet and dry words.

Not having an immediate obligation other than creating and advancing his prose, he continued this exercise until he had gathered a significant number of words. He then tried to construct phrases with all the words he had assembled. The essential purpose was to create innovative prose, or so he thought. But then he thought about Lyubochka who had directed him west. He thought about Leda and the absence of words to describe her absence. And he thought about Lulu and her uncertain silhouette. Calixto could not dismiss the impact those three women had on him. He then understood that real writing would not take place until he could verbalize what those experiences represented.

The sun stepped on him, and the winds pushed him around. Calixto felt the force of the elements and realized he could not fight against them either. So he offered his skin to the sun and his hair to the wind. He allowed for anything existing outside of his skin to have its way with him. Inside, however, he tried to establish some control. He began by thinking about Lulu and admitting he could not effectively grasp her image. A fleeting image had no handles. He considered Leda and accepted the fluid nature of her soul, and in so being, her unsubstantial quality. As for Lyubochka, he felt a genuine admiration for her calm demeanor and her intuitive nature. The three of them could exist at the same time inside his mind; they just needed to find their own private corner. So, once at peace with the divergent feelings those three women elicited, Calixto felt at ease with himself, relieved, free to unleash his creative power.

The hours marched in front of Calixto without disturbing him. Absorbed in his writing, he ignored their passage. He also ignored the arrival of several people who came to share the beach with him. From time to time he would look up from his writing and watch people frolicking on the sand and bathing in the ocean. For him, they did not exist as people; they were entities that turned into a blue substance that blended with the horizon. Everything he saw or heard existed only for a fraction of a second before joining the magnificent body of water extending in front of him. And in such a state he remained until the moment a hand landed on his left shoulder. Calixto turned and saw a wrinkled hand pressing him down, but when he looked up to find out who that hand belonged to, the sun blinded him. He then stood up, and when his eyes adjusted to the new light, he found himself in front of the deeply carved face of the old man he had met at the bookstore. He could not imagine how the old man found him on this remote beach. But there he was, standing in front of him, not saying a single word, impassive, as if he had been there for ages. Calixto felt the same uneasy feeling as when he sat in front of the old man at his store.

A strange nakedness. And when he was about to react, to say something, the old man beat him to the point and asked him if he had made advances in filling the void. Calixto did not answer the question. And somehow the old man had not expected an answer because at once he showed Calixto the copy of his own book, *No Somos Pero Somos*, and told him he was enjoying it tremendously. When Calixto asked him what was he doing in Adraga, the old man said he had come to talk to him about the book and the void. And when Calixto asked him how did he manage to find him in Adraga, the old man reminded him that he had worked for the resistance. The old man then sat on the rock next to the one where Calixto was sitting and proceeded to read *No Somos Pero Somos* in silence.

The ocean behaved as if nothing had happened. It remained placid in its immensity. And Calixto found that comforting. He then sat down in front of the old man and continued to write. He was creating new prose at the same time the old man was consuming prose he had created in the past. Calixto felt as if they were both on the same plane, like a Möbius strip, a cycle twisted on itself with no beginning or end. And sharing a common plane with the old man made Calixto wonder what his name would be. So he asked the old man what his name was. The old man looked at him, and clearly puzzled said his name was of no importance. Then Calixto asked again how did he want to be called. The old man took pause, he regarded the ocean as if something would emerge from it, and then asked Calixto to call him Theo.

When the afternoon arrived, it found the two men still sitting in front of each other. They had not spoken since the morning. And it was not until Calixto said he had nothing more to write, that Theo said he had nothing more to read. Then they stood up and agreed to walk back to Almoçageme to find something to eat.

*****

The walk back to Almoçageme turned into a crawl. Calixto had to slow his pace so that Theo could keep up with him. The old man did not seem out of breath, but his steps were significantly shorter than those of Calixto. In addition, at every turn of the road, Theo would look behind him and around him, as if he were afraid of being followed. Calixto asked him if there was something wrong and Theo responded that nothing was wrong, that everything seemed right, as far as he could ascertain. They eventually made it to the *quinta* where Calixto was staying. Theo greeted the host in the most familiar way, and after exchanging a few words in Portuguese, they were seated at a table in a quiet corner. The host brought a bottle of Douro and poured two glasses. He then asked if they were interested in dining at once. Calixto indicated he was ready, but Theo asked the host to wait a little longer because he had to discuss a serious matter before dinner. This request surprised Calixto. He could not imagine what serious matter Theo intended to discuss with him.

After toasting and drinking half of his glass of wine, Theo told Calixto that everything he had read in *No Somos Pero Somos* was a lie. Calixto accepted the premise but pointed out that he only wrote fictional lies, not real ones. He was not interested in the real lies people tell; those were better dealt with in real life. He was more interested in the creation of lies intended to exist within a fictional world. Theo listened attentively to the explanation. He remained quiet and drank some more of the wine. Then he asked Calixto if those lies, the fictional ones, would not necessarily get closer and closer to reality. He thought that was the real danger, that one could inadvertently breach the line between fiction and reality. He then added that approaching that line from the fictional side would be a reversal from the direction in which writers commonly travel. For Calixto, whether that porous line was breached coming from the real or the fictional side had no importance, and he said so. Before continuing their conversation, Theo insisted on Calixto drinking some more of the wine. He said both of them had to be equally influenced. Calixto obeyed. Then Theo spoke about the need to create false appearances during the times of Salazar, how the resistance had taught him to pretend, how nothing was what it seemed to be. He said that each person in the resistance was a novel. Calixto imagined the unbearable experiences Theo had endured. He also understood that a reader like Theo would read a novel in a completely different manner from another reader whose life did not seem like a novel itself. This time Calixto was the one who remained quiet and drank some of the wine. Theo faced him, a hard face he had, and murmured something Calixto did not understand.

The host brought a few olives and a basket of bread to their table. He asked again if they were ready to order. Theo presented him with his hard face, and the host understood to leave them alone for the moment. When Calixto reached for a piece of bread, Theo was quick to hold his hand, preventing him from grabbing anything. He let go of Calixto's hand and said that instincts could often betray the man, that we should not necessarily do what we felt like doing. In his opinion, reigning in one's instincts was not deceitful but protective. Calixto mentioned that he saw no need to protect himself in such a manner. A subtle smirk broke the hardness of Theo's face. And then he asked Calixto if he really had the words he needed to write his new book.

Do I really have the words I need? And why does he question that? In front of the ocean, I feel overwhelmed by words; there's no shortage of them. He was there; he saw me writing. But maybe what the old man senses is the void, that void Lispector wrote about. And these questions must be important for him since he came all the way from Lisbon to find me. I wonder what I represent for him. Perhaps a friend lost or murdered during the times of Salazar. Maybe I look like his son. Maybe he's looking for words himself. Or maybe his own void is larger than mine. I don't know. But he seemed at ease reading while I was writing. I must admit I also felt at ease. We both shared the same plane, the plane of language. I believe we were both creating at the same time. I was forging phrases while he was deciphering them. He created his own version of my book. Every text is reinvented when read. Perhaps the real creative communion happens when a writer writes while his writing is being read simultaneously.

So Calixto said that even if the words became scarce, he had conceived of a way to procure them. And he said this in such a convincing fashion that Theo did not see the need to question him, he just accepted the statement. Calixto then grabbed the piece of bread he was longing for and consumed it with great delight while Theo watched him attentively and drank still more wine. With a quick gesture, Theo summoned the host, and they finally ordered their meal. By the time the food arrived at the table the bottle of wine was completely empty. Theo asked for another bottle. They ate in complete silence, facing each other, sharing words that existed only in their minds, words that had yet to be written or read. When the meal was over, the night had descended in its entirety, and the two men were still sitting in front of each other. They were talking without saying a single word.

Eventually, Theo stood up and said he had to return to Lisbon, that he needed to open the shop in the morning because people deserved open access to books. He explained that the fact the current government was not a repressive one did not guarantee that other forces dissuaded people from reading good literature. For him, the most powerful force was undirected and purposeless freedom because it gave people more opportunities than they could handle. People were bound to sink into the pit of the lowest common denominator, he thought. Calixto noticed how Theo's hands started to shake, and his face became even harder. He could not tell if it was the alcohol that made him tremulous or his grave concern for the infirm situation of the reading public. And as Theo started walking away from the *quinta*, Calixto realized he had left the copy of *No Somos Pero Somos* on top of the table. He picked up the book and ran after Theo. When he attempted to give him the book, Theo said it did not make any sense for him to keep the book. Yes, he had not finished reading it, but he would only continue to read the book in Calixto's presence and only if Calixto were to be writing at the same time right in front of him. Then he just left.

Back in his room Calixto sat at the edge of his bed and looked out the window. He tried to find the reflection of the moon on the surface of the ocean. But the night insisted on being dark and offered no light whatsoever. Then he tried to listen for the waves. He thought he heard them, but that would have been impossible. He listened more attentively to all the sounds the night brought to the window. There were a few scattered words he could not understand. Perhaps the host was talking to someone. He then opened his own book, *No Somos Pero Somos*, and read random sentences. He tried to imagine how those words sounded inside Theo's mind. Did the words have the same timbre, cadence, and melancholic character of his own voice, his Calixto's voice? Or, most likely, did Theo hear his own personal voice, his Theo's voice, as if he himself had written the words down and was now talking to himself? Theo had only started reading the book after they had met, after having the opportunity to hear each other's voice. So he supposed that Theo read *No Somos Pero Somos* having his voice, Calixto's voice, inside his mind. This was an uneasy feeling because Calixto did not want to exist as a voice in other people's mind. But he could not stop wondering what voice would readers hear inside their minds when they had never met the author and heard his or her real voice. Readers had to invent a voice, any voice that seemed appropriate, he considered. But that left much to the vagaries of chance. Perhaps, he thought, readers hear versions of their own voices. They match their own joy with the joy of the book, pain with pain, and fear with fear in an ever-changing sequence of emotions dictated by the text. Calixto continued reading passages from his own book until the night quieted everything down and his mind fell asleep.

*****

The morning arrived with urgency. The clear light doused Calixto with such audacity that he had no other option but to get up at once and consider the day. He recalled the events that had transpired the previous night. He thought about Theo and his capacity to behave as a doppelgänger, a reflection of his own needs. He would have liked to talk to him that very morning before setting out for the new unknown. But Theo was probably in Lisbon opening his bookstore, taking care of the needs of anonymous readers. So Calixto grabbed the copy of *No Somos Pero Somos* and confronted the day on his own. He started walking towards Adraga, hoping to meet the vast ocean face-to-face once more. But then, by pure chance, his feet struck an abandoned path that led away from the beach instead of toward it. He stopped walking at once and stood calmly on the desolate path. He accepted the unexpected desires of a random morning, but he still wanted to return to the beach where he hoped to find a new stream of words. So he stood there, motionless, waiting for the competing drives to settle down. Once his mind found some peace, he corrected his course and headed toward the ocean. He then walked at a steady rate until the blue grew immense right in front of him.

Calixto searched for the same rock where he had sat the previous day. That vantage point had provided a clear angle to watch the ocean and source the words he needed. He found it without much effort and sat down immediately to prepare himself for the vagaries of a day of prose. But as he started to write, he felt an intense urge to move closer to the edge of the surf and walk along the beach. He could walk north towards a promontory where the rocks and the ocean met. The wind maneuvering around the rocks was certain to be strong there, salty. That wind would likely produce sounds, and on that account, create words he had yet considered. He could use those words during his writing day to give his prose the fugitive sense of falling, spiraling, burning. He could then walk back under the sun to his sitting rock, carrying the bounty of words in his mind, and then continue writing. Convinced, Calixto set out to meet the edge of the surf. As he reached the unquiet water, the surf charged him with an impetus he had not expected, only to retreat quickly, not because of cowardice, but because the ocean pulled back on it. He stepped forward and backward in an attempt to remain at the very edge of the white surf. And to this end, he stepped over hard sand and quicksand in an insane rhythm that tested his balance. He soon realized this back and forth movement prevented him from walking north across the beach to the rocky promontory where he expected to find the shimmering words. So he walked away from the edge of the surf and watched its movement from the safety of hard sand. Then a strong wind blew from the ocean, and the surf lost its white head. He felt sorry for the surf, so incessant and so feeble.

Once at the north end of the beach, Calixto climbed the dark rocks and took a good look at the expansive ocean in front of him, a body so vast he felt compelled to join it. He grabbed the copy of *No Somos Pero Somos* that Theo had left behind and hurled it into the brave waters. He gave his words to the ocean. His writer's body was now inside the body of the ocean. He then grabbed on to a hard rock and closed his eyes. He focused on listening to the wind, to the swirling words. Soon he realized how the position of his head changed the way the wind spoke to him. If he faced the wind straight on, both ears equally captured the words rushing by. This proved to be confusing. But if he turned his head ninety degrees to the right or to the left, exposing only one ear to the wind at a time, he had a better chance to listen to the words. So Calixto held onto the rock while oscillating his head from one side to the other as if saying "no" to the wind, but in reality, accepting all the words the wind had to offer.

Drunk on words, Calixto walked back to the spot where he had planned to write until dusk. All the relevant forces coalesced to catapult him forward into daring prose. And he started writing and looking for the edge, the line at the verge of a precipice, a precipice that contained nothing but pure bliss. And the words were flying, and the images were dawning, and the unconscious was humming, all as it ought to be when he saw the silhouette of a woman walking toward him from where the sun was shining. He could not distinguish who it was when looking into the harsh sunlight. But when the silhouette came close enough to block the sunlight completely, Calixto found himself facing Lyubochka. She did not say anything to Calixto; she simply sat down next to him and looked out to the ocean. Then, in the most casual tone,

Lyubochka asked him if he had found what he came looking for. Calixto was looking for many things, some of which he was not even aware he was looking for. And he knew that, the blurry line between the known and the unknown. So all he managed to say was that he had found the ocean just as she had suggested.

Calixto continued writing with the same impetus as before. Now, however, he had a witness. Sitting next to him, Lyubochka observed as he wrote every single word. She made no comments or remarks, nor did she react to the meaning of the words. But she watched attentively as he wrote and wrote. Neither of them had proposed this arrangement, but they did not fight it either. And this communion continued for a while until the moment when Calixto stopped writing abruptly. He seemed dubitative, unsure what to write next. He waited for a few minutes, but nothing occurred to him. He then looked far into the horizon hoping to find vagabond words somewhere out there, between the ocean and the sky. And as he regarded the grand openness, so did Lyubochka. He wondered if she was also looking for elusive words or if she just wanted to share that uncertain moment. He decided to hold his gaze on the horizon for a moment longer. Not only because he had not found what to write next, but to see if Lyubochka would accompany him in the prolonged effort. And she did. She placidly sustained her gaze, unperturbed by the sun or the seagulls. The ocean stretched as far as anyone could see and it did not care that it was being watched by people on the shore. It continued to undulate, to grow small wavelets on its back, to reflect the sun, to allow currents in the deep of its belly, and to send the surf out to the beach. Lyubochka was aware of the ocean's indifference. So she interrupted the long period of contemplation and asked Calixto if he knew the meaning of every word he had written that day. He responded that every word had a meaning but that he did not always know what that meaning was. Then she said she did not understand the ocean either.

For a moment Calixto considered asking what led her all the way from Lisbon to Adraga. But afraid of the potential answer, he withheld the question. Instead, he proposed his own answer. He told Lyubochka there was no need for her to come all the way to Adraga to confirm the ocean was, in fact, just here; that she had made the trip because she felt bored at the bookstore and needed the dynamic force of the ocean to bring life to her day. She smiled but did not respond to his statement. He then proposed to continue with their writing. She quickly remarked that the one writing was him, that she was only an observer. Calixto wanted to disagree, but he did not. So he stopped looking at the horizon and concentrated on trying to write in front of Lyubochka, his witness. By that time, the sun had moved further to the west, and the rays came at an obtuse angle, bouncing off the surface of the ocean and reaching straight into his eyes. This made writing a little more difficult for he needed to squint or block the sunlight with his hand. Lyubochka did not seem bothered at all; she just closed her eyes and let the sunlight bathe her face and the salamander on her neck. He admired her natural peace, how her face became a canvas for the drawings of light and wind. But determined to accomplish his mission, Calixto continued to write in silence, under the sun, in front of the ocean.

Who found whom? I just wonder. I walked into her store on my own accord. She said the ocean was just here. I walked west to Adraga because I wanted to write at the edge. Or, perhaps I walked west to Adraga hoping to find her here, even if that would have been unlikely. If that were indeed the thought process that led me to this beach, I would have to admit I wasn't aware of it. But the truth is that here she is and here I am. Then I wonder if my walking is driven by the need to write or the need to encounter elusive souls that I can barely understand. And there was Theo. Did I come here looking for him as well? I don't think I did but didn't I? And both of these esoteric people interact with my writing in strange ways. They seem to foster the prose, or better yet, exist alongside the prose. So I wonder if writers should write alone, or if we are supposed to write in the company of those who seem to know something about us that we've yet to understand. I fear the answer to that question. For the moment there's the ocean, there's the intense blue, there's the wind, there's the placidity of Lyubochka's face. For the moment I exist as a writer.

Calixto wrote with intensity. From time to time he looked out to the horizon. Other times he gazed at Lyubochka discretely, as if he was not interested in her, pretending he did not care what she was doing. He did care, and she knew he did. But both continued to do what they were doing. Then came the moment that Calixto had secretly feared and had not yet accepted. Lyubochka stood up and said she needed to return to Lisbon. He regarded her, broken inside but firm on the exterior. He said he was not finished writing for the day. She looked straight at him and produced a smile he had never seen before on anyone. And with the same facility with which she arrived, she left. Calixto considered running after her and asking if she could stay until his writing was finished. But he soon realized the baseness of this request. His writing belonged to him, all of it, and no other person could permanently influence it. These fleeting experiences could affect his writing temporarily, yes, but the influence would only be circumscribed to a specific moment and place. And holding onto that line of thought, he watched as Lyubochka walked along the beach until she made a right turn and disappeared from his view.

Calixto felt alone at that moment. Yes, he had come to Adraga alone, but the fact that he felt lonely indicated that something had happened to worsen his condition. A man who walks alone is a man who walks alone. A man who walks alone, and then interacts with people in ways that change the man, is a man who is no longer walking alone. So he wondered if meeting strangers were somehow eroding his condition as a lonesome walker. Even when he had never considered himself as a lonesome walker, he suspected that he was, to some extent, a loner. But walking entailed moving from one place to another, a displacement. And inherent in displacement one found loneliness. But displacement also produced chance encounters with souls he had never known before. Would not those new encounters annihilate the sense of loneliness? Perhaps, but if he felt a sense of affiliation with a new encounter, and the new affiliation would, all of a sudden, come to an end, would not that lead once more to essential loneliness? Calixto did not have an answer to those questions. He was battling the strong sentiment of loneliness after Lyubochka's departure, and at the same time, he was facing the strong urge to continue writing in front of the ocean. Then he thought of all those other writers that had come before him, all of those who had persevered in spite of essential doubts. And pacifying his thought process, he looked out to the horizon, regarding once more the line between the two blues, and he wrote a few more words.

At the end of the day, when he felt completely drained of words, Calixto decided to enjoy the product of his hard labor. He regarded the vastness of his writing, the countless paragraphs and innumerable words he had woven in the last two days. He then attempted to read a few passages to connect with the feeling of the story. But he found the sentences made no sense. He turned one page after another; he tried to understand what he had written so arduously. And once again, the text scurried through the crevices of his mind as water between his fingers. Nothing meaningful remained, only the loneliness.

He walked back to Lisbon, a defeated soldier with a deep vagueness in his soul. Calixto knew the future in Lisbon already existed ahead of him. He knew about the inevitability of arriving in the old city, of looking for fresh bread. But what he could not fathom was how to recover his writing and his sense of being. Was he supposed to avoid people to sustain his loneliness, or was he obligated to search for new encounters with unknown people in the unknown streets of Lisbon? This was not clear to him when he checked back into the hotel. And for that reason, he decided to do nothing and allow for the passage of time to bring clarity. Although he was tired from the long walk back from Adraga, he could not fall asleep. He sat in silence and meditated as the day took all its time to pass by.

Several centuries later, or so it seemed, Calixto realized the passage of time was not providing any clarity. So, in spite of feeling the weight of lead pulling him down, he walked out into the street hoping for an epiphany. He walked up and down and around the city blocks. He avoided making eye contact with strangers for fear of unintended consequences. He just moved his body from one place to another. For a moment he considered whirling, like the Sufi Dervishes, to search for the source of all perfection. But he could never sustain such intensity. Finally, in the middle of a tiresome street, he sat on the curb and watched the passersby. He imagined the infinity of thoughts those other walkers had in their minds, their fears, their dilemmas. And somehow, he identified with them. A sense of collective nihilism dawned on him. Not wanting to roll down the street like a worthless pebble, Calixto picked himself up and tried to walk with his head up and his gaze forward. And that was when he saw once more the image of a woman who resembled Lulu walking about 50 meters ahead of him. The woman was walking rather fast, so Calixto accelerated his pace to try to get a better glimpse. He was not sure that it was Lulu, but the resemblance was significant enough not to be ignored. Although he tried, he could not keep up with her speed. He walked as fast as his tired body permitted, trying to get a glimpse of her right ankle and the three red stars, but the woman still gained distance on him until finally disappearing at the top of a hilly street.

Resolved that no resolution would be had that day, Calixto made his way back to the hotel. He refused to think he was retreating from the world, from the ubiquitous uncertainty. He recognized his arrival in Lisbon proposed no other expectations than to write copiously and to be in the vicinity of the ocean. He had met both of those expectations. So the sense of uneasiness he felt that moment had to be the result of his failure in Adraga. Perhaps, he thought, those chance encounters had altered the delicate mechanism of his inner peace, perhaps the waters were not that still anymore.

Once in bed, dreaming about dreaming, but in reality, just lying down with his eyes open, Calixto watched the street lights coming through the window and splashing against the wall of the hotel room. The long day was over but, he feared what the next day would bring. He imagined waking up in the morning with a clear mind and no trace of apprehension. But he also worried he would stare into an abysmal morning. And after switching between hopeful thoughts and aberrant fears, Calixto finally concluded that the morning would arrive regardless of his expectations. So he abandoned himself to the flow of the passing minutes, to the flickering street lights reflected on the wall, and he fell asleep.

The morning did arrive as Calixto had expected. He prepared himself for the arduous work of being a writer assailed by uncomfortable doubts he could not even name. He looked out the window to confirm that the world was the same as he last saw it the night before. And he was pleased to see that nothing had changed, just the angle of the sun rays. He was determined to exist on this day as a *tabula rasa*, to allow the events, the people, and the words to find him supple, agreeable. He wanted this day to be different. To find a new footing on the sidewalks, he changed his typical walking shoes. And he did not pack his laptop computer, settling instead for a simple pad and pen. The idea was to enter this day completely unencumbered.

The first thing to impact Calixto as he ventured onto the narrow streets of the Alfama, was the sensation that his memory had abandoned him. For a moment he doubted he was a writer because he could not really remember what he had written before. He paused, he reflected, he took several deep breaths and delicately, at the speed of a falling feather, the memory of having written *No Somos Pero Somos* landed in his apprehensive mind. This seemed a difficult way to be a *tabula rasa*. Did being supple and agreeable require having no foundation, no history? Unable to entertain those questions in the early morning, Calixto forged ahead on his walk. The sole of his feet palpated the cobblestones and the crevices on the sidewalks. He glided along the streets as if he belonged in that old part of town. And he allowed all impressions to impact him, olfactory, visual, tactile, all of them. And he felt light.

Calixto then tried to remember what the central theme was of *No Somos Pero Somos*. Nothing came to his mind, just a white vacuum. He considered the title and tried to remember what the book was about. The vacuum blossomed. Then he realized the symmetry in the words composing the title. But this did not offer any clues into the meaning of the book. He resisted caving into the sensation that his past had died. Perhaps, he thought, to find new words and carve new prose, one needed to forget all the words used in the past and all the phrases previously composed. If the writing past was eviscerated, perhaps, a true *tabula rasa* could be had. But Calixto could not accept the destructive nature of such a construct. He wanted to write at the edge; he wanted to create fresh language. But he was not interested in destructing previous creations. After all, Michelangelo did not destroy his David before painting the Sistine Chapel. So he suspended all analytical thinking and abandoned himself to feeling and experiencing what the day had to offer.

The sun took refuge behind a low layer of clouds. He could still see the clear yellow disc, but not strong enough to make him blink. He accepted the tepid sun. He then heard singing coming from far away, fado perhaps, and he accepted not knowing what the song wanted to convey. Then he captured the smell of freshly baked bread. He knew this was inevitable, that at some point in his walking trajectory the smell of life would strike him. But what he was not expecting was to come face-to-face, once again, with Leda. And that was exactly what happened when he turned a corner in pursuit of the smell of life. Leda was walking up the street with a fresh baguette under her arm. Calixto stopped in his tracks and waited for Leda to approach him, not sure exactly what to say or do. Leda kept walking up the street until she reached him. She then excused herself, went past him, and continued walking up the street. When Calixto saw her walking away, he went after her. He was following the unknown, he was following life, or perhaps he was following the concept of his own self as reflected by the tranquil waters of a placid lake.

Once Calixto caught up with Leda, he asked her if she knew where she was going. She said she knew just as much as he did, no more, no less. He then said that his day was not yet determined, that he was open to everything and anything, that he had no clear idea of his destination. Leda congratulated him. And as they had done before, they walked next to each other for a while. Once they reached a small square flanked by a building clad in blue tiles where the Tejo could be seen in the distance, Leda asked him if he intended to be a writer that day. Calixto responded that he intended to be a writer every single day but that life, somehow, managed to insert itself in the middle and derail his intentions. Leda said that life struck everyone every day. He knew she was correct, so he did not counter her assertion. He wanted that day to be nubile, clean. So he asked her if she would suggest a few words to ignite his writing day. Leda heard him and offered him a very clean, unencumbered smile. She then took a piece of her baguette and savored it as if she was savoring life. Calixto wanted to share that bread; he also wanted to hear any words Leda would suggest. But all she offered him were the waters of a tranquil lake.

Calixto looked over the building roofs, far to the west, to the river that moved parsimoniously. The Tejo did not care about his day. The universe clearly did not care about his day either. So he then wondered why would Leda care about his day or his writing. Perhaps she did, perhaps she needed to stumble across him on a random street to find meaning in her own day. But if she needed him as much as he needed her, in that *tabula rasa* of a day, she was not revealing such need. So Calixto took the risk to ask again about those words tattooed on her arm. Leda heard his inquiry and regarded him for a while. She ate another piece of bread with natural detachment. She also looked out to the Tejo and seemed to read its waters. And gracefully, speaking as if a morning mist came out of her mouth, she pronounced the words tattooed on her arm and she told Calixto those were the words he was looking for.

Calixto fell deep inside of himself. He attempted to unravel the meaning of those words to no avail. He tried to relate the sound of Leda's words to the sound of other words known to him. And nothing came close but the cacophony of a garbled phrase. He knew the words were meaningful to her, but he could not make any sense of them. Leda had offered him a spark that did not light any fire. Ashamed, Calixto admitted he did not understand the words, but that he believed they were rather important to her. Leda listened to him, and her face glowed under the tepid sun. She then admitted the words represented the myth of who she thought she was, and because he seemed to be on some kind of quest, she thought the words would be useful to him as well. That kindness comforted Calixto even though he remained in virtual darkness about Leda and the words tattooed on her arm. He was unclear what to expect from her; he did not know if to continue questioning her, follow her, or just turn around and walk away. But respecting his plan to be open to everything that day, Calixto took Leda's arm and read the unintelligible words out loud mimicking her pronunciation. He then thanked her for the offer.

Calixto then focused on the three-story building clad in blue and white tiles. He realized the tiles covered the entire façade. On further observation, he discovered the tiles depicted a naval battle. There were ships, sailors, waves, swords, cannons, even sea monsters, all entangled in the most intricate battle. He could not recognize the forces depicted, what king, what country. But what caught his attention was a three-headed sea monster devouring an unfortunate sailor. It was brutal. The sailor stood no chance against the creature. And he could not help but think about the number 3 and its many iterations. Today, immortalized on the façade of a three-story building, a three-headed creature was massacring a powerless sailor. And he could conceive that if the story continued if the tiles could tell what happened next, the monster would have carried on his carnage until stopped by a cannonball. Cutting one head out of three would not have been enough to stop him. He needed to be struck directly in the heart.

He then asked Leda if she saw anything peculiar in the story illustrated by the blue tiles. With a distracted air, Leda regarded the tiles. She spent a long time looking while sustaining a pleasant smile on her face. Her eyes traversed the façade without focusing on any particular detail. She appeared to be peacefully drinking in the story. When she finished, she told Calixto that the story was probably a lie, that reality could never look that way. But that as an interpretation of how people feel when vulnerable seemed rather accurate. She then added that being eaten by a three-headed monster seemed particularly cruel. Calixto asked her if it would have been any better if the monster had only one head. Leda smiled and did not answer his question; instead, she asked him if he was going to write about sea monsters. He had not intended to write about monsters of any kind, but accepting this day as a *tabula rasa*, he accepted such possibility but clarified that the real monsters, the ones that could bite your head off, were within yourself. Leda looked at him peacefully, and before she could utter a single word, Calixto went ahead and said he knew what she was thinking, that she would ask him what his inner monsters were. Leda smiled again and explained that since he had posed the question himself, it was up to him to answer it. Calixto then fell deeper inside himself. Unable to answer clearly, he ventured to write the words Leda had offered him, those tattooed on her arm. He tried to write them phonetically, as she had pronounced them. He looked up to the sky and waited for the air to bring back the sound of the words. Once he connected with the sounds, he wrote three words on the pad. He took a deep breath, looked at the blue tiles, and handed the pad to Leda. She donned a pure smile.

And without saying anything else, Leda moved on with her life. She walked away from Calixto, down the street with her baguette under her arm. She did not look back even once. Calixto felt like shouting those three words so she would perhaps stop walking. But he did not do that. He simply watched as she walked down the street and became a fluttering leaf in the river of people. He had not expected Leda to appear in his life that day, but that being a day where anything could have happened, he was not surprised that she came and left as she did. Or, at least, that was what he wanted to believe.

Look at the battle portrayed on the façade of that building. Who initiated the aggression, what were the circumstances, who was the victor? I wonder if the three-headed monster took one side over the other, or was the monster operating on its own, eating away unanimously. That monster is the very representation of evil. It inserts itself in the middle of a naval battle as if it belonged there. Can evil exist as a force of its own, independent from those who seem to sponsor it or to suffer from it? Does evil take sides? Maybe evil is at the reach of our fingers, ready to be conjured by all, ready to execute our darkest wishes. Maybe evil is an integral part of who we are, of what makes us human. If I let my guard down, if I let my inner drives come to the surface, would they inevitably contain a destructive force? It seems we ascribe evil qualities to some people more frequently than to others. Are those the ones who fail to control their dark inner impulses? If that's so, we're all evil to the core. But that's not what I wanted this day to propose. I wanted this day to open me up, to bring a certain virginal newness, not the thought of the darkness within. But that's the danger, to look into our nature, that's the danger.

By the time Calixto had concluded that there was nothing to conclude, he was already about a block away from his hotel. He had walked plenty and considered plenty. What was left now was to resume his writing and move beyond doubts and shadows. He then turned a corner and stepped into the street that led straight to his hotel when a rancid smell, a powerful animal emanation, attacked him all of a sudden. When he looked to where the stench was coming from, he saw a man dressed in a striped tunic standing on the sidewalk. He stopped and could not help but to scrutinize the face of this man. And he noticed an angular bone structure stretching a brown leathery skin from one side of the face to the other and a dark hollowness below the eyebrows. Disturbed by the poisonous smell, he gave the man a wide berth and walked straight back to the hotel.

In the quiet of his room, his mind was unquiet. Calixto could not ease his mind into the writing process. The moment he started to write a simple phrase, the image of the strange man standing on the sidewalk besieged him. When he closed his eyes and tried to destroy all images, the strange animal smell stifled his breathing air. He closed all windows and turned the lights off. He concentrated on composing a single sentence. But the presence of the man wearing that striped tunic threatened to imprint itself on the *tabula rasa* of his day. He remained in silence for a while, hoping for time to undue this wicked maneuvering. But instead of fading away, the presence established itself with a sense of inevitability unknown to him until then. Resigning himself to the immediate reality, Calixto gave up all hopes to write a single word and bolted out of his room in search of the man in the striped tunic.

Then came the wind. The early morning breeze that had caressed his encounter with Leda grew into an anomalous force that scattered seagulls and kept flags rigid and horizontal. The old shutters on the old windows flapped and clapped. On the street people bent forward to cut through the wind with their foreheads. Calixto walked towards the place where he thought he had seen and smelt the striped tunic, but he found nobody. He saw a dog barely standing against the wind, holding its body close to the ground, but no trace of the man he had seen earlier. He walked forward to a corner offering a view of the Tejo river. He saw the water snake undulating, ripples crisscrossing its back, boats bobbing. He felt the force of the wind and felt small.

If a force like this one exists, invisible to the eyes of all, how could I replicate its power with words? Words are not seen; they're read or heard. They're symbols, representations. Invisible forces they are, the words. And as I come out on the streets, open to the winds, in search of a smell, of a person perhaps, am I not looking for words instead? Maybe the person I saw, that hard face, that striped tunic, maybe the stench I perceived, are nothing but a compilation of words that impacted me, creating sensations I confused. I can search until dusk for an image or a smell. I can walk until coming across those sensations again. But would I be able to harness those forces and create words or phrases, worthy of the intensity of the winds I now feel?

Calixto took the wind straight. He faced its force. He kept walking around the street where he had encountered the striped tunic. The winds had swept the entire area. The only smell that remained was the ubiquitous staleness of the Tejo. But he kept on walking and looking for that angular bone structure and the dark hollowness below the eyebrows. And just as he was becoming hopeless, he turned a corner and came face-to-face with the striped tunic.

Part II
The Striped Tunic

This nakedness hurts me. The uncertainty hurts me. I hope she will be well…, in the night she will. She will learn to belong to her own self, different from the confused belonging laid upon her. She will need to forget, not the night—she belongs to it. She will need to forget the hurt and those who inflicted it. Nadya, I leave so you can be who you need to be. I leave you so you can exist. And I let go… The waters of the river take me away. I glide, I float, I become the current.

At the train station in Breil-sur-Roya, I cover my body with newspapers and wait at a safe distance away from the sight of regular commuters. People come and go. Those who see me ignore me. Three black men move fast and board a train as soon as the doors open. They do not look back. An old woman stands next to another group of five black men at the end of the terminal. They seem nervous. They do not move much, they simply stay next to the old woman and talk to each other. They laugh, briefly. A few minutes later another train stops at the station. The five men board the train at once, their heads down. The old woman does not say goodbye to them, she just turns around quickly and walks away from the platform. On her way out of the station she stumbles upon me. She stops and looks at me. I look at her.

—When did you get here?
—I've been here for some time.
—When did you cross the border?
—What border?
—Ventimiglia
—The river doesn't know borders.
—One way or the other, you need clothes.
—I need to forget.
—Really…, you need clothes.

The old woman leaves the station in the direction of the parking lot. She quickly returns carrying a pair of pants and a shirt. She offers them to me. I have not worn such clothing

in decades. I smile but do not stretch my arms to accept the
clothes. She lays them next to me and stands there waiting for
me to don them.

—I normally wear a tunic.

—What kind of tunic?

—A striped tunic.

—Are you Moroccan?

—No.

—Where are you from?

—I come from the desert.

—The desert is a big place.

—Yes, it is a big place.

—One of the men from Eritrea left a tunic in my house; I
may be able to find it.

—Why would you want to do that?

—Because you said, that's what you normally wear.

—And why would you care about normalcy when you
seem to be doing something outside the norm?

—What do you mean?

—Those men are boarding the train.

—What I'm doing is normal. Helping people is normal.

—Where are they going?

—Nice. They're going to Nice.

—And what's normal about that?

—They need to register their abnormal circumstances.

—And then what happens?

—Nobody knows.

—Yes, that's actually normal.

The old woman leaves. I wonder who does she really
think I am. I wonder that myself. Who am I, really? She may
think I am an immigrant like those she seems to be helping.
Not completely inaccurate. But what I escape is not war or
financial turmoil. I run away from my past, that past that
keeps on dying a little every day. Not the deaths. I do not run

away from death. Death is something that needs to happen. Witnessing death does not make any one part of it; it just makes one aware of its existence.

After a while, the old woman returns carrying a tunic over her shoulders. She gets as close to me as any stranger would. This time I do stretch my arms to accept the tunic. The garment is the color of the desert, and that pleases me. It lacks stripes or any other markings. But what touches me more is the aura of sadness weaved into its fabric. A certain desolation, a certain hopelessness makes the tunic heavier than it needs to be. I discard the newspapers covering my body and don the tunic as I have donned many of its kind before. And the moment the fabric engulfs my body, I sense the weight of the old continent over my shoulders. And I accept the imposition, for such is the reality of those who leave behind what they know and what they love. This is a young imposition, the man from Eritrea who left the tunic behind is only at the start of his journey. The continent, Africa, has borne its weight before.

I enter the lobby of the station where common passengers await their train. I wear the tunic with distinction. As I sit on one of the rigid benches, a young woman holding a baby in her arms gets up immediately and sits at another bench far away from me. I do not sense hatred, fear perhaps, but not hatred. The old woman who brought me here sits next to me and whispers in my ear. She tells me to remain quiet and to prepare myself for the arrival of the next train to Nice. She says I should board the train and remain quiet until it arrives at the center of the town. She tells me the police may board the train in the nearby village of Sospel, and if they do, to pretend to be a French citizen. When I ask her what does that mean, she says I should talk about the weather with the officers. The old woman means well, and I thank her for the advice and for the tunic before she walks away from me.

I wait for the train to arrive. And as I am waiting, I wonder why I move away from my past toward an uncertain future. What can the future provide? I leave behind enormous parts of myself. They do not belong to me anymore: the desert is dead, the courtyard in Marrakech was taken by the winds, the professor and the perfumer died together, they failed to find each other, the fat poet joined the moon, the one-armed man was swallowed by his own fears, and Nadya, infinite Nadya, rests secure under my original tunic. Ahead of me lies a large precipice offering space but no answers. I step out of the waiting area and come to the edge of the train tracks. I look south and follow the train tracks with my eyes. The two rails keep a constant distance between themselves. And without touching each other, they stretch their backs in parallel as far as my eyes can see, indifferent about what comes ahead.

When the train to Nice arrives, I board quickly and find a seat next to a window. The car is practically empty, and I enjoy the absence of eyes looking at me, of faces turning away from me. I abandon my body to the movements of the train but hold on to my train of thoughts. I prefer to walk, to forge my way one step at a time. To be taken by the device of fuel and engineering may be a necessity at this time, but one I will dismantle as soon as my needs change. But what are my needs? I know I need to arrive. Where or when I do not know. Many things that could have happened have already happened. So arriving may be an illusion, the sense that something else could happen that has not yet happened. And the likelihood of such a peaceful time or place is questionable. I am moving away, and as a result, I reject my past. Such a stance is reactionary. But are we nothing other than creatures that respond? Would screaming of pain or fighting for freedom make me a beast? Is a four-legged creature different from me?

The train enters a tunnel piercing an inconvenient mountain. For a moment there is darkness. And I know the rail tracks lead the train through this darkness, unquestionably, blindly, expectantly. And if such is the nature of the movements of the train, could I not move ahead with the same certainty? Perhaps I will arrive because the path will take me there. Wherever the "there" may be. If I, then, were to consider my nature as fluid, I would be happy with joining the currents driven by the force of gravity and lunar attraction. I would then arrive at a large body of water, larger than my own body, where my individuality would be softly diluted. As the train comes out of the tunnel, the intense light from the southern sun falls on my tunic, on my face. I feel the heat. And my body absorbs the radiant energy, and I feel an internal and unique sensation of being alive as myself. I turn inside myself and relish in the warmth of my inner rivers. For the moment, I follow those waters.

When the train finally arrives in the center of Nice, I step out and join the crowd looking for an exit. Once out in the open streets, I realize the police did not board the train. Whether I feel lucky about that omission is irrelevant at this point. I have other concerns. At this point, I need to follow a clear line toward the unknown. The unknown contains everything that has yet to happen; that is, everything that exists outside of the desert, Marrakech, or Saorge. I sense the unknown is a vast place, even if I know nothing about it. But I am ready to venture into the unknown, to take what comes ahead.

South from the train station lies the sea. I approach the sea with some trepidation as the vastness proposes abandonment. But the sea seduces me into looking into it. I let the turquoise color overwhelm my senses. I let the colors percolate through me. And inside, I feel an unnatural warmth. The warm air that flooded the courtyard in Marrakech had a drier quality. In the desert, even when I traversed long distances exposed to everything the day and night had to offer, the dry air cut through me like an iron knife without making any promises.

What makes this warmth different is its seductive quality. I feel as if something extraordinary is about to happen. I want to believe that magnificence is on its way, but my mind, aware of the idiocy of perceptions, rejects such foolish hopes.

As I look at the sea, I wonder where to go next. I could go back to Marrakech, but the four orange trees would probably be flowerless at this point. I could rejoin the desert and the caravans, but the winds would have probably erased my name. In the mountains of Saorge, people will confuse me with their local murderers. My past does not move ahead like the train tracks, or like the waters of a river. My past is essentially dead. So forging ahead is the only solution, forging ahead with force and conviction. I decide to absorb the sun rays as they lie on me, I decide to gather all possible strength.

I also decide to mark my new tunic, to turn it into the likes of my old one, the one that protects Nadya in her dreams. Recumbent Nadya, of my inevitable silence. In a store selling all sort of tools and irrelevant items, I ask a young attendant for white paint. The attendant asks me what is the white paint for. I tell him I need it to paint white stripes on my tunic. After regarding me for a few seconds, he brings up a can of thick and oily paint. I thank him. I ask him for a thin brush which he provides right away. He then asks to be paid for the paint and the brush. I agree that he should be paid for the goods he provided but that at this very moment I do not have the money. He looks at me and keeping his distance; he tells me to leave the store at once. I would not take from this man anything that belongs to him. I just need to get a little closer to my own nature. He will be compensated, not immediately but at the proper time. I then walk away from the store with paint and brush and head towards the sea. Soon I reach a long promenade that extends majestically from east to west in front of the sea. I descend onto the beaded beach and find a place away from the crowd. Once I settle myself, I pull off my tunic.

Naked, I proceed to paint white parallel stripes up and down the tunic as if I was performing an ancient ritual. Nobody seems to care about what I am doing, nobody interferes. The stripes are not perfectly parallel, but they still represent the forward movement, the eternal search for what lies ahead. Once I complete the job, the tunic looks like the one I wore for several years before laying it on top of Nadya. It is not the same tunic, and the stripes are not the same stripes, but the function of the garment remains the same. The exterior world will be separated from my interior world, my body will be covered, and above all, my animal instincts will be contained.

In the mid-afternoon the sun stumbles down the horizon. The rays touch the surface of the sea and bounce towards me. Fractured rays those are. A large silver plate expands in front of me; it boils, it reverberates. I feel the heat. I wonder why the grandness, why the extensiveness. When the realm of our own lives is threatened, the sea seems immense and impassive. Perhaps the sea knows how to exist. It remains calm when it needs to be calm, it becomes upset when harassed by the winds when the moon pulls on it, it yields; but overall, it remains the sea, expansive, deep, engaging. Why are we different? Why do we crest and rise when we could be calm and flat?

With my newly striped tunic, I walk into the belly of the town. I manage to dodge most eyes, most approaches. Step-by-step I move into the core of this town that does not belong to me. I guess, in local terms, I am an immigrant. A strange concept, as I have migrated throughout my entire life without anyone making a point of it. In the desert, everyone is from somewhere else, and nobody cares where that somewhere else is. I sense that in this territory "belonging" is a precious commodity. The more belonging you claim, the more secure you are. I can be wrong in my assessment since I know little about this place. But if Saorge was an example of the rest of the villages in this Gallic country, belonging is preeminent. And facing this difficult reality, I decide to continue my journey south, west, or in any direction that will deliver me to a place of openness.

I understand I am a shadow. And like a shadow, I move back to the train station where being a shadow is almost normal. A train for Barcelona leaves in the next hour. I will board that train. Once in Spain, I could move south and perhaps approach the northern shore of Morocco. But why would I go back to the place I came from? Am I desperate for a sense of belonging even when belonging has nothing to offer? All I have to remember is that my father killed, but I am not my father. I remember the desert made me do things I would now abhor, but I am no longer that person. I should look ahead and forget all those experiences. I should launch into the future and bring my thoughts with me. Even if my thoughts do not provide any solace, I have to bring them with me.

The train for Barcelona is not really the train for Barcelona. It is the train for Marseille. Once I get to Marseille, there will be a train for Barcelona, I assume. Once the train enters the station, I board swiftly and avoid crowded cars or those with children. I find a seat in a corner away from the window. This is a corner for those who want nothing to do with the world. That does not define me. I do want to engage with the world, but the world proposes absurd circumstances I would rather avoid. I lived as a hermit in Marrakech not because I hated humanity, but because the winds that invaded the courtyard were more humane than the humans that roamed that ancient city. I even disrobed myself in Saorge. Yes, I was fortunate to find the kind hand of Nadya, she who preferred to exist in the darkness of the night. But I also found delusional hatred directed at me. So this forsaken corner in this mediocre train belongs to me at this moment. I lean towards the cabin wall, away from the corridor. I cover my head with the hood of my striped tunic, and I hope to be delivered to Marseille later today.

I think I fell asleep. The sunlight comes into the car from a different angle. Perhaps the direction of the train has changed. I look around me and realize that nobody has come to sit next to me. The car is completely empty. I take advantage of the solitude to stretch my legs and arms. I uncover my head and let the sunlight hit me directly on the face. A warmth so universal, so welcoming. And even if this tunic is not my original one, I feel comfortable wearing it. It seems to blend with my skin, with myself. And as I am enjoying my solitude, the door to the car opens up abruptly, and the train conductor steps inside. He takes a good look at me but says nothing. He takes a deep breath and starts coughing. At once he turns around and exits the car. He closes the door behind him with force, vehemently, perhaps with disgust. Maybe the tunic, I do not know.

The train moves at the speed of an easy morning. On the left side, as the train pulls away from Nice, I see the sea, magnanimous, extending far into the horizon, not caring much for the shore left behind. I understand the sea, that feeling of abandonment, that capacity to extend far into the unknown without concerns. For a moment I wish I were the sea. I envy its vastness, its solitude, its beatitude. And I realize the sea has neither meaning nor pity. But the sea I am not, and I am completely aware of that. When I feel defeated, like not measuring up to the sea, the train turns away from the shore and climbs the nearby mountains. When I feel like the sea is my territory, the train makes a turn toward the blue openness and follows the shoreline. I feel the train cares for me. It is a simple machine, the train, but intrinsic in its movements, and in the consequences of those movements, it approaches the likes of a demigod.

When the train finally arrives in Marseille, I move fast

onto the platform and search for the next train to Barcelona. I study the time table and discover the train for Barcelona will depart in about two hours. That allows me enough time to rest and collect my thoughts. Barcelona is not where I want to spend my time; it only serves as a corridor leading to the south. And once in the south, I will find my way back to Marrakech. A few seats flank the lobby of the station, and I drop my body in one of them. Once I let my guard down and relax all my muscles, I feel a wind, implacable as winds can be, tunneling through the open train tracks. I join the winds and try to drain my mind of conceptual biases. And without any forewarning, the notes from a violin start an imperfect melody, subsequently followed by a viola, and then a bass. I simply listen to the melody and begin to forget where I am. I let the weight of my body disintegrate, I disconnect from the voices around me and detach from the immediate reality. Then my body feels light, and the striped tunic begins to flutter in the air. The violin plays a beautiful passage, and I follow the notes as they ascend into the sky. But this lovely moment is interrupted by a loud voice announcing the departure of the train to Barcelona. Once back in the realm of those who fail to dream, I sprint for the platform where the train is already waiting. I look again for a corner with no windows and hide my head inside the hood of the tunic. The world remains outside in all its intensity.

*****

Why she enters the car is clear, all the seats are empty except the one I occupy. Why she chooses to sit next to me is perplexing. But that is exactly what she does, with her red hat and red shoes. I simply observe her as she opens her handbag and pulls out a book. She places the book on her lap but refrains from opening it. Instead, she turns her face toward

514

me and gazes into my tired eyes. Her face has a disconcerting intensity. People with those faces have lived improbable lives. We remain facing each other for some time without saying a single word, and I begin to suspect that inside of her, there lives a beast.

She stops looking at me; she opens the book and starts to read out loud. I recognize the text, Odysseus returning to the island of Ithaca, the Sirens, that magical song urging him to plunge into the waves. She projects her voice with conviction. I close my eyes and hear the ancient words against the sound of the train as it glides through the tracks. And for a moment, I feel like I am sailing back to a past that is no longer there. I do not question the words; I just let them take me where they will. She continues to read as the train continues to glide. And the train continues to glide because the horizon is willing to engulf its advance.

—Do you mind if I read out loud?

—For as long as the train keeps on riding.

—Do you think Odysseus should've tied himself to the mast?

—He had no choice.

—I don't have a choice either. That's why I read.

—But you choose to read out loud.

—That's not a choice, that's a necessity.

—Are you afraid of silence?

—I'm not afraid of anything.

—I didn't think you were.

—Why the tunic?

—Why the red hat and the red shoes?

—Because I'm not afraid, that's why.

—Are you afraid of the waves?

—No, I don't hear the song of the Sirens.

—How about the song of the beast?

—What beast?

—The one inside.

—There's no beast inside. Everything is outside. Look at my hat, my shoes… I show who I am.

—Do you know who you are?

—Of course, I know.

—But who are you, really?

—Someone who doesn't hide inside of a smelly tunic.

—No, you're clearly not hiding that way.

—Who cares about hiding? Tell me, where are you going?

—I'm going back.

—Back where?

—Back to a past that doesn't exist.

—Then you're going nowhere.

—Perhaps you're right about that. I may be going nowhere which isn't different from everywhere.

—Well, I'm going to Lisbon. That's where they need me.

—Who needs you there?

—Everybody.

—Everybody needs something. The question is what that something is.

—I think I'm something! Not anything, but something! That's why everybody needs me.

When I do not respond to her comment, she turns to her book and continues to read. I fear she may get closer to me or try to touch me. But this may be a projection of my own wishes. However, I do not want to touch her. On the surface of my awareness, I do not want to do that. But maybe below my superficial level of consciousness, I want to rip her apart. I really doubt I harbor such a drive. But for the sole purpose of protective restraint, I sit on my hands, bend my head down, and try to disengage from the experience of having seen her.

She continues to read. And with the turning of pages, the volume of her voice escalates. The gods and the goddesses, the sirens, the sailors, the rocks, the fear of shipwreck.

Shipwreck, perhaps shipwreck is what I really fear, not her touch necessarily. I listen to the story and try to remain calm and quiet. But the volume of her voice reaches the point where it overcomes the sound of the train on its tracks. I can no longer hear the march of the train. I can no longer hear where I am going. So I bolt from my seat in one abrupt motion and come to stand in front of her. She then stops reading, crosses her legs, and begins to swivel one of her red shoes. When I manage to hear the motions of the train once more, I sit diagonally across from her. And from this point of view, I realize she is not as young as I had thought, a certain hardness to her chin, the eyes experienced. I have met numerous travelers in my life, in the desert, at the hotel in Marrakech. But I have not met a woman who follows on the tracks of Odysseus with red shoes and a hat. There, perhaps, lies the need. The need we all have for the destruction of our own comfortable expectations.

—Did I offend you with my reading?

—You couldn't have offended me, even if you tried.

—Then why do you sit away from me?

—I'm not sitting away from you; I'm sitting close to myself.

—What's the difference?

—There's no difference. It's all a matter of perspective.

—And from your perspective, what do you see?

—I see you're in need to be needed.

—The only thing I need is to follow Odysseus' journey. Did you already know he would not jump into the waves?

—He protected himself.

—That's what you're doing now.

—I'm not tied to my seat.

—No, you're not. But your striped tunic seems to contain you.

—My striped tunic contains me as much as your red shoes and hat give you away.

—Are we talking about possession?

—No, we're talking about boundaries.

—I don't recognize boundaries.

—I realize that.

—So what would happen if I were to cross over to your side and sit next to you?

—I would probably hear what's buried inside of you.

—And what would that be?

—The beast, perhaps.

We stop talking to each other. She continues to read in silence, and I concentrate on the passage of trees outside the window. I wonder why she wants to go to Lisbon. Because people need her there, she said. But that is unlikely at best, if not delusional. This woman goes out into the world thinking she is needed. This woman wears the color red with intentness. She is not any woman. And as she continues to turn one page after another, in silence, without looking up from the book, the epic story unravels. I wonder what aspects of the story touch her deeply. Is it Penelope? Is it Circe's magic? Or does she identify with Odysseus himself? I can only guess, however, even a woman like her could harbor a beast inside. And that is what I wonder, what is the nature of her beast?

With the passage of the hours the silence between us matures. Not a word has been spoken for a while. In spite of the menacing sense it conveys, I do not stop contemplating her. She is aware that I am looking at her. And I am aware that she is aware. She probably feels needed when I look at her. Even though I do not need her, I do feel compelled to watch as she reads the book. And that is what happens with the passage of the hours, she reads, and I watch.

Outside the train, the world travels fast. Trees, mountains, houses, everything merges into one continuous mass flowing on the other side of the window. I know I do not belong to that world. I do not belong to the world inside the train either. I am just moving, away from my past, but perhaps toward my past. All I know is that I am between one time and another, between one place and another, even if those times and places are unclear to me. And as my mind tries to unravel that which resists unraveling, and as my eyes watch that which behooves watching, I hear the voice of the conductor announcing the arrival of the train at Barcelona Sants.

The woman closes the book and puts it back inside her handbag. She fixes her red hat. Then she turns toward me as if expecting something. I wait for her to speak, but she remains quiet. The train comes to a full stop inside the station, and people begin to exit onto the platform. The conductor announces that this is the last stop and asks for all passengers to exit the train. She continues to watch me as I am watching her. The sound of the crowd begins to die away as people leave the platform to find their connections or to exit the station. We remain alone, in front of each other, inside the empty train.

—The train for Lisbon will depart very shortly.

—You said they need you there.

—They do. But you may need to go there yourself.

—I don't need to go anywhere.

—That's why you need to go there.

—Are you asking me to come with you?

—No, Odysseus, I'm not asking you to come with me. You have your own nymphs to deal with.

*****

The train to Lisbon behaves like a relentless caravan. It stops along the way to take on people, to discard people, to breathe. And those who join the journey expect to be delivered ahead of themselves. By need or by desire, the passengers on the train believe in the future. And in this caravan I come across the same evasive eyes as before, people who turn their faces away from me. An elemental fear boils inside of them. Some of them harbor the beast inside. I am certain of that.

Under the brim of her red hat, her eyes are focused on my presence. Maybe she thinks I am returning to some kind of beginning. Maybe she thinks she needs to protect me. Or maybe she needs to believe that there is some truth in the book she is reading. The many hours ahead will allow for some clarification, or perhaps they will provide none. The train will make a long arch through the north of the peninsula before arriving in Lisbon. And I am pleased to avoid a direct approach, for nothing worthwhile is ever achieved that way.

The only other passenger in the car left a few hours ago when he could not open the window. He must have felt vulnerable. Now there is only her, under the brim of her hat, and myself wrapped in my striped tunic. That external layer, hat or tunic, keeps the outside world from venturing inside, away from the white center inside of us. I wonder what would happen if she were to take her hat off. Would the words of Homer flood the car?

The train heads west at a dismal pace. It tries hard to reach the sinking sun, but it fails. And that opens the door to the dark hours that begin their slow march. The woman turns on the lights in the car. I expect she will adjust her position with regards to the light to continue reading. Instead, she lifts up the brim of the red hat, looks at me, and seems surprised to see me there sitting in front of her. She closes the book and hands it to me.

—Do you mind opening the book anywhere? Just pick a random page.

—What would I do then?

—Just read what's on the page.

—What if I don't like what's written on the page?

—Why wouldn't you like it?

—Because it may talk about returning.

—It may also talk about Penelope.

—I wouldn't like to read that either.

—Why not? It's a beautiful image.

—There's no Penelope for me.

—So you're not returning then. I thought you were.

—I'm not returning because there's nothing anywhere to return to.

The book weighs three thousand years in my hands. Out of fear, I resist the impulse to open it on any page whatsoever. What if the ancient words speak to me? What if the text tells me a truth I prefer to ignore? That is the danger; a book may be bolder than yourself and reveal what you refuse to accept. So I do not move a single finger, paralyzed, I watch the woman as she watches me holding the book. She then points at the book and looks straight at me. Under the brim of her red hat, she holds her gaze for three thousand years. I can bear inordinate pain but not this eternal gaze. So, hesitantly, I open the book and stumble on this passage:

"Come closer, famous Odysseus—Achaea's pride and glory— moor your ship on our coast so you can hear our song! Never has any sailor passed our shores in his black craft until he has heard the honeyed voices pouring from our lips, and once he hears to his heart's content sails on, a wiser man. We know all the pains that the Greeks and Trojans once endured on the spreading plain of Troy when the gods willed it so—all that comes to pass on the fertile earth, we know it all!"

Not wanting to read any further, I close the book and return it to her. She then takes it in her hands as if she were taking me in her hands. And I know that in her hands she can raise a storm. But she then puts the book away and opens her face, her heart, her mind to me.

—I'm afraid of what may happen when I arrive in Lisbon.

—But you told me you were needed there.

—That's the problem; there's an expectation.

—Who expects what from you?

—Everybody expects everything from me.

—Is that a burden?

—Yes, a horrible burden.

—Don't listen to the honeyed voices pouring from their lips.

—I wish I could ignore them, but the song may be coming from inside of me, not from the outside.

—We all have a beast inside.

—Can that beast sing?

—Yes, it can. I've heard its song numerous times.

—Can it be ignored?

—No, you can't ignore it. You have to accept it. You have to tie yourself to the mast; you have to wrap yourself in a tunic, or hide under the brim of your hat.

—And then what happens?

—Nothing happens.

—Nothing?

—No.

The dark hours continue their march. They arrive one after another without any concern for those who resent them. After the conductor announces our arrival in Vigo, the train seems to bear south exposing the moon at the bottom of the sky. It is a moon almost round, almost white. Perhaps a moon that has been maimed. And its incorporeal light enters through the window to shine on us. Under this light, the red hat and shoes of the woman seem less aggressive. Her face looks pale. But her eyes are not softer, still fixed on me, they burn a little. And I wonder what she sees. Perhaps the son of a murderer, perhaps an ancient hero, or perhaps a striped tunic covering a body in flux.

Deeper into the night the Portuguese conductor enters the

car. She turns on the lights. At once she walks over to the window and opens it halfway. She inhales a good amount of fresh air and says that it would be better to leave the window open for a while. She turns to the woman whose name I have yet to learn and asks for her ticket. She produces a ticket. The conductor seems content with what she sees. She makes a little hole on the corner of the ticket with the hole puncher chained to her belt. She then approaches me but does not ask for a ticket or anything else. Instead, she turns around and starts talking to the woman in front of me.

—Is he traveling with you?

—He's in the same car.

—Yes, but are you together?

—We're not together, but we're going in the same direction.

—If you're not with him, why do you tolerate the smell?

—What smell?

—It smells like a dead animal in here.

—Oh, no… He's alive. You can verify that.

—Has he spoken to you?

—Yes, he speaks, but he doesn't make any sense.

—I'm moving on. If I were you, I would leave the window open.

When the conductor flees the car, she slams the door behind her. I then get up from my seat to turn the lights off and to close the window again. My life has been invaded by many winds before. I do not need more intrusions. In the calm quiet of the car, under the soft lunar light, I engage with the woman under the red hat.

—What's your name?

—They call me Erendira.

—And who are they?

—The people who need me, they call me Erendira.

—And what do you call yourself?

—I don't need to call myself.

—How do you call yourself in your dreams?

—In my dreams I'm always inside of myself, looking out through my eyes. I don't have to call myself in my dreams.

—So how should I call you?

—You don't need to call me; you're right in front of me.

—You're right, for the moment I don't need to call you.

—What about yourself, what's your name.

—My name is… my name.

—And what's that?

—I don't remember.

—Does anyone ever call you?

—No, nobody needs to call me.

—So how should I address you?

—You can address me according to what you see.

—I see a striped tunic.

—Then, that ought to be my name.

Under the lunar light, Erendira goes back to reading her book. Sometimes she moves her lips as if reading out loud, but I hear no sound. From time to time she looks up from the book. Her face seems transformed then as if the glory or the horror of the story is being played inside her skull. She continues her quiet interaction with the book until she falls asleep. Her chin comes to rest against her sternum, the brim of the red hat covers her entire face. I contemplate the fragmented image of this woman sleeping in front of me. I barely know her. But as my eyes hover above her skin, I sense the vibrations of the ungodly beast. The beast must be taking residence deep inside her body. That explains the ebullient aura engulfing her. The beast is there, crouching, hiding.

Meanwhile, the train continues to glide south, oblivious of the people who travel in its belly. It simply marches at a prescribed rhythm, following the tracks, stopping only when necessary. The train produces its own noise, a machine noise, different from the noise of animals. And nobody is ahead of the train, and nobody follows the train. The train could be a caravan, but it is not. The train could be alive, but instead, it feels dead to me. And I let the train take me wherever it wants to go because I could not change its course. Knowing that it goes south is sufficient for me. Different from Erendira, I am not needed anywhere. The opposite is closer to reality; I feel brutally despised. For the wrong reasons, I suppose… or I expect.

The moon begins to die, not because it wants to die, but because the day needs to be born yet one more time. And as the moon relinquishes its supremacy, I feel its loneliness. The moon parades through the night alone while most of the world turns its face away from it and falls unconscious. I would join the moon in its exodus if I could. But I do not have that option. A yellow light replaces the white lunar light as the train enters the density of a large city. And the new yellow light seems to penetrate deep into Erendira's skin. Inside, the beast is awakened. She begins to toss and turn; she stretches her arms and legs. And from deep inside her entrails she releases the somber howling of the beast. A song dark and powerful, horrifying and alluring. A song she could not hear herself even when it emanates from her own body. Then I realize she is searching. Maybe for love or for revenge, maybe for immortality, or maybe for her own self.

The train slows down its forward motion. Crawling, it continues to penetrate the thickness of the city. The conductor opens the door but does not enter the car. She announces we are arriving in Lisbon. Erendira surfaces from her deep sleep and enters the day. The first thing she does is to turn her face toward the yellow light filtering through the window. She then straightens her body and fixes her hat. Once upright in her seat, she takes a long look at me, as if deciphering who I am and why am I sitting right in front of her. She then talks.

—I see you're real.

—What else could I be?

—A figment from my imagination, maybe a character from a book.

—I could say the same about you.

—Yes, that's the tragedy.

—Would you want to be an illusion?

—No, I'd rather exist, even if that's an imperfect existence.

—Are you imperfect?

—Completely imperfect. Can't you tell?

—All I can tell is that you prefer the color red.

—All I can tell is that you hide behind your tunic.

—Do you think that's an imperfection?

—No, only you would know that.

—I don't know any longer. I really don't.

—Then you must be perfect.

—I couldn't be any more perfect than you are.

—Then we're both perfectly flawed.

—Perhaps, or perhaps not.

The train comes to a complete stop. The light inside the station is not yellow any longer; it has become greenish, somewhat sickly. The crowd descends onto the platform with their luggage, their children. I stay inside the car waiting for people to exit the train. Erendira does as I do; she remains inside the car. And I wonder if she wants to keep me company or if she has no idea where to go. I am not certain where to go myself, other than south. So if she were to depend on me, she would be essentially lost. But she took this train with determination. She wanted to come to Lisbon because this is where people need her. So she should have no reason to waste her time with me. She should step out of this train and head for the place where people are waiting for her.

But Erendira does not leave the car. Instead, she sits up and takes out the book from her handbag. Looking straight at me, as if taunting me, her lips draw a smile before lowering her eyes to start reading from the book. This time she reads out loud, projecting her voice with impetus. She reads for the world to hear, for the world to participate in the experience. Her voice resonates inside the car to the point I start feeling uncomfortable. I stand up and open the window while she continues to project the ancient epic poem out to the world. People on the platform begin to gather outside the open window to hear the poem. And as she continues to project her voice, as she continues to declare the verses written three thousand years ago, more and more people come to hear the story. Her voice ascends and fills the air space inside the car while spilling out onto the platform. Her face becomes as red as her hat and her shoes. And for a moment her voice becomes the story, and she becomes the book. She is perfect. This moment she exists as a perfect representation of the Odyssey.

Then comes the conductor wearing her badge and her crooked hat. She says everyone needs to leave the train. She asks Erendira to lower her voice and then disappears down the corridor. This time she does not slam the door behind her. Erendira closes the book and puts it back inside her handbag. She becomes a silent abstraction, a Homer for those who know no Homer. And I understand why people need her. Not only in Lisbon but anywhere she may decide to go.

*****

The floor of the train station is the color of dried blood, not the color of the reflective eternal sand. People step on the floor, oblivious of the dry blood under their feet. I have stepped on the eternal sand oblivious of its reflective miracle. We all step on something we do not understand. But this is how the world commences. Without a past to return to, the world commences every second. Like when I ran on the river's shallow edge, stepping over dark pebbles, one foot sinking while the other barely surfaced just to sink again in a circular race with no beginning or end. And as I follow the crowd out of the station into the gray outdoors, I lose track of Erendira and her red hat and red shoes. Maybe she was carried away by her own voice. Maybe she followed the song of the sirens. Or worse, maybe the beast devoured her from inside herself. I wonder?

The world outside the station is wide and alien. People move within a gray brume that engulfs every step they take. They briefly re-emerge from the brume only if the sun manages to grace them for a second. Then the heavy brume blankets everything, the street, the park benches, the dogs. I venture toward a wind that rises from the lower streets. I descend unannounced, unseen by most people, under the same brume that covers everything and everybody. I avoid facing the faces that would likely turn away from me. I do not hide, but the brume hides me.

At the end of a descending street, I come to vast open space similar to Jemaa El-Fnaa in Marrakech. But I find no monkeys, no oranges, and no snakes. There are only people interacting with people, or the brume. At the edge of the vast space, a body of water opens up majestically. The gray body of water extends as far as the brume allows me to see. There is no defining line far out on the horizon for there is no defining horizon, only brume. But the body of water ebbs and flows, it rises and plunges like a sea, or like a river that meets a sea. I stand in front of this gray body and consider it as a desert. I stand in front of myself and consider my mind as the sea. And I wonder if all the fluctuations I have experienced in my life have no other purpose but to extend me out into the horizon. If I were to become one with the gray horizon, the events in my life would have had no consequence. And at this moment, just when the world seems to be commencing, I resist to believe that life ahead of me is nothing but gray brume.

The outline of a slender sailing vessel cuts through the brume with brutal elegance. It tacks once, twice, before approaching a dark dock extending out from the quay into the gray body of water. The sails are quickly taken down. A few ropes are thrown to a few hands standing on the dock. The ropes are tightened, and the sailboat is secured. Three people descend from the boat onto the dock. The brume covers their faces and their bodies. I cannot tell if they are content to have arrived or desperate to leave again. They come from beyond the brume, and I wonder what have they seen. Perhaps they can share with me what they know? But perhaps they are only products of the brume, the grayness.

One of the three people that came off the sailboat walks toward me. When the person gets close enough, I manage to see the face. It is a brutal face, perhaps a face that has known the desert. The person starts talking, and only by the pitch of the voice I realize it must be a woman. Even if the deep crevices on her face challenge my gender expectations, the sound of her speech contains a certain tonality not often found in men. She talks at a vertiginous speed, making it difficult for me to understand what she is saying. And the more she talks, the less I understand. I then raise both of my arms and gesture for her to slow down, to stop talking. She stops talking. And the brume is quick to fill the void created by her silence.

I consider this woman and her need to venture onto dry land and start talking to the first stranger that would listen to her. I consider her face and wonder if she has been abused. I consider the impossibility of my presence in front of this gray body of water receiving the nomads of the world. Perhaps this happens because I am a nomad myself, perhaps because nobody else would listen. But I have nothing to offer this woman, not even a past. I hold both of her hands and look with care at her face, at her lips now shut. What I find is a languid desecration, an abominable terrain. I ask her to speak slowly, to tell me what seems to cause her trouble. She then starts talking again at a slower pace.

—Our children have drowned.

—What are you saying?

—Out there, in the middle of nowhere, they threw our two children into the sea.

—Who did that?

—The same people that put us in the boat.

—Where are those people now?

—They also fell in the sea. The brume took them.

The woman starts to sob. She then starts talking again, but her words get trampled by her sobbing. She then runs away from me toward the other two people that came with her in the boat. The three of them have a discussion, they gesture. Then they walk together at a fast pace away from the boat into the grayness. I follow them with my eyes until I no longer see them. What am I supposed to do? I am an immigrant who is facing the world. This woman found me; she shared her distress with me. This woman left me. In the train the woman with the red hat and shoes also found me. And she left me as well. I found Nadya in Saorge. Or perhaps she found me. She did not leave me; I felt I had to leave her. So why do we leave people we need? Why do we need people to leave us? I do not know.

I come to realize that of the thousands of people I have encountered in the desert, within the courtyard of my hotel in Marrakech, in the old village of Saorge, through the many roads and paths I have traversed, across the many years I have existed, the only thing that stays in my mind is the minds of those people. Not all of them, but those that managed to leave an imprint. Our mind is the only valid currency we possess. It is in our power to lend it, to cherish it, to exploit it, to throw it away. Our mind transacts with the rest of the world. And that mind cannot be usurped, cannot be incarcerated, cannot be bled from the outside. Some people wrap their minds inside a body of lies; others build a fortress of insurmountable walls around their minds; others are not aware of what their minds are all about. People could say that I wrap my mind inside a striped tunic. But my mind is not suffocated; it can float through the very fabric of my tunic and come to face the world. Our minds are not open or closed, like our eyes cannot be open or closed, nor our lives can be open or closed. It is all a matter of acceptance, of facing what the world places in front of us, of not running away from the unknown. Because even when we want to shut our eyes, fold inside our lives, or close our minds, we know the unknown is still there.

And I accept this very moment as my personal unknown for there is no other way to interact with the world. Why the woman with the red hat and shoes sat in front of me on the train, I do not know. Why she needed to read aloud out of the Odyssey, I do not know. Whether I will see her again, I do not know that either. And why a stranger revealed to me an improbable tragedy in the gray mist of this plaza, I will probably never know. And what will happen next in this journey to nowhere is a monumental unknown. But in spite of these uncertainties, I will not turn my face away from the mystery, from that which I cannot see, from the unknown that grows in front of me. I celebrate the moment, and I feel free, unbound, true to the very essence of myself, true to my mind.

I embark on the only journey available to me, away from everything that has happened and toward that which is about to take place. And there are numerous old streets in this old town willing to take me there. I chose one street, not because it looks particularly interesting, but because it seems to climb a hill while the other ones remain flat. And as I begin to climb, a sense of foreboding invades my mind. I try to ignore the feeling and continue climbing. But with every step, my apprehension grows. Then a door opens into the sidewalk and out comes a young woman holding the hand of a little girl. The moment the woman sees me approaching, she pulls the child toward her and holds her tightly. I continue climbing. And as I go by them, the woman turns her face away from me while the little girl, curious, looks at me just for an instant and then hides her face in her mother's skirt. If they react in an identical fashion to the unknown, does it mean they are mother and daughter? Is fear of the unknown hereditary? I will never know the answer to that question. So for the moment, I continue climbing. After another block, I stand still on the sidewalk to rest and gather my breath. A man, then walking down the street, stops abruptly and looks at me with interest. I also look at him and notice an expression of yearning on his face. He must be one of those people who search. I would have offered him some mint tea if I were in Marrakech. But this mutual scrutiny does not last too long as this man seems to find in me something disagreeable for he makes a large circle to avoid my proximity and continues to walk in haste. I watch him walk away with a firm step as if he knows exactly where he is going. But if he is certain about his destiny, why would he stop to regard me? He is clearly searching for something.

When I finally reach the top of the street, a gust of wind takes me by surprise. The wind seems to accelerate up the street pushing everything on its way. I hear the old window shutters flapping all around. Above me, a few seagulls balance themselves afraid of falling off the sky. I grab onto my tunic which threatens to fly away. I could let the wind take me where it will. After all, that is what ancient sailors did when they cast their boats off into uncertain waters. The winds took control of their destinies. And the world blossomed. At this moment I consider releasing all of me, letting go of the anchors that barely hold me down, unwrapping this tunic that binds my flesh. I could open the doors to deep desires, the ones that could frighten me. I could flourish from inside my skull.

Resisting the wind, I stand with my feet hip-width apart. With ease, I let my thoughts go where they need to go. I can now taste the sweetness of the unknown. And I am not afraid. I simply exist in the moment. But all of a sudden, a man turns around the corner from where I stand and comes to an abrupt stop right in front of me. I recognize the face of the man I saw earlier. It is a face bursting with fear as if this face was bearing down into the abyss of its own hollowness. And I sustain his gaze, as I sustain the universe.

Part III
Both, The Writer And The Striped Tunic

Calixto

For Calixto, to come across a face that had not bowed to contretemps was momentous. It was the kind of face that existed unhinged. And he found it by chance at the edge of the Iberian peninsula, perhaps at the edge of nothingness. He had encountered loose souls before, some who made an impact on him, but this face spoke a different tongue. If a face could will itself into the world, this one had entered many enclosures; those deep diagonal crevices could only speak of hardship. And for that reason, he looked at the face for a long time. He stayed right in front of this man who exuded a questionable smell, but whose face proposed impossibilities.

Sustaining the man's gaze proved a challenge. Calixto wanted to absorb the full essence of this man's soul. But he could not match the intensity nor the weight of his gaze. He bowed under the pressure. He felt obligated to abandon the eye-to-eye contact and look down to the ground. He felt defeated. But the man in front of him did not seem to notice his discomfort. Instead, he asked him if he was a writer. A bolt from the blue, the question shocked Calixto. Yes, he had been asked that question before, but the fact that this stranger would venture into that inquiry at once molested him. So he answered by saying he was a writer but different from most other writers. When Calixto looked at the man for a response to this statement, he saw the man's facial crevices deepening. Not sure what to make of the reaction, Calixto said he was a writer in search of writing.

There was no verbal answer. And the silence forced Calixto to continue looking directly at this man who was not on the verge of answering anything. Then the wind picked up its strength once more, making the striped tunic flap feverishly, releasing an abundant acrid smell. The man was the tunic, and the tunic was the smell. But Calixto held his ground. He remained standing right in front of the striped tunic while holding his breath until the wind calmed down. Once the world returned to a calmer state, he asked the striped tunic how come he knew he was a writer. The striped tunic then laid on the heaviest gaze Calixto had ever endured, an immaterial force as heavy and palpable as lead. And from underneath the heaviness, Calixto muttered an answer to his own question. He said that perhaps he looked like a writer. The striped tunic, however, said that nothing in his appearance would have led him to believe he was a writer. But that the oblique perplexity he showed when he stopped right in front of him, in spite of the strong winds that were blowing that very moment, could only be displayed by people who wrote about other people. Calixto was not prepared to contest that explanation, so he agreed with a simple nod. Then he added that in his extended walks he often came across a variety of people, some he could not understand, some he could not resist.

After such a confession, Calixto held back his explanatory address. He feared that opening up to a stranger, revealing his anxieties to a man who looked like a beggar, could be a serious mistake. But still, even if he had kept his inner thoughts private, somehow the striped tunic had understood he was a writer. And that level of exposure disturbed him. Not because he was ashamed of being a writer, to the contrary, he would have defended his inclination in front of the world. But the fact that his inner drives were easily identified by this stranger made him feel naked. So he volunteered no other information and resolved to attempt to sustain the striped tunic's gaze.

The two men stood in front of each other without exchanging another word. They regarded each other; they probably developed a theory of the other person's thinking, their motivations, their preconceptions, their biases. They probably concocted a history of each other explaining who they were, where they came from, their city of origin, their parents. They must have dreamed a past that would have detailed a causal chain of events leading them to stand right in front of each other at that point in time. For the striped tunic, the past was probably a dead entity. For Calixto, the past was a conflicting array of forces not yet clear to him. But regardless of the differences in explaining previous events, both of these men were at a crossroad in their own lives.

And that was when the wind became even more vicious. The invisible force swirled and swirled pushing them close to each other. The window shutters clapped noisily as the two men got closer. The dry leaves left altogether, and what remained behind were the solid stones as witnesses. Even the civet smell emanating from the striped tunic was lifted and dissipated by the strong winds. The proximity made Calixto close his fists tightly and close his eyes. He was uncertain as to the danger of such proximity. The striped tunic, on the other hand, had endured desert winds even stronger than that one, so he remained impassive, open to the world in front of him. They both said a few words, but the strong wind took those words and cast them away as dust. Whatever was said did not remain, and for that very reason, the words did not matter.

The striped tunic then started to walk down the street in the direction of the river. Calixto, unsure of what the encounter had meant, wanted to reach for the stranger and explore the reasons for his arrival in this part of the world. But when he took a few steps down the street, the striped tunic turned around and asked him why was he following him. Calixto said he just wanted to know where he was going. The striped tunic said he was just following the roar of the river.

This man is different, unlike so many that have crossed my path. There's a sense of unending to him as if he came from a place far away, yet going towards every place far away from here. Could he be a mere presence? No, he couldn't, he carries too much weight on his shoulders. Maybe he's a future character in one of my books who comes to introduce himself. But that would make him ethereal, and the putrid smell he emanates suggests something blatantly corporeal. He could be a carrier of words. He could be a writer himself. Or maybe he's nothing to the world. I can't tell. He goes to the river because of its roar. I'll follow him. I want to know what the river wants to tell him.

The striped tunic

All the rivers behave alike. Yet they are all born alone at their source and know of no other river unless they experience a confluence, forcing them to interweave their waters with the waters of another river. This happens by chance, not by choice. They all live a life of flowing and roaring until the very end when they meet the river ocean, the one that flows around the circumference of the earth. What if, like all the lesser rivers, I flowed and reached the river ocean? Would I find it to be as vast as the desert? What if the river ocean harbors one or a hundred beasts, all howling and nobody is out in that vastness to hear their song? As I descend to the lower levels of this city, I come across numerous people with languid faces. They may be river people who do not know about the river ocean. Or maybe they think the river ocean flows and flows without ever touching land. But if the land is bounded by the river ocean, the river ocean is also bounded by the land.

Every one of my steps sounds twice as they hit the cobblestones. The first sound is the one under my foot; the second is the sound under the foot of that writer I just met on top of the hill who now follows me at close distance. He seems intent in tracking my movements, for when I turn right onto a side street, he follows me there. I stop walking, and he does the same. And as I continue to walk toward the roar of what seems to be a very large river at the end of an immense empty plaza, he follows my every step. I wonder if this is the same gray body of water I saw under the brutal brume. Perhaps it is. Blatantly, the writer continues to follow me in an open and honest way. I stop abruptly and turn around to look at him. He stops, looks at me for a second, and then turns around to look behind him as if, in turn, he were being followed by somebody else. But there is nobody behind him other than a few frolicking pigeons. The writer knows that I know he is following me, so I turn around and walk all the way to the end of the plaza. Here a magnificent river opens up in front of me. A vast and boisterous body, boiling with life. Its roar is massive, immense, hard to understand. I listen for subtle, simple messages, but the torrent becomes a chorus of unintelligible voices. Then I hear his voice, the writer, who comes to stand next to me.

—Why were you following me?

—The one who followed me all the way down to this river is you.

—Up there, on the hill, you were stalking me.

—What makes you believe I'm interested in you?

—You know I'm a writer.

—Knowledge is powerful. Isn't it?

—What else do you know about me?

—Do you really want to know how powerful I am? Does it matter?

—Nothing really matters only the words we say to each other.

—Then stop asking questions and tell me why do you write what you write.

—I told you I'm a writer in search of writing, isn't that enough?

—It depends.

—On what does it depend?

—On your level of honesty.

—I'm honest; I'm transparent. Can't you see?

—I'm not sure I can see through you.

—What do you see when you look at me?

—Do you really want to know what I see when I look at you? Does it matter?

This writer yearns openly, and he knows it. He allows me to peek into his personal vertigo. People must find him tender, vulnerable. Certainly, people who approach him instigate his doubts. Any mind in a drifting state would want to latch onto him. Those in search of words would be happy to join his crusade for writing. I cannot tell where he is coming from or where he is going. But it seems clear to me he is in the middle of a journey that is confusing to him. Why else would he follow me down to this river, me, a stranger who has offered nothing to him other than a mirror for his own doubts?

At the quay, there are stone steps that descend to the water level. I go down the steps and sit on the last one barely touching the water. I then sink my feet in the cold water and watch them disappear from sight at once. I was cut off from the ground many years ago. I was tossed out of my land. And when my feet feel the freedom of the river-waters, they thirst for a certain belonging. They would grow roots if they could. But that is not at all possible in this middle earth stage in which I find myself. Then I open my tunic and unwrap my body with slow and deliberate gestures. I fold the tunic and lay it neatly on the stone step. I allow my naked body to slide down from the step until the river-waters swallow all of me except for my head that bobs up and down at the rhythm of the wavelets. The cold river-waters surround me, and my muscles feel tense and relaxed at the same time. I immediately remember descending into the Roya river after leaving Nadya sleeping and dreaming of a longer night. I felt sorry then. Now I feel a certain relief and freedom. Not from her memory, that one will never die, but from the shifting world that surrounds me.

After a few minutes of treading water, I feel a numbness taking hold of my body. With a strong push from both arms and a violent kick against the water, I resurface and come to sit on the moldy stone step. I unfold my tunic and don it at once. Water can refresh the body but not the mind. My past, the dead one, is not soluble. Neither is the uncertainty that lies ahead. Upon the plaza, the writer observes my actions as if trying to unravel a mystery or find a hidden meaning. His expression is softer now. Maybe he finds me just as vulnerable as himself.

The afternoon decides to intervene between this writer's curiosity and my need to avoid people. The afternoon drapes the sky with a certain gray-reddish color that invites isolation and a return to one's own house. I have nowhere to go. I expect the writer will leave and seek solitude at his writing desk. But this is not what he does. Instead, he stands a few meters away from me and continues to watch my every move. He seems to be analyzing and memorizing my gestures. As for what happens inside my mind, he has no way of knowing, although he could be inventing a thread of thoughts appropriate for one of his books. And there he stands, watching, saying nothing, and watching.

My need for a place to sleep becomes more and more intense as the afternoon deepens its colors. I must find a secure place before nightfall. As I look around, I realize this plaza must be the lowest possible part of the city. Multiple streets climb up the surrounding hills promising more secure nooks for the night. Letting chance be my guide, I choose the first inviting street and start walking up at a moderate pace. Behind me, at a safe distance, the writer follows. I turn randomly one way and then the other, exploring numerous streets while still gaining height. The street lamps shed their first yellow light making the city resplendent. And I continue climbing until I come to a landing where the horizon opens up, allowing me to see far into the distance. I cannot tell where the city ends. Neither can I tell where I end?

The writer, who has not missed a single step, comes closer to me and regards the open horizon, trying to figure out what is it I am looking at. There is nothing there but yellow lights and a city that does not end. His expression is not a disappointed one; to the contrary, he seems excited to stand next to me looking out to nowhere.

—Why did you go into the river?

—Why did you follow me up the hill?

—Because, somehow, I need to.

—Then you understand why I went into the river.

—You needed to wash yourself. Was that your problem?

—I don't need to wash myself; I have no stains.

—Then, where are you going now?

—For a while, I thought I was going where the river would take me. I'm not so sure anymore.

—Where do you come from?

—From the same place you come from. A land somewhere.

—Why Lisbon then? What brought you here?

—A woman, Erendira, said she was needed here. She read from an old book about a traveler who could not make it back home.

—Are you trying to go back home?

—I'm going everywhere which is the same thing as going nowhere.

—Sometimes I feel I'm going nowhere.

—Then you must be a wise man.

—For how long will you be in Lisbon?

—What's the essence of time?

—It has none.

—Then, time is not of the essence.

—You must be a writer as well.

—I never wrote a single word in my life.

—That's not possible.

—According to you, it isn't. But that's your prerogative.

—By the way you use your words, I assume you must have read extensively.

—You're confusing words with thoughts.

—What's the difference?

—You know what the difference is, you're a writer.

—I follow your thoughts as you express them by means of your spoken words.

—Yes, but those words are not written anywhere, the wind takes them all away.

—The words remain in my mind; they're written there.

—But you must know that our feeble minds retain very little, and what they retain gets all twisted with time.

—So why don't you write your thoughts down?

—I wouldn't want such an anchor.

—Then write fiction.

—That's what you do, correct?

—I write lies, mainly, not because I want to deceive anyone, far from the truth, but because I think reality is as much a lie as any good fiction.

—You're clearly searching for writing, as you said before, but maybe for something else.

—Aren't you searching as well?

—I already told you I'm not a writer.

—Who are you, really?

—That's a question for another time.

I maintain my pace and continue to walk uphill. The writer stops following me, and I watch as his figure becomes smaller and less significant with the growing distance. I reach a point where I can no longer see him standing on the sidewalk, perhaps because he became increasingly smaller, or perhaps because he just went home. I simply let him disappear from my consciousness. Somehow, I know this is temporary. The writer is searching, and his search will bring him back to me rather soon. How could it be any other way?

Further ahead, in a dimly lit alley, I see a red door. The impulse to traverse it and look for a courtyard with flowering orange trees floods my tired mind. I bring myself to the front of the red door and consider knocking. But before I manage to touch any wood, a woman opens the door and stands in front of me with a resolved expression on her face and a burgundy scarf around her neck. I sense she has been awaiting me for a long, long time.

She steps to the side, and I enter into her house as if I entered into my memories. Nothing on the walls, nothing in the corridor that leads to an inner courtyard where there are no flowering orange trees. I am about to turn around and leave at once when the woman holds onto my arm and leads me to a wooden bench in the corner of the courtyard. She asks me to sit down. I do sit down, and she sits next to me. Then comes a furtive wind, infusing the courtyard with the fragrance of loneliness, that unmistakable smell of bitter almonds. The woman does not react, she ignores the fragrance, maybe because it is utterly familiar to her, or maybe because she does not recognize loneliness. And I wonder why she lets me into her house, why she wants me to sit on this bench. I also wonder why I feel at home in this desolate courtyard.

After a while of nothing but silence, the woman exits the courtyard for a few minutes and returns with a silver tray carrying two cups and a teapot. She sets the tray at the end of the bench and proceeds to serve mint tea. She offers the first cup to me, and I accept it. She then serves herself a generous cup completing a ritual that must be as ancient as tea itself. While sipping from her cup, she looks at me as if trying to recognize a person from a time before this time. What she is trying to identify, I have no knowledge. But the way in which she looks at me reveals a profound loss, a loss hammered by time and disappointment. She then moves her lips as if she is about to ask me a question, but instead she sips more of her tea and continues to survey the territory of my face. I refuse to scrutinize her face for fear of finding traces of those faces I now need to forget. For that reason, I look up to the sky framed by the walls containing the courtyard, I take a deep breath and smell the bitter almonds, and I drink some of the mint tea.

—Your sandals are torn… from walking so long, I suppose.

—They've been torn for a long time.

—What took you so long?

—Time takes a long time.

—I wasn't expecting you, but I was.

—What were you really expecting?

—You, I think. I'm not so sure.

—I came in here because of the red door.

—Yes, the red door is the entrance to this void.

—And what are you missing?

—I miss that which I expect, you perhaps, or maybe someone else.

—Are you missing that which you're expecting, or are you expecting that which you're missing?

—Both, I suppose.

—Expecting will lead you to disappointment. Missing, on the other hand, will lead you to sadness.

—I don't feel sad, but I'm yearning.

—We all yearn, it's human nature.

—Isn't that sad?

—No, that's nature.

I accept another cup of tea from the hands of this woman who must have been awaiting me without knowing I cannot be awaited for because I come from nowhere and toward nowhere I go. But she seems to be experiencing something completely real that does not follow my internal discourse. As the tea flows inside my body, I start to feel more at ease. Then I dare to scrutinize the subtle lines on her face. They tell a story unknown to me. If I were to guess, the story is one of disillusionment. Although that may be the most common story of humankind, I do not recognize her version. If she were to be disillusioned with my absence, she would have been mistaken since I have never departed this place. But if she were to be disillusioned with my arrival, then I clearly do not fulfill the ideal of that which she has been expecting. And that sense of inadequacy makes me feel uneasy.

As time begins to exert its weight, the woman starts to show signs of discomfort. She stops drinking from her teacup, she squirms on the bench, and she loosens the burgundy scarf from around her neck. And there, tattooed on her neck, I see this wonderful salamander that yearns to jump into the world. As lively as the actual reptile, the tattooed creature seems to have been born from fire, and fire it wields with its intense colors and devilish eyes. I cannot help but to abandon myself to the power of this reptile and think of the numerous beasts inside numerous people who never had such a clear representation. I imagine that for this woman, waiting for anyone in the company of such an intense creature would have been miserable, or perhaps illuminating.

The woman notices my interest in the tattoo and removes the scarf completely. She turns her head towards the sky exposing her neck and the fiery creature in its full splendor. Wickedly, she does not look at me as I am looking at the salamander. Instead, she lets me regale myself with the image. After observing her not observing me, I feel a deep urge to reach out with my fingers and touch the salamander. But I recognize I would not be touching the mythical beast but her bare neck instead. So I restrain myself from touching this woman who may have expected my touch. And I realize I may be deepening her disillusionment.

—From what fire did this reptile come from?

—That was a while back.

—Is that what you're now awaiting, that fire?

—I don't know any longer.

—Then why do you show me the salamander?

—I thought you would recognize it.

—I do recognize it. It's a natural beast.

—The salamander or my yearning?

—They may be one and the same. They both sting, don't they?

—Yes, with equal force.

—That's natural.

I recognize this is not my courtyard. I also recognize I may not be the person this woman is waiting for. I might be the embodiment of a concept, but not the person itself. But perhaps that does not matter. If I can satisfy her yearning, would not that be sufficient? Why do we need to personalize everything? In the middle of this courtyard I could represent whomever she wants me to represent. Is that a hazardous proposition? I can also invert the equation and propose for her to represent that which I yearn for. After all, I found her behind a red door in the middle of a courtyard similar to the one in Marrakech. However, I am not exactly looking for her. I am looking for a way back to a place that may not even exist. Perhaps I am looking for the hand of someone who cannot offer me a hand.

On the north side of the courtyard, below the sill of an open window, there is a wooden table on top of which three books rest dormant. There are no other elements, animate or inanimate, in this courtyard. And for that reason, I feel the urge to explore those books and try to find why they happen to be there. The woman, noticing that I am looking towards the table with the books, moves quickly in that direction and grabs the book on top. She opens the book and starts to read out loud. I hear her voice pronouncing words and phrases that make me think of immortality. She then closes that book and takes the second one from the pile. She opens the second book somewhere in the middle and starts to read out loud again. This time she reads in a foreign language, Slavic perhaps. And before she continues reading, I interrupt her.

—Is this your mother tongue?

—If there was ever a mother, this is one.

—What you read sounded sad, or maybe the sound of the words is a sad one.

—Must be the sound of the words because the passage was about beauty.

—Isn't beauty sad?

—How would I know about that?

—You could if you ever lost it.

—I couldn't have lost beauty because I never had any of it.

—You couldn't have any beauty unless you had lost something.

—I'm not going to talk about that.

—Your loss?

—What loss? I haven't lost anything yet. I'm still waiting.

She keeps reading the book to herself in silence. The words must be full of meaning as the salamander on her neck seems to grow and tremble as the blood pulsates under it. The reptile seems to know the story. Then the wind gathers some speed and enters the courtyard, forcing her to hold the pages of the book in place. Bothered, she closes the book at once and removes her hair from her face. She then looks at me knowing very well I did not understand the words, but certain that I felt their inherent sadness.

With hesitation, she picks up the third book and opens it to what seems to be the very beginning. She starts to read slowly, pronouncing words in Spanish with difficulty. She tries hard to intonate and bring life to the text but without much grace. The salamander goes to sleep. She then puts the book back on the bench and throws her hands up to the sky, as if giving up, or as if asking for help.

—You don't know Spanish.

—No, but I should.

—Why should you?

—Because I want to read this book.

—Why?

—Because the author likes bread.

—He must like words too.

—I think he does, but I don't know him that well.

—Is he whom you're waiting for?

—There's no way for me to know that.

—Who's this person, where does he come from, what's his origin, who are his parents?

—All I know is that he's a writer who likes bread.

I take the book in my hands, and it feels surprisingly heavy for its size. Maybe it contains more words than a typical book, or maybe the words are heavier. The title, *No Somos Pero Somos*, implies an existential impossibility. But without reading the book, I would not dare to pass any judgment. I decide not to open the book to avoid an inevitable false impression. However, if this book is important for a woman who receives me in her courtyard without really knowing who I am, then the book must have caused a strong impression on her. An impression perhaps similar to the one I caused on her when I went through the red door. Both the book and I are unknown but somehow expected. Although it would be foolish to infer a connection between arbitrary elements that create a similar imprint, it would be just as foolish to deny an inherent link between them. After all, chance does not exist; it never has.

—Where did you find this book?

—It's for sale at the bookstore.

—Do you expect me to buy this book?

—Not this one. There are more copies at the store where I work.

—Do you work at a bookstore?

—We both do.

—You, and who else?

—My salamander and I. We never leave each other.

—You're interlaced.

—More than that, we know exactly what the other one is thinking.

—Is that a burden?

—No, to the contrary, a relief.

—If I went to the bookstore, would I meet the author of this book?

—Probably not. Is he supposed to be waiting for you?

—There's no way for me to know that.

—I guess there's no way for us to know anything.

—There's no way for me to know that either.

—Well, come to Livraria Mundo. You'll find the book there, maybe the author.

—How do I get there?

—The same way you got here.

Searching, searching. That is how we find ourselves in a place different from the one in which we are. Searching for an answer, for our past, for the object of desire, searching for the expected, for the unexpected, searching for what we lost, for what we will not find, searching for what is next. And in the next few minutes, I will find myself going through the red door and leaving the woman and her salamander in their courtyard, in their void.

Calixto

That morning, in his mind, Calixto had already walked around the world in search of the appropriate words to describe the impression the man in the striped tunic had formed on him. And in spite of its length, that walk had not produced any words whatsoever, but only an uneasy sense of emptiness. He knew he could venture inside his mind one more time or, alternatively, step out into the tangible world to find the words. He chose to step out into the world and walk as he normally did, and perhaps in the midst of such normalcy, the most abnormal words could be found. And those words would not be used in the labor of fiction, or in the artistry of lying, those words needed to touch something more real. He discarded a walk to the river because its fluidity would challenge his sense of reality. That morning he needed to stay close to the ground and feel the immovable solidity of the world beneath his feet.

With impetus and unwavering determination, Calixto ventured out and met a morning that made him feel transparent. His steps found a welcoming ground and no resistance from the green mist enveloping everything. He moved with ease. And possessed with such lightness, he directed his walk towards Livraria Mundo where he hoped to find Lyubochka. She could not provide him with the words he needed, and he knew that, but she could alter his basic expectations and somehow, open a sliver in his mind for unusual words to seep in. And as soon as he gathered some momentum, he thought of bread. He could not enter Livraria Mundo without offering Lyubochka life in the form of bread. He knew bread was important for her. And because he wanted to be fair, he was ready to offer a slice of life in exchange for words.

As he had done in previous days, he walked randomly until

finding the aroma of freshly baked bread floating in the air. He followed the trace and reached a small bakery surprisingly empty at that time in the morning. When he stepped inside, a man with a white beard and a white apron asked him what he wanted. He did not translate his thoughts and told the attendant he wanted a slice of life. The attendant asked him what sort of life was he yearning for. Calixto recognized he had spoken what was in his mind without linking his thoughts to the external reality. He corrected his request and asked for any bread soft in its core but with a credible crust. The bearded man said he gave all his breads enough credence, that it was up to Calixto to decide which bread to have. So Calixto pointed at a dome-shaped bread that resembled the world, an appropriate shape to bring to Livraria Mundo. The bearded man seemed to agree with his choice for he displayed an encouraging smile and told Calixto that he would be delighted by the inner and the outer aspects of the bread.

Once back on the sidewalk Calixto realized that, on pursuing the aroma of bread in the air, he had wandered away from the streets known to him. He had no idea in which direction to walk in order to reach Livraia Mundo. He knew that sooner or later he would find the place. But he felt he was carrying the world in his hands and wanted to be certain where to go. So he went back into the bakery and asked the bearded man if he knew how to get to Livraria Mundo. The bearded man heard the question and thought about it for a little while before asking Calixto if he was looking for a specific book. When Calixto said he was not looking for any book in particular, that he was in search of words, the bearded man displayed another encouraging smile. He told him to walk primarily east while ascending as much as possible and then wished him good luck in his writing. This unexpected confirmation of his condition as a writer made Calixto wonder if he had revealed his raw thought process once again.

But uncertainty did not comfort him, so he decided to follow the directions given by the bearded man and walked east and towards the sky while carrying the world in his hands.

As he kept ascending, Calixto noticed how his mind felt lighter. Lighter in the sense of the weight imposed by obligations. And the obligations that felt the heaviest were those related to accomplishment, the ones he imposed on himself. Would he be able to source the words he needed? Would he be capable of writing the prose he aspired to write? Surprisingly, those preoccupations became lighter and lighter with every step he took up the steep hills of Lisbon. And just before he became so light to the point of almost floating up in the air, Calixto arrived at the doorsteps of Livraria Mundo. He descended, he took a deep breath, and he entered the bookstore.

He thought of the ocean. He thought of the fire that gave birth to the mythical salamander. He thought of the placid expression Lyubochka had managed to sustain in front of him. And humbled by the overwhelming force of those elements, Calixto walked to the desk where Lyubochka was quietly reading and asked her if she cared for some bread. She regarded him as if he were an old friend, as if he had been standing in front of her for a lifetime. And with the simplest and most unencumbered nod, she accepted his offer. She said that bread was the essence of life and that having some of it at that moment would be just perfect. And without looking at him, she delicately turned her head and went back to her reading. Calixto placed the dome-shaped bread on the desk and proceeded to break a piece of it with his bare hands. He then offered the piece of bread to Lyubochka. She did not stretch her hand to accept the piece of bread. Instead, she turned her head, as delicately as before, opened her mouth, and waited for Calixto to place the piece of bread between her teeth. And in spite of fearing the salamander would lash out at him, Calixto went ahead and placed the piece of bread between her teeth. She chewed on the bread, swallowed it all, and continued with her reading.

Calixto felt as if a massive sun had burst inside of him. And not knowing exactly how to react, he abandoned the bread on top of the desk and went around the store reading book covers at random. He wanted to flee the bookstore as well but contained himself thinking he was on the verge of very important words or perhaps a revelation of sorts. But Calixto knew that neither words nor revelations would come forward without pain. So he took hold of himself and allowed a few minutes to go by while reading from novels in Portuguese. Once his mind felt more at ease, he returned to the desk and dismembered the bread a little. He took a piece and savored it with intensity. He then took another piece and offered it to Lyubochka. She grabbed the bread from his hand, and instead of eating it, she offered it back to Calixto. And just as she had done before, Calixto opened his mouth and waited for her to place the bread between his teeth. And she did just that. He then chewed on the bread and felt another burst inside.

Once they had shared the essence of life, both understood a little more about each other. And a small hint of knowledge could only propel a larger desire for knowing more. This time Calixto remained silent while Lyubochka took the initiative and asked him where was he from originally. He had asked her the same question before, and that placed him in the uncomfortable position of having to answer. But Calixto was not interested in his real origins, just as he was not interested in his real name. So he pondered for a while, walked around the store, opened a few more books, looked outside the door, consulted a large atlas, had another piece of bread, and then walked around the store some more. He then approached Lyubochka who pretended to be immersed in her book when in reality had been observing his erratic behaviors. With certain solemnity, Calixto said he was not sure where he was originally from. Lyubochka ignored his answer because she did not believe what he was saying. So she then asked him to forget about the concept of *origin* and to tell her where was he from. This time Calixto answered at once saying he was literally from nowhere. Lyubochka smiled and caressed the salamander on her neck. She went on talking about her youth and the many places she visited when growing up in Ukraine, many of which felt like nowhere. She said that nowhere was virtually everywhere during those days. And in the same light tone, she asked him if he felt like nowhere was everywhere around him.

So light she is, so seemingly nubile, so close to that nerve. I walk because I need to get somewhere. And once I get somewhere, I keep on walking to get somewhere else. But somewhere does exist, it isn't nowhere. Looking back is more complicated. I certainly come from somewhere, but I cannot find words to describe it well. Like there are no names to name anyone appropriately. In the absence of words, there's no certainty. In the absence of certainty, somewhere could become a ghost of itself, maybe disintegrating into nowhere.

Calixto explained that Lisbon felt like somewhere, that the bread tasted like the life he was living, and that if nowhere was central to his past, it was not a burden for him at that moment. She accepted the explanation and went back to her reading once more. Somehow she sensed it was a delicate question that needed further reflection, and for that reason, she dropped the subject. And what arrived next were minutes of silence during which Lyubochka read from her book, and Calixto continued to evaluate passages from various books he randomly pulled from the shelves of the store. The next arrival came in the form of a man wrapped in a striped tunic who entered the store emanating a questionable aroma.

The striped tunic

A bookstore called "Mundo" must be a crossroad of thoughts. Regardless of any particular language, origin, or destiny, all thoughts are bound to coalesce at some point. Perhaps this bookstore is such a place: an eye, a focus, a crux… Such a place must be devoid of fear. And I have no fear as my hand pushes the door open and I come to face shelves of books and the same woman who received me in her courtyard, now bent over a book, reading in the company of the sleeping salamander. She does not lift her eyes. Unperturbed she remains, maybe immersed in words, or maybe lost in her memories. As my eyes adjust to the dim light inside the store, I come to realize that many of the books are covered with dust. An old world this may be, or perhaps thoughts have ceased to coalesce in this place.

Resisting the urge to approach the young woman, I stand still and wait for her to acknowledge my presence. Sometimes the sands are uncomfortably still ahead of a desert storm. But what begins to move is not her, nor the salamander, but a man that emerges from behind a bookshelf and comes to stand in front of me. At once I recognize the writer that has been following me. This time, however, it was me who came from the world outside and entered this "Mundo." He makes a facial gesture as if wanting to smile, but nothing materializes. He then places a hand on my shoulder. Not a heavy hand, but a hand nonetheless. I have touched very few people in my life, and very few people have touched me. So, with the utmost delicacy, I lift his hand and drop it at the side of his body.

—Have you used that hand to write any words today?

—It's too early to try my hand at writing anything. So far, I'm just reading and tasting life.

—Are you reading your life or tasting your writing?

—That would be hard to answer.

—I know, that's why I ask you.

—I'm tasting bread and reading at random.

—That seems to be a common approach to life. But you don't seem to live a common life.

—How do you reach that conclusion?

—It's not a conclusion; it's an observation.

—How about yourself, what brought you to this bookstore?

—Nothing brought me here. I came on my own.

—But there must be a reason. There's a reason for everything.

—She's the reason, or perhaps the salamander, or both.

Upon hearing my mentioning her, the young woman finally lifts her eyes and looks in the direction where I stand confronting the writer. She does not seem surprised to see me in her bookstore. To the contrary, it appears as if she has been expecting me. She then closes the book and picks up a piece of bread lying on the table. She chews on the bread as if chewing on life. And somehow, I feel the force of diverse worlds coalescing. I turn away from the writer and decide to come close to the young woman as she is enjoying the piece of bread. The expression on her face is utterly placid, even blissful. I consider extending my hand to greet her, but I resist the impulse. I will not touch her. Why touch someone when we have thoughts and words that go beyond the mere physical sensation of pressure over skin? But what if I caressed her face, or taunted the salamander? Both invasive intrusions that would alter the tranquil coalescing of our worlds. So I let my arms hang loose next to my body, and I move forward with my words.

—What do you find in bread?

—It reminds me of my childhood.

—What about your childhood? A dryness, a softness, the breaking of a crust..?

—No, just the feeling of comfort.

—So you feel at ease at this moment.

—I do, but I don't.

—What bothers you?

—I feel as if nothing I expect ever arrives, as if I need to wait forever for everything.

—And what do you expect this very moment?

—Nothing, or everything, or nothing at all.

—But you seem so calm…

—I'm calm because I'm waiting.

—We all expect something. Sometimes, however, we forget what we're expecting.

—I don't know any longer. Maybe I've forgotten who was supposed to arrive.

—How about the salamander? It seems to spit fire with every turn of your head.

—The salamander knows.

—What does it know?

—Nothing, or everything, or nothing at all.

And like a bold desire, the wind bursts into the bookstore and causes havoc with the books, the breadcrumbs, and the moribund dust. The young woman runs towards the entrance and tries to hold the door in place. But the wind does not care and pushes the door with force making its way inside the store. I hold onto my tunic while I watch the turmoil. The writer takes shelter behind a bookshelf and says a few words that fly away. The wind blows, we go nowhere, but the wind blows. And just as suddenly as it made its attack, the wind retreats and vanishes, giving no reason for the assault. There are opened books on the floor, loose pages scattered all over, dust still swirling everywhere. The young woman traverses the debris and makes her way back to the desk. She sits down and resumes her reading as if nothing has happened. She bends down to the floor and finds a piece of bread the wind blew away. And with the intensity of a wanting soul, she savors the bread and continues to read in silence.

The writer emerges from behind the bookshelf with a chimeric expression on his face. His hands hold an open book, and he begins to read out loud. The words are in Spanish, a language unknown to me, but the inflection in his voice uncloaks a sense of longing as if something dear has been lost. The writer continues to read, and with every sentence, his voice becomes graver and louder. At the end of what seems like a mournful passage, he pauses to take a deep breath. When he recommences, the young woman joins him and reads out loud an identical passage from the book she has been holding all along. The voices produce identical words with an identical doleful expression although their pitches are an octave apart. They continue the duet for a few more lines, creating a gentle sonic wave that probably betrays the solemn meaning behind the words. When they come to the end of the impromptu recital, their faces transfixed, standing among the blown pages and dust, I realize this man and this woman are like tectonic plates that have just collapsed. And just as quietly as when he emerged, the writer disappears again behind the bookshelves leaving me alone in front of the young woman.

—I told you to come to Livraria Mundo, and you did. I said you might find the book and the author, and you did.

—You also told me you don't know Spanish.

—I don't. I just read the words.

—What do you think they mean?

—I don't know what they mean, but I know how they make me feel.

—And how do they make you feel?

—Probably the same way you feel.

—I think you're correct.

—Then I feel that way. That's exactly how I feel.

—Who are you? What's your name? Where do you come from?

—My name is Lyubochka, and I come from the Carpathian mountains. As for who I am, there's no way for me to know that.

—I think you're correct.

—How about yourself? Who are you? And… what about that tunic?

—Those are very serious questions for which I have no answers at this moment.

—And when do you think you'll have the answers?

—There's no way for me to know that.

—I guess there's no way for us to know anything.

—Again, I think you're correct.

This young woman, Lyubochka, is clearly searching. And it seems she is aware she may not find what she is searching for. The way she approaches an answer just to turn away when she is near. The way she seems happy not to know. She may fear the intensity of the truth, or perhaps she is not afraid of not finding any truth. The salamander seems to ground her, with its fire grabbing her at the neck. This time the beast is not inside her, as it is in most people. Her beast is an exterior one, leaving a wide space inside her to harbor questions instead of fears. She is a woman that can withstand silence. She is a woman unafraid of fear.

If this writer is the author of the strange book I have yet to read, I need to speak to him before he walks away. Yesterday it was he who followed me. Today I am the one going after him. I move among the bookshelves until I come to the end of an alley where the writer is sitting on the floor turning pages of a very large book. As I stand next to him, I discover he is not reading from his own book as I expected, but instead he is browsing a colorful world atlas. The pages display coastal maps of the Iberian Peninsula: all the way from La Coruña to Faro, from Faro to Almería, and from Almería to Girona. So much blue binding the land and the people in the land. I wonder what the writer wants to find at the edge of the sea. He then closes the book and looks up at me. He appears to be distant, in some far away shore, unencumbered, and probably happy. I consider giving him a hand to help him stand up but resist such impulse. He may not want to touch me, just like I do not want to touch him either. From his sitting position, his face at the level of my feet, he takes a long look at my torn sandals. He turns his face away in disagreement. And with impetus, he stands up from the ground and hands me the atlas.

—Can you show me the place where you were born?

—I was born in the desert.

—What desert?

—An open desert where the wind is free to move among people.

—Can you find it in this atlas?

—Probably, but that would not be the real place.

—Why, doesn't it exist on paper?

—Your words exist on paper. Are they real?

—You just heard them.

—I heard them, but I have not read them.

—I didn't read them either.

—So where did the words that you just pronounce come from?

—From my memory.

—A dangerous practice to trust your memory.

—What's the danger?

—That memory relates to the past, and that past may be already dead.

The writer drops the atlas on the floor, altering a thousand dust particles that take to the air making the light filtering through the windows completely visible. He makes his way around the bookshelves to the entrance of the store. There he stops and vacillates between the inside and the outside. But before leaving, he turns back inside the store and approaches the desk where Lyubochka is still reading. He asks her for a piece of bread. Lyubochka looks around for another scattered piece of bread. She finds a piece and brings it directly to the writer's mouth. He does not grab the piece of bread with his teeth. Instead he takes it with his hand and puts it in his pocket. Then he goes to the door, and without hesitating this time, he starts walking down the street. I follow him with my words.

—Where do you think you're going?

—To the edge of the sea.

—And what do you expect to find there?

—The spiral of words.

Calixto

During the night, between one nightmare and another, Calixto stood by the window of the hotel to breathe humid air and to consider the monumental walk from Lisbon to Cádiz. This would be a much longer walk than any he had ever attempted. He could not accurately calculate the number of days he needed to walk, and this molested him. Instead of feeling enthusiastic about the adventure and the massive release of endorphins the extended walk would produce, he felt asphyxiated. But Cádiz had been a point of departure before. The ocean was there and certainly a vantage place from where to consider its vastness. Then he thought about the three women that had recently intersected his life. An abrupt departure from Lisbon would certainly kill any possibility of seeing them again. Although deep inside, he believed those women would follow him anywhere he decided to go. But perhaps what caused a more pronounced sense of asphyxiation was the desire to walk away from the man in the striped tunic. He wanted to feel a strong repulsion against this man; he wanted to create a respectable distance between the two of them. But at the same time, he felt an uneasy curiosity about him and feared that, perhaps, deep inside his mind he yearned for his company. And that last thought kept him up for the rest of the night.

In the morning, Calixto packed all his belongings and told the hotel clerk he had an urgent matter to solve for which he needed to leave immediately. The clerk asked him if there was something wrong with his room. Calixto explained that the only thing wrong with his room was that it made him feel contained. The clerk nodded seemingly understanding but not understanding anything at all. Once on the street, Calixto perceived the unmistakable smell of freshly baked bread. He instantly thought about Lyubochka. And without hesitation, he headed to Livreria Mundo hoping to find her there. Through the door, he went to find her at her desk reading. Not really knowing what to tell her other than he was leaving, he told her precisely that, and nothing else. Lyubochka was not surprised. She then took the copy of *No Somos Pero Somos* that she was reading and asked Calixto to sign it for her. He held the book and took some time searching for a specific passage. Once he found what he was looking for, he asked Lyubochka to repeat after him. He read the passage in Spanish, out loud, and she, in turn, repeated the exact words after him. She then asked what was the meaning of the words. Calixto said he was not sure what the words really meant, and precisely because of that, he was about to go on a very long walk to the ocean, and perhaps beyond the ocean. Lyubochka reminded him that he had already visited Adraga to encounter the mighty ocean. He agreed, but then introduced the idea that all the oceans are not the same ocean and that only the river ocean shared its waters with all other oceans. Calixto then earmarked the page containing the passage and returned the book to Lyubochka. He left through the open door, and that was all he saw of her.

The journey started the moment the smell of fresh bread had dissipated. He walked as if every step would bring him closer to a certain truth, to a diaphanous place. He walked with the conviction that he would find a stream of words unknown to him. Perhaps not unheard words but unheard arrangements of words. And in such spirit, he traversed plazas and streets, bridges and tunnels, always heading south by southeast. He accepted the fact that not all situations along his journey would be agreeable, that the need to eat and sleep could arise at the wrong place. He even reflected on the potential dangers ahead. He could fall ill, or he could be robbed. But what he could not have forecasted was that a certain smell, or a stench perhaps, akin to that of a civet, would linger in the air throughout the entire journey.

On that magnificent March morning, Calixto approached the Tejo and found himself surrounded by thousands of people. It seemed as if half of the city had decided to follow him on his journey. People were enjoying themselves, all at once, walking over the river on a suspension bridge the color of burnt bricks. Halfway over the bridge, he stopped to look back at the city stretching over the hills. A few other people stopped to regard the open horizon, or to dream, perhaps. But the majority of people were intent on reaching the other side of the river, and they flowed like the waters below them.

At a steady rate he walked, and for the most part, nobody noticed or cared about him. This was not his land, not like any other land was his either. Land masses between one coast and another were particularly foreign to him. So he walked from one street corner to the next, along budding meadows, up and down gentle hills, under a sun not too harsh. Ahead of him, recumbent on its back was the promise of words. He wanted to write influenced by the immensity of the ocean, and the ocean circled the land he was walking through, and only at the other end of that trail, once he reached the port of Cádiz, would that ocean be awaiting him. And nothing could stand against his desire, he thought, when suddenly the silhouette of a woman materialized in the distance, growing steadily with every one of his steps. He recognized the shape, but coming across a known person in this part of the world made no sense to him. Even if the increasing proximity revealed a likeness to that of Lulu, Calixto held back his desire to clarify what could have derailed his reasoning and his plans. He simply stopped walking. He stood at the side of the road, still regarding the silhouette attentively, but without looking at her right ankle. The space between the two figures remained static, but not the inner workings of his mind.

There's trouble here. If it's her, then how did she find me? If it isn't her, then how come the resemblance? And if it isn't her and there's no resemblance, then what am I thinking? Three possibilities that promise nothing but complications. Once again the number 3. At the base of this triangle are two people, Lulu, perhaps, or perhaps not, and myself. At the top of the triangle are the three possibilities I just considered. And that makes it an imperfect triangle because it lacks balance. For it to be perfect, it would need to be a triangle of questions only or a triangle of people only. In that case, a third person needs to enter the scheme to bring it to perfection. And that makes me fear the stench floating in the air. Because I know what my senses are telling me. Because I know what my mind wants to resist.

Paralyzed, unable to solve the riddle, Calixto stood at the side of the road and waited for time to pass. He maintained his gaze firm on the silhouette which was as paralyzed as he was. Nobody moved, only time crawled by. The road remained empty; even the sky was void of birds. And Calixto understood he could not wait there forever, that he needed to continue walking if he were to reach Cádiz sometime soon. He closed his eyes hoping to find peace. He found darkness, not peace. But when he opened his eyes again, the silhouette in the distance was no longer there. It had vanished. It did not mean that Lulu, or whomever that person was, had stopped existing. It only meant that he could not see her any longer. Calixto assumed the risk of coming face to face with that unknown entity and started walking once more. He gathered speed, he was at the brink of running, and he kept that forward motion for a while until he found himself short of breath and needed to slow down to a sustainable pace. By then he had left behind the outskirts of the city, and the road began to open up. He did not look back for fear of seeing the silhouette again. Instead, he focused on a cypress that stood tall against the horizon and walked in that direction.

By the time dusk started to suffocate the day, Calixto had walked for several hours. Exhausted, but inebriated by the freedom of walking, he went on to find a place to sleep. The scattered buildings and houses on the country road were not promising. So he had to walk for another hour before coming to a village with a modicum of life. There he went into a small café and sat at a small table. When the waiter asked him what he wanted, he said he wanted a room full of words. Not understanding what he had meant, the waiter asked him again for what he wanted. This time Calixto ordered a glass of Alentejo which the waiter brought at once. He drank that first glass very quickly, hoping to reach a state of placidity and relaxation. But he could not relax much since the few people sitting around him started coughing and seemed truly bothered by something in the air. Some of them stood up and left the café. He could not have offended those people, he thought, he had not said a word to them. The waiter seemed unaware of the problem and seeing the empty glass on Calixto's table, came around and asked if he wanted another round. Calixto agreed. When the waiter returned with the wine, he apologized for the disagreeable smell and said he had opened all the windows to allow the air to circulate better. Calixto drank that glass of wine even faster than the first one. He then called the waiter back to his table, paid the bill, and asked if there was a hotel where he could spend the night. When the waiter asked him if he was bothered by the smell, Calixto explained he was not particularly bothered but that he needed to leave right away. The waiter pointed at a sign down the street and told him there was no other hotel in town but that one. Calixto rushed out of the café and headed straight to the hotel, uncertain if the air had changed around him.

The hotel door was open, but all the lights in the lobby were off. He walked through the lobby, careful not to trip on anything until reaching the concierge table. Then the lights came on, tired lights, bored lights. And a man came down a staircase at the end of the lobby and asked Calixto if he needed a room for the night. He needed a room for the night, but more than anything, he needed to rest his mind. He did not mention anything about his mind to the attendant; he only spoke about needing to rest. The attendant proposed that, if all he needed was rest, he could turn off the lights again and Calixto would be welcome to remain right there in the lobby and get all the rest he needed. Calixto thanked the attendant for his proposal but requested a room with a bed and a desk. Upon hearing the word "desk," the attendant immediately asked Calixto if he was planning on writing all night. He was planning on sleeping all night after walking for several hours, and he made that clear to the attendant. The attendant then concluded that if he was planning on sleeping all night, he really did not need a desk. But that if he insisted on having a desk in the room, then he must be some kind of writer. Calixto thought about answering the assertion in a straight and clear way, but he held back. All he asked was for the room and the bed, and if by chance there was a desk in the room, he would be pleased. The attendant seemed content with the answer and gave a heavy and ancient key to Calixto. He told him to climb the stairs to the third floor and to try the key on any of the four doors, that the key would open one of them but he was not sure which one. He then said that some rooms had desks and others did not, but that none had bathrooms inside, the bathroom was at the end of the hallway. And after saying all of that, the attendant ran up the staircase ahead of Calixto and turned all the lights off. In the dark, tired as he was, Calixto waited for a couple of minutes until he heard the steps of the attendant die away behind the thump of a closing door. He then grabbed the handrail and climbed the stairs in full darkness, slowly, until he reached the landing of the third floor. There he padded the walls until he identified the first door, he felt for the keyhole and tried the key. The door did not open. He went on to find another door and tried the key again. The door did not open either. There were no other doors to be felt on that wall. So he turned around and pierced the darkness across the landing hoping not to fall down the staircase. His hands then identified a third door. He felt for the keyhole and tried the key. The door opened, and he entered the room. A sliver of moonlight came through a small window barely illuminating the stark room. He confirmed there were a bed and a chair, but no desk. Calixto then dropped his tired body on the bed and fell asleep wondering why the third floor and why the third door.

Through the same small window, a ray of sun broke in the early morning and found Calixto ready to continue his long walk. He wanted to use as many bright hours as possible; he wanted to move far away from the little village and from everything that felt uneasy. He was hoping the attendant would not be waiting for him in the lobby. He had planned to leave the money under the heavy key and depart at once. Down the stairs he went, quietly, like a thief. But as soon as he stepped into the lobby, he heard the voice of the attendant at the top of the staircase asking if he had slept well. He responded that he had slept very well but that he was ready to continue with his travels. The attendant ran down the stairs and came to face Calixto as he was leaving the money and the key on the front desk. The face Calixto saw was that of a desiccated night owl who seemed anxious. He took the key and the money, gave them back to Calixto, and asked him why was he leaving so early. He insisted on Calixto staying longer and promised that if the room had no desk, he would move him to another room. That it was important to make him feel comfortable since not many writers came to the village. Calixto repeated his desire to leave and handed him the key and the money. And at that point, one of the windows burst open under the force of a strong wind that made everything in the lobby shake a little. The attendant rushed to the window and closed the shutters. But then the front door also opened up with vehemence. And the wind flooding the hotel was not only strong, but it also had a strange quality, as if it had been locked up in a moist cellar for a long time or as if it had been in contact with decaying mushrooms. The attendant shut the door and locked it. He then asked Calixto to excuse him and ran up the stairs disappearing behind a closed door as he had done the previous night. Calixto waited a few minutes in the lobby. He could hear the wind trying to force its way through the windows. The shutters were rattling. When nobody else came down the stairs, he realized the hotel was completely empty. He disliked the sense of that growing loud emptiness. So when the attendant failed to return, Calixto decided to try to open the front door and face the wind.

The striped tunic

This man who writes feels a need to go after his words; this man who travels the earth. But he does so by walking, moving at the natural rhythm of the human body. And I wonder if he finds the words in the very act of walking, or does he really need to be at the edge of the sea to find his words there. Either way, he seems to be in deep communion with nature of which language is only one of its expressions, no different from a mountain or a leaf in a tree. He showed interest in learning about my origins, but he did not speak of where he comes from. He could come from everywhere, just as the words he wields come from everywhere. Perhaps the words require a physical body to harbor them and bring them to existence. In that case, his essence would be a fluid one. But perhaps, he comes from the earth and blossoms from its core. The words are the man; the man is the earth, the earth is the source of many of the words men have uttered. But he seems to be an ocean man.

If he were to see me, he would probably think that I am following him. But I am not following him, neither his words. I am following his need. He is searching for words, he thinks, when in reality he is searching for understanding. And he needs to understand where he and his words come from like I need to understand why my past keeps on dying. In that sense we are not different; we both have a need for understanding. And I wonder what is at the root of such a need, what binds our feet together.

The writer emerges from the hotel in haste. He does not seem to care for what surrounds him. He does not look right or left. Determined, he undertakes his walk at a brisk pace, heading south, aiming at that shore he must have seen in the atlas. As he walks away with the strong wind at his back, the dust kicked up by his feet dissipates quickly. The same wind makes my tunic flap strongly between my legs, and to conceal such noise, I glide ahead towards the south. Along a lonely road, we walk in tandem for a long while. Our proximity is only known to me. He may suspect my presence, or perhaps even expect it. Why else would he have shown me the atlas? Even if he was not aware of his need for my following him, the need was there. And one need leads to another, as one step leads to another and one mind opens another. And so we continue walking, one ahead of the other, on this path to the southern shores. The sun climbs to its highest point and watches our steps, eerily quiet, revealing nothing. And for a few more hours the secrecy of my proximity remains intact.

As the day matures the shadows grow in length. I fear that my dark and stretched shadow will encroach into his reality. So I change my course to project my shadow into the fields and against the lonely houses, away from his body. I must avoid any sudden intrusion into his awareness. I will observe his movements, his turns, his leaps. And through his actions, I will determine his thoughts. And his thoughts will inevitably reveal what sort of beast resides inside him. As he is not different from every other man, he harbors his own, personal beast inside. And this I will do stealthily, in the quiet of a near distance.

When the night arrives, it finds us both exhausted. We have walked a great stretch of this world in one day. Yet, the writer seems intent in walking some more under the stars. He must be looking for shelter, or perhaps for the morning light. Ahead he continues until reaching a small enclave of houses where a few lights still shine through the windows. He turns a few corners until coming to a desolate plaza where he drops his body on an empty bench. He lies on his back, exposed to the night and the universe beyond this night. And as I watch him from afar, I wonder what he thinks of himself. Does he consider himself as a distinct entity or as an indissoluble part of the universe? Perhaps the words he uses link him to the great vastness. Or perhaps he is seeking a deeper connection by means of his words. But the connection already exists. His inner beast and the great vastness of the universe are made of the same material. They cannot be separated from each other. Just like my tunic and my body; they are one and the same. And even my past, in its dying form, belongs to the future of the universe.

I can hear his breath, soft now, placid, unencumbered by dreams or nightmares. And I observe as his body melts over the bench, his arms dripping on either side. He seems relieved to have walked so long. Even if the shore is far away, he seems to find peace in his total abandonment under the open sky. This leads me to believe the writer belongs everywhere, that he is a native of every land in the world. But he may not be aware of this reality, a reality I cannot impose on him. And for that reason, I need to maintain a safe distance. I shall not influence his search, his process of discovery. He needs to walk alone.

The wind dies down and the night reaches a beautiful stillness. I come to rest between bushes with fragrant white flowers that remind me of my past life among orange trees. I pull the hood of my tunic over my head and close my eyes. My mind travels back and forth in time. There is no use in holding onto my thoughts now. I let them fly away.

Calixto

Calixto had expected a long walk, but he had not anticipated the loneliness. One day of walking followed another day of walking where interactions with passersby were minimal. He began to think about the surprising encounters he had experienced in Lisbon. How the smell of freshly baked bread led him to women, he was now missing. He felt the need for company. And without realizing it, he started to suspect the image of Lulu he had seen on the road was an illusion. He then wondered if all the encounters he had in Lisbon were illusions as well. This was a disturbing thought he dismissed at once. He knew how to play in the fields of the words, in the diaphanous fictional space. But his mind always stayed in touch with reality. And there was nothing more real than traversing the world on foot.

The act of walking, especially when the walks were extensive, created a sense of vacuum in Calixto. A short walk did not have the power to produce a void, but the long ones were more challenging. After laying his head on a pillow, or a bench, tired from thousands of steps he had taken during the day, he felt as if a rush of air flooded into his inner vacuum. In the last couple of days, the air seemed laced with a pungent smell he could not clearly identify. Maybe the farmers were spreading manure on the fields; maybe the land was getting old. But this strange experience did not dissuade him from pursuing his goal. He simply accepted the flow of air in its natural form and continued to walk.

Walking south promised a future ocean. The ocean promised a vastness from where words would naturally emerge. Words would interlace with each other to produce provocative prose. He would then shape the prose and construct his next novel. His next novel would deliver him to a realm beyond that of *No Somos Pero Somos*. And in that realm, perhaps, he would feel completely integrated with every writer that had existed in time. After all, every one of the words in that novel would have been used in a similar context and with a similar intention by some writer in the past. He realized that literature could not be re-invented, that the highest goal was to commune with every writer of every time, past, present, and future. He wanted to feel free to literally play in the fields of the words.

So Calixto walked and walked some more. The hours behind him and the hours ahead coalesced to form a river of time. And in that river he navigated south, passing villages and fields, people and their miseries until he reached a massive wall of stone. The majestic wall had a square bastion in its center from which a purple flag flew with pride. Behind the wall was the old city of Cádiz. And behind the old city was the ocean. The Phoenicians, the Greeks, the Romans, and the Moors had arrived before him. They had all settled in Cádiz at different times to look out to the ocean, to marvel at the possibilities.

Calixto made his way through the narrow streets, convinced he was at the end of his journey. From this point forward he planned to move ahead by means of his words, not his feet. Cádiz offered him a promontory in front of the ocean from where to extract the words he needed. In spite of the excitement of reaching his destination, he acted with the utmost care not to reveal his identity as a writer. This time he wanted to remain anonymous, like a shadow. So when he walked in front of a bakery where the twisted *manoletes* were on display, he resisted the urge to enter and continued to walk ahead. He did not want to meet anyone by chance or by destiny. He preferred to bear the loneliness than to risk his progress.

After walking around the maze of white buildings and asking numerous people, Calixto finally found a small *pensión* willing to rent him a room for an undetermined amount of time. The room was the size of a matchbox, and the wallpaper was peeling off. But it had a small window that opened out over the ocean, and below the window was a desk with a chair. That meant everything to him. He rested his feet, but his mind carried on seduced by the warm air and the potential for words. Once his mind settled, and he felt the weight of having arrived, he got on his feet and took to the streets again. The purpose was not to walk in circles around the city but to buy a bottle of *Jerez* to celebrate his arrival. And not even a block from his room, Calixto found a simple bodega where he bought the fortified wine. Back in his room, he rested his feet again while enjoying the first glass of *Jerez*.

This is the soul of the earth. This wine is the blood of all the cultures that have dominated this land for the last three thousand years. I partake with them in the experience of living. They must have felt like I do now, content to have my feet grounded while looking out to the vast ocean in front. We are the same people, with the same dreams, the same fears, and the same need to express that which we harbor inside. By painting on the walls, by hammering the stone, by singing, by stringing words together. We need to usher out the creative lava inside of us. The wine helps, there's no doubt. The wine does to the mind what the blood does to the body; it keeps it alive. But there's a limit, I know. Too much wine and the mind loses its way. Too much blood and we need to apply leeches. But at this moment I celebrate my place in the fluid continuum. I raise a glass to honor those who came before me.

By the time Calixto felt restored, the moon had made its appearance and was reflecting a simple and clear light. Outside the window, the ocean had turned into a black undulating surface marked by silver streaks. He felt like touching the ocean with his hands. So he left the room once again in search of the shore. The streets were lively at that time. People paraded with a sense of abandon as if all that had to happen had already happened and there was nothing else to worry about. There was a vibrating energy connecting everyone on the street as if all the bodies were evenly tuned. People were talking to each other with vivid enthusiasm. He tried to understand the themes of the multiple conversations to no avail. The voices grew in volume and rose to an unintelligible level. As he went through a narrow alley, he came across a young woman leaning against a wall and singing alone. He managed to get her attention and asked her why were people so happy. The young woman said she did not understand his question and continued singing. Again he tried to ask her what was causing the euphoria. The young woman said that nothing was causing the merriment other than the clarity of the moon. Calixto looked up at the moon and found it clear indeed. But he had seen many moons before, some as clear as that one, and that had not made people so euphoric. Then the young woman told him to go to the beach where the moon was at its clearest.

The voices of the celebrants became fainter and fainter as Calixto made his way to the shore. In front of him, the ocean grew, it's black body vast and heaving. He took off his worn-out shoes and left them on the dry sand. Gradually, he walked into the lapping surf until he was knee-deep in the water. He felt grounded and fluid at the same time. That was the provenance he was searching for, extensive, connecting all the people in all the continents. He then bent and tried to grasp a moon ray reflected on the surface of the water. His hand grabbed only water. He then listened for the words of past writers, but only the sound of the surf reached his ears. He looked up to the moon again and found it extremely clear. And he felt a certain bliss.

Then came a gust of wind from the ocean and a salty spray

bathed his face. The force of the wind began to mount. Right in front of him, the moon rays revealed a herd of white horses galloping over the ocean's back. They jumped from one wave crest to the next, their white manes bursting in the air. The wind emboldened, lifted the sand on the shore giving off a smell of rotten algae. The stench was as rancid as the wind was strong. Calixto admired the violence of the elements, but as the surf began to ram against his chest, he decided to retreat to dry sand. When he turned his back on the ocean, he was shocked to see the man in the striped tunic standing at the edge of the surf. The white stripes on the tunic and the silver streaks on the ocean were one and the same.

The striped tunic

At the edge of the ocean, the writer looks for his edge. The surf traces an eternally undulating line of convergence. In front of him I stand, not as the ocean, but as an undulating counter-reality. His feet are dry and wet and dry, in response to the ocean. My eyes are open and closed and open, in response to the reflected moon rays. Outside of this moment, there are other moments, but this is the one that concerns us both. So I try to forget my past, and I hope he will try to ignore his future. And the river-wind tries to bring us together with its fluid force.

—What do you feel when you immerse your feet in the ocean?

—Maybe the same you felt when you immersed yourself in the river.

—But those are different waters.

—And why does the river seek the ocean?

—Because it has no other choice.

—And why do you insist on following me?

—Because we both respond to water.

The writer seems perplexed to stand between the ocean and me. He could dive into the heaving waters and swim to any land he wishes. He could also ignore me and return to the safety of dry land and the squalid room he rented. But he came here for a reason that will not resonate with any of those options. He came here to search for words. But in spite of the massive weight, the search imposes on him, a sense of peace surrounds him now. Under this clear moon, he seems lighter, almost weightless. Maybe he has found something, as unlikely as that may be. Or maybe he is getting used to my presence.

This writer must have a past. Even if he behaves as if the world is only about the moment, he must have a land he belongs to. Even if my own past is in a continuously disintegrating matter, that does not mean the writer shares the same conundrum. Why else would he flock to the very edge of this land, one of the most ancient shores? From where he now stands, voyagers have taken off to the unknown. And he may be seeking for such an opportunity. But to leave it all behind requires a land to treasure as your past. His impetus, his desire to venture, demands rooting. And in such elemental reality, we differ. He who seems to launch ahead extricated, me who lives an extricated life who wants a sense of rooting.

In total solitude, a stone bench rests a few meters behind me. This bench endures the salty air and the weight of humanity on its back. It does not move; it remains planted in front of the ocean. I come to sit on the bench and continue to observe the writer as he walks into the surf and out of the surf as if probing the limits of water. Far in the horizon, the moon illuminates a faint line where the ocean seems to bend away and cascade over to the west. The writer leaves the water behind and comes to sit next to me on the stone bench. For a few minutes, neither of us utters a word.

—What draws you to the ocean?

—Everything started there... you, me, the whole world. If it is the source of life, it must be the source of words.

—Why don't you enter the ocean?

—With my body?

—No, with your mind.

—That's not possible

—You're a writer, aren't you?

—I would suffocate.

—Are you afraid of death?

—Only sometimes. How about yourself?

—I'm not afraid of death, but of the loneliness afterward. In the meanwhile, parts of me are dying every day.

—What parts are you referring to?

—My past. It keeps on dying.

The wind starts shifting from south to southwest. Then an aberrant wave crests over and spreads itself all over the sand almost reaching the bench where we are sitting. The submissiveness of this sand reminds me of the dunes in the desert, those sand dunes that were continuously reshaped by the burning winds. The desert, the desert… The desert of my past exists in its proper shape as landscape. And the current condition of my memories is the desert of my past. Then another impetuous wave reaches close to our feet, and as it retreats, it scars the sand forming ridges that will be cured by the next wave. Do we only remember the visible scars? What happens when brutal insults leave no marks? I am certain the scars of the mind are real, and we remember them for as long as our memories are alive.

—But I do remember aspects of my past. Perhaps the way you remember a book you wrote a while ago.

—I forget what I write in my books almost as soon as I finish them. I must read them again to know what really happened.

—Aren't your books part of your life?

—As much as your past is part of your life.

—Then your books are dying as well.

—Perhaps, but I can always find a copy and read them again.

—As you see, I cannot relive my life, so the death of my past is imminent.

—Why don't you write about your past?

—I don't court vanity.

The writer responds in a short phrase, but the wind blows the words away before they reach my ears. I regard him and notice the steadiness of his expression. I sense he is determined, but I am not so sure what he is really determined to do. We remain in silence witnessing the battle of wind and ocean. Fluid forces, immense forces that shape each other. We hear the loud words of those fluid forces without knowing what they say to each other. An ancient discourse, I suppose. Then the writer gets up from the bench and starts to walk towards the village. A clear night this is.

Once the figure of the writer begins to vanish, I leave the stone bench behind and follow him under the clear moon. He mixes with the crowd in the streets but does not seem to interact with anyone. He is part of the tumultuous body of people celebrating in the middle of the night, but at the same time, he is completely separate. And that can only happen when the beast inside is growling. That which he searches, those words he yearns, are already brewing inside of him. The creative process must have unfolded under the bright light of his unconscious. And the beast can speak in words the bearer cannot listen hear. But at some point in the night, the beast will howl. A deep and uncloaking howling that will be. I want to listen to that howling.

Through the maze of streets, he walks. The moon whitewashes the white buildings, making them radiate in ancient glory. He accelerates his pace as if wanting to burn his path. Perhaps the urge to write has taken hold of him. I keep up with his pace at a distance, never to close. He then comes to a small plaza completely open to the night sky. There he stops abruptly and regards the clear moon above. I remain in the periphery of the plaza hiding among the moon shadows. The writer talks to the moon. He enters in a one-way conversation with the whiteness. What he says I cannot hear. He could be asking the moon to lighten his path. He could be asking the moon about a distant shore. But the moon does not respond; it has no answers. I wonder if he knows that all the answers are already inside of him.

After this brief interlude, the writer continues his walk until reaching the white building where he will spend this and many nights to come. He is absorbed by the front door. And a couple of minutes later, a light shines through a window that opens in the direction of the ocean. The writer has entered the realm of the words. I am certain he feels safe inside that room. No wind to fight, no disappointing moon, nobody following him. There he can allow for the words to emerge as they wish. I do not expect he will turn that light off the entire night. How could he?

Then time becomes fluid. For a long while, I hear nothing, only the lapping of the waves of time. But I know the writer is writing. Inside his mind, the words are coming together into sentences and paragraphs. I cannot imagine the themes; I cannot imagine the images he sees. I do not yet know what his fears are. But inside his mind, everything is converging, turning past and present into the same unit of time, mixing the real with the unreal; facing the elemental anxiety of not knowing what will happen next, distilling life drop by drop. And all the sudden, in the middle of the bright and quiet night, I hear a doleful cry as if uttered by a haunted animal. A possessed sound that comes from deep inside the writer's room. There is the beast; there is the howling.

Calixto

Calixto wrote uninterrupted for the entire night. He observed the changing angle of the moonlight as it filtered through the window. Transported by the moonlight, he received the words he was waiting for. And he received them in abundance. At first, the words were loose, unattached to each other, seemingly unrelated. But as they stirred inside his mind, they started to make sense. He realized the words somehow referred directly or indirectly to the man in the striped tunic. The associations were at first unintelligible. But he then came across the words "noisome," and "rancid" and knew at once what the signified was.

The verbs carried unusual force, and the nouns created elliptical associations unfamiliar to him. He knew he had started to write irreverent prose, precisely what he was yearning for. He carried on with abandon, not holding anything back. At one point in the writing, he tried to hammer out a description of the man in the striped tunic. The description attempted to combine the various impressions he had had since they came face-to-face in Lisbon. But as he put the words together, he became nauseous and had to vomit to release himself. Calixto worried he would fail to write an accurate impression of the man. He thought he had not seen enough of him, and even the little he had seen was revolting. He then considered exploring the fears the man elicited in him. At first, he resisted the impulse. However, the pull was magnanimous. And the more he wrote, the more painful it became. But undeterred he continued, knowing that his text was existing outside of pleasure, that bliss could only come with new disturbances.

The morning light arrived and found Calixto drained. Outside the window, the ocean was showing off its blues. The air was calm then. He realized he had written the whole night. The text glowed in front of him, but he would not dare to read a single sentence. He turned away from the text and continue to regard the ocean. He thought of the many sailors that had taken off from those shores. Many of them had no idea where they were going. Many of them never returned. And of those who returned, many of them left again. He understood them; he had walked thousands of miles and was familiar with the urgency of departure. But Calixto had always arrived somewhere at the end of his walks. Every one of his walks had a clear destination. He had yet to fall off the edge of the earth. But the writing he had done during the night was a different departure. It did not feel like walking as usual, but like swimming in obscure waters, unable to breathe sometimes, unanchored, without a north star. He had never vanished in the process of writing. And so afraid he was of where this new writing would take him, that Calixto allowed himself to fall asleep. And he drifted.

The sound of thunder woke him up in the early afternoon. When Calixto looked out the window, a gray curtain of rain was blocking the ocean view. All surfaces inside the room were moist, the wallpaper, his skin. The steamy wetness bothered him. He considered leaving the room to explore the old city and find some bread, but the rain seemed to gather strength. He then took off all his clothes and sat naked at the desk below the window. There he confronted again the writing he had produced the previous night. It seemed like an enormous creature with a mind of its own. He would have read one or two passages in regular circumstances, but he did not dare to take a look. Trapped by the rain, the humidity, and the unruly writing disgusted him. So Calixto got dressed and bolted out the door into the rainy afternoon.

Under the rain, he walked led by his sense of smell. After a few turns right and left he arrived at the bakery he had seen the day before. Inside the bakery, the air was warm and dry.

Then came the overwhelming wave of the smell of life. Calixto rejoiced in the surge and asked for a traditional *manolete*. He relished on a piece at once, and his mind traveled to Lisbon and the seemingly random encounters he had with women who liked bread. Without any success, he tried to decipher the meaning of those encounters. Perhaps those were irrelevant moments in his irrelevant life. But the intensity of the experiences and the oddity of the various women could not be easily attributed to chance alone. For a moment he hoped that one of those women would walk into the bakery and ask him for a piece of bread. But the rain kept most people indoors, and nobody else seemed to want bread at that time.

The rain continued to fall on Calixto and his bread as he made his way back to the room. He knew the ocean was testing him. It brought a mass of humid air from the north and dumped it at the shore and over the old town. He needed to be patient. The air would dry out, and the ocean would show its face again. And as he waited for the rain to stop, his expectations began to change in nature. He would venture out once more, not to look for bread or *Jerez*, but to go to that stone bench on the shore where the man in the striped tunic would certainly be waiting for him. He wanted to come across that leathery face. A turbulence of words had been unleashed the previous night, and he wanted more. That man had spoken about a dying past, a past on its way to extinction. He knew that could be a horrible past, but it had the potential to source a million words. And if the intensity of that past matched the intensity of the face, he would have words to write for a century.

The striped tunic

The writer will come to the ocean tonight. He knows no other option. There is that beast inside prompting him to come to the edge. And that beast needs my consciousness. He has walked long distances and written books before. But this is where he will find his absolute beginning. The future ahead of him is a blank page. And he cannot get away from his commitment to fill that page. And as soon as that page is complete, another blank page emerges. The absolute beginning is as vast as the ocean and as deep as the writer's soul.

On this stone bench, wrapped in my tunic, I await his arrival. I withstand the obtuse gazes of people who walk by. Nobody comes close to me. Even the surf folds back into itself before reaching my feet. The seagulls, however, take their risks. Screaming for food they come around and peck my tunic. They want my flesh. I gesture with my arm as if tossing food out to the shore. They recognize the gesture and move away from me hoping to get some food. They find nothing.

The night begins to settle and the rain withers away. If the moon reaches the same clarity as it did last night, I will look deeper into the writer's mind. There I will find the words he wrote last night, the words that taunted the beast. He must have reached deep inside his fears; he must have come across an image of himself. Of this, I am certain because the beast becomes aroused only when we regard our raw selves. He is unaware of what happened. He could not have witnessed his unconscious looking at his unconscious, which is why we can never come to know ourselves completely. And perhaps, this is why, on this bench, I wait for his arrival.

In front of me, the river ocean undulates and begins to reflect the moonlight. I step up and approach the surf. In the act of dipping my hands in the river ocean, I am touching the entire world. As the river ocean circles the world it touches every shore. And those shores extend beyond the coastline, reaching further inland towards the towns and villages where people live and die. Even if the world is unaware of my touch, I am aware of the connection between us. And by touching the waters, I am touching people. This kind of touch I prefer for it is pure and unaffected. As I look out into the horizon, I see nothing but the openness, so vast that it is hard to fathom. And like the blank page the writer confronts, this openness is an absolute beginning. And if I can touch the world by touching the river ocean's waters, so can the writer touch the world by writing on the undulating blank page. He touches the entire world even if the world is unaware of his touch.

When I turn around and regard the stone bench, I find the writer already sitting there. He has arrived. As I had predicted, the writer attends the instinctive meeting of our minds. He comes empty-handed, without paper or pen. If he is to discharge his function as a writer, he will be doing so from memory in the solitude of his room. I know that is what happened last night. The beast howled when he tried to write his visions of the day. I imagine the same miracle will take place tonight. Or perhaps the same horror.

—What draws you to the ocean tonight?

—The same reasons that drew me here last night. I'm in search of words.

—And what would happen if the words you find end up hurting you?

—There's always that danger, an intrinsic danger to writing.

—So you don't mind getting hurt, it seems.

—Not exactly. I don't mind writing, even if it hurts me.

—Then you must have been badly hurt before.

—Yes, while writing the book you heard me reading in Lisbon. There are many painful moments related to that book.

—And what's the pain about?

—I'm not completely sure of what causes the pain. That's why I need to continue writing.

—To extend the pain?

—No, to understand it better.

I come to sit next to the writer. Under our combined weight the stone bench remains impassive in front of the ocean. The writer, however, wrings his hands and shuffles his feet back and forth on the sand. Perhaps my proximity is disagreeable to him, or perhaps the pain has started to boil inside of him. I settle my gaze on the confines of the horizon and study the faint line between the two darks. The sky and the ocean reflect each other's darkness, but they are distinct from each other. And my predicament and that of the writer reflect each other, but we are also distinct.

—What makes you believe understanding could somehow reduce the pain?

—I imagine that by understanding I would be assigning a past to the pain. Then I could distance myself from it.

—Be careful with the past. I can die without you wanting.

—Have you already lost portions of it?

—Some, but not all. I still remember the desert and the caravans. The extensive movement under the extensive reach of the sun. Our lives didn't matter much; it seemed. That's when I learned about death. It was imposed on me.

—Who died there?

—That's impossible to know with certitude. Death existed in the desert; I know that. And death certainly continued its work once I left the sand and sought shelter inside four walls. But the deaths that coincided with my time in the desert were momentous. And most came not by the force of nature, but by the force of murderous hands. A man against another man. But the most painful was the death of my imperfect father, a murderer himself. When he stepped out of jail, the old man looked older, broken, his vacuous eyes hovering in the dead center of round shadows. One day I went to offer him mint tea and noticed his eyes to be heavier as if the weight of the shadows had become unbearable. I called his name, but he did not answer. I tried to raise him, but the body had no lift, no upward movement, it simply sank. And when the rigor stiffened my father's body, and the air stopped moving through his lungs, I understood the finality of my imperfect father.

—So you achieved some understanding.

—More precisely, I came to realize the impermanence of all things.

—Is that what led you to seek shelter?

—With no one to call my kin, I wandered through the desert, unable to rest my head. Eventually, I went through the city walls of Marrakech. There I stumbled upon a decrepit building with multiple rooms around a barren courtyard where a fountain grew green algae. There I remained in self-confinement, officiating the lives of voyagers like yourself. And there a man and a woman, both in a desperate search for each other, had the unfortunate chance to actually find themselves.

—What happened to them?

—Death happened to them. She wasn't aware of the beast she harbored inside and he wasn't at peace with himself. I saw through them. I saw their fears, their hopes, and their desperate search for something they could not see. I saw the vacuity that comes from not being whole. She created a perfume the likes of which I've never encountered again in my life. He played the music of his childhood, a bridge to a time he apparently never understood. And they coalesced under the open sky of my courtyard where four flowering orange trees witnessed their demise.

—By looking at your face, I can tell your past must be as immense as the ocean.

—But I don't know the future of my past. What I just

recounted may not exist tomorrow, either by lapse of memory, vulgar shame, or simple indifference. It is completely possible for events to vanish, leaving no trace. Or perhaps, the traces are those deep ridges you can see on my face. But I only have one face, not dignified enough to honor the lives of so many that have disappeared.

The writer regards my face with consummate attention. Under the bright moonlight, he seems to carve through every deep ridge unearthing a lifetime of turbulence. I remain steady and allow him to explore at will. He seems as brave as he is curious. And he carries on with his exploration until the wind becomes enraged and makes my tunic flap violently. He jumps back and steps away from me. As if afflicted by a nauseating sensation he turns towards the ocean and begins to breathe hard. He takes all the air the ocean can offer. He must be sourcing words, I think. He must be integrating the words that emanate from the ocean, from my body. And still seemingly revolted, the writer runs towards the village. The moonlight follows him, and so does the wind, and my consciousness as well.

Calixto

Inside Calixto's mind, a tumultuous insurrection erupted. He needed to reach his room and unleash a legion of words on the blank page. He needed the catharsis to happen at once. But the narrow streets boiled with people celebrating life. The dense crowd forced him to slow down his pace. He went from running to walking, to merely getting by. He took one side street after another to find yet more people talking, drinking, and smoking. The intense celebration had taken hold of everyone's time and the night stood immobile.

Pushing his way through, Calixto came upon an open plaza completely occupied by the uproarious crowd. He tried to cross through the middle but made very little headway. He then started to make his way around the periphery of the plaza when he came across the shadow of a woman resembling Lulu who stood alone at the portal of an old building. He stopped and regarded the image with suspicion. The moonlight revealed a profile identical to the one he had seen before. He could not understand the tenacity of this woman who insisted on following his steps from Nice to Lisbon and then to Cádiz. And he wondered if she had been following him for even a much longer time without his awareness. She could have been a presence all along, perhaps since he started writing. The tumultuous insurrection inside Calixto's mind soared.

Step by step Calixto approached the silhouette of Lulu. He took care to keep his face covered as he advanced at a slow pace. Then a young woman bumped into him and asked for a cigarette. Calixto made the gesture as if giving her a cigarette but there was nothing inside his hand. He then pretended to toast with a group of three men but had no beer bottle in his hand. He established a conversation with two women that were not listening to him. He became a silhouette of himself in the middle of the ebullient crowd. And unnoticed like a chameleon, Calixto reached the portal where Lulu was standing and looking at the bright moon. He came as close to her as he could without touching her. So close, he could hear her placid breathing. Then he tapped Lulu's shoulder, and that made her turn around to face him. He saw the face of a woman he had never seen before, bright under the moonlight, almost radiant.

She's not who I think she is. The image is not the person. But why do I keep on seeing the image? Why does the image follow me? Or, could it be that I'm the one following the image? No, that's not possible. She must be walking next to me, side by side. Maybe we always have an image that walks next to us. But what's the purpose? She doesn't talk to me; she doesn't reveal anything. She only makes me think that I'm seeing Lulu. The illusion sustains the illusion.

When Calixto finally made it to his room, he opened the window and looked out to the ocean. He felt connected to the striped tunic by way of the moonlight and the flowing air. And without wasting any more time, he started to write. The words flowed like a torrent. He found it difficult to channel the voluminous amount of images, feelings, and ideas. He began to tell a story based on what the striped tunic had told him on the stone bench. But the writing took a turn of its own. Time lost its essence. The past became the present, and the present became the past. The dead people the striped tunic spoke about emerged among the living. The desert became the ocean, and the ocean became the desert. And when he wrote the word "sun," the word "moon" appeared instead. For a moment Calixto thought he had lost control of the writing. The tighter he wanted the process to be, the looser it became. He felt as if he was looking down a precipice. But he knew that discomfort was at the heart of sublime, disinterested text. So he held back his reign and allowed the writing to write itself.

In a writing trance, he remained for a time unknown. The wind came through the window at will, and the moonlight continued to shed its light. And nothing in his writing changed until the moment Calixto started to describe the smell that emanated from the striped tunic. Then he became conscious of the writing process and had to stop to seriously consider the words. The first association he came across was that of the civet. The cat-like animal whose fecal and nauseating essence could become a radiant, velvety, and floral scent. He then thought of shame and imagined what the smell of shame would be like. He considered decay, death, and rot. He remembered the wounded beggars of large cities and their sordid presence. But none of the words or associations sufficed to accurately describe the olfactory experience of standing next to the striped tunic. He came to an impasse. So he gave up writing for the night.

The room felt small and confining, the air insufficient. Wanting to expand his lungs, Calixto stepped to the window. While looking outside, he realized that it was almost dawn, that the hours had passed without him noticing. Only a few people traversed the street below, most of them alone, a few dragging their dogs. The celebrating crowd from the previous night had vanished completely. At that time the morning had yet to propose anything. Accepting the void, Calixto went back to what he had written during the night. He was surprised by the number of words. Not only were they numerous but also marvelously interlaced. But even after reading through numerous pages, he could not decipher the nature of the story. In front of him was a text which felt intimately his own, and at the same time, alien. He confirmed the central character of the story continued to be the very man whose essence he had no words to describe.

The time of innocence had come to an end for Calixto. That morning he understood that his writing was not ultimately his. He felt connected to the universe by a flow of words outside of himself. He was not a conduit; he knew that he still decided on the order of words and the acuity of adjectives, but he was not a writer independent from the writing of every other writer who ever wrote before him. Writing, then, was not different from life. Our lives originate from the lives of those who have lived before us and share intimately with the lives of those around us. And he took comfort in that thought.

He would have loved to go walking in the misty morning, but the weight of the long night of writing felt like lead. The writing was safe, he thought. The mysteries in the writing were intact. The small window would not allow for any words to escape. So, confident that the integrity of the miracle would be preserved, Calixto let himself go deep. The wind continued to enter the room at will. The ocean held the world as usual. And when his mind was resting, life existed as life. His lack of awareness did not leave an imprint.

Later in the day the sunlight filtered through the window and bit Calixto's leg. He felt the warm bite and woke up not knowing where he was. For a moment he existed as if floating in a vacuum, unattached to any time or country. But the instant he saw the open window, he recognized the place, himself, and the impending writing. The first impetus was to read again what he had written the night before. But he resisted the impulse and put the writing away. What was written was already written. What needed to be written next was the only thing that mattered. And he foresaw that his night walk would take him to the shore, to the stone bench in front of the ocean where the striped tunic would very likely be reciting his life. But this certainty created a sense of doubt. Why would the striped tunic be waiting for him unless he had an essential need to tell the story of his life? He had insisted on the impending death of his past. Was he trying to save that past by recounting it? He, himself, had a past that had never been recounted. So why become concerned with the past of someone else? Yes, he was a writer, but writers have no obligation to tell any particular story.

The hours flowed completely unconcerned about Calixto's rumination. He served himself his first glass of *Jerez* to prepare for the expected. Ahead of him was the ocean with its waves and peculiarities. The stone bench could not move from where it lay. The striped tunic, with his unconceivable smell, would be waiting for him. He then served himself a second glass of *Jerez* to prepare for the unknown. Where would the writing take him that night?

The striped tunic

If I were to sail beyond the curve of the horizon, I would certainly arrive at the port of Tangier. But if I could reach all the way to Essaouira, as the crow flies, then Marrakech would only be a short distance away. I wonder what version of myself I would find there. My hermetic self could no longer exist inside the courtyard. That self would have died by now. Or perhaps, that self has been kept alive by the four flowering orange trees. And if I were to find my old self, would I recognize it? From within my current self, the world seems wide and distant. But this is the only world I have.

In the late morning hours, people come to the shore to bathe in the water or to bathe in their reciprocal gazes. There is merriment. However, nobody comes close to me. I sit on this bench alone, in contemplation of the human exchange developing in front of me. I recognize the archetypal gestures that have always existed: the quest for closeness, the desire to dominate, the need to seduce, brutal rejections. But these are the lives of others; they do not pertain to my world. And no matter how many hours I regard the human interaction, nothing occurs that will change the universe.

By the time dusk invades the shore, very few people can be seen roaming around. The sky becomes preeminent now; it appears grander than the ocean. It signals that other shores exist awaiting their turn to be touched by the night. And all we have to do is close our eyes and wait for the night to deliver us there. But the night has the tendency to make us confront the past. And this is what I fear most at this hour, the crushing advance of my memories, that vast legion of dead soldiers. When I try to lift them up, to entice their fighting spirit, I find that dead memories have no war left in them.

I imagine the shores of Essaouira and wonder if my memories would breathe a different life there. Would I need to withstand the same type of assault as I do now? Would the dead soldiers continue to confront me? Why would it be any different? At any shore, no matter where, the waters of the river ocean are all the same. But perhaps, the closer link to the desert that once bound my feet would liven up my past. A treacherous thought that is.

I see the writer far down the shore walking in my direction. His steps seem light, unencumbered. He must have dislodged a certain gravity from inside himself. Maybe he is learning how to tame the beast. Or maybe he is just oblivious. I cannot tell yet. But, clearly, he does not vacillate, he walks straight towards me. I knew he would return tonight. How could he not? And like an empty galleon, he docks at this stone bench looking for his bounty. He seems tired but eager at the same time. His face reveals a profound expectation. Yes, he may be expecting something from me, but most likely he hopes to embody his own expectations as a writer. I wonder what those expectations are, how real they are, how attainable?

He begins by saying nothing. And I accompany his discourse by remaining silent as well. A time of innocence this is. Then gradually, I sense the emergence of a dialogue inside my mind. The telling of a story, or perhaps a confession. I am not sure. If the ebullient words are mine, then it must be a confession for I have no desire for storytelling. And since I have nothing to confess but my past, this must be a resurgence of events I may have forgotten. Some people may refer to that internal dialogue as memories. But memories are nothing but our own confessions. We confess to ourselves in order to find peace with our past actions. And as the words become louder, I let them out of my mouth.

—Have you paid attention to the roar of the river?

—Right now I only hear the ocean in front of us.

—This is not an ocean, the river ocean this is.

—Then I hear the river.

—Why don't you write what it tells you?

—I would, but I cannot understand what it says.

—But you understand what I say to you this moment.

—Yes, I do.

—Then you know exactly what the river ocean is saying.

The writer regards me with keen attention. He wants to listen to my internal confession; he wants to get the words he needs. I do not resist. I let the words arrange themselves in the necessary order to elicit a past that escapes me. And the images flood my mind, they swell, and I flourish. I do not fear the past. How could I? The past was ordered; it occurred as if perfectly orchestrated. The present, however, shows itself with no consideration for order or sense. It wants to happen on its own terms. So I let it take the shape it wishes.

—Through the river, I reached a village where I had no ties by birth or ancestry. There, a woman brought me food and wine in the middle of the night. Others weren't so kind.

—Where's that woman now?

—She's probably looking for the longest night.

—Do you miss her?

—Do I miss her...

—Yes, do you feel for her?

—I feel for her, deeply. And we spent a night together that could have been the longest. But then came the horror. A horror that only humans can bring upon each other.

—Can you speak of it?

—No, I won't speak of it. It pains me to this moment.

—So where do you store those painful memories?

—My body is the only thing I own, and this tunic to protect it. I'm completely alone with no room to hold memories. The memories go through me; I cannot hold on to them.

—So what happens to your past?

—My past is nothing other than a big hole. My present: this bench, the ocean.

—And if you were to think of your past as your present, if what you thought today were a reflection of your past, what would you then remember?

—I remember I touched a man, something I had not done in years, and in consequence I killed him. He could only make use of one arm, the other one was already dead, but with that single arm, he wielded paranoiac hate.

—What did this man do?

—This one-armed man committed a crime against humanity. He murdered a poet, a gentle spirit who fed words to his mules and sourced words from the moon. And he shot him in response to his anomalous hatred. I had no choice, I had to touch him.

—Do you always kill everyone you touch?

—I don't touch people.

The writer shifts his body away from me on the bench. He creates enough distance between the two of us to prevent an accidental touch. This does not bother me as I am used to people keeping their distance from me. But in spite of his space considerations, he seems interested in what my confession may bear. He waits for me to continue talking. Somehow, he expects me to divulge the story of my past. But I have no desire to share my consciousness. If there is a story within me, if my past could be construed logically and with appropriate sentiment, then all there is to be had is a lie. Nothing can be held within a body that cannot hold anything.

—Why did you follow me all the way to Cádiz?

—I didn't follow you.

—So how do you explain your presence here?

—What makes you believe that I'm present here? I'm the bench and the ocean. My presence isn't mine. You, on the other hand, wanted to come to Cádiz with a clear purpose.

—But that doesn't mean you didn't follow me here.

—You walked here on your own. You have a need, and you pursued it.

—And you followed me.

—I have a need, and I pursued it as well.

—Do you mean to say that we have the same need?

—Do you find that possibility troubling?

—I just need to write my book. That's what I'm after.

—So we happen to coincide in time but not in purpose.

The writer gets up from the bench and walks towards the surf. The moon still shines, but it has lost some of its luster. While last night it seemed eternal, tonight the moon appears slightly maimed. But the writer does not care for the moon. If he had known the fat poet from Saorge, he would understand the moon has the power to extricate words from inside any of us. At this moment he only cares for the tongue of the ocean that comes to lick his feet. I get the impression he is a sensualist. But as I observe him, I realize he does not conform with getting his feet wet; he steps on the back of those ripples where the moonlight shines the brightest. He may still be a sensualist, but that inclination may serve the very purpose he espouses.

—Would you tell me your name?

—My name…

—Yes, how do people call you?

—I haven't been called by anyone in a very long time. And if I ever had a name, it now belongs to my dead past.

—So, how could I refer to you?

—What's in front of you this very moment is the only thing you can refer to.

—In front of me, there's a striped tunic.

—Then that's all there is to refer to.

—But there's also the ocean.

—Yes, but we're not the same.

—Then there's only the striped tunic.

—There's nothing else.

—What about what's inside of you, your thoughts, your desires?

—Just listen to what the river ocean is saying.

The writer then starts to kick the water, sending droplets up in the air. He does so with intensity as if he wants to walk on the surface of the ocean. The moonlight penetrates the water particles and makes diamonds out of them. And the frenzy unravels in front of me. The light, the water, the writer, the words, my past. The writer then sheds all his clothes and immerses himself in the river ocean. The more he thrashes in the water, the more diamonds fly up in the moonlit night. And then he starts to swim away from the shore, deep into the arms of the river ocean. He swims like a dolphin, into the water and out of the water, but always following an elongated moon ray that extends far into the edge of the night. And then the wind starts to gather speed. It blows from the land towards the ocean as if wanting to embark on a long journey. And the waves begin to crest, and the moonlight jumps from one wave to the next, creating jagged angles and broken paths far into the edge of the night. I look out in search of the writer but cannot see his body any longer. He cannot help but satisfy his need. He is going deep into the source. He wants to listen to what the river ocean is saying.

Calixto

He floated on his back, Calixto, and his recumbent body moved up and down under the moonlight. The waves behaved like benevolent angels at the service of the ocean. They could have swallowed him, but they spared him instead. In reality, the ocean did not mind that Calixto had pierced its undulant body. So the ocean allowed him to continue floating on its vast surface. Finally, the waves and the wind returned Calixto's body to the shore far away from where he had started his swim.

He crawled until he reached dry sand, and there he stood, overwhelmed by the numerous words he had gathered from the body of the ocean. He was alone, naked, but ecstatic with his bounty. All he needed was to return to his room, if he could find it, and immerse himself in the writing process. So he took to the streets of the old city hoping to find his way. He went for the darker streets, avoiding the clear moonlight that would have revealed his nakedness. He waited in the shadows for people to pass by him, he dodged all lamp posts. But the white buildings reflected the moonlight so perfectly that Calixto was inevitably bathed in the nightglow. Trying to become a shadow turned out to be impossible.

Calixto then decided to shed all fears and expose his naked self. So he took to the streets running at full speed. He went by people who were surprised and amused at the spectacle. But nobody tried to stop him; he ran unopposed. The speed he kept made him miss a few turns and to confuse one street with another. But he eventually managed to reach his room without a major accident. Once inside the room, he opened the window and looked out to the ocean. He had communed with that immense and fluid body. He had extracted a wealth of words from it. And he trembled. The sweat dripping from his entire body got mixed with the blood trickling from the cuts on the soles of his feet.

I feel whole in this nakedness. I extend beyond myself. People wouldn't want to see me this way, but this isn't about people. This is about the bodies that hold the words. I wonder if that man ever sheds his striped tunic. The stories and words he harbors inside must be immense. And he only insinuates a few details from inside that shell. He says his past is dead, but maybe his past is only covered. Maybe he needs to swim in the body of the ocean as well. If his body were to merge with that of the ocean, the fusion of words could be exceptional. Or maybe he just needs to get rid of that tunic and let his past come alive. There's so little I know about him. The inverse is true; he seems to know me, he seems to see through me. He must know how I feel in this nakedness.

After opening the gates of his unconscious, Calixto started to write abundantly. He did not even bother to get dressed. He silenced the internal critic and allowed the prose to gallop unbridled. For Calixto, every day contained a moment when he thought he would touch immortality, what followed next was the stuff of novels. He considered the relationship between an artist and reality to be an oblique one, and indeed, in his judgment, there was no good art that was not consciously oblique. If he wanted to respect the reality of the world, he knew that he could only approach that reality by indirect means. And the path he was following that morning was an obliquely unconscious one.

The hours and the words accumulated. He had no desire for food but did not skip on a glass of *Jerez* every so often. In an effort to transcend traditional narrative, Calixto needed to wield words under the constraints of the novel's tremendous weight. Consequently, he needed to discard many rules to bring forth this vision. On that account, he was creating an anti-democratic experience that promised to leave out the middle-class, or middle-reader, the populous group which had generated the traditional novel. He explored the inner world of the striped tunic, experimented with nonlinear formats, employed multiple points of view, embraced philosophical constructs, used lyrical language, and made clear and not-so-clear allusions while not explaining everything in an expository way. He was writing outside of the traditional mold, but he was not the first, nor would he be the last one. His challenge was how to manage that difficult and complex task, how to pull off the high wire act without crashing down to the floor.

I would like to know what's the ultimate purpose of writing novels. What's the real value of reality in fiction? Should the novel be clear and open to all? Who are the readers? And in a more existential vein, does it matter to the universe whether I write a novel or take a piss in the ocean? When the path becomes an ocean, and the waters burn, when a step is nothing but a dream, when leaping forward grows flowers on my skin... I then know I'm a writer. So I plunge, deeply.

And ahead he continued until the dawning of the hours. And he saw no respite during the long day. Finally, consumed by hunger and exhaustion, Calixto wanted to rest. But the desire to feed his mind with words and to be in the presence of the striped tunic was stronger. So he barely dressed and took to the streets. He did not care if the streets were crowded or empty if the wind was calm or beastly. He walked towards the stone bench in search of the essential elements that sustained his writing. And the closer he got to the ocean, the faster his heart rate became. And his steps gathered force, and the walking became a furious run towards the shore. Fast, fast, faster...

Calixto reached a point on the shore from where the bench

could be spotted in the distance. He then gathered all his strength and went for a final sprint. But as he got closer, he stopped his frantic race at once. The shape of the person sitting on the bench was not that of the striped tunic. It was the familiar silhouette of Lulu. He did not know if his eyes were telling him the truth. After a full day of writing fiction, the world had become somewhat unreal. So Calixto closed his eyes and waited some time, hoping the image would dissipate. If he were to open his eyes and the image of Lulu was still there, there was a chance it was really her. Difficult to explain, but possible. If upon opening his eyes the image would have vanished, then he needed to explore his expectations or go even deeper into his unconscious. Regardless of the outcome, he knew a piece of reality had become dislodged.

When he opened his eyes again, Calixto saw with clarity the loose shape of the striped tunic sitting on the bench and looking out to the blurred line between the ocean and the darkening sky. After calming down his breathing, he launched towards the bench at a normal walking pace. His concern with the vision of Lulu would not be unraveled then. At that moment, what mattered to him was the striped tunic and the ocean. And both were there waiting for him.

He came around the bench and sat next to the striped tunic. He tried to find the spot on the horizon where the striped tunic was focusing. But what Calixto saw was a vast body of water blending with the vast body of the night sky. He wanted the striped tunic to continue talking about his past. But all he got was silence. The striped tunic remained motionless and did not say a word. And even when a light breeze came from the ocean, it carried only white noise, not a single word. There he was, in front of the essential elements, deriving nothing from them. He feared death, or perhaps oblivion. Calixto then wondered if the striped tunic was indeed sitting next to him. So he closed his eyes again and waited.

I cannot decipher him. I might be able to write an entire book about him and never know who he really is. Perhaps he may reveal himself to me if I reveal myself to him. But I get the sense he already knows me. He knew I was coming to this bench tonight. He prepared himself to receive me. In silence, that is, but here he is. Or, is he not? Is he only a product of my fiction, a mere embodiment of words I have written down? And if so, what difference would that make? I need to open my eyes now. I will open my eyes.

The striped tunic

—How far are you willing to go?

—I have come very far already.

—You have only come as far as it is comfortable. Are you willing to venture further?

—In search for words?

—You think you're looking for words, don't you?

—Yes, I've been looking for words, and I've found them here.

—This is only the portal. Look at the river ocean in front of you. It extends far into the horizon; it touches every shore. Land is the secure ground of home; the ocean is like life, the outside, the unknown. There are words out there, and much more.

—But I cannot take it all.

—You don't have to take the river ocean; the river ocean will take you.

The writer looks spent. I am not surprised when the beast howls there is no rest to be had. He went into the body of the river ocean last night, and I believe he found some words. Not only has he found them, but he must have written them down. And tonight he comes back to this bench because he believes in continuity. What yesterday procured, today will likely procure it again. A comfortable thought that is. But if he wants to identify his real need, he would have to take to the ocean and go beyond this night. I will take to the ocean myself. But I will do so to rejoin my past, to start over again.

This night is the preamble; he does not know this night is the last of its kind. Ahead is the next phase of both of our journeys. Different journeys those are but intimately interlaced. If he were to join me, which he will because the need is already there, he will source the words he yearns for. He will also find himself in a different place from this place.

And as I think these thoughts, I regard his long and tired face and wonder if he has the strength to carry on.

—I told you about the longest night.

—The one that brought horror and pain?

—Yes, but on the longest night, there's room for more than horror.

—What else is there?

—There's everything: hope, joy, mystery, marvel, pain for sure, perhaps eternity.

—Has anyone ever experienced a night as long as that?

—Probably not, but we all want to live through it.

—Is that what you're after?

—Perhaps, but I'm after my past at the moment. The longest night may be there for me eventually.

—And what do we make of this night?

—This will be a long one indeed, but not the longest.

—It already feels heavy for me. I can barely stay awake.

—Again I ask you, how far are you willing to go?

The writer does not respond to my question. He turns away from me and deposits his fatigued gaze on the horizon. I imagine he wants to float on the water, or perhaps he would like to sink into it. He can see the horizon just as well as I can. For him, it represents the rest of his life, his life in words, his life as a wanderer. For me, the horizon is nothing other than the natural extension of the river ocean. And by means of the horizon, by reaching out to its confines, I will arrive at the same point from where I started. And in so doing, I may commence a past anew. We will both take to the ocean tomorrow. And if the winds are fair and fill our sails, we will dock in Essaouira after two nights. From there we can make our way to Marrakech, by foot if he prefers. But I have yet to find out how far he is willing to go.

—The ocean is the path. Behind us is the land you already know. Burnt land that swallows your past as well as mine. You came to the shore because you recognized the limit. You're standing at the limit right now, and it doesn't move. You went beyond the limit last night when you entered the waters. And you found your words, and you saw some of yourself in the words. Stop weaving dreams in your mind. Because the only thing we have, of men, are their words.

—But how can I follow that path? By drowning like the rest of them?

—Come and join me, we'll sail together. Now go back to your room and rest if you can. Collect the material things you need and come to this bench by high noon.

—Where are going?

—Look far into the horizon. That's where we're going.

In the early morning, I reach the port where a bearded man prepares his boat for sailing. I observe him for a while. It appears no passengers wait to board the boat. A younger man, his only crew I suppose, helps him get the boat ready. I approach them when they sit down to have coffee in the cockpit. After talking for a while, I explain we are two people who want to reach Essaouira. The captain's plan is to sail as far as Casablanca where he has some business to manage. He agrees to continue further south if we work as crew. In that case, he would dismiss the young man. He would not have to pay him, but he would not pay us either. He clearly wants to keep his money. And I clearly understand that he is a smuggler. He seems suspicious of me, and I do not blame him. Men of his nature deal in a world where everything is shady, and no one is truth worthy. When he extends his hand to seal the agreement, I do not shake it. He does not take offense; he probably does not want to touch me either.

With only a few hours before departure, I decide to purify my body in preparation for entering the river ocean. I traverse the old town until finding a traditional hammam tucked away in a side alley. The gloomy-eyed attendant does not ask any questions nor does he demand any money. He simply points in the direction of the room where I am supposed to disrobe. The air inside the space feels heavy; a mixture of vapor and smoke forms a tangible curtain in front of my eyes. I then recognize the sweet smell of burnt opium, thick and rich, like a flower on fire. I remember frequenting places like this in Marrakech before taking shelter behind the red door. I remember them well. After carefully removing my tunic, I follow the narrow hallway to a small room clad in white stone where the vapor is even denser. Here I will rest my body; here I will release all the impurities that dealing with people has forced inside of me.

Time then becomes immemorial. I feel as if everything that has ever happened to me occurred centuries ago. I look into the abyss of my past, and the immense void gives me a sense of vertigo. I close my eyes, and I breathe. I inhale the warm vapor. When I look into the abyss again, it seems to grow, to unfold further. I lie down on my back, and the heat radiating from the moist white stone penetrates my body. The heat flows through me. And I feel as if every molecule composing my body vibrates slightly, creating space around them, letting go of anything clinging to them. I feel the rivers of unwanted thoughts, toxins, memories, and fears flow away from my body. I am being vacated.

I think of what awaits me. An immersion into the river ocean. A likely immersion into my past. A probable confirmation that my past is moribund. A telling of tales, a telling of stories. An unraveling of the writer's true fears. A vigilance for the obscure vices of the bearded captain. A vision of Essaouira. A landing on the ocean sand. A long walk towards the desert sand. An encounter with the unknown. Or perhaps, what truly awaits me is nothing at all. Maybe an intimate vision of the bright moon and a simple exchange of breaths with the river ocean. My body cannot tell me, and my mind, in playful intercourse with the vapors in this room, slackens its grip on reality.

Once I become aware of my breath again, once I start to feel my body, I realize the immediacy of my journey. I make my way through the misty spaces and find my tunic, my only shelter, awaiting me. My purified body accepts the shelter, and as a unity of interiority and exteriority, I leave the hammam and head for the stone bench in front of the ocean. I fear the day has escaped me; that time has moved faster than I expected. But when I reach the stone bench, the sun has not reached its apex yet, and the writer is nowhere. I then re-establish the order of time and wait a few minutes before high noon.

The writer strikes twelve steps as he approaches the bench. He comes to face various levels of uncertainty. A brave man he is. On his face, I notice a certain degree of apprehension, but at the same time, a glimmer of inquisitiveness. Does he exercise his free will when coming on this journey? I am not sure. I believe he needs to come. A force outside his consciousness must be at work in his mind. Otherwise, if he were entirely sensible, he would have changed course and rejected this journey. But there is a path we all follow, our very own path, informed by everything within ourselves, and by the universe around us.

—What brings you back here?

—You asked me to be here at noon.

—Yes, but that doesn't mean you had to come.

—It's my choice.

—Is it really your choice, or does it feel like it is your choice?

—At this very moment, I wouldn't know the difference.

—Then, you're looking for more words.

—Words mean the world when the world means little to me. That's all I can say.

And that is all he says. The writer follows me to the port without asking any questions. He walks with the same determination as when he walked all the way from Lisbon to Cádiz. He wanted something then; he needed to find his inner beast. And today is no different. He clearly needs something, even if he is not completely aware of the nature of the need. When we arrive at the port, we find the bearded captain sitting in the cockpit of his sailboat smoking a cigar. He takes a good look at the writer, at myself, and I imagine he doubts whether we are capable of managing our duties as crew. Or maybe he is setting a price on our heads. He tosses what is left of the cigar in the water and invites us to come on board.

The captain does not ask for our names nor does he ask for passports or any identification. He goes around the boat as if we do not exist, making sure everything is ready for departure. He checks all the lines, the winches, the sails. I move towards the bow, from where a gentle breeze is coming, and my tunic starts to flap like a loose sail. At once the captain demands that I move downwind to the stern. He says it is safer there, but I think he has other reasons. When he finishes making all sort of preparations, the captain comes back to the cockpit and sits across from me. He lights another cigar and begins to smoke, placidly disconnecting himself from everything around him. This may be how he deals with his own insecurities before taking to the sea. He inhales and exhales his fears.

The wind begins to die down, and the captain emerges from the seance with his own demons. He takes advantage of the quiet wind to hoist the mainsail and release the boom. With the sail flapping slightly, he lets go of the spring lines, and the gentle breeze pushes the boat away from the dock. Then he trims the mainsail and unwinds the jib. As the boat starts to sail into the ocean, I watch the face of the writer. I cannot decipher what he may be feeling at this time, but I know that deep inside him a tempest of words is brewing.

Part IV
The Red Door

The striped tunic

Around me, there is no visible land, only the vast horizon extending in a circular way. No matter which way I look, at the very far end the ocean touches the sky. Without my feet touching the ground I feel displaced. I know where the land is: one hundred meters below the hull of this boat or two days ahead at the shores of Essaouira. And the fluidity of the space engulfing me allows my mind to drift securely, freely, with no encroaching limits. Floating in silence, I take the risk to delve into a few deep recesses of my memory. Nothing at first, just a dim light over a milky white surface. I try to break that white surface with my thoughts, but they fail to puncture it, they simply slide away. I must be patient.

The writer has not spoken since he boarded the boat. He has not written a single word either. He must be accumulating visions and sounds. I wonder if he also accumulates ideas, philosophical propositions, unanswered questions. I also wonder if he lives his life separately from the life of his books. Are they one and the same? A thorny proposition that would be. But somehow he must die a little with each book he writes. Or perhaps, he gives a little of himself with every book. That would also be dangerous since after writing several books there would be nothing left of himself. If that were the case, writing would be an exercise in self-annihilation. No, he would not go to that extent to obliterate himself. Perhaps he lives a more extensive, larger, and deeper life because of his books. If so, most engaged minds would choose to write books. Ergo, they would come to face their inner beast. There is the fear. And the fear makes him break his silence for he begins to speak.

—Where are we going?

—Does it matter?

—I'm sure it matters to someone; you, or the captain…

—Does it matter to you?

—It does, but it doesn't.

—Then you must be in the middle of writing about something crucial.

—I'm writing what I need to write.

—And what determines what you need to write?

—Life, what happens around me, everything…

—What's around you right now is the river ocean, the captain, and myself.

—That's precisely the reason why I'm here.

—So, then, our destination is of no consequence to you.

The captain keeps his distance. He is essentially sailing the boat by himself and does not seem eager to ask for help. And this worries me for I expected he would like to exploit us. For the moment he seems content to manage the boat on his terms, he gives no orders and no explanations. I assume he follows the agreed course south to Essaouira, an assumption I better confirm before nightfall.

The wind starts to accelerate, and the waves begin to grow. The boat responds with brisk movements that make it necessary for us to hold on tight. The captain gets a wide grin on his face and chews on a few words I cannot understand. He then asks me to hold on to a line and to pull as hard as I can when told. He prepares to tack. When he steers the bow across the wind, he screams at me to pull the line. I pull hard and the boat heels to an uncomfortable angle. The captain's grin widens. He takes the line from me and fastens it to the winch. He then hands the wheel to the writer and tells him to keep a steady course. And without saying anything else, he disappears belowdecks.

The boat inserts its bow into the conversation between the wind and the ocean. It glides forward interrupting the eternal discourse. The ocean responds by sending spray up in the air for the wind to catch and throw at us. It is not an angry response; it is an invitation to join in the conversation. I would speak to the river ocean just like I have spoken to the air in Marrakech—with honesty. They know my secrets although I cannot decipher theirs. But unlike men, they will never divulge what has been whispered in their ear. We will speak to each other in the quiet of the night. I have two long nights before landfall to converse, to speak my memory.

—Do you know the direction in which you're steering?

—The sun is ahead of us; we must be heading south.

—True at this time of the day. But what if it were a red sun instead?

—I imagine west.

—And in the dark, which way would you steer?

—I would pick a star and follow it.

—How about the path ahead of you? Can you see it?

—All I see in front of me is water, and the horizon bending far away.

—That's because there's no inherent path. You make the path as you go.

—But if I turn around, I can see the boat leaving a wake behind us.

—That path vanishes, and you'll never step on that same path again.

—So, there's no path.

—There has never been one.

A natural rhythm settles the boat and our minds. Nothing seems to change, while at the same time, everything is changing. The ocean carries our weight on its supple back, the wind opens its arms, and the sun looks down with casual interest. And we carry on leaving no trace or memory of our passage. A few minutes ago we existed, as we exist this very moment. What happened in between that moment and now could be a memory. But if we are not interested in recalling it, then nothing happened between then and now. Just the boat gliding through the vastness. Perhaps the passage of time is different on solid ground. Perhaps the magnitude of our impact is larger as we traverse forests, meadows, or sand. But our legacy cannot only be a solid imprint, like a fossil. Our legacy has to include the immaterial imprint on our mind and the minds of others. Time, then, is marked by what we feel and by what others make us feel.

The captain emerges from belowdecks with an air of boredom. He makes his way forward and sits with his legs dangling over the toe rail. With some difficulty, he lights a cigar and the white smoke blends with the wind. For a long while, he remains there, taking puffs from his cigar without looking aft, refusing to engage with the writer or me. And from time to time he looks far ahead as if trying to find a landfall, or perhaps another vessel. Then, suddenly, he starts singing in a language I do not recognize. But I do not need to understand the words to tell he is hurting. It is a deep and dark melody, heartfelt as if mourning an object of desire. He carries the tune to the end after which he goes back to his former silence. I wonder how he relates to the ocean, to his past, to his pain... The wind extinguishes the cigar. He tries to light what remains of the cigar but fails to do so. He takes a good look at the truncated cigar as if studying its physiognomy, and after whispering a few words, he tosses it into the water. He continues to look out to the horizon, but I wonder if his eyes are open.

After a while, the captain comes aft to the cockpit and looks at the compass. He inspects the shape of the sails carefully, the tell-tales. After trimming the main and the jib only so slightly, he takes hold of the wheel. He makes a minor correction to the course the boat is heading and hands me the wheel this time. In a low and morose voice, he tells me to keep the course steady until dawn. I regard his face for a second, and what I encounter is an empty expression. He simply looks abandoned. Then he turns around and buries himself belowdecks under the weight of his emptiness. I have seen men like him in the desert, unattached, floating over a thin and fragile life.

—My dear writer, the course is already set.

—I'm not a writer today.

—What are you then if not a writer?

—I'm the path.

—I thought we had agreed there's no path.

—I'm the path but not in the sense of a trail, a walkway, or an alley. I'm a channel.

—And what goes through you?

—Your past goes through me.

—My past is barely breathing.

—Speak your past then, before it suffocates.

—Where are you going with this?

—You probably know. You said the course is already set.

Calixto

They started to land on his awareness, the words, in rhythmic coincidence, with the same soft undulations as the waves that struck the boat amidships. The striped tunic had dislodged a narrative starting with events that occurred in forsaken corners of the Algerian Desert. He spoke in a calm voice, precise, without undue affectations. People in his story were referred to by name or attributes. Sometimes the only description a person would receive was a state of mind, as if someone could only exist as the embodiment of anger, jealousy, or bliss. Other times people were described by their actions: the murderer, the bearer of fortune, the wind gatherer. Places were named using the local dialect, often ancient names, or by their geographical relation to another place, or by their climate. But the essential characteristic of the narrative was that events seemed interconnected in ways that were obvious, sometimes, but in deeply obtuse ways other times. He was recounting an entire cosmogony of people, places, and events.

Calixto did nothing but listen to the narrative and try to feel as the striped tunic felt during the recounted events. He was not afraid of missing details or particular twists in the story. He knew very well that his own memory would reconstruct the narrative and employ ample license in the process. But what mattered to him most was the emotional charge attached to the events. That was the past worth recovering, the feelings elicited inside the striped tunic and in those around him when everything took place. The rest could be replaced or even discarded, but those feelings were precious.

In a metaphorical and poetic way, the striped tunic was offering not so much answers to particular questions about his past, but ways of beginning to think about his past. He was peeling off his tunic and revealing his naked self, tender and vulnerable. He spoke uninterruptedly for several hours, and he did so candidly as if nobody but the ocean could listen to his confessions. And when the moon rose, the striped tunic had only reached the early stages of his journey.

The night ushered a truce between the wind and the ocean. They both recoiled and left a clear and calm realm for the boat to traverse. And the voice of the striped tunic acquired a diaphanous transparency making his narrative take flight under the moonlight. What seemed overwhelming in the early evening hours, the complexity of the narrative lines had become more and more understandable as the night deepened. Calixto was developing a mental map of a past that did not belong to him, but in the exercise of its recreation, that past was assuming life anew, it began to breathe, to exist once more. And he knew those words would be dispersed by the breeze, that the chance they would be heard again in the order and cadence imparted by the striped tunic was practically null. In the absolute night, Calixto understood he was the only witness to the miracle.

Soon after the morning broke, the captain made his appearance on deck. He did not bother to greet anyone. He moved around verifying the boat was in proper order and on the right course. Then he went belowdecks for a while after which he emerged with coffee and bread. He served himself first and then invited Calixto and the striped tunic to partake. He said a few inaudible words without expecting a response. It seemed evident he knew their exact location and where they were heading. This was a familiar passage for him, and his apparent boredom revealed so. He confirmed once again the course and told them both not to change anything, to keep a firm hand on the wheel, and to alert him if any other vessel showed up in the horizon. Then he vanished down the hatch.

Calixto took charge of the wheel. The striped tunic went forward and lay down in front of the mast. There he rested his body but not his mind. He started to sing what seemed like an epic poem. For a moment Calixto thought he heard the words of Homer, that the events narrated were those of the Odyssey. But as he paid attention, he realized the story was a continuation of what the striped tunic had recounted the night before. Recited in dactylic hexameter, the simplicity, speed, and directness of the narrative, the brilliance, and excitement of the action, and the imposing humanity of the characters disarmed him. He wanted to listen to the striped tunic for the next one hundred years; he wanted to travel on that boat as far as the farthest corner of the ocean.

And then the wind began to blow harder. The small waves became longer, and the white horses started to gallop on the surface of the ocean. Then the waves began to rise and crest over. And foam blew in streaks along the direction of the wind. The boat heeled aggressively, and Calixto had to firm up his grip on the wheel. In the midst of the wind force, the striped tunic stood up and held on to the mast. He pushed his back against the mast and braced himself by holding on as hard as he could. And with his chest open towards the bow, he continued to recite the epical poem of his past. The turbulent wind and the excited words intoxicated Calixto. And for a moment, he thought he had witnessed immortality.

As the hours matured, the wind gradually calmed its temper. The boat sailed south by southwest at a steady and comfortable rhythm. The voice of the striped tunic had not ceased for a minute during the course of the day. He had sustained the arch of a fascinating story that revealed a dense past, worthy of a thousand lives. But what fascinated Calixto the most was the inner workings of the striped tunic's mind. He had never imagined that a mind could have such a deep understanding of other people's minds. His epic poem revealed a significant gift for intuition, but an even more powerful capacity for observation. He was capable of distilling a person's ultimate fears. And once Calixto realized that he had been followed, observed, and spoken to by that piercing mind, he felt completely naked and exposed. He felt transparent.

Up in the sky, the clouds became thinner and thinner until they were no longer. There was a clarity of light that made the late afternoon resemble the morning. But soon enough the color red started infiltrating the horizon far to the west. Calixto kept looking ahead, thinking he would see land arise over the horizon. But nothing materialized. Another night of sailing would follow, and in that night the striped tunic's story would grow and deepen. Calixto was afraid his memory would not be capable of containing the epic tale. He was afraid of forgetting what the striped tunic was afraid to forget himself. Without control of that journey, without faith on his capacity to recall, without a clear sense of what would happen upon landing, transparent as he felt that moment, Calixto let go of the wheel, and the boat turned immediately to the wind. The sails began to luff at once, and the boat got trapped in irons.

Soon enough the captain made his appearance on deck. His bored air had not changed. His eyes seemed heavy as if tired of watching an ocean that did not mean anything to him. He did not seem interested in what had happened; he only asked if they had seen another vessel. When nobody responded to his question, he took the time to look out in all directions to confirm they were alone in the visible confines. He then set the boat once again on its course and gave the wheel to the striped tunic. He said the night would be calm, that if they kept the course, they would reach Essaouira in the morning hours, and if they kept their mouths shot nothing bad would happen. He then took a long look at the striped tunic, and he could not help contain his disgust. He coughed, he grabbed his throat as if choking, and he went belowdecks almost head first.

That was the beginning of the longest night Calixto would ever experience. He was about to face a density of time commensurate with the density of the emotional story the striped tunic would unleash that night. And it all started with a revelation of vulnerability when the striped tunic spoke about his fear of dying. When Calixto asked what he meant by death, the striped tunic explained that death had nothing to do with the loss of life, but with the loss of an emotional past. He went on to clarify that there was a feeble past, the one that contained vacuous events, maybe multiple vacuous events, but all devoid of an emotional connection. That past could be recounted, even chronicled, but meant nothing and could not really die because it had no life, to begin with. Then there was the past made of a deep emotional fiber. That past had touched someone at an unconscious level; it had penetrated the deepest rooms of the mind and caused inner vibrations. That past was alive, even if the person had no memory of it. And that was the past worth unearthing, recalling, immortalizing.

The striped tunic held on to the wheel and kept a steady course. The ocean kept coming at them, and so did the night, and the wind. And as if speaking to the universe at large, the striped tunic continued to recount the most improbable story Calixto had ever imagined. And as the night extended its reach beyond that of the hours, time lost its essence. The words coming from the striped tunic's mouth interlaced with the voluminous words emerging from the very ocean. And what was told was told as a unity of nature. Mind, emotion, time, life, and death were all existing on the same plane. And the story was not the story of a man or a woman, of a country or a continent, but the story of the emotions of all who live and have lived on the face of the earth.

The boat glided over the silky waters leaving no trace of its passage. The moon rose and fell into the ocean without making any sound. The wind continued to circle around the earth. The birds began to approach the boat wondering why.

And the minds of Calixto and the striped tunic were one with the words. At that time, far ahead in the horizon, toward where the sun had started to usher the day, there was the vision of land emerging.

The striped tunic

The golden walls of Essaouira try to split a land from its ocean. A fruitless effort for no structure rooted in land can keep the air from flowing free. Like in my courtyard of Marrakech where the air visited at will. And with the air come the sounds and the smells. Sometimes the howling of the beast can be heard throughout the village when carried by the innocent air from one open courtyard to the next. For those who observe and listen, the lives of others are always present under the open sky.

As the boat approaches the port, there is yet no sign of the captain, and I wonder what his intentions are. I cannot steer and dock the boat. Neither can the writer. The ocean begins to boil at the mouth of the port making the course of the boat erratic. I try to control the situation by turning the wheel right and left, but the wild movement of the boom makes it impossible. We are bobbing up and down with no clear direction. And soon we start to come close to other boats that sail in and out of the port.

The thrashing must have alerted the captain who now comes to take hold of the wheel. He maneuvers well enough to rectify the course, and we find ourselves heading straight for the dock. The captain yells a few orders. He hands me a line and tells me to stand by the bow. He hands the writer another line and asks him to stand by the stern. He then glides slowly inside the port and comes alongside the dock. At once he jumps on the dock and asks us to throw the lines to him. He fastens both lines, and the boat comes to rest. But as soon as the captain has secured the lines, two men in uniform come to greet him.

The three men argue, they gesticulate. I feel the hostility between them. The men in uniform stand next to each other and block the only access to land on the dock. The captain finds himself trapped between the two men in front of him and the water behind him. Then, in a flanking maneuver, the men in uniform get on each side of the captain and escort him off the dock. They disappear through an opening in the golden wall. And I get a sense this is only the beginning, or perhaps the end, depending on the perspective. I ask the writer to go belowdecks and to remain silent. Then I sit in the cockpit and wait. There are times when a man lets adversity come to find him, and those are always better than the times when he goes out to find adversity himself.

After some time, the two men in uniform return to the boat. They come without the captain, which leads me to believe he has encountered some adversity of his own. They board the boat without asking permission and come to stand in front of me. The expression on their faces is not serene; they seem anxious, or bothered by doing what they probably do not want to do. They expect me to start talking, but I remain as quiet as I am wise.

—Where do you come from?

—I come from everywhere, and toward everywhere I go. But as the uninvited, perhaps you could tell me where the two of you come from?

—We're the ones who ask questions here.

—Does that preclude you from answering?

—What does "preclude" mean?

—It means to prohibit or to arrest you from doing something.

—We do that, we prohibit, and we arrest.

—So, you're not arrested, are you?

—No, no, no… we're the ones who arrest other people.

—Therefore, you can go ahead and answer.

—Let's be clear. We're the ones who ask, and you're the one who answers.

—That's perfect. What would you like to know?

—Where did you meet the captain?

—I don't know the captain.

—But you're in his boat.

—I don't know if this boat belongs to him.

—Ok. What brought you here?

—The boat did.

At this point, the breeze turns around and starts to blow inland. The two uniformed men look at each other and step away from me. They take a minute before continuing with their questions.

—What's your land?

—The desert.

—There are many deserts.

—Not really. There's only one desert where all the sands coalesce.

—Coalesce?

—Yes, join together, combine, mingle.

—Forget the mingling for now; we're not getting any closer to you. Where do you intend to go from here?

—I want to go to where my past feels safe.

—What does that mean?

—It means nothing to you, but the world to me.

The two men turn their backs and confer with each other. The breeze takes their voices away. Then they disembark without saying anything else to me. They walk down the dock and disappear again through the opening in the golden wall. I wait for a few minutes, and neither the captain nor the two men in uniform come back to the boat. I then ask the writer to gather himself and to prepare for a long walk. And, as hastily as possible, we leave the boat behind, the port, the ocean. We traverse the ancient village avoiding any contact, like the fugitives we are not. I walk ahead this time, and the writer follows me. And as we head east, I recognize the fresh scent of flowering orange trees.

Marrakech, Marrakech, why do you haunt me? I found refuge within your walls; I contained my impulses behind the red door. And then death happened, as it does, without asking. Would the fountain still sing to me? Would the air feel free to visit? Would there be another tender soul wanting to touch me? That was then, and there is no certainty that it would be the same now. To the contrary, everything already experienced is by definition consumed, extinct. And that is the problem with the past, that we keep on murdering it as we move along. But perhaps what remains alive is what we felt. I know how it felt when the fountain sang to me, that has not died, it reverberates inside of me. I can still feel the sensation of touching somebody. I can still feel the moist seduction of mint tea traveling through my throat and releasing a certain goodness. I also felt fear when persecuted. And when I instilled fear on others, I was then afraid of my own self. I felt all of that.

Reaching Marrakech is a question for which I have no answer. It is a desire based on the fallibility of the present day. It is the need to look into the precipice. And if I keep on walking east, climbing the gentle hills, I will reach the plateau from where the desert extends with the majesty of an ocean. Then, through the clear desert air, my eyes will confront the spectacle of the Atlas Mountains. At their foothills, I will find Marrakech in its redness. But that encounter will happen in the future, a time devoid of emotional experience, a time that has yet to be lived. I cannot predict the wounds that will be inflicted on any mind once I reach Marrakech. And even more obscure, how would I feel about those wounds?

And as the day becomes the night, and the night becomes the day, we sustain our march. A silent march this is, for the writer and I have not exchanged a word since we both set foot on dry land. I am aware of his need for words, the sole desire that seems to propel him forward. In which case he must be suffering at this very moment. But perhaps he aims for more than words and a story to tell. Perhaps he just wants to touch immortality like most living things. Or perhaps, he needs to write in order to exist in this world that grants no reason for existence. I cannot decipher the pure essence of his need. And for that very reason, I am content to walk and hear him walk behind me, for I know he is wrestling with the beast inside of him.

Calixto

Once he saw the red stones guarding the entrance to the ancient city, Calixto understood that people had disputed their right to belong inside those walls for generations. And he also understood he had no right to the terrain inside the mind of the striped tunic. He had listened and memorized the epic tale, but he had no right to narrate that story as his own. An apocryphal writer he would be if he were to simply write what he had heard over the past few days. Furthermore, his story would not resemble the true life of the striped tunic. He had no chance of reaching the inner confines of his mind. The narrative would then have no merit; it would not honor the very reason of its existence. He then realized he was in possession of an extraordinary wealth of words he could not handle. So when in front of Bab Agnaou, the gate to the eternal city, he stopped walking altogether and stood facing the afternoon sun.

The striped tunic stood next to him, calmly, and did not ask the reason for halting his march. They both admired the gate and the surrounding redness. And when the striped tunic asked him if he was ready to drop all expectations and enter the city as a child, a child that had yet to write his first few lines, Calixto answered that he was indeed nubile, for at no other time in his life had he felt so naked. And together they crossed the Bab Agnaou and pierced the core of the ancient city. And the walls grew around them, and the narrow streets channeled their steps, and the sounds of people living their lives, transacting with each other, loving one another, vibrated in the dry desert air. Inside the walls of Marrakech, Calixto felt vulnerable.

They walked in what Calixto thought were concentric circles. The alleys turned always to the left even when a right turn would have offered a more inviting option. But for

Calixto, the difference between one option or another had virtually disappeared. He was at the mercy of the striped tunic, who was at the mercy of his own tumultuous memories, or at best, at the mercy of his sequestered passions. And as the day lengthened its reach, the march through the village had become an enigma. And when Calixto was about to halt his march again, they reached the fabled Djemaa El-Fna with the snake charmers, acrobat monkeys, storytellers, musicians, and dancers. Here Calixto was assaulted by the confluence of a thousand stories. All of them vibrant, engaging. Words were rising and clamoring, a frenetic exchange of meanings was traversing the square from corner to corner. And Calixto understood the greatness of this source, a source of words that could challenge that of the ocean.

Exhausted, both men lay on the ground next to a pile of oranges that would likely be sold in the morning hours. They had no words for each other; they simply let the night traverse through them. But the night brought to Calixto's ears what he had never heard, or allow himself to hear: the wrenching, piercing howling of the beast, the horrid unconscious voice that haunts everyone, every night, in the deepest level of their somnolence. Frightened at first, Calixto bit his lip and braced himself. But as he listened to the lamenting voice of numerous beasts unknown to him, as the howling grew and multiplied, as he came in touch with a multitude of selves vying for expression in the empty hours of the night, he felt a certain lightness and calm. He realized that he was not alone, that he bore no responsibility for their suffering, but that he could be, perhaps, their verbal conduit. And as Calixto and the striped tunic remained prostrated in their sleep, the night continued to deepen and the beasts continued to howl.

The striped tunic

Dawn makes a raucous arrival when it unleashes several layers of wind on the Djemaa El-Fna. The merchants have to secure their wares, and more than one yells a blasphemous word. The violence of the untouchable substance touches every single person occupying the square. And the prayer from the nearby minaret is severely dismantled. I speak to the writer and tell him we need to find a red door, but he only hears the brutal sound of the wind. So fluid, so invisible, so malleable, yet so destructive. I grab onto my tunic and start to walk toward the narrow streets of the Medina without saying anything else to the writer. And when he realizes that motion is imminent, he gets on his feet and follows after me.

I know where the red door is and what lies behind it. I know there will be four flowering orange trees standing in the corners of the courtyard. Would they remember me in the same way I remember them, with affection? Or would I be nothing to them like I am nothing to the rest of the world? I think the fountain will still be singing, but what would the song be? And what I cannot unravel are the desires behind the red door. Or perhaps, more realistically, the desires inside my own mind. Arriving in Marrakech a second time is not a return; it is a continuation of the same search I started within the heart of the desert. Do we ever change as people? Maybe our fears are the ones that change.

I walk aimlessly through the old streets and find enormous satisfaction in not being recognized. My striped tunic is only one among many, and my face so ragged, so anonymous. I move as fluidly as the wind among people. I could flow as a simple conscience. And as such, I expand over the roofs of the Medina, and I breathe once again the air that sustained me for so long, before the deaths, before the impetus to flee. The writer must sense my inherent need for he asks no questions;

he follows me unambiguously at a close distance. I imagine he intuits my need to make peace with my dying past, a past I spoke to him in full detail. If he was repulsed by it, he would have killed me already.

The shadows advance with the hours. And with each step, I come closer to the inevitable encounter with the threshold of my past. And that threshold, where my past and present come together, is no different from the threshold where the ocean meets the sky. They are both inaccessible; we can pursue them knowing we will never touch them. But they exist nonetheless, and we bow to them. So I begin to correct my path and veer in the direction of the red door. I traverse familiar squares and nefarious streets, I enter the womb of the Medina, I hear the clamor of words I now ignore, and I pierce the final alley at which end stands a red door.

—Is this a dead end?

—No, this is the beginning of my future.

—But this alley leads nowhere.

—It is what's behind this red door that concerns me.

—What's behind it?

—Everything that I've started to forget and everything that you can't help but write down.

I look at the writer, and I get the impression I am looking at myself. I think of my past, the time that has elapsed up until this instant, and I think of the time that is yet to come. And with utmost care and deliberate gestures, I remove my striped tunic and torn sandals. I extend my arms and offer them to the writer. Without saying a word, the writer gets rid of his clothes and dons the striped tunic and the sandals. And I speak to him for the last time.

—Where would you go next?

—I need the backing of the ocean.

—To write or to dream?

—To exist.

—Then go away from yourself, but close to shore and even closer to your feelings.

—I'm going back to Lisbon.

—And what can Lisbon offer you?

—Bread and a salamander.

After listening to his words, I turn my back on the writer and face the red door. I push the red door open and step through it in full nakedness. Inside there is a courtyard with a fountain in the center. In each of the four corners of the courtyard, there is a flowering orange tree vibrating with life.

Jorge Armenteros was born in Cuba, his family leaving for Madrid, Spain, then Tampa, Florida, before finally settling in Puerto Rico. After graduating from Harvard University, he acquired an MD at the University of Puerto Rico and completed his residency in psychiatry at Bellevue Hospital in New York City, later obtaining an MA in Spanish and Latin American Literature at New York University and an MFA in Creative Writing at Lesley University. Armenteros is the author of the 2015 International Latino Book Award winner *The Book of I* (Jaded Ibis Press), and the *Striped Tunic Trilogy: Air*, *The Roar of the River*, and *The Spiral of Words* (Spuyten Duyvil Press). His author interviews and book reviews have appeared in The Writer's Chronicle, American Book Review, Rain Taxi, and Gargoyle. Armenteros resides in the South of France.

www.ingramcontent.com/pod-product-compliance
Lightning Source LLC
Chambersburg PA
CBHW011936210726

48290CB00011BA/2696